Joey W. Hill

Ice
QUEEN

ELLORA'S CAVE
ROMANTICA PUBLISHING

An Ellora's Cave Romantica Publication

www.ellorascave.com

Ice Queen

ISBN 9781419955648
ALL RIGHTS RESERVED.
Ice Queen Copyright © 2006 Joey W. Hill
Edited by Briana St. James.
Cover art by Syneca.

This book printed in the U.S.A. by Jasmine-Jade Enterprises, LLC.

Electronic book Publication March 2006
Trade paperback Publication November 2006

Also by Joey W. Hill

෧

About the Author

℘

I've always had an aversion to reading, watching or hearing interviews of favorite actors, authors, or musicians because so often you find that the real person does not measure up to the beauty of the art they produce. You find their politics or religion distasteful, or you find they're shallow and self-absorbed, or a vacuous mophead without a lick of sense. And from then on, though you still may appreciate their craft or art, it has somehow been tarnished. Therefore, whenever I'm asked to provide personal information about myself for readers, a ball of anxiety forms in my stomach as I think, "Okay, the next couple of paragraphs can change forever the way someone views my stories." Why on earth does a reader want to know about me? It's the story that's important.

So here it is. I've been given more blessings in my life than any one person has a right to have. Despite that, I'm a Type A, borderline obsessive-compulsive paranoiac who worries that I will never live up to expectations. I've got more phobias than anyone (including myself) has patience to read about. I can't stand talking on the phone, I dread social commitments, and the idea of living in monastic solitude with my husband, a few animals, books and writing is as close an idea to paradise as I can imagine. I love chocolate, but with that deeply ingrained, irrational female belief that weight equals worth, I manage to keep it down to a minor addiction. I adore good movies. I'm told I work too much. Every day is spent trying to get through the never ending "to do" list to snatch a few minutes to write.

This is because, despite all these mediocre and typical qualities, for some miraculous reason, these wonderful characters well up out of my soul with stories to tell. When I manage to find enough time to write, sufficient enough that the precious "stillness" required rises up and calms all the competing voices in my head, I can step into their lives, hear what these characters are saying, what they're feeling, and put it down on paper. It's a magic beyond description, akin to truly believing that my husband loves me, winning the trust of an animal who has known only fear or apathy, making a true connection with someone else, or knowing for certain that I've given a reader a moment of magic through those written words. It's a magic that reassures me that there is Someone, far wiser than myself, who knows the permanent path to that garden of stillness, where there is only love, acceptance and a pen waiting for hours and hours of uninterrupted, blissful use.

If only I could finish that darned "to do" list.

Joey welcomes comments from readers. You can find her website and email address on her author bio page at www.ellorascave.com.

Tell Us What You Think

We appreciate hearing reader opinions about our books. You can email us at Comments@EllorasCave.com.

ICE QUEEN

Chapter One

ℬ

"Catch a tiger by the toe, eeny, meeny, miny, mo."

Marguerite glanced up from her purchase order as her hostess, Chloe Marcel, came into the kitchen area. Genevieve Wisner, her other waitstaff person, slid by in front of her with a tray of teacups as Chloe propped a hip on the doorframe. Fortunately, Gen was a tall woman, whereas Chloe was a tiny thing not even five feet tall and committed by genetics to look fourteen years old though she was nearly twenty-eight. Marguerite had discovered her working a kiosk at the mall that sold a wide variety of body-piercing jewelry. She'd liked the woman's easy manner that drew customers to her side like old friends, the selection of high-quality jewelry and the fact that Chloe, while passionate about piercings, only had one. A navel piercing that she rarely revealed by her clothing choices without having to manually turn up the edge of her blouse or tug down her waistband. Marguerite had also liked the simmering mischief in her eyes. However, since hiring her as hostess for Tea Leaves, informally known in the Tampa area as the Tea Room, she'd learned to be wary of it.

"What are you going on about, Chloe?"

"I'm thinking about better parts of a tiger than his toes."

Genevieve rolled her eyes, setting down the tray. "She's in one of *those* moods, M." She used her favorite nickname for their boss, having pointed out more than once that Marguerite's cool reserve and authoritative presence would qualify her to head up the MI-6 of the James Bond movies. "She's comparing men to animals again."

"It's not like we get many here, you know."

"Men, or animals?"

9

Chloe grimaced at her. "This is a terrific, lovely place, Marguerite, but we do need to figure out a way to market it to men of marriageable age. Or at least the age of sexual interest."

"Got it." Gen nodded. "Age twelve to ninety."

"I'll plan a construction workers' convention here just for you, Chloe." Marguerite tapped her pen on the desk, considering the matter from her side office while Gen grinned, placing the teacups from the Coalport set carefully in the sink water to handwash them, as they did with all the porcelain sets. "Do you think they'd prefer something manly, one of our strong black teas served up in a reproduction YiXing? If clay was good enough for the samurai, it should be good enough for them. Of course, since the samurai left their swords outside the teahouse, we might ask our guests to leave their tool belts at the door."

"Maybe everything else but the tool belts." Chloe grinned wickedly. "Here, take him today's sample." She took away the dish towel and pressed a tiny cup into Gen's hand. "You go take a look and tell me if I'm right or not. Money isn't the only thing oozing off this guy. I'd have given him a lap dance if he'd said another word in that voice, or kept looking at me with those tiger eyes."

Genevieve made a resigned face but obediently went back out the swinging door.

Chloe looked toward Marguerite. "Even more intriguing, he says he's here to meet with you. And that you're expecting him."

Though the apprehension curling in Marguerite's stomach at Chloe's description had already raised her suspicion, the hostess's words confirmed it. He was an hour early. Marguerite suppressed a surge of resentment, laced with a bit of uncomfortable panic. She'd wanted time to close up the shop. While she'd wanted the strong foundation of meeting on her own turf, he'd taken that edge by coming when she would have to be something different from what he knew, revealing a side of herself she'd not intended to give to him.

10

But then, it wasn't the first time Tyler Winterman had unsettled her. Why had she decided to approach him to help her resolve her dilemma, knowing that about him?

Pride, in a simple word. If she had to do this—and she'd been told it was required—she wouldn't do it paired with someone whose skills were less than her own. Her hope was that she wouldn't have to embrace the task at all, which was the less galling reason she'd invited Tyler here. He might agree with her plan and go along with it. If he didn't... Well, she preferred not to address that at the moment, especially when a flush swept her skin like the brush of a heron's wings at the thought, making her heart flutter strangely and the muscles in her thighs tighten.

This was a mistake. One she could not gracefully undo.

Genevieve re-entered, a smile playing around her mouth. "Beware the day Chloe comes in here and compares a customer to a bull. We'll have to run out there and collect all the china cups before the metaphor becomes reality. She's right. That one's a tiger. I feel ten times prettier, just having talked to him."

Gen didn't know the half of it. Tyler was a Southern gentleman, always rising when a woman entered the room. She'd seen him kiss a woman's hand as naturally as an English duke. When he was with a woman, he saw to her welfare with the easy authority of a man who believed it was his responsibility to look after her. That essence was what Gen had picked up. Anything female felt enormously delicate in his presence, as if his sweeping glance put her in skirts, corset, décolletage, piled-up hair. Marguerite knew all of that. Felt it and so much more that disturbed her about Tyler.

"Marguerite?" Chloe spoke. "Is this guy some kind of trouble you need me to get rid of? I could tell him you had to leave early, let you slip out the back."

There was no running from this. Maybe that was good. Yes, she decided. It *was* good. Time to face up to it. Destroy the illusion her mind had created that had made her avoid him for nearly two years. Maybe that was her true motive in inviting him here. Facing this task would uncover the man behind the myth, and then she could firmly place him on the shelf with other bedtime stories.

"This isn't one of your extreme tests for yourself, is it? Marguerite, you've actually gotten paler."

"Don't be ridiculous. He's a man, not a leap from an airplane at ten thousand feet." Though suddenly, the first time she had done the latter seemed less daunting than this situation.

"Need a chair or a whip to face your tiger, then?" Genevieve dispelled the moment with a twinkle in her eyes.

Marguerite rose. "With my two circus clowns in the wings, I feel fully protected from any wild beast."

"Cute." Chloe did smile then, though Marguerite felt their attention follow her closely as she moved to the kitchen door.

She looked back at them, summoning the cool, tranquil expression they knew. "I'll be back in a moment."

Courtesy demanded she acknowledge his presence, even if she couldn't meet with him for the next thirty minutes. But perhaps courtesy was not what was called for here.

She didn't notice men the way Chloe did. When she allowed herself to notice them as sexual beings, it was in the boundaries of The Zone, the BDSM club she frequented. It was a part of her life Chloe and Gen knew nothing about. When she chose her submissive for the night, she focused on his eyes, looking for signs of a need that she could not describe in words. And they recognized her as the Mistress that could fill that need. She never lacked for a partner.

But Tyler she noticed, despite the fact he was not a submissive. He was well acknowledged as one of the most powerful and sought-after Masters at The Zone by the female submissives.

Whenever she was close enough to feel the heat of his energy, which seemed to be whenever they were under the same roof, even at a club as large as The Zone, she felt his dangerous edge. The ruthlessness and resolution moved like an intriguing shadow just beneath the surface. Something in his eyes made her feel she could need *him*, and he would take care of those needs, of anything she needed.

As she moved out onto the floor, she saw him right away. He wore tan slacks and a perfectly ironed and fitted cream-colored Oxford shirt, open at the throat. His jacket was hooked on the point of the chair, and he wore brown, polished dress shoes, the casual elegance suiting Tea Leaves.

He didn't blend though. Instead, he looked like an intrigued, benevolent god who walked among men. He emanated difference and yet something so familiar, as if she knew him like the touch of the sun.

She had tried to describe him in her mind before, as if using words would sculpt a definitive closed boundary around him, keeping the essence of him from touching her identity and altering it somehow. Her failure to do so forced her to acknowledge she was captivated by more than his physical attributes. Her body reacted to his presence, the sound of his voice, his scent. There were times she would pass an area at The Zone, catch that scent, and know he had been there only a moment before.

His physical features were nothing to scoff at, however. Dark hair kept cropped smoothly short on his nape and around his ears. Just enough feathering on top to draw attention to the way it scattered carelessly across his high forehead. He was in his forties, so she suspected if he let it grow longer, the peppering of gray would become silver streaks. A tall man, probably six foot five, his shoulders coaxed a woman's fingertips to trace their breadth. And then those fingertips might tremble off the edge, slide down the curve of hard biceps, linger on a forearm, find themselves captured by a large hand that looked capable and confident of handling something fragile without damaging it, much as he handled the whimsical sample cup now.

13

In short, he exuded the confidence of a man in the prime of his life, where the physical and mental abilities were at once together, a man who understood what he wanted. And whatever that was, it created a restless force to him that had the ability to reach out and physically touch her whenever they had the slightest proximity to one another, like now.

She'd never had to deal with him out of The Zone. As she crossed the floor, it suddenly felt as if they were all alone. Her heart rate sped up, choking her with its throb of panic.

Stop. It's bad enough you have this reaction to him. You don't know why, which makes it irrational. Stupid, even. You invited him here. Remember?

With the expression of the pleasant proprietress firmly in place, she moved toward him, giving him a slight nod to let him know she was on her way, a courtesy. However, she stopped to pay attention to her customers, an unspoken reprimand to him for coming before the closing time she'd specified.

"Mrs. Allen." The lady she addressed was approaching eighty. It was an age at which Marguerite expected a woman could safely allow one's looks and appearance to lapse but most of her senior citizen clientele were better put together than women half their age. They came to Tea Leaves wearing silk blouses, suits with a tasteful pin on the lapel and sturdy but stylish shoes. Their nails neatly manicured and legs always, always clad in silky hose, never a run to be seen. Sometimes the perfume might be a bit overdone but Marguerite found it comfortable. The smell of older Southern women, the scents of their powder and papery skin mingling with White Diamonds or Chanel #5.

Mrs. Allen smiled at her and clasped her hand, and Marguerite immediately covered it with her other one, savoring the contact with someone she genuinely liked, who eased rather than disturbed, the familiar rather than the unknown. She realized at once her grip might be a bit desperate, for Mrs. Allen looked startled. Marguerite loosened

14

her hold and gave the woman's knuckles a gentle pat. "After your friends treated you to the Staffordshire set for your birthday, I thought you'd never go back to Brown Betty."

She nodded at the little brown ball of a teapot, its surface polished to a shine that allowed her to see the impression of her own reflection, distorted and distant. The connection of their hands was magnified, as if it was the truly important part of the picture, and she supposed it was.

"Miss M, you know that was the prettiest thing. And you were right. The same tea could taste entirely different in it. I'm so glad you had us try that new brand of Earl Grey. But me and the Brown Betty..." Mrs. Allen gazed fondly at the squat ball of a teapot. "We have ourselves a standing date each week. We're a sturdy pair of practical birds is all."

"Stolid classics," one of her two friends at the table put in.

This incited a chatter of notes and laughter among the three women that made music in her tearoom. It would join with a similar composition at the next table, then another, the different conversations weaving into a complex arrangement that was a song of sanctuary. Marguerite imagined its energy filling and surrounding her tearoom every day, even spilling onto the street and bringing in new people, those seeking tranquility. She fed off it, used it now, absorbing it in a deep breath as she gave them one last smile and released Mrs. Allen to face the less tranquil element who had entered her domain.

As she passed the last table, he rose, that Southern gentleman she expected. Her height of five ten with an added two inches of heels to bring her to a willowy six feet didn't faze him. That centered element to him made him perfectly in sync with the atmosphere she strove to provide. It was how he affected her that sent a ripple through the composition, that warning note that a transition in the symphony was about to occur.

He didn't smile, utter polished platitudes or flash a smile to throw up the barricades of acquaintances. His gaze passed over her leisurely. She was sure he had thoroughly inspected her when she came out from the back, as sure as she was that he was doing it now to be certain she was aware of his scrutiny.

It made no sense at all. Tyler was a sexual Dominant. She was a Dominant. There should be the attraction of mutual admiration but why this? This indefinable, overwhelming feeling?

"Our meeting was for six-fifteen," she said.

If he was taken aback by her lack of greeting, he did not show it. He remained standing, studying her, and then he did the most remarkable thing, because men did not touch her. Not without her expressed permission, and usually only after they had begged for the privilege.

He reached out and touched the hair she'd artfully arranged along her temple. "I've never seen you with a curl." Inserting his finger into the coil, he caught it with his thumb to stroke it with his forefinger, stretching it out straighter as he did so, then letting it go, watching it bounce back into place. It caused a pleased and warm look on his face that made her feel at loose ends. "Always, when I see you, you're wearing it tied back in that severe tail."

She knew she needn't worry. He wouldn't fill in that sentence with "...when I see you at The Zone", the place where they knew one another best. Or rather, the façade they both knew best. They both knew the strict rules of confidentiality for all members of The Zone, maintained in the outside world.

"Yes," he said at last. "I'm early. I wanted to see your place, how you run it. I can't get that impression after closing. Why does my being here early bother you?"

If it had been anyone else, the automatic answer "It doesn't" would have bounced out of her mouth. But she was sensible enough not to bluff with a man who only had one equal at The Zone for interpreting body language and tone, and that was herself. It raised her hackles though, for him to exercise his power as a Dom at this moment, calling her out and making it clear, albeit in a mild and courteous way, that he wouldn't accept an evasive answer.

People lied all the time in the real world with a bouquet of pleasantries to deceive no one, only to make evasiveness palatable, acceptable. In The Zone, Doms didn't allow subs to do that. It was all about getting to the pure naked core of every thought, no dissembling on any level.

"That's not really something I care to discuss. It's my problem, not yours." That was as honest an answer as it had been a question. And it was all of the answer he was getting. "You're welcome to be here. If you need anything, let Chloe or Genevieve know. I've got some things to finish in the back but I'll be out when they lock up in about thirty minutes."

He nodded, those amber eyes never shifting from her face but making slight movements, revealing that he was watching her lips as she spoke, the sweep of her lashes, even the sparse movements of her hands. "I'll be here. Go finish your day. I'll wait as long as you need."

Like she needed his permission.

Her lips tightening to suppress a retort, she turned precisely on her heel and headed back the way she had come, intensely aware of the curious looks from Mrs. Allen's table. Her regulars would be wondering about that corkscrew curl move but she kept on her cool smile and moved briskly enough that no one engaged her. Her track took her into the reflection path of the large Victorian mirror mounted to the left of the kitchen entrance, so she could see him.

He was watching her. Quite deliberately, making her acutely aware of the swing of her hips beneath the fitted skirt, the glimpse of the back of her knees and curve of calves that would be displayed as she walked in her heels. His regard made her aware of the fact she'd chosen seamed stockings, and this pair had a tiny embroidered rose in black thread just above the delicate anklebone. Even the soft brush of that curl along her temple was intensified by the memory of his touch there.

His gaze met hers in the mirror right before she entered the kitchen. One corner of his mouth tugged up in a smile, and from the expression in his eyes, she wouldn't have put it past him to mortify her with a wolf whistle. She escaped through the door, but her own lips were twitching with a near smile, reminding her that she liked Tyler Winterman. She was just deathly afraid of the effect he had on her.

Taking the two steps up into her side office, she closed her door. Chloe and Gen were used to her doing that at the end of the day so she could focus on receipts. It gave her an excuse now to collect her thoughts. And watch Tyler.

The large Victorian mirror was a façade for a two-way mirror, the window side mounted on the wall of her raised office so she could keep an eye on the floor. It helped her anticipate when Chloe and Gen could use a hand, or she needed to come out to greet a frequent or new customer, underscoring the sophisticated charm and service her tearoom was known to lavish on its clientele.

In this instance, it gave her the opportunity to study him further. He had left the bistro chair, and was now perusing her display wall. It offered pieces from the full tea sets that clients could request for the serving of their chosen beverage, everything from English porcelain to Japanese and Chinese clay. With one hand, he touched the tuocha, a compressed tea shaped like a bird's nest, then he moved on to examine the copper shine of the Russian samovar with its ornate dragon tap.

She had originals under glass that ranged from one hundred and fifty to one thousand years old, the latter being the YiXing set from the Ming Dynasty. Her very first tea set was also under glass, a child's set of colorful ceramic cups and matching small teapot. It sat within the ankle span of a doll whose best days were long over, underscored by her brittle hair, faded satin gown and scarred face.

Her hands clutched the desk edge, knuckles white as she watched him study that symbol of her past which she had arranged with quaint charm. It gave patrons the picture of a little blonde girl getting the set, the doll when it was brand new. Cherishing it, deciding to grow up and have her entire life be like a tea party. Civilized, every detail thought out. Well designed, beautiful. Peaceful.

The room was laid out such that none of the tables were too close to that display wall, so that a person could move comfortably past its offerings without hovering over seated patrons. In this case it gave the ladies in the room the opportunity to study him easily under the guise of interest in the displays that most of them had seen many times before. She had three age groups in the room; Mrs. Allen's set, who were well into grandmother realm and perhaps holding out successfully for great-grandchildren; a pair of women in their forties, now empty nesters; and a table of six chic professional women who preferred this spot on Thursday afternoons rather than a golf course, nightclub or bar hangout. And every one of them was watching Tyler. Not blatantly, but with quick flicks of their eyelashes, secret smiles among themselves, a feminine chuckle. It set her teeth on edge. Why had he invaded her world before she had the inner gates to it closed? She felt as if he were contaminating it in some way, disrupting the atmosphere like the arrival of a Chippendales stripper in a library to deliver a birthday gram to the quiet steward of all those dignified books.

But he didn't have the effeminate prettiness of a Chippendale. Chloe was right. Tyler commanded attention because he was like a tiger. Mesmerizing and possessing something that suggested it was wise not to turn your back on him, any more than it would be a wise move to run.

He turned at last, made his way down the wall until he reached her mirror. Being a tall man, it was easy for him to rest an elbow on the mantel.

Other male Dominants did not affect her this way. Perhaps it was the Domme in her that admired the strength to his bearing, his profile. The predatory readiness that pulsed from him was equally balanced with the assurance he would be the first to hold out a chair for a woman, help an elderly woman down the stairs at the bank or ask a girl crying in the mall what was the matter. How could he make it better? The moment any woman met his gaze she'd know he *could* make it better. In short, he was a walking fantasy, and there was nothing more dangerous to Marguerite's world than that.

The motion of his body suggested that he had put a hand in the pocket of his slacks, a comfortable, masculine pose. His attention appeared to now rest on a photo of colorfully dressed tea pickers in India, which was grouped with lovely landscapes of the green hills of the tea gardens in Malaysia. Beyond that were some of her favorite Japanese tea theme scrolls and watercolors drawn by tea masters.

The desk pressed against her thighs as she leaned forward. The surface was too wide for her to touch the window. Inching her skirt up, she slid onto the wood top, folding her legs beneath her as she reached out.

It didn't matter why she felt like doing this. She didn't want to think about why she was tracing his shoulder on the glass, imagining how it would feel, the fabric of his shirt, the solid man beneath. Flattening her palm against the cool surface, she visualized touching his hair, the line of his throat, feeling the heat of life pulsing there as she passed her knuckles over it, just a gentle caress.

He turned toward her, studying the mirror rather than himself in it, and she saw his shrewd assessment, his quick realization that it was likely a two-way. Outlining his mouth, she watched as the sensual lips curved into a faint smile. He winked and placed one finger on the glass. Entranced, she moved hers to it, pressing finger pad to finger pad. She supposed he thought she was frowning at him or ignoring him, and that was fine. But as they stood there for a moment or two and his finger stayed in place with her print against it, she began to get that uncomfortable feeling she often had, that Tyler saw more than he should when he looked her way. Moving off the desk, she took her seat and returned to her paperwork, trying not to look up again.

She held out for about three minutes.

He was still at the mantel. He'd taken out a palm organizer and was keying something into it. Checking his messages, she supposed. Tyler was a significant name in the erotic film industry, using his talent to help producers and directors put high-quality erotic content for women on the screen. He'd even co-written a couple award-winning scripts himself, and served as advisor on countless others. Although she'd heard that he'd cut back some the last couple years, she imagined he had a full schedule just maintaining his going concerns. *Evolution of a Domme*, his latest investment, had swept the erotic film awards. It had even garnered a Golden Globe nomination, for the first time breaking a barrier shattered previously only by darker, more destructive erotic films with larger name actors.

She watched, curious, as he lifted the organizer. He placed it flat against the glass, his body shifting so to the others in the room it only looked as if he was casually relaxing at the mantel.

What are you wearing back there?

It startled a snort out of her, and she clapped her hand over her mouth, though there was a reasonable amount of soundproofing. As if he knew her reaction, he grinned, a slow, sexy smile. Pocketing the organizer, he strolled away, wandering back past the display wall.

Tucking the memory of that smile to her breast like she was clutching her doll, she used it to ease her concerns about this meeting. It would work out. Of course it would.

And it was nowhere near the worst thing she had faced in her life.

Chapter Two

ॐ

As thirty minutes ticked away, the anxiety returned. A nagging feeling of apprehension that made her wonder again how she'd reached the logical and seemingly well-thought-out decision that she could have this discussion with Tyler Winterman in any capacity that was safe. She shouldn't have entertained it at all, except she had no choice. There were things in her life she knew she needed in order to keep other things under control. Fate recently had determined that Tyler was the key to one of them. Not so much him as his cooperation at the very least.

She bid Chloe and Gen good night, locked the rear service entrance and then stepped back out into the tearoom. Chloe had locked the front door and dimmed the lights to evening security mode, just enough light that the passing patrol car could see into her downtown shop. It surprised her that her hostess had done that with Tyler still in the room. Then she saw, with a mental note to slap Chloe in the morning, a small trio of candles burning in the center of his table. It set an atmosphere she did not wish to cultivate.

Marguerite picked up a douser on the side table and gestured courteously to him to stay seated as she approached. Laying it over each candle, she felt him watching her movements. It put the room in even dimmer light but she knew every inch of her own place, though it seemed different with his presence.

"I'd like to have our talk in the private tearoom, if you don't mind. That way, no one's confused about whether we're closed for the day or not, and we won't be interrupted."

"Should I bring my cup?"

"No. Just leave it there. Chloe is still new to judging customer tastes. That's one of our stronger black teas. I think I have something more to your liking." She laid the douser on the tablecloth, keeping her eyes on it. "It's a small matter, but earlier I didn't give you permission to touch me. I'd prefer you not to do so."

He was a Dom with a very cool temperament. She knew he'd understand and not create a row, though she questioned the wisdom of making an issue of it, based on what she was intending to ask him.

"Not comfortable being around men who aren't on their knees?"

Tyler had no problem with woman Dominants, so she assumed the question to be based on curiosity. It didn't make his exceptional intuition any less irritating.

"Not used to it, certainly."

He rose, and she'd misjudged how close she was standing to him. She made herself wait a second before she stepped back, wanting it clear she was doing it to give him room to follow her around the table, not because being confronted by his height and broad shoulders at less than a foot distance washed her with a disturbing heat.

She turned on her heel, ostensibly to lead him to the private room but also to avoid prolonging the face-to-face proximity with nothing between them. When she reached the brocade curtain that separated the private tea area from the main floor, he was close enough behind her that his long arm drew the fabric back for her. His fingertips grazed the small of her back, the contact just light enough not to be a blatant disregard of her request. What was it Lao Tse said? Energy was in the space between things. The light touch made her decide that such energy could become compressed into a flash of heat upon impact, shuddering up one's spine.

Tyler noted the shiver that rippled through her. He knew Marguerite did not welcome touch. Even her submissives were

23

allowed very little liberty in that area. She touched them; they did not touch her. On infrequent occasions she allowed a slave to service her orally, and the undulations of her body while he did so were as sensual and controlled as a swan on a lake. She appeared to draw pleasure from it but Tyler sensed that the pleasure for her was in the choreography, the emotional reaction of her sub when she granted him the pleasure of her most intimate taste. He knew there were those who thought she climaxed during those sessions. He had his doubts about that.

But he didn't read rejection in her shiver now, simply surprise at being touched at all, and uncertainty in how to react consciously. Her body did it for her, instinct filling in the void, and that reaction made his own body respond.

She stepped away, reluctantly drawing his attention away from the slim and statuesque line of her back and shoulders to his new surroundings.

The room had a pleasing simplicity. One large original watercolor of a blue heron graced the wall behind the round table. The table was draped in a gray damask which dropped the proper twelve inches on all sides, revealing teak legs shaped like the elongated heads of Chinese dragons. A rock fountain grouped with several bamboo plants and a palm in the corner gave the impression of a tropical forest. And behind Marguerite was a picture window overlooking a tiny courtyard with a statuary garden.

The room spoke of confidences, seclusion and sanctuary. She'd obviously desired all three for this meeting, intriguing him. The table settings emphasized a ritual of civility. Personal control.

"What type of flavor do *you* think I prefer?"

She cocked her head. "The subtle, the delicately made. You're the type of person who wants the mystery inside the flower bud."

"I can still appreciate the different nuances of the stronger flavors." He studied the orchid in the center of the table. "With the very delicate, you sculpt something down to such a whisper of form, there's nothing else it can be. It's in strength you find surprises, variation."

Marguerite realized he was too good at discerning her own interests, the philosophies in which she'd immersed her life. And he was far too intelligent for her peace of mind.

She changed the direction briskly. "Well, all that said, this is a second flush Darjeeling. It might remind you of a muscatel wine."

"It might be worth the cost, then. I could buy a box of a hundred tea bags at the grocery store for the price you charge for a cup of it."

She winced. "Barbarian. Darjeeling is the high end of teas. It's produced in India, in the foothills of the Himalayans."

"Have you been there?"

She nodded. "You can see Mount Everest in the distance on a clear day. There's a misty climate there. For tea, the perfect composition of soil, air and rainfall. The first flush, the first harvest, of this particular tea is very expensive. They usually serve it at an invitation-only tasting with a great deal of fanfare."

Certain that the information was similar to what she gave her clientele when they asked such questions, he wondered that any of them could get past the distraction of the woman to focus on the words. She was different from any Domme he knew, and now that he was seeing her in her world which was anything but mundane, she intrigued him even more.

Her shop was in a downtown neighborhood where people hung out in the quieter side streets. Cars navigated around them, the people acting as if the vehicles were in their front yards, which seemed almost true. It was a poor area of mostly black faces but there was a sense of community. He'd done enough background research on her to know that

Marguerite's shop in the elegant old house had been well received and her location did not seem to dismay her upscale client base. She'd bought the block of six lots, chosen one of the hundred-year-old structures as her teahouse and torn down the other run-down edifices, one of which had been used as a crack house. When he'd driven up to the teahouse, he'd noted that on two of the lots she'd created a park with swing sets, a sandbox, comfortable benches, gazing pool and a privacy hedge. On the opposite side of the business was a lush garden with walking paths that looked as if it was maintained by one of the local landscaping companies. He'd surmised that the tall privacy fence directly behind the house gave her a backyard of her own, which included this private courtyard he saw now.

From what he'd seen when he came in, the play park and the path garden were apparently open to the neighborhood children and their parents, anyone seeking a moment of peace and beauty. But two adamant rules were printed on colorful, tasteful signs at the multiple entrances to them. No alcohol or drugs were allowed on her property.

His gaze shifted to the Japanese scroll to the left of the doorway. "What does that say?"

She went to the side table where there was a stovetop and a kettle steaming and checked the temperature reading. "'God is in the silence. God is in the empty space.' Please sit down." She glanced at him. "Southern male etiquette has been acknowledged and is appreciated. But it's easier to prepare the tea for you if you're sitting, since this is a smaller area and you're not a slight man. Either chair is fine."

It had been set for two people with woven bamboo placemats, napkins neatly arranged and fanned in pewter rings, silver spoons and saucers with a red and gold oriental design. Rather than facing over the expanse of the table, the two cup settings were next to one another, a more intimate arrangement that surprised him. A small round cake was in the middle of the table, a sharp-bladed short knife waiting for precise cuts of the dessert.

"You prepared for me." He realized it with a pang of chagrin. "I apologize for coming so early. You're right. It was rude."

She inclined her head but he sensed no censure to the gesture. The Ice Queen was what they called her at The Zone. But as he took a seat to watch her, ice was not what came to mind. She could not be described. Like the most perfect piece of art, a person had to stand in the same room, breathe in what she was, be this close to touching her.

In the club, she wore the clothes of a Mistress. Not always what one would expect but garments that clearly underscored her ability to command obedience from any sub whose path she chose to cross. But here in the real world, she wore beautifully tailored dark slacks and a blue silk blouse. No jewelry, not even her ears pierced. No rings.

The feature that struck most men first about Marguerite was her hair. So pale as to be almost the color of moonlight, and eyes that were such a light blue that he was reminded of the shifting images one could almost glimpse in a spring's clear waters. Pale skin. Tall and elegant, never the slightest slouch to suggest she had any self-consciousness about her height.

She affected him in a way he had great difficulty in describing, a way that he knew would cause his few close friends within the BDSM community to doubt his sanity. When he looked at her, he knew he was meant to understand the secret to her soul in a way he suspected no man ever had.

When he decided to come to this meeting, he'd made a conscious decision to start down that path, and not stop until he reached the nexus of her.

"Your place reminds me of the Victorian solarium, run by the acknowledged society queen. A place for ladies to talk politics, religion, home. But not really a male sanctum."

She glanced toward him. "Do you know in Morocco it's the man's job to pour the tea in households, and he holds the pot high above the cup as he pours, to create a frothy top to the tea? I think it's welcoming to either gender. Men just don't tend to take advantage of the environment. But Chloe agrees with you. She thinks we need to do something to attract more eligible males."

"Well, I suppose you could have ladies drinking tea naked. That table of elderly matriarchs had promise. I'll bet they were wearing some pretty sexy lingerie beneath their fancy dresses."

Her lips tightened in an almost smile but then she drew it back into herself. He nodded toward a box on a shelf to the left of the stovetop where it could not be adversely impacted by the steam. "What's in that?"

She took it down, the gracious hostess, bringing it to the table so he could see it better. The box looked to be carved out of ivory.

"This is orchid tea," she explained, lifting the lid of the tea caddy and showing the foil-lined interior. He bent forward and examined the dark rolled leaves interspersed with the pale twists of the orchid blossoms. She raised a silver scoop shaped like a scalloped shell. "Centuries ago, when tea buyers were testing different teas, the supplier would leave a scalloped shell on the top of the container as a scoop so the buyer could smell and handle the tea." She scooped some of the infusion up in a simple movement, and extended it to him. "I'll serve you the Darjeeling tonight but see what you think of this."

Her hands had the long-fingered grace of meadow grasses stroking the flank of a passing deer. Tyler reached out, took the spoon from her so he could gently encircle her wrist and turn her palm upward. Tapping the spoon's contents into her hand, he lifted her palm closer to his nose, his lips mere inches from the pulse he felt racing beneath his grip, making him want to tighten it. He didn't. He inhaled, smelled a woman who wore no perfumes but the fragrances of her café. The tea's fragrance was soft, tantalizing and soothing at once, the energy of life married to its tranquility, balancing the drinker in a like fashion, he suspected.

"Much better," he agreed. "I find that much more to my liking." He let her go slowly, his touch whispering across her skin.

She remained motionless, staring at him, the hand in the air where he left it, cupped around the spilled tea.

One thing Marguerite knew about Tyler. He did not idly flirt. If he reached out, touched or caressed a woman, whether it be with his fingers, his voice, or the powerful regard of his gaze, it was because he had his sights firmly set on acquisition. It was possible he was merely enjoying the sexual chemistry that a man and a woman could have in their current setting, an acknowledgement that their common tie was in fact their sexual pursuits but this felt far more...personal.

She turned away at last, feeling his regard as she measured out the proper amount of tea and dropped it into the first teapot, a simple white bone china piece she used for steeping before pouring the mixture into the final tea container. With a quick glance at the kettle temperature again, she lifted it to pour the heated spring water on top of the tea leaves in the pot.

"Isn't it supposed to be boiling?"

"Not for a green tea. Just below boiling is more suitable."

"Does it matter?"

She finished the pour, set the kettle aside, and covered the steeping pot. "It matters. It all matters with tea. The amount of moments you steep it may be personal preference but the container, the water you use, the color of the teacups, it's all important. Tea is a touchstone, a way for my clients to reclaim their balance. I try to give them that."

"Do I look unbalanced?"

He looked as though he wouldn't show a line of hull in a full course gale. Instead of answering, she picked up the tea strainer.

"Sounds like you've studied this from the Zen perspective." Tyler's attention drifted back over to the single orchid on the table. It sat in a small clay container lined with smooth stones carefully arranged on the surface, wet with a shallow amount of water. He noted that the gray glaze of the pottery shone softly in the muted light from walls sconces on either side of the heron.

"Yes. And there are Taoist principles involved as well. Even when the leaves are picked and rolled, every degree of breakage creates a change in flavor, in pleasure received."

"You could say the same about a cherished submissive."

Her nod appeared to acknowledge appreciation of his insight. He was beginning to be fascinated with her economy of movement to convey a wealth of response. Or, he mused, she could be conveying very little. The potency of her slightest movement allowed the one in her presence to conjure all manner of meaning into it.

Raising the white teapot in one hand, a matching porcelain strainer in the other, she began to pour the tea into the teapot he assumed they were going to be using, a Chinese porcelain with a bright design of green leaves, red blossoms, and gold work.

"May I pour you a cup?"

She could do anything she wanted for him, Tyler acknowledged dryly to himself, though he gave her a simple nod. He noted the lack of teacups on the table at the same moment she turned back to the side table, bent and opened what appeared to be a dish warmer from the waft of warm air that drifted from it. She brought two teacups of a matching design and poured.

"Keeping the cups warm also affects the flavor?"

Her lashes flickered. "Yes."

"You know," he observed, "the perception of D/s is that every interaction is rigidly controlled by either the Dom's Will, or rules both parties have set up. Or even the rules of the environment, like The Zone." He watched her sit in the chair next to him, adjust it out so she was facing him. She picked up her cup, examined the bright red contents, then raised it to her nose, inhaling. He watched with interest as the tension in her shoulders eased a fraction. That she was listening to him, he had no doubt. He could count on one hand the times he'd actually seen Marguerite meet another person's eyes for more than a second at a time, if at all, but she still managed to convey her absolute attention. As if she was meditating on the words as they were spoken. It made it easy to pause and collect one's thoughts, for he'd never known her to interrupt someone before they were finished. It was as if she was tuning into something that wasn't the speaker's voice but the place the words came from, knowing when the thought was complete, the well empty.

"But that's just the perception, the rules of engagement. Inside those boundaries, there are no boundaries. A simple sexual encounter can become a much deeper, more meaningful interaction, going in ways neither sub nor Dom expects."

"It's similar," she said, picking up on the direction of his thoughts as if she were inside his mind. "With tea, it's the preparation, the selection that centers the mind, the spirit, opens the tea drinker to a much wider experience once you sit down in the embrace of those preparations."

"What is it you like about that photo, the one with the women walking with the baskets on their heads?"

His abrupt change of topic didn't appear to surprise her. "It captures a moment, a single expression of the complexity of their lives."

He thought about how she'd prepared the tea, the simple sensuality of it, and thought about the beauty of this single moment, its complexity.

"It makes sense now," he mused. "I've seen you spend an hour prepping a sub mentally. Your audience is riveted all that time, not a shift among them, a cough, a murmured comment.

It's a miracle to watch." He raised his cup. "So. To the preparation of tea."

She touched the edge of her cup to his, and then they drank for a moment in silence.

"I invited you here to talk about the mentoring requirement at The Zone."

He nodded. "I figured as much." At her startled look, he explained. "Not many people know it, and I'd appreciate keeping it that way, but I'm a thirty percent owner of the club."

That seemed to give her pause. "Did you help create The Zone?"

"No. But a couple years ago, when they wanted the major renovations they're working on now, they needed more capital. It's a good investment."

"But you're more than just an investor, if you know about my mentoring requirement."

"I choose investments carefully, and I monitor them. It's one of my conditions for turning over my money. It came up because it was a management oversight, and they wanted me to be aware of it. It's not a grand concern, obviously, because you're an accomplished Mistress, always very careful to protect your subs and play within the rules of The Zone."

"Despite that, I'm required to endure a checklist of submissive experiences and a mentoring period under another Dominant."

He met her gaze. "It's policy for all Masters and Mistresses. It was supposed to have happened during your first ninety days at the club. When you came in, you didn't list whether you were coming in as a sub or Dom, and it didn't get flagged in the computer when your preference became obvious. It wasn't your oversight," he added. "I spoke to Perry Stevens, the club manager, and the other owners. We agreed the Dom mentoring is pointless. You've proven yourself enough in that area to satisfy policy. We just need you to do the submissive training."

"Well." She put her cup down. "Knowing that you're part of the operating decisions makes this easier than I anticipated."

"Less to explain, certainly." He leaned back in the chair, stretched one long leg out so it was parallel to the outside of her chair.

"And possibly less of a problem for both of us." She tented her fingers over the top of her cup, and he watched the steam warm her skin, create moisture. "Tyler, we're both well-known Dominants at The Zone. As you said, I've never had a single rule infraction or complaint from anyone I've handled. I obviously know how to care for a submissive. I've been going to The Zone nearly two years. Is it possible that whatever box on my record that needs to be checked can be checked, and we can call this done?"

The glance flicked up again, the pale blue eyes holding his for three blinks. Then her gaze shifted to the window, contemplating the view, waiting for his response.

Tyler thought the matter through from several angles. There was no one more accomplished than Marguerite at bringing a sub pleasure, and yet he'd never seen her dig into the "why" of a submissive's desire to submit, as if that was something private she did not feel she had a right to know. It had to be a precise art akin to surgery, managing to navigate a person's psyche to the point she could leave untouched that deep emotional core, so closely integrated with a sub's response. And perhaps she chose to leave it untouched because a Mistress could not touch the emotional core of a submissive without impacting her own psyche.

"You've disappointed me, Marguerite."

Marguerite stiffened. "I'm not seeking your approval, Tyler. If I've offended you, I apologize. I'll simply withdraw my membership from The Zone and go where they'll accept my current level of expertise without challenge."

"Is that what you think the sub session requirement is about? Confirming your expertise?" His brows rose. "This mentoring requirement is more than about understanding how to safely treat a submissive, Marguerite. Oh, that's the liability matter, and I don't mean that in the legal sense. The Zone takes its responsibility to keep everyone safe very seriously. But by walking in a submissive's shoes, you're able to understand some of the emotional transitions that occur." He nodded to the table, gestured around them. "You take such care to prepare for something as simple as a meeting with a casual acquaintance. I thought that you'd appreciate the opportunity to see more deeply into a submissive's heart, so that your future sessions as a Dominant could try out even more extensive territory."

"Maybe you think about me too much."

Tell me about it. One of Tyler's closest friends and a Mistress at The Zone, Violet Siemanski, now Violet Nighthorse since she'd ensnared and married Mac a couple years ago, had told him as much. Often.

"What I think is that leaving The Zone wouldn't be as easy for you as you're making it sound. It meant enough to you that you called this meeting between us, took the time to offer me your gracious hospitality." He fingered the cup, looked at the orchid sitting in its carefully placed isolation on the table, nothing to disturb a contemplation of its solitary beauty. His gaze shifted, and he wondered if she was aware of the same effect she had, her body straight and outlined only by the monochrome gray wall, her features pure and elegant.

"You take tremendous care in all that you do. I look around and see this beautiful tearoom, all these details, everything paradoxically invested to create one special, incredible moment, not just for the guest but for the proprietress feeding off that moment. That one amazing moment where everything is clear, fine, everything gone but the purity of the soul. Wouldn't you like to see it through a sub's eyes, just once?"

She smoothed the tablecloth, moved the teapot. "I'm where I want to be on that, Tyler."

"If the issue is you don't want to risk emotional exposure, that's normal. Most Doms are apprehensive about this part of the requirement but I can tell you from experience you come out on the other side of it more enlightened and a better Mistress. And we set the rules up front. What you can handle, what you can't."

I can't handle any of it. She forced herself not to move the teapot again. Instead, retrieving her cup, she took a sip and closed her eyes to absorb the taste. Waited until the sensation reached her toes to raise her lashes again and respond.

"That may be true but this isn't something I'm willing to do, Tyler. There are clubs that don't have this requirement."

He nodded. "But I've always felt that one of the strongest qualities of The Zone is that it's not about tricking. If that's all you're looking for, the one-night stand thrill, then The Zone isn't the right home for you."

"Tricking. That was a low shot." She cut him a glance beneath her lashes.

"So is asking me to lie for you, and expecting I would do it. But while we're on it, what do *you* call taking a different partner each week, not committing or emotionally investing yourself?"

"I call it none of your business. This isn't about how you can play with my mind. Curb your Dom's natural tendency to expose my vulnerabilities, or it will end here with a cup of tea, and a very expensive bill for it."

"Cost doesn't concern me." He took a sip, mirroring her. "Especially when it's worth the price. I believe your private Japanese tea ceremony is your most expensive service."

"It's only offered to the guests I choose. It's a privilege."

"A privilege that must be paid for."

35

Her blue eyes were frost. "Yes. As all privileges are."

"A good Dom doesn't ever play with his sub's mind. But he does seek out the vulnerabilities."

"You're casting stones in a glass house, Tyler. You take students, not lovers. You teach them everything about being a sub, and then let them go."

"You don't know anything about what goes on emotionally between me and those women." He kept his tone mild, though he felt the surge of temper, and acknowledged the effectiveness of her strike. She handled herself well when cornered. "While I have them, they're mine."

"My experience is no less emotionally intense for being more brief."

"What is it they can give you in that brief time?" He asked it, genuinely curious.

"Enough."

"You don't achieve the bond you think you do. If you truly reached it, your sub wouldn't let you go."

She blinked at him. Once, twice, three times. Slow, deliberate movements that reminded him of a cobra's regard when rising out of a snake charmer's basket. "Would you like to know the history of this tea caddy?"

"Pardon me?"

"A brief subject change. You'll note it's made of ivory."

"I noticed that," he acknowledged, watching her closely. Something had shifted between them, and he was not certain where the tide of the conversation was going.

"It's over a hundred years old," she said. She stared at him another silent moment, then continued. "I keep it to remind me that beauty and cruelty often go hand in hand. Even with the knowledge that it was taken from a creature whose wisdom is far more ancient than ours, I feel pleasure in its beauty. The duality of human nature. We're savage artists."

She lifted her cup, held it poised just beneath her lips.

"You know how people pretend things aren't awful that really are?" She took a sip, and Tyler marked how steady the motion was. Almost uncanny in the preciseness with which she took it to her lips, put it down on the saucer again. "Like going for an annual physical. We all pretend it's something civilized. We joke with the nurse or doctor but the stark reality is that we go to a room with no windows, and we strip off our clothes for strangers. We lie on a table with our legs in the air or bent over a table so they can shove things into our most intimate areas." The cup went up again, then down. Tyler's gaze followed it, noted how her hand lay next to it, perfectly still, her manicured nails gleaming in the light so her fingers reminded him of polished silver at a table setting. "Our fear of some awful disease drives us to that untenable situation."

"Sounds more like our fear of being vulnerable." Tyler leaned forward, clasped his hand over hers on the table and deliberately slid her teacup and saucer away from her, to his side.

"What are you doing?"

"Making a point about the nature of a submissive. You were saying?"

She stared at him, those pale blue eyes so focused in their frost he expected to feel a sheen of ice form across his face. "Give me back my cup. Please." She issued the courtesy like a threat.

"No. Tell me what your point was."

She sat back in her chair, a pose of ease but every movement was calculated as she removed her hand from beneath his and laid it in her lap with the other hand atop it, those nails curved into a loose claw.

"We go around in our SUVs, pay our taxes, mow our lawns. But underneath every person's veneer lies the Trail of Tears, the Holocaust, the atom bomb, the massacre of Christians in the Sudan. Lurking in the shadows of our darkest motivations is the eighty-year-old homeless woman raped by bored teenagers, the child who huddles alone, afraid of attracting attention. The baby who gives up crying because no one ever comes. Then there are the animals who suffer in labs from our fear of death, who are hunted for sport and captured for amusement as if we have the right to confine life just because we're bigger and stronger. All the while the land is raped and poisoned by our greed and selfishness. Every event in our lives is a chance for the civilized to be stripped away, exposing the darkest side of who we are. Our veneer is our only hope of maintaining the illusion that we can be something better."

Tyler noted she now had one hand gripping the other tightly, nails digging into her flesh. "My point..." she said quietly.

Her leg uncrossed, a simple, pleasurable act to watch. A blink too late, he recognized the diatribe and sexual tease for the distractions they were. Surging forward, she clasped the handle of the cake knife in her hand, flipped her grip on it and planted the blade in the narrow space between the third and fourth fingers of his left hand resting on the table. She sunk it clean and deep, cutting through tablecloth and solidly into the wood itself so the knife stood on its own, the blade quivering.

Tyler maintained his stillness, even as every muscle tensed in readiness. He'd been in circumstances before where his life depended on razor-sharp intuition, on knowing exactly how to react. Even so, he felt the fury simmer in him at the challenge he would have met equally if he sat across from a man.

"Do you want my violence, Marguerite? Am I that much of a threat to you?"

She stared at him a long moment, her delicate nostrils flaring, her face inches from his. "My point—" she repeated in measured tones, though he almost felt the vibration from her body, an overwhelming tension she was not permitting to become trembling, "—is that savagery is our true nature, Tyler. Like this cake knife, created for such a lovely purpose, to share an elegant dessert. It's a killing instrument, able to be something else only until someone's veneer cracks."

Leaving the knife, she found her teacup without looking for it, tenting her fingers over it like a spider. "Don't fuck with mine."

Deliberately, Tyler pulled his hand free of the restriction of the knife. Covering her tense hand on the teacup, he pushed it, with her hand still atop, back to her side of the table, easing her back to her chair.

She resisted each inch. Not a fight, but enough so that he had to exert pressure. Their eyes remained locked together until she reached the point where she would need to slide her hips, and then suddenly she gave way, gracefully easing back from his touch. Settling into the chair as if he had simply held it out for her as was her due. It was impressive, but he was logging other signals. The pounding pulse in her throat, the intensity of her gaze. The fact that she, who had so many carefully cherished items in her shop, had so brutally and quickly destroyed the top of a valuable antique table.

"Marguerite." He rose, removing the knife. Holding her gaze, he lifted one of her hands and laid the handle of the knife in her palm, closing her fingers over it. "I'll take you through the sub requirement if you choose to accept me. But I won't lie for you. You decide what's more important. Your veneer, or what The Zone provides for you. You're not a coward. Don't act like one."

She didn't look at him. Merely sat motionless and focused on the scene outside the picture window. The gathering night, a bird taking her last sip of water from the lap of a stone Indian goddess. The light flutter of the leaves of a silver green eucalyptus tree from an unseen breeze.

Marguerite didn't have to look at Tyler to feel his movements, the impact of his expression. She'd faced dangerous situations before but suddenly antagonizing him seemed one of her more foolish calculated risks. Perhaps because she'd not calculated at all, simply reacted. Compelled past control, which had never before been a problem for her.

He released her, moved past her chair. Leaving. She watched the bird move to the ground to scavenge what could be found there. She tried hard to concentrate on that, the mental reminder to replenish the feeder, instead of trying to see Tyler's reflection in the glass, ashamedly hungry to see his form.

She was successful enough that she jumped, unprepared when his hands came down on her shoulders. The fingers of his right hand curled in her braid, digging in so the tension tilted her head to the right and exposed her neck to the heat of his mouth closing over her jugular.

The power of the sensation exploded in her body with the violence of a grenade. It was something she'd never felt before. A man's touch, uninvited and overpowering, had never felt like this. Never something she thought she'd welcome.

He'd chosen a method of retaliation to her mad act which simply swept the floor and the walls away, leaving just the magic of his lips on her skin.

Suckling her, he scored her with his teeth. Muscles were drawing taut low in her belly, and she felt the amazing sensation of wetness on her thighs. Cupping the silk-clad curves of her shoulders in his large hands, he tightened his grip as his fervor increased, his lips moving up her throat to her jawline. She found herself leaning to the right and back, almost cradled in the curve of his right arm. Overwhelmed by this unexpected turn of events, she couldn't grasp why she was allowing this or what was happening to her. Only when he moved from the line of her jaw to the corner of her mouth did fear and sanity return.

"No...no." She struggled to get the words past her lips. Turning to press her head against her shoulder, it put her forehead against the heat of his hand, his hard knuckles.

He stopped, his lips at her ear, his breath caressing her. His left hand dropped down to where she clasped the knife in two tight fists. She hadn't realized she'd brought her hands together in such a manner. When he closed his palm over the pointed end and bore down, she jerked as the blade punctured his flesh. He turned his palm up so she could see the blood well up from the Venus mound. It trickled along the life line as he tilted his palm and guided the slow, thin flow of blood down to his index finger. She inhaled sharply as he traced the line of her neck with the warm wetness.

"I'm not afraid to bleed for you, Marguerite." His voice was a rough whisper against her ear. "I'll tell The Zone you're thinking it over. Don't disappoint me. Or yourself."

Chapter Three

ℰℐ

His visit to the tearoom on Thursday had been an enlightening trip. Tyler had never been in Marguerite's place. He supposed he'd been honoring an unspoken code not to come without invitation into the territory of a Zone Domme. He'd expected it to be a well-run establishment. He hadn't expected the experience to include art, culture, spiritualism. A return to a time romanticized in memory that she'd made fact with the environment she provided, the knowledge she demonstrated, the offerings she had collected and shared. A complex and very intelligent woman.

He smiled at himself, at his infatuation with Marguerite Perruquet which had only increased the more aloof she made herself toward him. At times he thought she was doing it deliberately to goad his interest and perhaps she was, even if unconsciously. For he knew without a doubt he had an effect on Marguerite, no matter her usual coolness toward him. He wouldn't classify yesterday's attempt to spear him to her table as dispassionate. Or her body's reaction to his lips on her soft throat.

As he drove into The Zone parking lot on Tuesday, Tyler didn't have to see her black BMW to know she was here. When he got inside, he didn't even have to see the crowd of club attendees clustered around one portion of the glass floor. He felt her.

Marguerite had become his obsession. She couldn't draw breath without him feeling the loss of oxygen in his own lungs.

He didn't know how or when it had happened. He'd known her for some time, admired her techniques at The Zone. What had intrigued him first was the way she never met anyone's eyes. Not as though she was avoiding confrontation. It was as if she perceived people with a sense other than sight, so sight was unnecessary to her to establish a connection, communication or acknowledgement.

Certainly the man in the room with her tonight, restrained in such a complex layer of straps that Tyler doubted there was any muscle capable of free movement, was not feeling neglected. Brendan had waited months for the pleasure of serving the Ice Queen for the second time, because she almost never took a sub to a private room twice.

Tyler fully expected she would break Brendan down until each cell of his body was attuned to her every movement, every blink or shift of her weight, every aspect of her existence. She was right, what she had said at her tearoom. In two hours she achieved more than most people might in a relationship in which they'd invested two years. For her subjects, he suspected she was the trip of a lifetime. They planned, hoped and dreamed for this short moment.

She would take them to a point where they would die for her, for the simple touch of her hand. When she was done with them, she would walk away without even a glance over her shoulder. He could count on one hand the number of times she'd allowed her subjects to believe they'd brought her to climax, one of the many reasons she'd earned her title. Never with their hands, definitely never with their cocks. Fully underscoring the slave's status. Only with his mouth could a sub serve her. As he took a seat, Tyler recalled one of those rare times, when he'd considered himself fortunate to be present.

It had been about six months ago. She'd been straddling the chosen man's face while he was restrained on a bench that had been tilted at a forty-five degree angle, his head toward the floor, his feet in the air to increase the sense of helplessness. She hadn't removed her clothes; she rarely ever did. However the tight lace bodysuit in a shimmering black had allowed the sub ample ability to feel the soft lips of her pussy rubbing in slow circles against his mouth.

When she'd lifted her head, apparently in the throes of the climax, her gaze had locked with Tyler's through the glass ceiling, where he sat in the upper mezzanine watching. She'd shuddered, fighting something, her head bowing back down so her face was in shadow. He'd watched a flush spread across her neck, the line of her cheek. Something shattered, so distinctly he was surprised to still find his drink dangling loose in his fingers. The shattering was within himself. He couldn't describe what he felt. He just knew something had happened between them in that brief eye contact. As surely as he knew that she'd been faking that orgasm until she looked up at him. Somehow that had pushed her into a place she hadn't intended to go.

Look at me.

He wanted to see it, wanted to see her lose control. She gave her subs mind-blowing orgasms, so totally focused on their pleasure they seemed to overlook that she herself remained cool and unflappable through the process. Like she was a guru guiding them to spiritual enlightenment. For spectators, it increased the sensual mystery, but he had sensed the heat beneath it, as if it were stifled and unable to find expression.

A compulsion he could only thank God for had made her look up at him again. As she fought to stay fully in control of the situation, of herself, barely moving, he'd formed the words with his lips, not thinking, just acting.

Come for me.

A gasp broke from her lips. Despite the obvious struggles of her mind, so vibrant he could see the swords clashing in her eyes, her moist lips parted and a sound escaped. The audio was not on but he guessed that sound would have been small, plaintive, like the cry of a dove cut short.

Triumph filled him, and more. Sudden, raging desire, so primitive that he did not have the rationality to question the fury that rose in him, wanting the sub's lips off her cunt. He wanted his lips, hand or cock there.

Yes. His lips moved again, his eyes burning.

When her lips drew back from her teeth, her throat contracting, he had a sudden uneasy moment, thinking her fight to deny the natural reaction of her body would cause her to go into a seizure. A hard convulsion jerked her on the man's mouth, taking her to an almost painful culmination, everything in her resisting the pleasure, the inevitable.

As he returned to the present, Tyler acknowledged that it was problematic. The Ice Queen was a Dominant. No. THE Dominant, the Domme of all Dommes. She didn't belong to anyone, though her lovers, temporary though they were, belonged to her for all time. He suspected that like a sorceress, after leaving her emotional mark on them, she could summon them back to her with a spell as an army to do her bidding.

Even more ironic to him was that the women who had always drawn him, intrigued him, were acknowledged submissives. But that one look, that one connection and he knew that he wanted Marguerite Perruquet with a hunger that couldn't be called anything else or explained away.

He knew there was a whole spectrum of psychological analyses on the BDSM culture and its adherents. Much of it judgmental, colored by the moral biases of the researchers and some abhorrent excesses of their complicated lifestyle. He had understood a long time ago that BDSM was a faith you had to feel to understand. Many of those who felt it even then denied its pull on their senses because it was so counter to what was considered normal sexuality and political correctness. He took pleasure in unexpected responses in himself but watching her climax had exceeded pleasure. It was pure, predatory need and it was growing stronger, telling him he had to have her.

He settled into his favored spot in the mezzanine where he would have the best view of the room she had reserved for the night and ordered a drink.

* * * * *

Marguerite stood in the corner, motionless. She was to Brendan's right. He could see her with some eyestrain. For the moment she was letting him struggle for it, though she kept her own gaze forward, focused on the air, focused on her own breathing. Nothing existed outside her and Brendan, just the heat and life of their two bodies. The glass above displayed Brendan well to a couple hundred attentive people, clustered around the opening. The Doms would watch from the upper mezzanine. Jeremy was in the room with her, The Zone employee and trained paramedic who was here to assist. But all of that was just a buzz of blurry sensation around the sharp clarity of Brendan's naked body, bound securely on his stomach on the spanking bench. His knees and calves were strapped to the floor so he couldn't move, his muscular ass tense. The bare back gleamed, the canvas she would mark. A permanent reminder of her presence in his life for all time.

She wondered how many people carried similar brands inside where no one could see. At least this was a brand that would not be susceptible to infection forever, as some internal brands were. Wounds that never healed, that could always be torn by something as simple as the persuasion of a man with amber eyes. When he'd arrived she'd felt his presence through the glass as easily as if she could see him the way she saw Brendan now.

She didn't freeze up. Accepting that her clarity would include three rather than two tonight, she let the thoughts of him pass through and out her consciousness.

When she moved at last, she stepped out of the shadows in supple thigh-high white boots with lacings up the back and four-inch heels. She'd perfected the art of sauntering in them, heel, toe, heel, toe, pause, one heel digging into the floor as she idly let the toe rock back and forth in the air. She ran her hands over the grips of the three irons, resting at the moment in a bed of glowing briquettes. Lifting one iron, she noted the hue of the metal, set it back down. Not hot enough yet. The safest brands were ironically third-degree burns, because they cauterized the wound, deadened the nerves forever.

She would be doing a trio of brandings across the small of Brendan's back, just above the rise of his buttocks, using strike irons not cautery pens for the maximum amount of pain. The design would be a fleur de lis with two decorative elements on either side of it.

"Not quite ready yet, Brendan." She dipped her knees to trail her fingertips up the back of one of his thighs, felt his shudder. From talking to other Dommes who sought more real-life information from their subs than she did, she knew that he was an amateur swimmer who removed all his body hair when preparing to compete. Tonight he'd done it for her as well. It felt odd, the way his leg was smooth like a woman's but so much harder from the lean muscle tone. She wondered what threading her fingers through the hair on Tyler's leg would feel like, combing through the coarse strands, feeling his muscles shift under the heat of her palm.

Turning abruptly on her heel, she paced away. Became motionless once again just outside Brendan's view. Breathed. Closed her eyes. Breathed. Yes, there it was. The center. And it again told her that the thoughts of Tyler must be accepted, allowed to flow and mingle with this moment's impressions. By actively trying to shut them out, she would drain the energy she intended to provide to Brendan tonight, to make him capable of attaining a level of focused devotion that would cause any Domme to crave him for her own.

Of course any Domme would count herself fortunate for that privilege now. Brendan was bisexual and beautiful, living with a male lover who was also into the submissive scene, was likely part of those in the audience tonight. With glossy dark hair that fell to tanned shoulders, Brendan had an ancient

Greek athlete's physique and green eyes so pure in color they were like smooth jade stones. His body was unmarked, not a single piercing or tattoo. But he wanted her mark. Had begged for it.

* * * * *

She'd had her night with him and she never went with a sub twice. Regardless, two months ago, he'd knelt before her, where she sat at a table at The Zone with two other Dommes.

He'd waited, kneeling at her side for a good ten minutes until she'd given him permission to address her. Brendan never crossed lines. His pleasure was in absolute service, not rebellion, so his manners were impeccable. She'd heard that he taught drama at the community college, which she suspected explained how effectively he adopted a courtly demeanor in all his interactions with Mistresses at The Zone.

"Please, Mistress Marguerite. I know your rules and I would never offer any disrespect to you, but I've thought about this long and hard since our night together."

"And gotten long and hard while thinking, I'm sure," one of the women said, observing the crotch of the gray dancer's tights he wore. It was his only article of clothing except for a collar with several hooks in it to accommodate the tethers of a Dom or Domme who chose to seek him out this night. He was popular, so he'd come to her early, apparently to put in his plea before he was chosen for the evening's games. The Dommes watched him, their hungry gazes recognizing the precious treasure of devotion like pirates with a pleasure yacht in their sights. Marguerite knew that when he was done with his entreaty, one would likely choose him for her games that night.

"It's difficult not to get hard when thinking about Mistress Marguerite." He bowed his head. "I ask, if ever you would consider it… Please, I wish to be branded by you. With the fleur de lis, the mark of a prisoner, for though I know I'm not your chosen, I would declare myself as yours whenever

48

you desire me, even if that should be never. Even if I'm just a worshipper at your temple who never gets to touch the Goddess or hear her sweet voice anywhere other than in my own mind again."

"Goodness, Marguerite, you do make an impression," the other Domme commented, the amusement in her voice not quite able to obliterate the not unpleasant expression of envy.

When Marguerite continued to say nothing, simply sipping her drink, he bowed his head even lower. "Why should you honor me with your mark when I'm undeserving even of putting my lips on the sole of your shoe? I've taken up enough of your time, Mistress, Mistresses. Forgive my presumption. I ask your leave to depart your company."

"You don't have it." Marguerite made a noise in her throat as his surprised gaze almost lifted. He dropped it immediately. "I'll determine if you're deserving or undeserving, presumptuous or unpresumptuous." Straightening her knee, she extended her foot gracefully. She left it in the shoe, no intentions of giving him the excessive liberty of touching her flesh.

Bending, he pressed his lips hard to the bottom of the black heel. His eyes raised briefly to take a hungry snapshot of her face, showing her those clear, pleading eyes she could not find it in her to resist.

It twisted things inside her, his words, his expression, the beautiful power of his body, so eager to please, to rut, to fuck if a woman commanded it of him.

No teasing came from the other Dommes now. There were moments a sub could humble his Mistress with his devotion. While Brendan did not belong to her, he was offering her that exceptional level of loyalty based on their one session together. She knew what they said about her, that her reputation deserved such responses, the things she was able to pull out of a sub in such a short time, like this. It didn't mean that the gift did not affect her.

"I'll think on what you said. In the meantime, prove how much you want my mark. Until I tell you to cease, every Friday you will submit to a session with Master Tiberius."

Master Tiberius was a pain administrator the Inquisition would have envied, bringing subs to orgasms so interlaced with agonizing physical strain that they did not know how to separate pain from pleasure. And she knew Brendan was deathly afraid of him, of having the walls shattered that pain could destroy.

"Yes, Mistress. Gladly."

The lack of disagreement or hesitation startled her. She lifted his chin, allowing herself to stroke his smooth cheek with her fingers. His lips were soft, pale pink, but then all the subs she chose had that quality, innocence still preserved in their features despite the transition to full, fine manhood.

"You're not afraid."

"I fear Tiberius but I fear your displeasure more, Mistress."

"Go then and do my bidding this week. And the next, and the next, until I'm satisfied and tell you to stop."

She'd stopped over Tiberius' favored room at times during the next couple months, breaking her pattern to come to The Zone on several Fridays. Not to play, just to see Brendan and how he was doing. Gagged, nipples and scrotum clamped, his anus stretched with plugs of impressive size, balls forced through cruel stiff straps, Tiberius' flogger leaving red marks on his flesh until Brendan screamed and came, again and again. And he would risk the Master's wrath to look up, find her and bow his head to show he would endure anything for the chance to bear the mark of her servant. Even though he would be a servant that he knew and she knew would never be called to serve her.

* * * * *

50

She hadn't made an idle choice. After two months of Fridays, Brendan was ready for what she would do to him tonight. He could not only bear the pain; she intended that he would find pleasure in it.

She knelt at his face, cupped it in her hand and touched those soft lips. She'd let him kiss her pussy in that first and only session, she remembered. It had been through her clothes and just the press of his lips. She'd made him remain completely still with his mouth on her clit for several minutes, his nostrils flaring to take in her scent, his jaw tense to keep him from moving as ordered, though it was obvious he wanted to disobey with his whole body. Even that still touch was a liberty she didn't often allow those she took into the private rooms. Once, she'd allowed a sub to fuck her with a dildo strapped around his jaw while he serviced her clit with his mouth but she hadn't repeated the experience. It had done too many strange things to her, things that had kept her from coming back to The Zone for a month. Intimacy was too dangerous for her.

Taking down the front zipper of her snug bodysuit one set of teeth at a time, she revealed what she had cradled between her breasts. A lifelike phallus, warm with the heat of her skin. She put it into her mouth to lubricate it with her own saliva. It was not particularly large. After the sessions with Master T, she knew Brendan could easily take it.

"Shall I put this in you, Brendan? Up that sweet, fine ass of yours?"

"Yes, Mistress. Please."

"Did you clean yourself for me?"

"Yes, Mistress. Thoroughly. Tim helped me." He referred to his roommate and live-in lover. "But I mean, we didn't... I saved myself for you tonight, Mistress."

She nodded, rose, this time walking the length of his body so closely that her thigh brushed his side. She noted that just that brief contact raised fine gooseflesh on him. Stepping over his anchored calves, she positioned the dildo in both her hands before her hips as if it was attached to her in the way it was attached to a man and guided it in. She'd had Jeremy grease him up further, so even with her saliva, it was a smooth glide. She put her pubic bone against the base once she had it started down the passageway and let go. Gripping either side of his buttocks, she used her carefully balanced forward weight to push it slowly inward, her hips brushing the inside of his quivering thighs. She made a mental note to thank Master T for his thorough work, though he'd already sent her a dozen long-stemmed pink roses for the gift of Brendan these many weeks.

Brendan moaned his pleasure.

Running her nails down his cheeks, she watched the red marks rise up on his flesh, then slid one finger in the crevice and caressed the stretched rim of him around the plug. When he gasped, she saw his testicles tighten between his spread legs.

"Are you hard for me, Brendan?"

"As steel, my lady."

She liked the improvisational title. "But you won't come."

"Never without your permission, Mistress."

She reached down, cupped his balls, found the rigid line of his cock up against his belly with one straightened finger. Rubbing her fingertip idly over the pulsing vein in its center, she watched his ass clench in reaction, his tiny jerks as he involuntarily tried to thrust into her touch.

"My apologies, Mistress."

"You don't displease me, Brendan. I want you to hold nothing back but your seed. When I put the iron to your flesh, you will not make a sound or movement. Do you understand?"

"I...I understand. I can do that."

"I know you can." Tiberius would have been sure to train him that screams could command greater degrees of pain. She would use the lesson to show him how euphoric the internalizing of intense sensation could be.

She savored the feel of him in her hand another moment. The hard length, its heat, the pulsing want it conveyed. She wondered how Tyler would feel, his size and thickness, how his heat would taste in her mouth.

She stopped a moment. That was an unusual thought. She'd certainly tasted a sub's cock before, usually when he was strapped and turned upside down on a wheel so he could stare at her pussy while she enjoyed taunting his erect member at her eye level. But that wasn't what she imagined with Tyler. In her mind, she moved down his body to her knees, taking him in her mouth while his hand came to rest on her head, tightening in her hair, driving her down on him.

Good Goddess... She straightened abruptly, stepped back, paced away to collect her thoughts. Did another circle of the room. Deep breaths again. *Accept. Analyze later.*

"Are you all right, Mistress?" It was Jeremy who spoke in a low murmur, but she could tell from the flick of his lashes that Brendan had heard.

"Nothing that Brendan can't fix for me," she said softly. A pleased flush rose in her captive's cheeks. She moved back to him, slowly. Heel, toe, heel, toe.

Tyler watched her from above, his brow furrowed. He'd picked up on her agitation as well, a mere ripple in the normal pond of tranquility surrounding her, though she seemed to refocus herself now. She was stunning tonight. The white bodysuit fit her like skin. A ripple of reaction had gone through the crowd when she stepped from the shadows for she'd decorated herself with diamonds. A choker at her throat, teardrop clip-ons at her ears and an ankle bracelet on the left boot. His lips curved as he imagined asking her what man had given her those. Imagined her tart reply that she didn't need a man to give her diamonds.

"This skin..." She was passing her fingers over every bump of Brendan's spine now. "Is mine. As is the muscle and sinew, every dark corner inside you, any disease or infection, every thing. I accept all of it. It is *my* skin I'm touching."

Hypnotic. Her voice filled the air as some enterprising staff person bumped up the sound system so it reached every corner of The Zone.

"She's like a priestess, isn't she?"

Tyler pulled his attention away from them to see Lisbeth, another Zone Domme, take a seat next to him. Lisbeth was in her fifties, beautifully maintained and wealthy and a very good Mistress to her subs.

"Her acolytes are trained and prepared under the tutelage of the other ordained priests and priestesses, like Tiberius, while she watches from afar." Lisbeth considered the tableau beneath them, her expression absorbed by it. "Then, when they've earned it, when they're ready mentally and physically for the punishment she'll put them through, she takes them to enlightenment." She took a sip of her vodka and tonic.

"You sound reverent."

"And a bit intimidated by her. When she turns those pale eyes on a sub, he wants to give her everything and yet he's petrified, wondering if she'll ask for more than he can give. And then she plunges a hand into areas he doesn't know he has and wrests it out anyway."

He turned his attention back to Marguerite thoughtfully. It was another piece of the puzzle. Perhaps Marguerite provided her subs a transcendental experience because her goal was not her own sexual pleasure but to see them reach spiritual bliss through physical release. And that's what she did, every time.

"We judge one another all the time, don't we?" That sensual voice came through the speakers. Marguerite was pacing around Brendan. "But when we do that, we're just projecting our perspective on someone and not really seeing them." She crouched, so close to Brendan their noses almost touched. He looked dazed by his lust, mesmerized by her. "When I look into your eyes now, I see beneath the surface, everything you've built or constructed. Minds don't know each other. Only souls. That's where I'm going, Brendan. Straight to your soul. I see who you are and you see me. We know each other."

"Yes, Mistress. God, yes."

She studied him another moment, then rose. Marguerite went to the metal container holding the briquettes, lifted the first iron. Taking two steps to him, she laid her hand precisely on the center of the small of his back. "Not a sound, Brendan," she reminded him.

She laid the brand on his skin with the deliberate precision of an aristocrat putting her seal into wax and held it. Jeremy's nostrils flared, emphasizing that the most uncomfortable aspect for bystanders was the unfamiliar smell of burning human flesh.

Every muscle in Brendan's face contorted, his jawline frozen in rigid agony, his shoulders trembling with the effort not to do anything to anchor himself. Marguerite's countenance was a study of focus, her full concentration on what she was doing and how she was doing it.

"Feel the pain, Brendan. Accept it." She lifted the iron, handed it to Jeremy. Reaching down, she worked the plug in slight movements, her fingertips whispering against the sensitive bulge of his sac as he breathed hard through his mouth. There was a light sheen of sweat on his skin. When she held out one hand, she was handed a soft cloth which she patted in the dip of his spine on either side of the fleur de lis brand.

"It hurts now, almost more than when I did it, doesn't it? That will go away, because the nerve endings will die. But the nerves around it will compensate every time you move for a while, bringing you pain. Reminding you of your gift to me."

"My...pleasure, Mistress."

There was a soft murmur among the watching audience at the devotion in the trembling male voice, even though he knew he had two more coming. Two that would hurt worse because of their proximity to the first brand.

Tyler could only shake his head in amazement. Even Marguerite for once displayed a less than perfectly controlled reaction. Laying her cheek in the middle of Brendan's back, she swept her ponytail to the side so the strands of her hair spilled over his shoulders, the line of his cheek, across his mouth. Pursing her full lips, she blew soft, cool air along the brand. He shook in response. She cupped his buttock again, twitching the plug with her thumb and forefinger, her head moving as he writhed at the stimulation. "Two more to go, Brendan. I could do them at the same time but I won't. Do you know why?"

"Because my pain is your pleasure, Mistress."

"Yes. Yes, it is. And I like to savor gifts." She rose, one lithe movement from the erotic squat where her knees had been splayed, the white material straining over her ass, the dark shadow of the cleft visible, showing Tyler, showing them all that she wore nothing underneath it.

As she turned, Tyler's eyes narrowed.

"What?" Lisbeth asked, apparently catching his reaction.

"She's not wet."

Lisbeth lifted a brow. "With that pristine white, she could be wearing something inside to keep from staining. For some Mistresses, part of the turn-on is completely controlling their external reaction to the slave. Keeping them guessing, not giving them the advantage of thinking they've aroused you, though of course they know you wouldn't be doing it if it didn't."

"Of course." But his gaze drifted up as Marguerite straightened, caressing Brendan's hair, allowing him to place a fervent kiss on her palm. Her nipples, clearly visible in the bra that had to be open-cupped or thin beneath the outfit, were not drawn to taut points that arousal indicated. In fact... He leaned forward, studied her skin. She wasn't even perspiring.

But he wouldn't say she wasn't aroused. He sensed the still explosiveness of her, the total attention that was possible with intense sexual sessions with a submissive. It was as if her physical response was hidden somewhere that no one else could see or find it. He wondered if even she could feel it, or if it was somewhere contained inside her like a bomb she had no idea she was carrying. When he kissed her neck, he'd had a clear view down the front of her blouse, the full curve tucked into white lace. He'd seen gooseflesh rise on her skin then. If he'd commanded her to be still, if he had inserted his finger into that neckline, down the column of a perfect throat, would he have felt her nipples harden beneath his fingertips, her body tremble? And if he'd pressed the heel of his palm in between those elegant thighs, would he have discovered damp heat? Somehow, he knew he would have. Even as he knew he wouldn't now, despite the sexually charged atmosphere.

He suspected either he was losing his grip on reality or the pathway to Marguerite's soul was a truth like the law of gravity, something so obvious that it took really looking at it to see it.

Down below, Marguerite ran her fingers down Brendan's bare spine, watched his quivering increase. Sometimes she knew she could stay nearly motionless like this by a sub, watching and feeling as he succumbed, entering a peaceful trance while she merely trailed a line up and down his spine, along the sweep of ribs, the curve of buttock, the straining thigh. The tranquility would enter her as well. She could absorb its emanations and take it home as nourishment until the next week.

The ceiling being open for public viewing did not disturb her. The more she needed those emanations, the deeper she could go into the scene. She reflected she had been in need of an exceptional catharsis tonight. While she was the only

Mistress approved to do scarification at The Zone, she did not doubt Brendan's honesty or his devotion in asking her specifically to do it. It added to the power of this moment.

"Watch her," Lisbeth whispered to Tyler. "She's there, but she's not there. She neither loves nor hates him. Simply accepts him. She's inhuman."

Tyler's fingers caressed the stem of his glass but he didn't respond. He kept his gaze fixed on every nuance of the tableau below. Myriad emotional and physical reactions boiled through his system as he watched her build to her finale.

Marguerite positioned one mirror before Brendan, one behind, angling them so he could see the affected area of his back, the first brand and the smooth expanse of skin where the other two would go.

"It looks beautiful on you, Brendan." She picked up the next brand. One step, two steps. "Keep watching this time. Don't take your eyes off of it. And again, no sound, no movement."

"Yes, Mistress," he said hoarsely.

Tyler noticed that this time some of the audience had to look away as the brand came down. Jeremy actually covered his nose and mouth with a handkerchief out of Brendan's view range. Though she held no watch or timer, Marguerite appeared to know exactly when to lift the brand. Tyler suspected the temperature gauge he'd seen her check on the teakettle the other night was only for her staff or if she got interrupted. While concentrating like this, she probably could calculate milliseconds in her head.

Brendan's eyes watered with the effort to keep them open. A trickle of blood seeped from the corner of his mouth where he'd apparently bitten down on his tongue to keep from screaming. When his breath came like a rasping bellows, Marguerite nodded to Jeremy, assuring him that the young man was fine, that his response was normal. She handed him the iron and went back to the head of the bench.

Stroking Brendan's sweaty hair off his brow, her hand descended and covered his mouth and nose, cutting off his air and causing a surprised exclamation from the audience.

His body jerked in shock but Marguerite kept her face close, her voice a whisper that nevertheless carried well over the speakers.

"Take the pain into yourself, Brendan. Make it one with everything you are. Breathe in and out of your soul. If you want my brand there, you have to let it reach deep down into you, past the flesh. Burn the deepest part of who you are."

As she spoke the words, Brendan's eyes started to roll, the precursor to a faint. Marguerite took her hand away, a smooth move without hurry. She spoke in the imperious voice of a Mistress. "Your deepest breath, Brendan. Now."

His chest expanded. He gasped, his eyes blinking, focusing again. Tyler noted without amusement that there was a rush of air as the audience around him and on the main floor below drew in almost at the same moment Brendan did, not realizing until then that they were holding a collective breath.

Miraculously he did look more tranquil, even as his body continued to make convulsive jerks from the pain and the near-orgasmic state of his body.

"Mistress," he said, just gazing into her face. "Mistress."

She brushed her knuckles against his cheek, rose. Stopped and let him press his lips with passionate adoration to her thigh, just above the knee, continuing his quiet chant. Not her name but the one word that represented all she was to him at that moment.

Marguerite turned, bringing her other leg to the opposite side of the low bench so she was straddling his head, facing toward his buttocks. Sinuously she laid her body down along the length of his, her elbows on either side of his hips. Taking hold of the plug, she seated it more deeply, beginning slow thrusts in and out which inspired his buttocks to clench, his hips to rise to meet her, the little amount of movement that his bonds permitted. Tyler could see Brendan's eyes, his brow and the bridge of his nose as he continued to work kisses along the inside of her thigh, covered with the thin white barrier. In her position, her pussy was pressed against the back of his neck out of the range of his mouth but Tyler was sure the young man could smell her scent. He would be hyperaware of where she touched him, the crevice of her buttocks brushing the hair on his skull, her belly pressed between his shoulder blades, her breasts just above the brands.

She raised up, putting pressure on his skull as she effectively sat on the back of his head. Taking the zipper of the one-piece bodysuit down to her waist, she spread it open. The lace bra she wore was for support, not coverage, the cups open as he'd suspected. She held out the edges of the suit to keep the zipper from touching him as she lay back down on him, using the strength of her upper body alone to hold herself. Just barely putting her bare breasts against the raw wounds, she dragged her soft nipples over the area, tracing the skin outside of the brands.

He stiffened from the pain but even as he did, the shuddering desire on his face registered that he knew what she was doing. She lowered her head, using her mouth to deftly move the plug. Despite the obvious torment he was feeling, Brendan writhed at the stimulus, whimpering between lust and pleading. The angle at which Tyler sat showed Brendan's erection was enormous, ready for release.

"Astounding." Lisbeth shook her head. "Brendan's never been into large amounts of pain. This threshold... I've never seen anything like it."

"I know the lightest touch brings pain, Brendan." Marguerite's voice came through the speakers. "Do you wish me to continue?"

"Ah... God, yes, Mistress. You feel so good to me." Brendan's face was contorted with the conflict between torture and pleasure.

Tyler was sure that the touch of the Ice Queen's bare breasts meant that the fires of hell could have been consuming Brendan right now and his cock would have been hard, straining to spew for her. To one of her submissives, it was like getting the best parts of heaven and hell together.

"That's enough now. I've no intention of causing you infection. And it's time for the last one."

Marguerite rose. As if rewinding, she took her leg back over his face with the same graceful movement and posed there at his side. Elegant, haughty and bare-breasted. The restrained man nuzzled her thigh, tears of pain running down his face even as his body shook uncontrollably from head to toe.

"He's in the zone now." Tyler heard another Domme near them comment.

"Zone, hell." Lisbeth snorted. "That poor baby is gone. Up in the tornado, hell and gone from Kansas."

Putting her hand down, Marguerite cupped his jaw and broke the contact. She circled him, let him watch her as she picked up a rigid rubber phallus, a jaw-stretching size.

"Are you close to coming?" Marguerite asked her captive.

"Yes... Yes, Mistress."

"I thought so. You're very hard." She reached down, gripped him. He groaned. "That's when I'm going to lay the last one down, when come is shooting out of you."

"Mistress..."

"Yes, Brendan?"

"I...you're giving me such a gift. I know you'll think I'm selfish. But when it's over, if you'll consider it, I want...I wish..." His gaze flicked up to her, Whatever it was he wanted, he mouthed it, for it didn't come through the speakers. Her body was positioned where Tyler could not see his lips. But whatever he said, she reacted to it. Something like pain crossed her face for just a moment before it was gone and she was the Ice Queen once again.

"You've asked a great deal of me, Brendan. Sshhh. Just let this happen. Open up."

He obeyed and she inserted it. "Bite down. You'll hold that cock in your mouth through this last one because I won't have you going through your tongue." His eyes looked down, ashamed of his weakness. "No, you've nothing to feel guilty about. You've given *me* a great deal tonight." When she turned, Tyler saw the faint gleam on her abdomen from Brendan's perspiration. For some reason, where nothing else had, seeing that dampness made his loins stir with territorial need.

"She's being more intimate with him." Lisbeth put a name to what his fogged brain could not. "I've never seen her interact to this level with a sub before."

Jeremy had the last brand handle in his grip but she gestured to him to hold it in the fire a bit longer. Instead, she came back behind Brendan. Out of his line of sight, she picked up a strap-on cock as big as what was currently protecting his tongue and stretching his lips. She ran the straps around her hips, between her legs, her hands smoothing, molding her curves as she did so, testing the fit of the crotch strap with one finger to make sure it wasn't pinching her labia. The caressing motion made several of the audience groan in reaction. Tyler shifted, crossing his leg back the other way while Lisbeth hid a smile.

Then she stepped forward at last, removed the plug and slid her strapped-on cock into the greased opening. She eased in, her thighs pressing against his, leaning over him, her body arched over the branded area, breasts hanging loose, wobbling with her movements.

Jesus Christ. Tyler was hard as a rock. He wanted to put his hands on either side of that slender rib cage to lift her onto him, impale her inch by inch on his rigid cock, which felt as enormous and stiff as what she was taking to the hilt into Brendan now.

Brendan's breath rasped around the gag as she seated herself home and began to stroke him, in and out, her hands gripping his buttocks, spreading them, thumbs playing around the rim, nails digging in. Brendan's face conveyed the intensity of it, the agony of the pull near the burn wound warring with the incredible pleasure she was causing him. Reaching down, she wrapped a fist loosely around his organ. Coming away with some of his cream, she brought it to her lips.

Tyler was on his feet before he realized it. Up to the railing as others gave way before him. As if she knew, her gaze rose, met his. Putting the fingers in her mouth, she sucked. Let them slide out, down. Using her damp fingers, she wet her nipple, played with it as she rocked in and out of Brendan, whose breath was beginning to rasp with the same rhythm. As Tyler's burning gaze fastened on her fingers, the nipple elongated, tightened. She jerked her attention from him, back to Brendan.

"Mistress..." It was a muffled cry around the gag but Brendan's distress was clear.

"Come for me, Brendan," she said, her voice even, cool, caressing, as if the raw moment had never happened. "I want to hear you this time."

His body stiffened and she gave a quick nod to Jeremy. Never breaking her rhythmic thrusts in and out of Brendan's backside, she took the handle of the brand. Lifting it above her head, her lower body changed its pattern, undulating in the S-movements of a belly dancer. She swept her gaze over the crowd above her, ignoring Tyler this time. Slowly she brought the iron down, pressing it to Brendan's skin.

He screamed, a scream of torment and pleasure mixed. Like an animal, without understanding of what he was experiencing, if it was pleasure or pain, or beyond comprehension of either. His cock began to spurt, his orgasm sweeping over him, drowning him in all the mixed sensations.

Still thrusting, she handed the brand back to Jeremy. Loosening her hair from the ponytail so waves of white silk cascaded down her back, she dipped her head like a beautiful, coquettish mare. The strands rippled over the raw area. Tyler knew the touch of silk would be like the scrape of razors against skin throbbing from the simple touch of the air. Brendan bucked, the muscles rippling along his back, his thighs, his shoulders arched as he kept spurting, groaning, crying her name.

"Mistress. Mistress…"

And then Tyler heard it taken up, echoed, whispered among the faithful clustered around the expanse of glass.

Mistress. Mistress. An acknowledgement of her absolute Dominance, her ability to command total capitulation from the soul of another. A remarkable gift that had been offered by a sub whose body she likely would never touch again. Maybe never even exchange a greeting with him, for subs were not supposed to address Masters or Mistresses unless they were addressed first.

She pulled out slowly at last, twisting, bending at the waist so her hair rippled down his back, over the brands, over his buttocks and thighs. When she straightened, tossed it back, she had her eyes closed. When she opened them, she stared straight at Tyler.

The look in her eyes said it all. This was her swan song here. She was snubbing her nose at him and The Zone requirement, leaving them the memory of a Mistress who was a force of nature to herself. A Goddess laughing at man's pitiful attempts to teach her what she already knew, possibly had created herself. The message was clear.

Fuck you.

His jaw tight, Tyler turned to find Lisbeth looking at him peculiarly.

"What?"

"I think I'm losing my mind."

"And why is that?"

She tapped her manicured nails on the side table. "I believe I just saw one of our strongest Mistresses bratting for one of our most powerful Masters, throwing down a gauntlet and daring him to do something about it. And him standing there looking at her as if he was going to pick it up, turn her over his knee and use it on her. What's going on, Tyler?"

Tyler turned back to the glass floor. "You're losing your mind," he said.

Or I'm losing mine.

But Lisbeth's words suggested another theory to him, despite his moment of frustration.

Perhaps Marguerite was throwing what she knew in his face, in a desperate attempt to cover what she didn't. What she knew she should face but perhaps could not. Maybe he *had* pushed too hard at Tea Leaves. Maybe he should have chosen a different way to approach it. And maybe he *could* choose a different way.

Chapter Four

ഇ

When Jeremy freed Brendan, Marguerite stood back and watched The Zone employee help him sit up as he checked vitals. Brendan was forced to lean on the other man while the world oriented itself and became what he knew it to be, though she was sure the band of fire across his lower back made his immediate future different. She stood away from him, in front of him, her clothes back in place. She explained the aftercare while he drank the glass of water Jeremy pushed on him. His gaze watched her hungrily, so she made sure her voice was firm, cool, reminding him of her boundaries and what would and would not happen after this night.

She saw the reminder sink in, the acceptance come into his eyes more easily than she would have expected. It suggested that tonight's experience had changed his reality, taken him to a different plane of understanding of himself and her. Brought him an inner tranquility. The post-euphoria of a successful pain session, she told herself, knowing it was at least partly true. When she gathered up her bag of items and put it over her shoulder, he rose from the bench and knelt before her, despite the pain she knew the position must be causing him.

"Thank you, Mistress."

She nodded, walked around him without touching him and left the room.

The carpeted hallway outside was blissfully empty. Moving quickly toward the women's changing room, she nearly ran into the door before giving herself time to pause and turn the bronze door handle.

They offered individual changing rooms along with an open vanity area. She went into one of the rooms, closing and locking the door. Sinking down on the bench, drawing up her feet so no part of her could be visible under the door, she laid her head on her knees, closed her hands around them. Then she let the shuddering take her, rack through her body like a sudden fever.

Why had she done that? Why had she taunted Tyler when every molecule of her focus should have been on Brendan?

She knew why.

But it took several more indrawn breaths for her to say it in her mind. Breathing in, lifting the diaphragm, breathing out, letting the energy channels open, releasing the buildup of nervous tension.

He was right. She wasn't a coward, though she had never wanted to be one as much as she wished to be at this moment.

She took off the boots, stood before the mirror in her bare feet. When she walked through The Zone, the people there saw what she wanted them to see. When she stood here, she saw someone much younger. Someone she had created the Ice Queen to protect, someone who was not strong enough to survive this world. Pale skin, pale outfit, pale hair. A ghost with the glitter of diamonds to give her life.

God, she was in a mood. Time to go home and treat herself to a cup of chamomile, an herbal infusion. She couldn't do tea tonight, not as wound up as she was. Reaching into the bag, she pulled out a cream-colored tunic and donned it over the bodysuit, belting it with a sash tied loosely on her hips. She found a pair of short heels for her feet and dropped the diamonds in their velvet box, tucked them back into the bag. When she tied her hair back on her shoulders, she was normal-looking enough for the street, the mundane world, though she had one stop to make first before she could escape to it.

When she stepped out into the hallway, he was sitting on the wide carpeted staircase that led up to the main floor.

Because of the excellent soundproofing in The Zone playrooms, there was no audio evidence of what might be going on behind the nearly thirty doors along the hallway. There was an almost hushed stillness in this area. All the music, voices and light on the main floor above were contained behind the heavy wooden doors at the top of the stairs.

It always made her feel as if she were alone in the great hall of a castle. The vaulted ceilings offered equal visions of pleasure and pain, silhouettes of bodies, the gleaming curves of exposed skin, a ready hand or brushing of lips. Nearly two hundred scenes painted along the arched expanse, a masterpiece created exclusively for The Zone by an anonymous patron, though everyone suspected famed erotic artist J. Martin. Life-sized erotic statuary was placed between every third and fourth door along the hallway, the silent sentinels guarding a world beyond the comprehension of most people's lives. But not hers and Tyler's.

She walked toward him, a straight line, her gaze fixed just past his shoulder, neither of them smiling. He sat on one of the lower steps, a hand on the dividing handrail, the other on his knee, a masculine pose. An authoritative pose. A still one, because he was a master at stillness, at giving nothing away by body language.

The dark slacks and white dress shirt open at the throat suited him. Stark black and white that didn't detract from the etched planes of his face, the intensity of his eyes fixed on her. He'd shaved before he'd come tonight, so his jaw was smooth, perfect. Her fingers curled with a sudden desire to touch it, feel that satiny texture that a man had after a shave, to lean in close enough to flare the nostrils and try to identify the aftershave he used. What would it be like, to be part of a man's intimate life like that? See how he took care of himself every day? She'd never thought herself interested in such a thing before. The Zone's front door was a door she literally and emotionally closed behind her every time she left, such that she'd had Mistresses or submissives come into Tea Leaves and it took a couple blinks before she realized why they seemed familiar, or seemed to know her.

She stopped twenty feet from him and resisted the urge to defensively tighten the belt of the sash. Instead she remained motionless, studying the pattern of the carpet that ran on the stair alongside his hip. What did he carry in his pockets? Keys, perhaps Chapstick or gum. Were there pictures in his wallet?

She wanted to forget everything she'd resolved in the changing room and walk away. This could not go well. She could not do this.

"Was that entirely necessary?"

She didn't pretend that they both didn't know exactly what he was referencing.

"If you recognized it for what it was, then yes, I suppose it was."

Not even by a tremor did she betray what was going on behind those pale eyes but somehow Tyler got the impression that the exterior of the formidable woman before him had become glass since she'd left the room she'd shared with Brendan. He'd surprised a street dog in an alley once, a female with glittering eyes and a very impressive set of teeth. Every line of her lean, muscular body had indicated she would be aggressive if pressed but he understood her primal fear of being trapped, helpless. He'd stepped aside and she had shot out of the alley, escaping his perceived threat.

With the same instinct, he sensed Marguerite was at the end of some emotional tether and was showing her teeth to get him to step aside. And it wasn't just the emotional drain from an intense session with a sub. It had made him hurt for her, to watch her studiously avoid touching Brendan at the end. Like watching a mother refuse to touch her infant as it came naked and shivering from the womb, turn her back so it would not completely shatter her to give him up.

"Will you come sit by me a second?" He nodded to the spot on the stair beside him.

She looked startled by the mild request, the softer inflection. After a moment, she came up the steps, smoothed her tunic beneath her and took a seat in the informal position as easily as she might settle herself in more elegant furnishings. Of course—he suppressed his grim amusement—she sat on the other side of the railing from him, the one that cut down the middle of the wide staircase.

"You were magnificent tonight," he said. "This will probably rank in the top three experiences of that kid's life until he's on his deathbed."

"It was very moving to me as well."

"Watching you is like watching a highly trained horsewoman handle a fractious stallion. Though, admittedly, Brendan's more like a yearling." When he smiled, he was surprised to see an answering curve of her lips. She read him well. Knew when he was being sarcastic and when he wasn't, honest versus passive aggressive or overtly aggressive. But then why was he surprised by that? She had an exceptional ability to read people, which is likely why she'd approached him so warily, sensing his still somewhat roused temper.

"Wouldn't you like to be that steed for once, waiting for the lightest touch on your mouth, the release of the crop, finding your pleasure at the will of another? Just to see what it's like for your subs, what you do for them?"

She drew her knees up to her chest, locked her hands over them, rocked. "What do you want from me, Tyler?"

Everything. That one word encompassed it.

"I'll do it." She spoke before he could say anything else, startling him. "I'd already changed my mind and decided to do it, just before I came out here. It's a requirement and I value what The Zone brings to my life. I shouldn't have asked you to lie. That was wrong. I apologize."

He inclined his head. "Apology accepted. And thank you."

"For what?"

"For choosing me." Most of the Masters at The Zone would have given both of their testicles for the right to top the Ice Queen. She could have chosen any Master or Mistress approved for the mentoring program. It was a thought he preferred not to dwell on.

Mirroring his movement, she nodded her head. "So when will we meet at The Zone to do this? How many nights do you think it will take?"

"I'd prefer to have you come to my home on the Gulf for the weekend."

"I'd prefer to keep it in neutral territory."

"The Master determines the location. That's part of what it's about. You're giving up control for the sessions." At her frown, he added, "Look at it this way. I can cover almost all of the required areas in that one weekend. Come at six o'clock on Friday. I'll leave the directions to my house on your Zone email account. Bring the clothes on your back and a change to wear home Sunday. You won't need anything else in between." He rose before she could respond. "And before you run off, I want to show you something, something new to The Zone that hasn't opened yet. You'll be the first to see it. I'd like your opinion."

He offered her his hand. When she rose, declining his touch in favor of the handrail, he kept his hand extended, waiting. "Marguerite, we may have to touch each other this weekend. In fact, I feel fairly confident of it. Consider this practice, a small step. Take my hand."

"It's not the weekend yet."

"Marguerite."

She sighed, put her hand in his with little grace. He lifted a brow. "Are you cold?"

She lifted a shoulder. "I'm always cold. The Ice Queen, remember?"

Cold was also a sign of nervousness. Though her face was not revealing it, he realized her body was. Closing his fingers over hers, he started up. He stopped short at the second step to look back. She hadn't moved, her eyes fixed on their fingers loosely linked over the rail, his tanned masculine skin against her pale, delicate fingers.

"You act like a man's never held your hand before." He said it gently, not teasing.

"Last night you said that we would set up rules. I have three." Her gaze flicked up.

"Let's hear them, then." He eased her forward and they were walking up the steps, then the rail was gone and he was walking next to her, their fingers still intertwined. He headed down the opposite wing of stairs, past a barrier that said employees and contractors only, instead of making the left turn that would take them back to The Zone's open areas. He matched his pace to her stride in the short heels.

"No kissing. No actual sex. And I'd like to do this clothed."

He stopped midway down, looked at her. "The kissing I can allow. Reluctantly. And as far as sex goes..." His brow lifted. "You don't do sex? Ever? Where are you from?"

"Kentucky." She gave him an even look. "The rural part. Where we only have sex with family members. Tyler..."

He lifted a hand. "You have every right to set the limits on sex. But clothes are nonnegotiable. You know they're an important key to understanding a sub's vulnerabilities."

"All right." She agreed so readily, he realized she'd probably offered the three as a calculated strategy so she could get the one she really wanted. It was a child's trick. With an inward smile, he admitted it had worked successfully on him.

"There are some marks on my body that I don't wish to explain."

"Like this?" He raised her hand, rubbing his thumb over the scar that looked like a starburst in the center of her hand, turned her wrist so he saw the matching scar on her palm.

"Like that." She closed her hand into a fist, though he continued to hold it in his grip. "Going through this type of training doesn't mean I have to bare all the corners of my soul."

If done right, it does. But he nodded. "Fair enough. Are you in counseling for anything, Marguerite?" She looked at him sharply but he pressed on. "I don't want to harm you emotionally, any more than I would physically. You're obviously carrying dark things around. I'm not sure The Zone exactly qualifies as a therapy center."

"You'd be surprised," she said sweetly. "Besides, what's a shrink going to tell me? That the world's a beautiful sunlit meadow flanked by some truly wretched dark forests and if I take enough of his drugs I can stay inside that meadow, or at least as close to the perimeter as my vampire soul will let me get? Thanks. No."

"Vampire soul?" He lifted a brow. "You don't drain life, dearest." He tightened his grasp so she couldn't draw away. "On the contrary, I feel more alive when I'm around you."

"Where are you taking me?" Marguerite grasped for something safe, since he seemed determined to drag her into murky waters.

"This is the new wing. We're hoping to open it up for rental sometime in the fall. This foyer will be the twin of the hall we just left. The same artist will be doing frescoes, sculptures and a ceiling mural with different scenes, an original work just like that one. There will be ten new playrooms here instead of thirty. We've made them larger for more expansive role-playing, bigger groups or small parties. Special effects technology will give it even more options."

"I suppose that's where your contacts in the movie industry made you a very desirable partner."

"One of the many reasons I'm a very desirable partner," he agreed, giving her a wink, an astonishing bit of flirtation that did in fact amuse her. "Here it is." Unlocking one of the doors, he gestured her in, snapping on the lights.

The floor of the large room was still plywood, the walls only primed. A great deal of electrical work was going on, equipment hanging from the ceiling. Tyler stepped over and into a frame built of two-by-fours that looked like it was intended to be sheet-rocked into a hidden control room.

"I thought you said it's almost finished."

"It is. The hard part. Programming the lights, the sound." He gestured to the speakers. "With this kind of setup, you want to get everything right before you rough in the floor, walls, et cetera, because when we're done almost none of this will show. There'll be access panels for repairs but those will be well concealed. Would you stand in the center of the room for me, in that circle marked with orange tape?"

Boys and their toys, she concluded. He was intent on what he was doing, his fascination with the control panel obvious. She wanted to brush the soft strands of hair over his forehead, see if he would smile distractedly at her. Instead, she went to the circle. She froze as the room went completely dark.

"Tyler—"

"Hold on."

Spotlights came on from various positions on the ceiling, strobing smoothly over the room. She jumped as the light revealed a man and woman whirling past her in a tight turn. She spun at another motion behind her and let out a startled yelp as this pair of dancers passed right through her, molecules of light and color. Like the other couple, they were doing a graceful ballroom dance across the room, the woman's skirt flowing out from her like the glittering sweep of a peacock's fantail.

When he pressed another series of buttons, the dancers changed. Now she found herself on the stage of *Swan Lake*.

74

Prince Siegfried knelt before her, his holographic face lifted to her with a surreal sad expression as if he was looking at his precious Odette. The music came in then, the strains of the classical piece. The prince gracefully leaped from her, his muscular body perfect, movements of effortless grace among the froth of lace-clad ballerinas. The music drifted off, the images fading.

As she looked over at Tyler, he gave her a smile, though she noted there were shadows in his amber eyes as he watched the ballerinas fade to ghostlike images before disappearing entirely. But his fingers were moving. Now the speakers offered her a primitive, tribal piece. He made more adjustments to the lighting and the room was full of shadows like flickering firelight. Overhead a wash of stars were flung against the night sky, surrounding a heavy yellow moon. She was by a large fire surrounded by African women wearing colorful scarves wrapped tightly about ample hips, their upper bodies bare, jewels glittering on their arms and necks. Medallions struck against their breasts as they stomped and circled, slowed, sped up, dancing for the gods above to answer their prayers.

Or perhaps they were simply moving the way the music told them to move. The heavy beat resonated inside her most vital organs, making her want to join them, to let go of thought and simply move, open her body to the night. The women turned outward, moving forward, their thighs spreading out, hands reaching up to cup their full breasts. The whites of their eyes, the dark irises, glowed with firelight.

It was marvelous. She saw where Tyler was planning to take it. Even now, unfinished, the detail shone through. She noted he was studying something about the bonfire, making some adjustments. If he found something wrong, she suspected he'd be driving the special effects team insane tomorrow, because he would demand that it be perfect.

The program changed. She was in a club, Latino couples moving in silent, erotic dances with lots of close, undulating movements. The men stripped down to their jeans, the women in slit skirts and silken tops, club wear meant to titillate, their hair brushing their partners as they moved together almost as one body, feeling the music.

There were storyboards leaning against the wall which showed the design of gleaming hardwood that would be the floor, the chandeliers done in an art deco platinum that would hide further projection equipment, the walls in simple white, for they would be further areas to project the décor desired for each programmed scene.

As if reading her thoughts, a silhouette of figures appeared on the white expanse of the wall before her, spotlighted over the dancers' heads. The shadow of a woman, a man kneeling before her, his arms obviously bound behind his back. The woman adjusted cloth at her elbow, revealing that she wore elbow-length gloves. As she put her hands on his chest, she pushed him back slowly, moving him up to his heels so the impressive shaft of his erection was visible, jutting up from the black column of his thighs. Keeping one hand at his throat, collaring him to stillness, she reached down and gripped it. His head fell back to his shoulders in shuddering reaction.

The woman straightened, her lips moving in another command that could not be heard, that did not need to be heard. Her submissive came forward on his knees again, started to lean forward. Stepping around and behind him with one, two long-legged, sauntering strides, she drew attention to the jut of her breasts, the curve of her hip, somehow all the more prominent because only the dark outline of her could be seen. Gripping his wrists, likely where the bindings joined, avoiding direct contact with his fingers, she put her hand to the small of his back and pushed him down. An apparent rough move but with her hands on the bindings it was a controlled descent. She braced her weight and made sure his face went safely, slowly to the floor, leaving his haunches high in the air. It was a poignant scene, her total control underscored by her careful protection of him.

When she prodded him with a spike heel, he automatically lifted his buttocks even higher. She stood back, arms crossed under those proud breasts. Marguerite could tell she held a slender switch in her right hand.

Tilting her head, she visualized the moment in detail. "This is me. With Marius, last fall."

"You've a good memory." Tyler moved through the flickering world of the dancers, coming to her side. He considered the images above them. "We pulled quite a few remarkable pieces like this from the security tapes. All transformed to silhouette work of course, though later we might ask the permission of the participants to portray them in full detail, within the walls of The Zone only, of course."

"But you didn't feel you needed permission for this."

"No. You're perfect for this medium. Elegant, statuesque, your every movement precisely choreographed. You were the first person we thought of when we came up with the idea, which is why I'd like to know what you think of it. I don't know of a tougher customer at The Zone than you." He raised her hand to his lips, pressed her knuckles to his mouth. From the look in his eyes she thought he was suppressing the urge to nip. Perhaps to keep the wariness she was feeling from evolving into full-blown retreat.

"It's all...fantastic." She gave him honesty because she didn't see any reason to dissemble. This was not about the two of them. "Literally and in the complimentary sense. Your detail..." She looked toward the dancers, was amazed to see the occasional gleam of skin that suggested perspiration, pulled off by some miracle of light and shadow. "You'll have people lining up to use this room."

"I hope so, because the capital cost is steep. We brought in guys who do work on movies that pull in millions but I think it will be worth the experience. We're going to try and offer five different playing scenes and add five more every year, make them even more interactive."

"The cost doesn't matter to you." She shook her head. "You've got more money than Kuwait. What matters to you is how people react to it. Will it have a glass ceiling? Will they be able to see the images up there?"

"Some of the rooms will have the glass ceiling. Some of them will just have cameras to project onto the large screens upstairs, because of the wiring we need to run through the ceiling. But in either case they won't see the holographic images. Just the suggestion of lights and shadows."

"Good. That's the way it should be. The focus remains on the actual people in the room. Seeing their movements without the images will be intriguing. Absorbing." She pulled her hand from his grasp and backed to the center again, closing her eyes briefly as a couple, the woman in a colorful red strapless dress with flared skirt and her partner in jeans and a black T-shirt, rumbaed across her, the flickering light making a canvas on her white outfit, her pale skin.

"You should do an exhibitionism scenario, for couples that don't want to do it for real, or for a Master or Mistress trying to break a sub into it gradually. You could have a tight circle of people watching. Do a soundtrack of whispers."

She stood next to one man taking a break, hands on hips, deep breaths expanding his bare chest, his pants snug enough that the bulge of his genitalia was impressively noticeable. His shaved head gleamed, dark eyes vivid in the flickering light as he watched his partner nearby bending over in a tiny miniskirt to adjust her shoe, her dark hair falling forward to cover her face. Though he was somewhat transparent, Marguerite put out her hand to touch, trace air, imagining what that gleam of muscle might feel like. Then she turned on her toe, stepping into his body, facing the imaginary circle of faces, visualizing a sub in the center.

"The sub could be stripped naked while 'they' all watch. The score is a jumble of whispers mixed up with a jazz piece…

Murmurs, suggestions and you could change the background tape to the Dom's specifications. 'Make her play with her pussy…' 'Look what beautiful nipples she has', 'I want to fuck him next…' Adding to what the Master or Mistress is saying."

Tyler nodded, his eyes moving over the open expanse of floor, seeing what she was seeing. Imagining it the way she was imagining it. "Maybe you could help me plot out a script, be part of the production process."

"Maybe."

He smiled. She found herself needing to swallow, feeling the press of those firm lips on her hand again.

He moved back to the control room area, in its wooden open frame that would one day be hidden behind finished walls. She found she might like it better like this, where she could see what lay behind the magic. Seeing all the genius and sweat that had gone into it made it a far greater magic, more valued than the ability to wave a hand and make it happen without conscious effort or commitment.

When he looked up at her, her gaze drifted to the line of his shoulders, the strong line of his throat, the way his shirt stretched over his chest as he moved his hands over the controls. The smooth slope of his waist where his trousers were neatly belted, the lean curve of his hips beneath the cloth as he shifted his weight to one hip. She wondered what Tyler would look like in jeans, the snug fit at the crotch. She rarely watched him perform at The Zone. For one thing, he rarely opened the ceiling screen, preferring privacy. His skills were relayed by the subs who experienced them. Nothing about Tyler suggested they were exaggerations.

But none of that explained why he made her breath quicken when he looked at her. Or why, after all the men she'd Dominated, her confusing sexual and emotional images about Tyler were *never* about Dominating him. Instead they lingered over touching his skin, getting close enough to inhale his scent at her leisure and feeling his arms around her. Simple, romantic images. Other more darkly sensual images sometimes beckoned to her from the shadows of her subconscious but she refused to go there.

She had a *crush* on Tyler Winterman, that was all. A two-year obsession that she'd been able to keep under control by keeping her distance. A crush.

He'd stopped the club dance music. A low note pierced the quiet of the room, stilling her thoughts with its clear, beautiful pitch. As it built in strength, it blended into a melody of female voices, all crooning the same note. Then one broke away, began a soft blues song of longing, of lonely need. Bass kicked in, thumping through the room like the heartbeats of all the souls of shadow and light slowly undulating around her, moving to the rhythm in sinuous motion against one another. She saw hands move down low on hips, grip, rock together, breasts pressed tight against male muscle. The woman who had sung that first long note came back in, a strong R&B talent that gave romance to the primal sound. Every beat of it, every stroke, seemed to be urging lovers to take that step toward movement, toward each other.

Up on the opposite wall, the silhouette of a different woman lay on her back and a man lowered himself onto her, penetrating her as she arched up. Slowly he began to rock his hips in and out, in and out, taking her up.

Tyler was behind her, his breath on her neck. So close the curves of her buttocks brushed the front of his trousers, the tops of his thighs. His hand came up under hers so it was raised into the air, curved over the top of his. Flexing his fingers so they came through the spaces of hers, he crossed them so they were over the top of her knuckles. He brought their now laced hands in to fold them across her body, low on her waist. With his other hand he gripped her opposite wrist but didn't lift it. Her arm was sandwiched between her thigh and his arm, both arms in a straight line pointed toward the floor. He closed the gap between them so his body was pressed completely against hers, chest to her shoulder blades, waist to the small of her back, his hips against hers. The shape of his cock rubbed against the sensitive cleft of her buttocks such that she instinctively tightened there. She felt him harden further. His thigh moved forward, pressing into hers. Before she could decide to bolt, he began to move.

"Dance with me," he said huskily. "Follow my movements."

An early training session. At least that's what she told herself to make it acceptable. His thigh shifted again, his hand pressing against the hand on her wrist. He rocked with her, shifting hips, moving them in rhythm with the beat of the R&B score. Tyler kept them in the open circle area into which the dancers did not come, though on their turns the light flashed over the women's hair mere inches from Marguerite's face. They were on a crowded nightclub dance floor, surrounded by bodies responding to one thing. The sound of the music, the message of it, too demanding to be denied.

He took her down lower and her hand curled up into a fist in his as his thigh rubbed the back of hers, as their knees bent, then straightened. She leaned back against him and he lifted the hand he held by the wrist to the side of her face. Threaded her fingers through her own hair and then up, bringing her touch and the strands of her hair alongside his neck.

Marguerite closed her eyes, felt the beat of his pulse, dug her fingertips into his skin and her hair as he turned them. When she opened her eyes, she had a brief impression of bodies, light, shadows. She could feel his heart beat against her back, the press of his cock firm against her. Every time the bass thumped, it vibrated through their bodies, meshed with their heartbeats.

The hunger broke through like a wind tearing loose the lock on a shutter, slamming it open. She mewled, a soft cry of aching want as he laid his lips on her neck the way he had last night, only this time he didn't move or even bite. Just kept the pressure of his mouth there as she realized he was bearing almost all her weight. He rocked them and spun, shifted them in the steps of the dance.

Without thinking, she tried to slide her hand free, move down her waist for that throbbing scream for fulfillment. Instead of letting her go, he went with her, went down her body. She quivered in his grasp, arching in rigid, silent passion as his hand and hers covered her pussy through her tunic. With his clever fingers still laced through hers, he shoved away the tunic material impatiently and touched the soft lips of her pussy through the thin white fabric beneath. Brushed over them, and though she knew her fingers were there too, it was his firm touch that her body reacted to like a starburst, sudden, explosive.

Tyler swore under his breath at the surge of wet heat against his fingers. *She could be wearing something inside…* Not likely. Marguerite had not gotten wet for Brendan, but at his touch she was as soaked as a woman after climax. The Dom roared up in him, wanting to take, possess, devour.

"No, no…" She was gasping, twisting. Before he realized what she was about, she had pulled away, disappearing among the lights and wildly dancing figures of their illusory companions, as illusory as the woman herself.

Tyler swore again, turned on his heel to shut it down and go after her. He cursed himself for rushing her, cursed his lack of control, something he'd never had a problem with before. He wasn't in the mood to analyze it, though. His raging hard-on made it difficult enough to get to the control panel and told him the obvious. His mind was the organ he'd used the least in the past few moments. But he'd be damned if she'd elude him when his flaring nostrils had her scent, when his fingers were damp from the proof that she wanted him.

* * * * *

Marguerite strode out into the back parking lot, her motions too jerky, nothing feeling smooth. She felt a trembling in her limbs she didn't want to feel. She was shivering, cold and hot at once. She couldn't do this, couldn't afford this. She'd just have to leave The Zone, maybe stop this part of her life altogether. Damn Tyler Winterman. She was fine as long as she stayed away from him. What the hell did he want from her? She'd opened the D/s door in her life to find some answers to her past. Well, she'd found them, understood as much as she needed to do so. It was time to move on.

That's what she told herself, though the idea of never coming here again, never seeking that connection with one of her chosen submissives in the exceptionally safe surroundings of The Zone, burned in her gut like an ulcer.

When she reached into her purse for her keys, her arm was seized, twisted with an explosion of pain calculated to scatter her wits. She found herself shoved hard up against the door of an SUV, a position which blocked her from the sight of the back entrance of The Zone and the security cameras. The silver point of a knife pushed against her throat and the whites of a pair of cold dark eyes were all she could see of the masked face before her.

"Purse, bitch." He yanked it from her grasp, his grip on the knife tight and sure, conveying the confidence of a man who often took from others the things they weren't willing to give.

Well, she was a professional in that area as well. She let her knees go out from under her and dropped to the ground. He swore, following her, trying to hang onto that purse strap. Curling her knees up to her chest, she formed a ball and kicked out, plowing into his stomach, thrusting him off her. It wrenched her shoulder as he lost purchase on his prize. As he stumbled onto his backside, she sprang up, stomping on his lower midsection, the same place she'd kicked him, following it up with a sharp jab with her blunt street heel into his crotch, the soft nest of testicles. He howled.

"Son of a bitch," she snapped. When he rolled away from her, she turned her back on him and headed for her car.

"Just plain bitch," he rasped. He latched on to her ankle, twisted and brought her to her knees. With a roar, he was up and on her, lifting her, slamming her against the side of the SUV. He punched her stomach. Despite the painful loss of air, Marguerite hissed at him and knocked her forehead into his, dazing them both. She scratched at his face with her fingers, trying to find his eyes with her thumbs.

She was seeing a haze of red anger, furious with his hands on her, the flash of his bared teeth, his smell, everything about him affronting her. She wanted every scrap of his existence eradicated but behind all the berserker rage, she knew he'd just gained the advantage. He had her by the throat, one hand tangled in the front of the tunic as he rapped her hard into the side of the SUV. He was trying to make her let go, give up and let him take what he wanted.

"No, no, no…" She tore at his face, kicked at his legs with feet that were just grazing the ground and struck at his shoulders but she couldn't bring any power into the fight in this position. She was losing.

Abruptly, she was dropped, crumpling hard to the ground, her ankle twisting beneath her. The robber spun away and it took her a moment to realize the wild pinwheeling of his arms and legs to regain his balance was because another force was holding him by his collar and the waistband of his baggy trousers. Swinging him around, Tyler rammed his head into the window of the car next to the SUV with a solid thunk. A thin chink signaled the window had been compromised. When Tyler pulled him back for a second blow, she saw a spider web of lines running out from the point of impact, a momentary impression before the window disintegrated into nuggets from the second ram.

When Tyler yanked him back this time, the man slumped to the ground and stayed there, shuddering with pain and the shock of the likely concussion.

Tyler gave him enough of a look to confirm he was out of the game. Then he was beside her. Marguerite had already managed to struggle halfway to her feet, using her hands behind her to crabwalk up the side of the SUV. She suddenly realized the car alarm had gone off, was wailing frenetically. Voices were coming from the back of The Zone, alerted by the alarm or the fact that Tyler's actions would have been caught on the camera. She realized with a great deal of satisfaction she was still holding her purse and shouldered it more securely.

She supposed it was smart thinking, hitting on a high-priced S&M club. The clientele surely wouldn't want to fill out police reports. But her assailant hadn't counted on the type of person who would be a member of such a club.

She nodded at Tyler, a brief move but one she hoped expressed the courteous thanks expected at such a moment. "I've got to go," she said. Reaching out, she touched Tyler's startled face, his strong jaw. Her thumb passed just below his eye, which still reflected a protective rage that made something tremble in her belly almost more severely than her legs. "I'm going... I don't want to do anything to him. I shouldn't have lost control of the situation. I let anger take over. Emotion."

A variety of expressions crossed his features. His hands settled on her shoulders, holding her in place. "You lost control because you were dealing with a career criminal who had at least fifty pounds on you."

"I wasn't talking about that."

"I know that. You don't have to be in control, Marguerite. Not all the time. Not of this. Not of us." Tyler cupped the side of her bruised face, fighting his rage, his desire to turn around and rip the man's head from his shoulders and kick it across the parking lot like a soccer ball. "Why the hell did you fight him?"

She stared over at the man. "Because no one's ever taking anything from me I'm not willing to give."

"Is that why you're so pissed at me?" He guided her face back, made her look at him. "Because I made you give something you weren't willing to give?"

"Tyler, everything you've gotten from me so far is something I wasn't willing to give. I can't give. But I don't want you to stop." Her voice dropped on that last sentence, so that for a moment he wasn't sure he'd heard what he'd heard. Then it registered. Enflamed him.

She let out a small sigh. "And that pisses me off more."

"I need money, man." The thief spat blood. "What the fuck is wrong with you people?"

Tyler was forced to turn from her. When she would have moved, made her escape, his hand snaked back, caught the edge of her tunic in a strong grip. Holding her, two of his fingers found a rip in the thin white fabric high on her thigh. He stroked the scrape gently, even as he leveled an expression of cold anger on the man on the ground.

"Wal-Mart is always hiring, asshole."

Two security people had arrived. Tyler nodded to them. "Tell you what. The lady's not interested in pressing charges but if I ever see you here again, even in the neighborhood, I'm going to treat you to your worst nightmare. I'll take you inside those walls and let some of the scariest women you can imagine put clamps on you in places you've never thought of, beat you with canes, stretch your balls until they drag the ground and fuck you with a railroad spike until you bleed. Got it?"

"Tyler."

She sounded more like herself now, her voice no longer that vacant whisper of a few moments ago that had galvanized his rage. Tyler looked up and her eyes were level, cool, remote. She reached into her purse, withdrew what looked like a handful of hundred-dollar bills and dropped them so they landed in her attacker's lap. By putting her hands over Tyler's hand on her tunic, she asked him to release her with insistent fingers. When he reluctantly complied, she knelt, reaching out to touch the robber's face, the bloody lip. She brought her face close and Tyler tensed but there was no reason to worry. The robber was frozen by this unexpected turn of events and a pair of arctic blue eyes.

"You can have my money." Her voice dripped with disdain. "Snort it, drink it or give it to charity, it doesn't matter, because ill-gotten gains do nothing but curse you. We make our own fate, our own karma, no matter our circumstances. If you have the integrity and strength of character to understand that, then you'll mail that money back to this club to the attention of Mistress Marguerite. If you don't, then God help you, because that money won't."

Rising, she nodded to Tyler and the security detail. "Please let him go. I'm going home."

She turned, a tall, elegant woman with torn and dirty clothing, her hair falling down on one side. She began moving toward her car, limping badly. Ten steps away she bent slowly and retrieved her keys.

Marguerite made it five more steps before Tyler caught her. He didn't stop her as she had expected. Didn't turn her around and make her explain or demand she act a certain way. He put an arm around her waist and supported her, taking her weight, pressing his hip against hers so she had no choice but to capitulate and let him help, despite the dangerous shudder that ran through her limbs, telling her how close she was to feeling the aftermath.

Taking her keys from her hand, he deactivated the locks on the BMW. The lights went on, a warm, welcome sight. What was it about your own car that was always so comforting? She understood how shiny Cadillacs appeared in the front yards of the poorest homes. A car felt like freedom, security. The ability to stay or to go, wherever, whenever one wished.

"Anything broken?" He asked it quietly.

"No. I'm sure the ankle's just twisted. It'll be fine with some ice. The rest is just some bruises and cuts." She was also sure her back was going to be nicely black and blue in the morning. Mentally, she ran down what bath salves she had on hand at home, what medicinal teas she could use in compresses to minimize the aches and pains.

"I saw most of the fight running across the parking lot," he commented. "You're a tough lady."

She didn't bother to answer that. He opened the car door for her and she got in, feeling his hand at her elbow, her waist, guiding her.

"I'm following you home. I won't try to come in but I'm going to make sure you get there safely. And don't argue with me, goddammit."

She laid her head on the headrest, looked up at him. Aware that he was holding her hand still, caressing her fingers. What could he do? Run that bath for her, carry her up those two sets of stairs she would have to face? As soon as she imagined someone doing that, the idea of taking care of herself became exponentially harder. She pulled her hand away. "Fine. I appreciate your concern, Tyler. You're a kind friend."

He dropped to one knee so they were at eye level, put one hand on either side of her face with infinite, inexorable tenderness.

"We're not friends, Marguerite," he said. "Come Friday. Don't back out."

Giving him a desperate look, she broke free, reached for the door. "Let me go, Tyler. Please."

It was a long moment but he at last stood up, stepped back. She shut the door, started the car and pulled out, forcing her body not to shake, her stomach to stop its nauseous heaving. Forced herself not to look back and see his eyes which conveyed how much more he wanted to give her. Far more than she could accept.

Chapter Five

ഇ

"I understand there was a scuffle of some type involving you and Marguerite out in The Zone parking lot the other night. Did she whip your ass?"

"Cute. No. I assume you know the real details."

"Oh, yeah." Violet Nighthorse's voice was dry, even over the cell connection. He assumed she was maneuvering her Stealth through Tampa's traffic with the professional ease and terrifying maneuvers of a NASCAR driver. "Mac won't let me go within ten feet of the exit doors at The Zone without him. Like I'm not a cop, just the same as he is."

"The man loves you to the point of imbecility."

"Yes, he does, doesn't he?" The smile in her voice was obvious enough to make Tyler roll his eyes.

"God save me from goofy newlyweds." He sobered. "She fought him with the fear and rage of a cornered animal. Then slam, the drawbridge whips up."

There was a moment of silence on the other end. "Knowing you, it must have been hard as hell to let her drive away."

"I followed her home. Made sure she got into her door. She didn't even look my way but she knew I was there. I sat outside until I saw her light go off. Hell, knowing her she turned it off to get rid of me."

"Well, you're obnoxious and intolerably arrogant."

He chuckled, rubbing a hand over his face. "Always a good friend. And probably right. But I know she's drawn to me. You feel it from a sub, you know you do."

"You think she's a switch?" Violet didn't bother to hide the disbelief in her voice.

"Yeah, I do. When we're interacting just the two of us, I think she might be playing the wrong side of the fence altogether. Then I see her top someone and she's so damn gifted at it. It's like she's two people."

"One of the most terrifying Mistresses I've ever seen and you think she's a sub in Domme's clothing? Tyler, did you have a recent head injury I don't know about?"

"Now I know why I've been seeing of three of everything. Brat. Shut up and listen. Marguerite is the perfect Mistress. Never out of control, never emotionally ragged. It rings false to me. It's like being a Mistress is the closest thing she can get to what she really wants without losing control, because the control's more important to her than anything else. There's something wrong, Vi."

"You've said we're all damaged, Tyler. That's part of life. Your psyche gets bumped, bruised. Wounded."

"Maimed, mutilated." He allowed himself a tight smile. "I guess what I'm saying is I think Mac's instincts weren't off."

Her tone sharpened. "What do you mean?"

"I mean, back all those months ago when Marguerite was his lead suspect in the murder of male subs. She's not a murderer but I don't think he was off in his evaluation. She's the real deal. Damaged to the point the civilized world doesn't touch her, not when she's cornered. Maybe not at all. She thinks of survival first, consequences second." He thought of the knife, embedded an inch deep in a table that probably was worth four figures. The untamed look in her eyes when she'd fought the mugger.

"Then maybe you shouldn't be messing with her mind, no matter what your gut tells you. Maybe she needs to be just who she is."

"Maybe she just needs to know she can really trust someone. So she can let go."

"Are you familiar with the damsel in distress syndrome, Tyler? The man who has to rescue a woman to prove something?"

His jaw flexed. "Don't go there, Violet."

"I won't if you won't."

"What combination of words will convince you that we're not having this discussion? Or will it take me snapping the phone closed?"

"I'll ease up." He heard her frustrated sigh through the connection. "But you're worrying me. You don't exaggerate things. You have the training to know what you're saying. Want me to see exactly what Mac found out about her when he was investigating the S&M Killer and ask him to dig a little deeper? I don't think they went too far with it, seeing as Mac managed to stumble onto the actual perp."

He thought it through. Was tempted. "Yeah, I do. But don't. I want her to tell me herself."

If she shows. He glanced at his watch. Six-forty.

"Tyler?" Violet's voice was soft in his ear.

"I know. I know. I just…" He shook his head. "When did a ninety-pound Dominatrix fairy become my confessor?"

"I weigh far more than ninety pounds. You call me Tinkerbell, I'm going to shove a Taser up your ass."

"Ouch." He sat down on his front porch steps, tried to listen for the soothing sounds of the sea birds instead of the sound of an engine. "On our second phone call about him, you told me you wanted Mac. In your voice, I could tell that wanting him had become everything to you. In the space of a breath, this guy you didn't even know had crawled up into your soul, busted it up. I didn't believe in that. I heard it but I didn't understand. So I was worried about you. You see the things I've seen, you can't… It's impossible to think something like that can happen. But then I saw you two together and knew it had happened for you. She's kept her distance, not letting me get within an arm's length. Now I got the excuse and…"

"Wham. You find she's sitting in the center of you, like she's carved a big hole in your chest and set up house."

"Yeah." His throat closed up as a pair of headlights threw a wash of gold across the lawn. He heard the purr of the black BMW, then her car was slowly rolling up his drive.

"She's here." *She's here.*

"Good luck. I'll be here if you need me."

"Violet." His hand tightened on the phone, though his attention remained on the car. "You're not my confessor. You're my best friend." Something he hadn't had in a very, very long time. "Thank you."

There was a pause. When she spoke, her voice was a bit thick, making him smile. She might be tough, perhaps the second toughest woman he knew, but she was still female.

"You're so full of shit. Stop charming me and go work on her. I've got a guy."

He noted Marguerite was moving a bit stiffly as she got out of the car. It swamped him with renewed anger at the man who'd laid hands on her, as well as a wave of protectiveness.

"So does Marguerite. She just doesn't know it yet. Bye, Violet."

She was here. And he had her for two whole days.

* * * * *

Marguerite had heard his home was beautiful, a sanctuary from a busy world. The graceful antebellum plantation house and all of its outbuildings, including a family chapel, had been transported from his home state of Georgia.

He'd planted them here on his acres bordering the Gulf, ninety minutes from Tampa. The extraordinary undertaking had been done to save the structures from demolition, when the property on which they sat was taken under eminent domain for additional highway expansion.

She'd learned that from conversation at The Zone, from people who included it as a footnote to their discussions of how his home was a D/s playground, containing a personal home dungeon beyond compare, if the stories were to be believed. Knowing what she was about to face, dungeon was definitely the word that came to mind, not the plush toy room that had been described to her.

But she was here. Though there might be lines on which she would stumble because of her own personal issues, she could stay in control of this situation. She was a Mistress. She knew a Dom had to strictly adhere to a sub's boundaries, and Tyler knew that as well. And she was a Domme going through sub training for a better understanding of the sub mentality, to enhance her future experiences as a Mistress. She was not a sub herself. She would and could keep certain shields in place. Tyler would certainly expect and respect that.

"You're late," he said quietly. She turned to see him standing there, the breeze off the Gulf riffling his hair, molding the soft fabric of his shirt against his upper body. He was wearing the jeans she had imagined in great detail several days before. She'd been right, and even understated it. The long columns of his thighs, the nicely outlined groin area. The man had a rugged sexuality that was oddly even more blatant outside The Zone walls. Here on his own ground, the sense of him being a Dominant was far more out front. The way his golden eyes examined her from head to toe, taking in the slacks and crisp shirt she'd chosen to wear with loafers, a more feminine version of male garments. A message that she would not dress sexually for him unless he commanded it, as she was sure he would. She would arrive as a Mistress and leave as one no matter what happened in between. That much she had promised herself.

"Are you wearing boxers or briefs under that outfit?" he asked.

As always, she was momentarily taken aback at his ability to pick up on the direction of her internal thoughts as if they were having a spoken conversation about them. Before she could respond to that, his tone gentled. "How are the bumps and bruises?"

"Fine."

"And the ankle?"

"Nothing an ice pack couldn't cure. It's just a bit tender. Nothing you need to worry about interfering with or slowing down our sessions."

"Hmm." He moved toward her, didn't stop when he reached the personal space boundary. His hand snaked around her, pressing on her back, on the bruises. Not expecting it, she flinched before she could tell herself not to do so. Tossing her braid over her shoulder to throw her head back to face him, she was childishly miffed when he managed to pull back just enough to avoid the lash and level an amused gaze on her. That gaze became much less amused when he brought his hand forward to cradle her face, his thumb tracing her lips. She had to make a conscious effort not to part them.

"We need to talk about the rules again." She sounded desperate, even to herself.

"I remember them. No kissing." He continued to stroke her lips. For some reason she couldn't take her eyes off his mouth. "You wanted to keep your clothes on. We agreed that's not an option. But I agreed to no questions about any unusual marks on your body and no sex. Unless you ask for it. I'm giving you thirty seconds to state any last-minute rules you've concocted and then it's going to be all about my rules. Okay? Go."

She pulled away from his touch, stepping back, which brought her up against her car. "I want two hours each day to prepare and take my tea. That time will belong to me, not be part of the training. There should be plenty of time between now and Sunday afternoon to cover the session requirements even without those four hours."

"All right. But if I choose to join you, I'll do so. You won't shut me out in my own home."

That was exactly what she'd hoped to do but it was a fair enough request. She nodded reluctantly.

"Anything else?"

Yes. Don't make me do this. She shook her head.

"Good. Here's one of *my* rules, Marguerite." He moved in, ran his touch down her back again, so tenderly that her bruised skin wanted to weep at the contact. "You won't lie to me about anything. As a sub, your care and comfort are completely my responsibility. If at any time something is beyond your capacity to bear, you'll use the word *chado*."

The Japanese word, translated to "the way of tea" or "the philosophy of tea". A smile touched his mouth at her surprised look. "I figured that would be an easy one for you to remember. At that time, we'll evaluate what's going on. I won't necessarily stop what I'm doing but we'll work it out. But all that can wait a few more minutes." Tucking her hand into his elbow, he laid his on top of her fingers. "You've shown me your place. Let me show you mine."

"Shouldn't we just get started? We have a lot of ground to cover —"

"Marguerite." He stopped and faced her but kept her hand. "When we walk up those front stairs and you step over the threshold of my house, from there forward I'm your Master and you're my slave. I can tell you're nervous as hell. So let's take a moment, okay? I'm not a complete tyrant."

There was something in his gaze that told her that was not entirely true. He could be as ruthless as one. "This isn't a course at the community college where you can answer all the questions correctly, proving to the teacher you're paying attention so he'll leave you alone." He tipped her chin, feathered his hand through some of the shorter wisps of hair around her face. "You're going to have my complete personal attention all weekend long."

"I thought you said you were trying to make me feel less nervous."

She didn't smile. Neither did he. "I might like you a little nervous."

He pulled her into a walk, and now he clasped their hands loosely between them. She'd never known a man who liked to hold hands so much. Though she didn't recall ever having seen him hold hands with his subs at The Zone, she found it a somewhat sweet, romantic gesture. She realized it suited him. She didn't know much of the man Tyler was outside The Zone, which made her wonder how much more she was going to find out.

The house had some minor architectural improvements that modern building technology could give it. However, Tyler had apparently made every effort to restore the home to its previous condition, honoring its past. It was painted the pristine white that a Southern belle like this deserved. He'd made the circular driveway a mixture of gravel and oyster shell and the groupings of azaleas around the foundation only accented the house's sweeping grace. He took her around the corner and she saw the rear and side areas had even more to offer. A lawn stretched out behind the house, followed by a mulched area that ran to the banks of the Gulf and had a scattering of sprawling live oaks draped with Spanish moss. There were tennis courts and a large glass pool house off to the right, connected to the house by a maze of gardens that even from a distance were beautifully designed, a series of linked circles that featured central pieces of statuary and fountains surrounded by lush green specimens splashed with blooms.

He strolled with her down to the wide lawn. "Slip off your shoes," he advised. "You know those stuffed animals you find in the card shops that are so soft you'd like to sink into a vat of them? That's what this grass is like."

Bemused by his easy enthusiasm, she watched him toe off his loafers and then did the same to sink into the cushioned coolness of the grass. "How do you get it so green, so close to the salt water?"

"I have two house staff," he explained. "Sarah is our cook and does the cleaning. Robert, her husband, does maintenance and repairs. He's also the best organic gardener in Florida." He guided her toward the water's edge. "He keeps the grass back just far enough. That's why there's the mulched area with the oaks to serve as a wind break. At least that's what he tells me to justify why it's so green. I personally think he met the devil at the crossroads. He insists he just has a knack for knowing how to work with nature. So, was I right about the grass?"

"It's very soft."

"Robert proves his reputation by keeping it this way practically year-round. We host Shakespeare in the Park here for the community theater in the spring and have even been known to show old movies on a wide screen and serve ice cream in the summer." His eyes glinted. "In the fall, I have a three-day D/s carnival I'm sure you've heard about. It's an invitation-only fundraiser, a thousand dollars per Master or Mistress and their chosen sub. We donate the money to the Tampa domestic violence shelter."

"Anonymously, of course."

"Of course. I just send it in as a donation from one of my trusts, since people won't accept money from a bunch of sexual deviants." She noted that he sounded amused, not offended. "Maybe you'll come to the one this fall. You could always come as my slave."

"Or you could come as mine," she retorted.

"I already am, Marguerite." He lifted her hand to his lips again, flustering her with that old-fashioned gesture he did so well. Even the words should sound silly, contrived, but he had an ability to make real what another man could not. "Don't you understand, when all is said and done, it's the Master who's the captive?"

"No." She drew her hand back. "I don't understand that."

"Maybe you will by the end of the weekend. It would be an honor to know I've taught you something about being a Mistress that you didn't already know."

"Who are *you*, Tyler? You keep pounding at my boundaries but I don't know anything about you."

"Hmm." He sat on a long bench, drawing her down next to him. "Lately I'm an amateur gardener and a bit of a handyman. When I moved here, I paid to have this house restored. Money makes a lot of things easier, but I wasn't as involved hands-on as I really wanted to be. That's one of the reasons I eventually chose to ease back on the writing and film production, take more time to be part of those details. Something else money allows you to do."

But she was sharp enough to catch a darkness in his eyes. That wasn't the only reason he'd taken the time off, she suspected. Not the most important one.

"Look over there. A heron, like the one in your picture."

Marguerite turned her head, watched the long-legged, graceful white bird step through the shallows, looking for dinner.

"He's like you. Perfect in his isolation. Everything goes in slow motion around you, Marguerite. You steal time when people look at you."

She'd intended to retort to the comment about isolation, but with the compliment the response died on her lips. Turning, he laid his head down in her lap, stretching out his long body along the length of the bench. One knee crooked up against the back, the other foot resting on the ground. When he looked up at her, the weight of his skull pressed into her thighs. His hair whispered against the fabric of her blouse, so tempting she had to curl her fingers into a tight ball to keep from touching it.

"I think you know everything about me, Marguerite. That's your special gift. From whatever plane you view the world, you see right straight to the heart. I don't believe in games, so I'll say I know that I attract you. I thank God for the gift and hope to keep earning it, because I know you attract me like the proverbial moth."

"Then it's probably not very professional for me to use you as my mentor."

He chuckled. "Nice try. You contacted me, remember? And there's nothing that says the mentoring can't be done by people with personal relationships. This is The Zone, not a corporate work policy."

"I think you've just come up with a charming way to avoid questions about yourself."

"Maybe I'm afraid if you know the sordid details of my life, you'll like me less."

"Than I do now? I hardly see how that's possible." She sniffed.

"Petulance looks very sexy on you. Don't get me stirred up." At his lazy grin, she shoved at his head and shoulder.

In a movement that was so fluid it did not seem hurried, he brought his hand up and captured both of her wrists. In the same smooth motion he reversed their positions, laying her head into his lap and putting her shoulders against his denim-covered thigh. His arm settled with deceptive casualness over her waist, anchoring her in the vulnerable horizontal position.

"Tyler, stop this. We need to get started." Where any intimacy that happened could be explained as part of her training. Not a spontaneous, accidental pleasure experienced in his company as she was feeling now, with butterflies feathering around in her lower belly.

He stretched his other arm along the back of the bench and cocked his head, looking down at her with those intense eyes that seemed to convey two messages. There was the surface gentle teasing light, and the darker shades. A man's desire coming through, stirred by her presence and making no attempt to mask it.

"If you could ask me one question about myself, what would it be?"

She didn't want to know more. She'd just been being defensive and he knew it. She sat silently, stubbornly. Watched his smile die away. But she studied the clouds over his shoulder and wouldn't watch the reaction grow in his eyes further.

"Look at me. Unless you're afraid to."

Of course that was an easy ploy to recognize, but she stepped right into it. The expression in his eyes was not what she expected. Not frustrated or angry, not hurt or rejected. Deep, focused, centered on her face. She reflected he was already figuring out things she didn't want him to know with that intelligent mind of his.

"How far will you run, Marguerite, before you realize you're not running away from me? You're running to me."

He put his hands beneath her legs and back and lifted her onto her feet as he rose before she could think of a response to that outrageous statement. "It's time to go up to the house. Sarah and Robert will be here periodically through the weekend. Out of respect for them, I typically hire off-hours Zone staff for cooking and assistance when I have larger D/s parties. But they've started helping me with smaller groups or when I'm alone with a sub, or when I need certain areas or settings prepared. When I anticipate needing them through a weekend they stay in one of my guesthouses. While I've no indication of their own sexual preferences they understand mine, so you need feel no concern around them this weekend."

She struggled to reorient herself as he shifted gears on her, physically urging her toward the house and that very significant threshold with a firm hand on her lower back. They paused briefly only to retrieve their shoes and slip them back on.

"Do you remember all the items on the requirements list?"

Commands, total submission, restraints, flogging and punishment, exhibitionism…submitting before another Dom… She nodded, a quick motion, her stomach constricting in a twist of nerves.

He took her to the front of the house, up the steps. As he opened the door, he looked down at her, unsmiling, his mouth a little stern now. She wished he could be one of the many men who was shorter than her when she wore heels, though of course she'd maximized the difference in their heights with her insolent desire to wear the gender-neutral deck shoes.

Why couldn't he reassure her, say something that acknowledged she was just playing at this role? Why did he have to treat her like she actually was a sub?

Because that was the point of the training. She knew that. It didn't work if it didn't feel real and Tyler had integrity. He wouldn't let her just skim through the basics. She'd talked to Lisbeth about her session. The woman had seemed so calm about it, like she'd been able to maintain some sense of…not detachment, but had actually enjoyed the experience of understanding what her subs felt. All Marguerite felt was a frightening sense of going down a dark tunnel where she wasn't sure what would grab her. What might reach for her in the dark, a hand covering her mouth…

"Hey." Tyler's voice, like the warming heat of a summer sun, reached through the cold and found her. His hands were on her face again, his eyes close. Those beautiful brown and gold eyes. The tiger. *Taigaa*, in Japanese, though the word that came to mind was *mouko*. Fierce tiger. Afraid of nothing. Willing to do anything to keep her feeling safe forever.

"You can do this, Marguerite. Slow, easy steps. Let me hear that beautiful voice of yours."

"I'm okay. I'm fine."

She was trembling under his touch. Tyler took a firmer grip on her cold hands, drew her over the threshold, stopped. Rubbed his hands along her upper arms. "See? Small steps. Just take it one thing at a time and you'll be fine. Angel, I'm not going to hurt you. You know that, right? Can you nod for me? Breathe a little?"

Tender humor mixed with the concern in his face could undo her. And give her reassurance. She was rather amazed at the combination. When she managed a nod, he put an arm around her waist, guiding her forward.

To her left was a sunken living room with a widescreen television, a white sectional sofa and a black glass center table. An alabaster statue of Isis rested on the table next to a small water bowl with floating fresh gardenias. Over the fireplace was an oil painting, a tall ship of the line plowing through a stormy sea. As he took her through the house, she noted that every room on the first level seemed to have windows and more windows affording the inhabitants panoramic views of the Gulf. There was absolute privacy here. The last neighbor she'd passed had been a few miles away, so it was easy to imagine him walking into his kitchen in his underwear to get his morning coffee, his eyes sleepy, a shadow on his jawline. All those wonderful muscles on display that she had felt under his clothes when she was pressed up against him.

She hadn't expected to feel desire rush in so suddenly on top of fear but inside his house, his touch and the sense of sanctuary that the comfort of his home suggested allowed it to happen. She'd have preferred the fear of her training to this—fearing the emotions he evoked, how he made her think these intimate things about him. The sky was now a violet blaze, night settling in. He had the gas logs going at a low setting in a cozy sitting room. He paused in there a moment, stopping her in front of its warmth. "Sarah will have us a small meal in about an hour. You probably haven't eaten yet."

She shook her head. "I'm not really hungry."

"You'll eat, because I'm going to be requiring a lot of you." His voice was the erotic touch of warm oil on bare skin. "And it's my job to care for you. As much as it is for you to follow my direction for your benefit."

Get a grip, Marguerite. They're just words. Words have no power to change who you are.

It was just the way the game was played. That's all it meant, though the focused way he watched her very movement, heard every word she spoke, made her stomach do a funny dip. Was this the way it was for subs? Every reaction of approval or disapproval from the Master ratcheting up the tension as well as the arousal another notch? And was it this easy to slip into the way a sub might feel? He hadn't even demanded she address him formally as Master but she'd felt the new relationship settle onto her shoulders like a staggering weight the moment she'd crossed the threshold. She'd always been a Mistress. It never occurred to her that the states of mind could be so easily tried on.

The foyer was a hallway that extended the length of the house. When he took her up a staircase to the second floor and turned her onto a catwalk that connected the two sides of the second level, she could look at the view of the Gulf out of the two-story-high window that framed the rear entry and rose high above it in an arc, a wall of glass. The water moved calmly under the rose sky which was beginning to be jeweled with early faint stars that would grow more ornate as the night deepened.

"This is an amazing home," she said out of politeness, sincerity and an awkward inability to come up with anything to say. He glanced down at her, reminding her again of their height difference before he tugged her to sit down with him on the catwalk. The slats of the railings were wide enough that he could slide his legs through them. When he directed her to do the same, they sat like two children, their feet dangling over the open space below. He put her hand on his thigh, his own hand curled over it.

"Here's one of my rules, Marguerite. You speak only when I ask you a question or if you want to say something, in which case you ask my permission to speak first." His thumb moved over her knuckles one at a time, tracing the bumps of bone, the veins running across them. "Do you understand why I would have that rule?"

"Because you're an egotistical male who doesn't want any competition with the sound of his own voice?"

He tightened his grip. "Marguerite, focus. Quit building up your defenses and think."

The admonition stung, mainly because he'd seen so easily through her tartness, more easily than she had. Closing her mouth, she tried to think beyond his touch. He'd turned her hand over now and was running his fingers over her palm, down toward her wrist. She wanted to pull away, to make him stop doing things that were creating taut arousal in her lower abdomen. She could handle this. She could. Then he leaned forward and pressed his lips to her sternum just below the pocket of her collarbone, inside the vee of the blouse. Her breath expelled sharply from her, her nipples instantly reacting. Her thighs wanted to press together, to contain the response between them, but of course her legs were between the slats and could not close. Her chin brushed his hair. Looking at his other hand braced on the railing just in front of her, she could imagine how easy it would be for him to let go of the railing and cup her between the legs of the slacks.

"I'm waiting for an answer to my question, Marguerite," he said against her skin.

"Because…" She swallowed, closing her eyes, wishing his tongue wasn't so warm and clever, able to make her heart pound beneath it. His chin rubbed the top of her breast, an innocent touch. "What…why are you doing that?"

"Because a Master is able to enjoy the gifts of his slave at any time he chooses. Answer the question. Or am I making it too difficult for you to think?"

The teasing, the arrogant implication, stiffened her resolve as she was sure he'd intended. However, she was learning that being able to identify the strategy did not make her any more immune to it.

A Mistress of incomparable experience and yet his lightest touch was making her react like an innocent, unused to sensual pleasures. Tyler wondered what she would think if she knew how powerfully that unexpected discovery affected him.

Her voice came out strained, her brow furrowed like a student puzzling out a difficult math problem. He smiled against her skin.

"A slave who doesn't have to make...conversation will focus on...things."

"Feel the Will of her Master far more keenly, physically and emotionally." He raised his head, making sure his approval was evident in his eyes. "Similar to what's implied by 'God is in the silence'. Many enlightening lessons are to be found in quiet."

A flush spread through her cheeks and drew his attention to the delicacy of her eyelashes, as fine and pale as her silken hair.

"Come with me. We'll come back here, don't worry." Rising, he easily plucked her out of the slats and set her back on her feet, guiding her forward again with a hand on her lower back, his fingers lingering on the beginning swell of her buttocks.

He took her across the catwalk and down the rear staircase, to an oak door carved with a pastoral scene. While sheep lay placidly in a meadow, a shepherd serenaded a reclining shepherdess with his pipe. Marguerite reached out to touch the fine detail as he turned the skeleton key in the lock, the key also serving as a doorknob to pull the door open.

It was an atrium, a large chamber with a domed ceiling which had been painted with a simple scene of clouds and pale blue sky. Only... Her eyes narrowed. On closer inspection, she saw wispy outlines of angels floating in those clouds, elegant fingers extended toward the feathers of swans backing against the wind, soaring. It was a study of whites, the shadowing giving the features of clouds, birds or angels.

"It's called 'Living a Child's Summer Day'," he explained. "Inspired obviously by the way children lie on their backs and look into the sky. The artist told me that there are over two hundred and twelve images in it. I haven't found them all myself yet. Sometimes I think magic has touched it and the images actually change from day to day."

She managed to tear her gaze from it to see that the chamber was a gallery. The walls were hung with original paintings. Sculptures had been placed on pedestals strategically scattered across the room, such that one could either wander among them or stay in one space and simply turn in a circle. And as she had that thought, her eyes came to rest on two cushioned straight-back chairs positioned in the center of the atrium, back to back. There was an ice bucket next to them.

"I'd like you to sit here." He guided her into one of the chairs as she eyed him, distrustful. "And while we're in here, you may speak freely, whatever comes to your mind."

Kneeling by her, he took one ankle in his hand. There was a muted ripping noise as he loosened a Velcro strap she hadn't noticed at the base of her chair and wrapped it around her ankle over the thin dress sock she'd worn with the loafers. "A simple lesson in restraints," he explained. "Nothing too fast or aggressive, just easing you into it."

She peered down the other side, noted there was a matching one there. Her heart started pounding up into her throat again.

"Would you ease a sub into it? I don't want to be treated differently."

Tyler took the other ankle in hand, fastened it to the opposite chair leg so her legs were spread, restricted. "Handling subs doesn't come with an Equal Opportunity Employer policy, Marguerite. Every one is different. If she was new to it, uncertain of what her feelings meant, yes, I would take my time. To rush it would be selfish, but even more than that I'd be depriving myself of a great pleasure. To watch the minute signs of nervousness, the moistening of the lips..." He raised his head, passed his finger over her mouth. "The quick darts of the eye, the pulse riding high in the throat..." He stroked there and she shuddered. "The trembling, the knowledge that this is something the body and soul are begging for, even as the mind and its fear and its inhibitions try to interfere, to slow a process that's inevitable... It's one of the sweetest aphrodisiacs I know."

"I've never broken in a virgin sub."

"You've denied yourself a real emotional pleasure then, for both of you. I can't imagine any sub not wanting to be under your command for his first time. Now the hands."

He stood up behind her, his hands coming down on her shoulders, molding over her biceps, moving to her elbows. Tugging gently, he eased her arms behind her, around the back of the chair. It flattened her against the upper part of the chair, straightening and arching her. Tyler could tell it startled her when he secured each of her wrists not in Velcro straps but in the handcuffs he picked up off the seat of the chair behind hers and ran through the slat of her chair back. He was still learning the territory, working on picking up the minute nuances of her expressions, body language and voice, but it was hard to focus when she was now all his, restrained and open.

Bending to her ear, he ran his hands up her upper arms again then rested them there, his grip light, easy. "Are you wet, Marguerite? Wet from me restraining you, holding you open to me like this so I could fondle your breasts or your pussy whenever I wish?"

"I'm...I'm wet. I think."

She had no flirtatiousness or artifice to her. From her sudden stiffening, he knew she'd realized that her words could easily be construed as an invitation, not as honest uncertainty. It made Tyler curse the obvious need to exercise restraint, not to take undue advantage. *Weren't you the one who just expostulated on the benefits of patience? Idiot.*

He went back in front of her, dropped to one knee, laying either hand on her spread thighs clad in the mannish trousers. Leaning forward, he felt her tense, quiver, as he brought his face down between them, his nose and mouth so close, so temptingly close...

He inhaled, closing his eyes, felt his cock harden even further than he'd thought possible. "You are wet," he agreed, his thumbs caressing her inner thighs. "And I'm going to make you much wetter."

Marguerite wanted to spit at him when he rose without doing anything else, almost as much as she wanted to rail at her traitorous body for wanting him to do more. Surprisingly, he took a seat in the chair just behind her so they were back to back. There was that rattling of handcuffs. She was astounded when she turned her head enough to see him fit one of his wrists in a second pair, work the slack between the slats of his chair. He clicked the other one in place, locking his arms behind his back in much the same manner. They were close enough that he was able to lace the fingers of his right hand with that of her left. Reaching out with his foot, he tumbled the ice bucket over on its side, so that two ice cubes rolled out. Marguerite noticed that there appeared to be something gray in the center of the cubes.

"Those are the keys to the cuffs. When it melts down, we'll be able to free ourselves."

"And exactly how is either one of us going to reach down to pick up the keys?"

He twisted his head, looked at her blankly a moment, then the meaning of her words apparently sank in. "Oh, Christ. Didn't think of that."

At her alarmed look, his grin broke through. "Just kidding, angel." He caught her fingers in his, tugged them so they were feeling the slat of the chair through which his cuffs had been threaded. "The slat of this chair is in slots, see? I just remove the slat, pull the cuffs free. Then I can pull my legs through the cuffs and pick up the keys."

"You..." She shook her head, resisting the urge to throttle him as he chuckled. He settled his back to her, both of them bound by the handcuffs, hands intertwined in a lovers' clasp.

"Tyler, why are we doing this?"

"It's a way to see if you can follow direction. And remember, one of the requirements was the restraints, the physical vulnerability."

"But why are you participating?"

"Maybe to remind you that we're in this together. You're not all by yourself." He caressed her open palm as she moved restlessly, clacking the cuffs against the wood of the chair.

And there was another point as well, though Tyler chose not to share it. He wanted to coax forth the Marguerite he'd seen in brief flashes at the tearoom, with her appreciation of aesthetics. He wanted the real woman when he roused her passions, not the prisoner fighting involuntary response every step of the way.

"Trust me, Marguerite. Look at the artwork on display before you."

Marguerite closed her eyes, wondering if she should count to ten as a method of regaining her composure. She thought that a multiple of ten might not be enough. So she resigned herself for the moment to following his direction.

She found herself auditing an eclectic assortment of erotic art. The one directly before her chair was a photograph blown up to life-size and framed in black. A woman was folded over the soft high back of a couch. Taken from a rear angle, the photo focused on her from waist to feet, showing her wearing frilly high-cut panties, garters, stockings and heels. Her calves had been crossed and tied, her arms bound behind her. Her face was in shadow, the whole photo artistically done in black and white, every detail of her submission starkly outlined except for one tiny touch of pink. The line of ruffles that went across the widest portion of her backside. *Cry Mercy* was the name of the photo.

Not a cry for mercy *from* punishment Marguerite knew. *For* the punishment, for the release that came with it.

The piece to the left was a photograph focusing on a man's erect cock. With his body displayed only from mid-thigh to well-defined abdomen, the man rested his hand on the base of the cock, a loose curl, his fingers massaging his testicles. It was easy to imagine him caught in a frozen moment of stroking himself for an avidly watching lover. She was absorbed by the hand, the long fingers, and made herself pull her attention from it.

Next came something familiar, the fresco of the three Graces, the Hellenic Period rendering, the two outside Graces facing forward, the middle one with her back to the viewer. The smooth bodies, small perfect breasts and heart-shaped buttocks, the partial torsos linked by their arms in sensual innocence, simply what they were.

"Describe what you're seeing to me as if I've never seen it. Tell me what you think about it."

She cleared her throat as her gaze shifted again. "It's a pen and ink drawing, in color. In the forest. It looks like a David Delamare. A man has been attacked by a woman with...wings and fangs. Like a harpy, only beautiful, with raven dark hair falling over her shoulders. She's crouched over his groin, her wings folded back, teeth bared. You can see where she's scratched his chest with her talons. He's bleeding. Naked, his garments and armor stripped...as if he's a knight...scattered in piles in the clearing where she's torn it haphazardly all off him. She's just started to lower herself onto his erection and though you can tell she's forced him to this moment, something has happened. He's gotten one hand loose to reach up to her face."

"Even though she could tear him to shreds, he now desires her more than fears her," Tyler suggested.

"Yes. But it's more than the fact he desires her. The way he's touching her face...he's offering...more."

"And what's she doing?"

"She's...looking down at him. You can tell it's...she's not sure. She didn't expect her savagery to be met with desire. With love. You can't tell if the next moment is going to be one of blood or passion."

"The interesting thing is that's an adaptation from a medieval religious engraving. It was intended as a rendering of an agent of the Devil trying to tempt and destroy the soul of a poor sinner but the artist took it and provided a different interpretation. Do you like it?"

"Yes," she said after a moment. "What are you looking at?"

You, he wanted to tell her. There were two angled mirrors that allowed him a clear view of her profile without her being able to see him. Her shifts in gaze, her expression as she studied the artwork, intrigued him. He wished he'd thought to open her blouse before he'd restrained her so he could see the small curves rising up over the top of her bra and know if her nipples were puckering into hard points. Her fingers were twitching against his, suggesting agitation, possible arousal. Or just the fact she didn't like his proximity, he reflected wryly.

"First, tell me if you like the one of the man's cock. And why or why not."

"I like it. The detail. The stillness. A moment of reality you don't usually get to study at your leisure before the view changes."

"Well, unless you have Viagra."

"That's not what I meant." There was a smile in her voice, though. It pleased him to know he could touch her sense of humor. "The hairs on his legs, the line of muscle in his thighs, the curve of ass, the planes of his abdomen. His hands..."

"You like his hands." He caught the slight inflection and pounced on it.

Her fingers flexed in his and he heard a quiet swallow. Testing, he began to move his index finger on a slow glide up the center of her palm. "Why?"

"Tyler." She stilled further at the caressing touch. "Are you... It feels like you're seducing me. Trying to seduce me," she amended.

"Does it? You sound surprised."

"It doesn't seem necessary."

"That's because you don't have to seduce or flirt with men, Mistress Marguerite." He leaned his head back on her shoulder, turning to brush her cheek, smile up into her confused eyes. "You are a seduction. A man looks at you and not even a siren's voice would tear him away from your side, or keep him from seeing to your desires. But the rest of us poor Doms..." His thumb drifted to her wrist, stroked that erogenous zone. He felt her shoulder shudder where it was pressed under his. "We must endure the torment of flirtation. The tedious, monotonous arts of active seduction."

Despite her best struggle, he saw that tightening of her facial muscles he was beginning to recognize as her version of a smile, the resistance to one.

"Tyler, I really don't like you."

"I'm glad you told me," he said gravely, wishing he was free to turn around and kiss a smile onto her mouth, a real one. He had a suspicion that those blue eyes could sparkle like diamonds when she was truly happy. He lifted his head, returning them to their back-to-back position where she thought he couldn't see her. "Tell me about his hands."

"They're...capable. You'd think the cock would be the focal point of the picture but because they've brought his hand into it, underscored its functionality by showing it stroking and stimulating him, you begin to think of the other things his hand could do if..."

"If?"

"If he stepped out of the picture."

"Nicely said."

"You still haven't told me what you're looking at."

"Marilyn Monroe's breasts."

"Excuse me?"

"It's a molding. Not from the real ones, because the artist unfortunately was just a boy when that wonderful lady passed out of our lives but he studied her movies, photographs. Interviewed two privileged gentlemen who had the honor of seeing them uncovered. He chose to mold them as they would have been toward the latter end of her life, when they were fuller, heavier, ripe."

Tyler paused, searching for the right words. "When I saw it, I saw what he intended. The breasts of a woman... They're her life, her vulnerability, one of the most powerful of her allures. Have you ever noticed when a woman touches herself for pleasure at The Zone, she often starts with her breasts, almost as fascinated with their perfection as men are? But while our interest is often atavistic, hers is more reverent, as if thanking Mother Goddess for a gift that ties the woman to Her. And I suppose that's why he also sculpted her hands beneath them, cupping them. The vulgar would say that it represents what she offered to the world. They'd mean it in a crass way that denied her value, the fact that she captured our hearts as much as our sexual fantasies. She was a woman in every sense of the word. Every man wishes he could have saved her, helped her see the world was a far better place than she knew and that she was stronger than she realized."

"I think you're idealizing her. She likely was as difficult and mundane as any of us."

"I reserve the right to make up my own story behind the art."

Switching gears on her, he curled his forefinger and thumb around one wrist. "You're fine-boned for your height. No jewelry, though. You don't wear it much but when you do... That was some show of ice at The Zone. If that robber had known you were carrying those on you, he would have fought a lot harder. Probably cut your throat."

When his grip tightened on her, just thinking about it, her fingers touched his, a reassurance that stilled him, made him loosen a bit. He cleared his throat. "Tell me your favorite piece of all of those you see in front of you. Don't think about it, just say it."

His sudden possessive protectiveness was almost more unsettling than his moments of physical seduction. Marguerite struggled to stay up with him. "They're all beautiful. You've got exquisite taste, Tyler."

"I certainly do." He pinched her knuckle and she wiggled her finger free.

"Now you're flirting."

"A Master? We never flirt. We merely wave our hand and command our sub to fall to her knees in slavish devotion. We never cajole, coax, flirt, seduce..." He tilted his head, this time toward her other side. Catching her braid in his teeth, he gave it a tug and succeeded in catching the band holding it. When she jerked her head away, he was able to pull it down six or seven inches, off the base, so that the braided strands started to loosen.

"Tyler Winterman—"

"Tell me your favorite. Stop being a polite guest, trying to say all the right things."

"The statue in the left corner. I like the statue. And the chair near it. Though it's not part of the artwork."

"Describe the statue."

"It's a man and a woman. It's done in brown clay and she's... He's behind her, his arms outside her arms, both in a vee, pointing down the front of her body, all four hands clasped just at her vagina. They're bent over. His legs are spread, hers together, and it's obvious he's inside of her. Her head is back on his shoulder, his is tilted forward, his lips on her opposite shoulder. They're perfectly meshed, unified. I like the lines of it."

"Get past the artistry. What does it say, what does your heart say when you look at it?"

I wish I was her. The thought came to her mind uncensored but she couldn't say it. "The look on her face...moves me. She's not thinking of anything but this, doesn't have to. Nothing is touching her, filling her but him. She's an empty vessel, filled by him."

He was silent. She knew he knew there was more. "And you like the chair," he said at last.

She let out the tense breath she was holding, relieved he hadn't pressed. "Yes. What do you call it?"

"A tête-à-tête." The design was like two chairs facing in opposite directions, side by side but curved as one pair, so the two backs formed an intimate S-shape that would allow a man to reach over and lay an arm around the waist of his lover. However, separated by the opposite arm, they had to maintain a seductive distance. "There were many subtly suggestive items in the Victorian era," he noted. "During sexually repressed times, I think people just get more creative."

"That chair seems to be more romantic than sexual."

"You think so?" He shifted to consider it, which rubbed his shoulder against hers again. He was so much broader there, reminding her how infrequently she allowed her subs to get close enough to her to compare the differences in their body types. "If you and I were sitting there, side by side, you know what I'd do?"

"I'm not going to encourage you."

Tyler smiled to himself. "Do you also realize that many of the most popular sexual role-playing games we've adopted are associated with that time period? For instance, I can imagine you as a prim schoolmistress, saying what you just said to me, the naughty student. I come back after class is over, having loosened my cravat, tossed away my neat stockings. I take away your ruler and turn you over *my* knee for once, throwing that skirt over your back, feeling the press of your waist against my thigh, seeing your trim pantaloons beneath. Wondering what it would be like to take those down your stockinged legs while you're struggling, kicking in those dainty little boots..."

"While I maneuver for a clutch grip on your crotch to get you to let me go."

He winced. "You and Mistress Violet have similar mean streaks." But he noticed her eyes had moved back to the photo *Cry Mercy* and her pale face had more color than before.

"Now if I were in that chair, I might try to steal a kiss. Or maybe go lower, kiss every inch of your lovely throat, down to the first button of that stiff shirt. I'd bite it off with my teeth, then the next one. Run my tongue in the valley between your breasts, nuzzle your soft skin, nip at the lace holding it. But what would your more romantic version be?"

She couldn't grasp any image now except the one he'd just painted. Imagining.

"I see you're fascinated with *Cry Mercy*."

Her gaze jerked up and he saw her realize at last that he could see every expression of her face.

"It's interesting, isn't it?" he continued in a mild tone. "How the photographer chose to keep everything in black and white except for that one ruffle of pink lace across the widest curve of her ass? And you can't help but think of another area so delicately pink and female, waiting for a tongue, a hand or cock to slide into its welcoming warmth. Now, answer me. What was your romantic version for the chair?"

The creases of her palm were damp enough to please him. He was equally pleased by the tension he felt in her body now that she knew there was nothing she'd been able to hide from him.

She drew in a breath, then another. He admired her ability to continue to regroup, rebalance, no matter how often he was seducing her off the pedestal.

"Just sitting like that, the closeness, the arrangement of the chair speaking for itself, saying that the two people in it have a connection, or want more of a connection than they ever had up to that point. The suggestion of things to come. That's romantic. And I guess you've proven it can be sexual, too. That's a dirty trick," she added. "The mirrors."

He lifted one shoulder in a brief shrug. "The point is the sub learns there's nothing she can hide from her Master, that she's to be open to him in all things."

"She doesn't deserve any privacy?"

"No," he said simply. "Not if the Master is going to give her the pleasure she deserves." *And needs.*

He removed the slat of the chair to free the cuffs from it. When he moved to the floor, he felt her watching him as he brought the cuffs under his hips and pulled his long legs through the loop of his arms in a lithe, practiced move. Bending, he fished the key to his cuffs out of the melted ice, unlocked them. Then he came around the chair to squat between her spread legs, laying one palm on each kneecap.

"You look like you've done that a few times in your life." Her breathing was beginning to elevate, he suspected because he was so close and she was completely helpless before him.

"More than a few."

Sliding his hands up her thighs, he studied her face as he moved inch by inch up the inside until his thumbs were resting just shy of the spread crotch, framing it. With her arms behind her, her breasts were well displayed before him, the white shirt pulled taut across them. He suppressed the urge to unbutton her shirt, fondle them in whatever underwear she'd chosen to wear beneath it. If she'd dressed to the skin in the same theme, it would likely be something as practical and nonsexual as the rest. Clothed even in armor, her breasts would attract him. "The strongest drive inside of a submissive, underneath all their emotional wounds, is for the Master to push aside any curtains or walls they may have erected to separate them from their true self, the naked, vulnerable soul. Because that soul wants only one thing. Do you want to know what that is?"

She tightened her jaw, looked through him until he touched her face. Not with forceful compulsion but a whispering caress that drew her gaze back to him.

"You'll answer me, Marguerite."

"I don't want to know. That's not what the training's about."

"Wrong. That's what submissive training is all about. Getting past those shields so she feels truly bound to her Master, a part of him as he's a part of her. The ultimate connection, where thought isn't necessary. They're together in the most elemental and perfect way there is."

She stared at him. "Let me go, Tyler. I can't do this."

"You can. You will." He framed her face, leaned forward, pressed his lips to her cheek, her forehead, the curve of her ear. Her body shook under his touch and he kept his touch soothing, gentle, stroking the wisps of hair around her face. He'd gone to one knee to accomplish the nuzzling caresses. His leg pressed against the inside of hers, the front of his shirt brushing hers, his breath warm on the side of her neck. "It will be all right, Marguerite. I won't let anything happen to you. I promise."

He drew back, just a space. Marguerite saw that his eyes were almost gold in the room's light. To his right she saw the brown statue she liked so much. The woman who could just be in the moment, a part of her lover, worrying about nothing further.

She closed her eyes, looking for something solid but the only thing she could feel was his touch on her body. "Why is my key still in ice?" She opened her eyes.

His lips curved. "I put it in a bigger ice cube."

Chapter Six

ॐ

He'd had Sarah lay them out a light meal in the breakfast nook off the kitchen. Moonlight glittered on the Gulf as the backdrop for a bistro table draped with a lace tablecloth, set with an elegant set of dishes, a silver soup tureen and a trio of candles of different sizes.

When she saw it, she stopped them with a hand on his arm, a bare brush of contact she instantly removed. "I appreciate..." She shook her head. "May I say something?"

"You may. And I'm impressed by your memory for instruction."

"I understand how this could be seen as necessary, this warm-up." She waved her hand at the table. "I appreciate all the effort you've put into it. But why don't we skip it and get to the rest?"

"Still trying to control the situation." He propped his hip against one of the chairs, crossing his arms across his chest to consider her. Marguerite could not think of a response because it was obvious that was what she was trying to do. But she wasn't a submissive, damn it.

"Just like the annual physical, hmm? Have the doctor get on with it while you pretend you're anywhere else, waiting for the metal probes to finish their routine of humiliation."

He was tossing her analogy back at her and she forced herself to remain calm, steady. "Tyler, I've read—"

"No. You haven't. Not closely enough. Pull out the requirements. I'm sure you're carrying them on you. Or have you committed it to memory?"

Thinning her lips at his sardonic tone, she removed it from the pocket of her slacks and handed it over.

"Restraints, exhibitionism, interactive play with other subs and Doms and several other categories I'm supposed to inflict on you or go over with you if you ever intend to do them at The Zone. Mummification, sensory deprivation, pain, et cetera ad nauseum. But then there's this paragraph beneath that laundry list. I'm sure you read it, reread it, hoped I wouldn't care enough to notice it."

"Tyler—"

"Be quiet."

She stiffened at his sharp tone. He guided her firmly to one chair, holding it out for her. When she sat, he put the paper down in front of her. "Read the last paragraph. Out loud."

"The Master must be satisfied that the mentored Dom or Domme understands the psychological issues during submission as a part of these components. That's fine print," she muttered. She saw him press his lips together against a smile and wanted to slap him. "I know submissives as well as you do."

"No, I don't think you do. Not from this side of it." He uncurled her fingers from the paper, made it drop to the floor. "Let. Go. Of. Control. In order to take control, someone else has to relinquish it. Willingly. For you, being a Mistress is breathing. Unconscious, unthinking effort. You don't think about the why of what you're doing, you just do it. Your rational brain isn't part of the process."

"Is that an insult?"

"Not at all." He looked surprised that she would think so. "There are many spiritual paths that spend a great deal of time teaching their acolytes to do what you do so naturally without analytical thought at all."

Analytical was not the word she'd choose for the way he was making her feel, or the thoughts that were running through her head.

He crouched, staring steadily at her, no smile now on his lips, no mercy in his gaze. "I'll say this one more time. I will be gentle. I will be slow. But you don't have the reins. You don't tell me what to do. You may ask anything you wish. But it will be up to me to decide to answer or grant your desire. You have responsibility for nothing this weekend except to serve my desires and submit to pleasure. Mine and your own. And first, we eat."

With effort, she bit back a defensive retort. She had known all along he wouldn't let her make this session into a silly game in her head to establish distance. To him, Mistress Marguerite had been left outside the front door. But she didn't know herself in this role, which gave him all the advantages.

Trying to get her mind around it, she thought about herself with Marius, Brendan or any of her subs. Thought about the way they looked at her. For once, she dared the emotional risk of trying to see through their eyes and understand. What came to mind was Brendan, the way he'd looked to her when the pain had taken over his body.

Maybe a sub initially floundered in a sea of uncertainty but found his calm in the belief that the Master or Mistress was the anchor, the lifeboat. That he or she would throw out the float on which the sub could rest, giving them a calm space to focus their desire. Could she trust Tyler enough to do that in this controlled environment that felt anything but controlled? Could she trust anyone to do that? And why was something that was so simple and safe feeling so threatening?

"Marguerite." He laid a hand on either side of her face. When she tried to look away, he held her fast. "You're stirred up right now. This is like using muscles you're not used to using, may have never used. For some subs what Brendan asked you to do, the branding, doesn't even seem close to edge play." His touch dropped, closed over her wrists as she tried not to let the anxiety take her. The fact he'd picked up on her thoughts as easily as if they were written on the paper on the floor unnerved her. "For others, this —" his grip tightened, "is the edge. I understand that. I'm going to push you out of your comfort zone but only to teach you to trust me. Just trust me. That's what this whole weekend is about."

If he wanted to beat her within an inch of her life or poke her with hot brands, that she could handle. She hadn't expected that Tyler's version of submission would include crawling into her mind. She should have expected it but perhaps she'd thought her status as a Mistress would have made that a forbidden road that any decent Master would have respected by not going past the roadblocks. Tyler seemed to be zeroing in on those areas she didn't feel should be involved.

But she couldn't help wondering if her subconscious had known the truth all along. In fact, a desperate part of her suggested that she may have chosen him specifically because he had that capability. Maybe ultimately, despite her protestations and manipulations, it had been her choice to be here, doing this."

He rose. "Don't touch anything in front of you. Put your hands under your thighs and I want your knees apart, your feet tucked in around the outside of the chair legs. Shoulder blades pulled back, touching the back of the chair so I can see the outline of your breasts against the moonlight outside. I want to feed you by hand while you stay in that pose."

"I told you I'm not really hungry."

"This isn't about nourishment, Marguerite." He pulled the chair on the opposite side of the table closer to her and sat down. His knees were splayed so one pressed against the point of her hip along the side of the chair, the other against the point of her knee under the table. "And our current conversational topic has been exhausted. You'll need to ask permission if you want to choose another one."

Keeping her legs apart was making her pussy throb in response. The pressure of the crotch seam of her slacks made the reaction more acute. She was too aware of how close his hand was. With his forearm on the table, he had his fingers draped loosely over the edge, inches from her thigh.

"You can look out at the water if you wish."

She immediately turned her head, realizing he hadn't commanded her to do it but given her the option, a direct acknowledgement of her weakness, her fear. She wanted to look at the beauty of the view primarily because she didn't want to look at his face.

He stroked her ear, tracing the shell and then his clever fingers were freeing her hair all the way from her braid, sending it rippling down her shoulder, along her jawline. His touch soothed her, eased the pressure on her scalp. She noticed the single orchid bloom in a vase on the table, the deep pink-purple of its delicate petals.

"I raise them." He noted her glance. "I started with the native Florida species and have branched out since. Seems we both have an interest. Do you grow your own?"

"Am I allowed to speak?"

"A slave must always answer when her Master asks her a question." He ignored the waspish tone. "And please do. I love nothing better than the sound of your voice."

That old-fashioned gentleman again, his eyes so intent, body so disturbingly close and attentive to the position of hers. "I don't grow orchids," she said at last. "Japanese tea ceremonies place special emphasis on the display of flowers during tea to match specific themes or just for contemplation purposes. I like the tradition."

He nodded. "Some sources say the very first flower arrangement came from Buddhist monks."

"Saving flowers uprooted by a storm by placing them into containers of water," she finished. "Out of reverence for life."

"Ironic, isn't it? When flower arrangements now are all about the deliberate cutting off the life of a flower?"

She didn't want to be reminded that he was an intelligent, interesting man. His sexual power was enough to overwhelm her at the moment. "There's a man who studies the art of flavoring teas with flowers," she continued. "He brings me his blends to try out and he'll bring me flowers to be displayed with certain teas."

"So he provided the orchid on our table the other day."

"Yes. It was a gift from some time ago."

"And how old is he?"

She raised a brow. "You think a certain age removes him from competition for my affections?"

He smiled. "I think past a certain age a man's heart couldn't handle you. I know mine races like a teenager every time I'm around you."

"He's a friend."

"How about me, Marguerite?" He cocked his head. Her gaze lingered on his firm lips despite herself. "Am I a friend?"

"I don't know yet."

"A cautious answer. You know what, Marguerite? I don't think I want to be your version of a friend, because a friend is someone you can put into a neatly labeled box. Waitstaff, flower man, Dommes at The Zone. People whose margins of existence don't really encroach on yours."

"Well, I didn't ask you to be my friend."

"Careful, angel. Speaking without a direct question," he reminded her. "I'm also not worried about tripping over your admirers because you don't invite them into your home, in here." He touched her sternum lightly. "You come out to hold court with them and take chaste strolls along the parapets. At the end of the day you roll up the drawbridge and leave them outside."

Tyler met her gaze, held her in its grasp. He intended to keep doing that until it was second nature for her to look him in the face. "And I'm already inside, whether you're going to admit it or not."

"Then you're a trespasser. My castle guard will locate you and I'll have you hung outside the castle gate and disemboweled as a warning to others."

He noted there was no amusement in her words. There was a slight break in her voice. She was attempting to ignore his words but the most significant factor to him was the fact that she hadn't denied it.

Ladling some soup into her bowl, he picked up a spoon. "This is one of Sarah's specialties. It's a potato soup with fresh vegetables from Robert's gardens and a mixture of spices I know nothing about except they're terrific and I usually want to eat about a gallon of the stuff before I come up for air. Now, as I'm feeding you for at least the next fifteen minutes, I want you to talk about yourself. You. Who is Marguerite? What does she think about, dream about?"

"So you can tell everyone at The Zone personal things about me? Brag that you know what they don't?"

"You're very skilled at that."

"What?"

"Changing the subject so we're not talking about you. Why do you do that?"

"Because most people aren't interested in other people except as it relates to their own stories."

"I'm interested in you." Brushing a finger over her cheek, he made her hold his a gaze an extra beat. "Only you. And perhaps I'll tell them Marguerite Perruquet is a remarkable woman, just as you expected her to be. Someone to admire. Open up." He inserted a spoonful of soup between her reluctant lips, casually picked up the napkin, dabbed at her mouth. Was pleased when he saw the exceptional taste of the soup register. "Or maybe after hearing you talk fifteen minutes, I'll say, 'God, she's a bore. You don't want to know.'"

Some of the tension in her shoulders eased. He saw something else in her expression to please him, just a glimpse. "Now that was almost a smile. Fifteen minutes, Marguerite. That's a command. I'll help you get started. Tell me about the doll and the children's tea set."

She went still. "It was a gift."

"When?"

"When I was a teenager."

"Seems the type of gift you'd give a younger child." He studied her face, the closed expression. "Fifteen minutes, Marguerite. Give me honesty and you'll be able to put one check mark on your little paper."

She sat back in the chair, her expression frosty. When her gaze shifted to the expanse of air over his shoulder, he noted it but let it pass. For the moment.

"My mother died when I was fourteen. I went into foster care. I had difficulty adapting, and a social worker brought me the tea set and the doll."

"Keep going."

"That's all."

"No, it's not." He put down the spoon. "The tea set was new when she got it for you, perhaps picked up at a drugstore. It isn't chipped, not even stained by the teas that might have been in it, remarkable care for a teenager to take with a cheap tea set. On the other hand, when she gave you the doll, it wasn't new. It was something that had belonged to her. I'll bet you brushed that brittle golden hair with a comb, just enough to remove tangles, carefully curled and parted it, tied it back with a ribbon. You removed as much of the scuffs as you could from the once peaches-and-cream cheeks, the bow-shaped mouth. The blue eyes were intact but the lashes were already stubby and sparse. You could have found a new dress for her, glued new eyelashes on, had new hair implanted by someone who restored such precious toys. But you've kept her in the condition she was given to you, just like the tea set. Because it was important for you to always have her be the same. Because people take exceptional care of the things that matter to them."

Her eyes had transitioned from frost to outright arctic snow and he made a mental note of where the sharp implements on the table were. Of course if she decided to dump the tea on his groin he wasn't sure he'd be able to stop that, based on the open position of his body to her, a calculated risk he hoped he wouldn't regret.

"Are you finished playing psychotherapist? Can you just get to the part where you prescribe me some mind-numbing drugs to keep me from having to listen to your bullshit?"

"I believe you're supposed to ask for permission before you speak."

"May I speak, then?"

"You may."

"Go to hell."

"Hmmm…" He considered her, his eyes drifting downward. "Is your bra front-closing or behind? Answer me and I'll change the subject."

She swallowed, a muscle in her jaw twitching. "Behind."

He touched the front of the starched stiff fabric of the dress shirt she wore and slipped a button, then another. She began to tremble again.

"You're shaking, angel."

"I can't stop." Her voice wobbled, even as her body got more defensively rigid.

"I know. It's normal. You haven't handled many first-time subs. They tend to get shaky."

"Even when they're just pretending?"

He glanced at her. Spreading open the fabric, he worked it off the point of her shoulders but no farther, intending to increase the sense of constriction on her upper body. "Arch for me, sweetheart."

She did, stiffly. His hands slid into the shirt and to the back, spanning her rib cage. It brought her into his light embrace, his chest close to her breasts.

Her cheek brushed his shoulder and the side of his neck, suggesting that it might be comfortable to lay her head there, relax in his embrace, see what that felt like. Marguerite felt torn between rage and lust and something softer, far more difficult for her to manage.

"You know—" his fingers were on the hooked clasp, "sometimes holding on to someone for just a moment can make you feel more connected."

"A hug, to make us feel on equal footing?"

His free hand clasped her throat, tilting her chin up with the pressure of his knuckle so her head was at somewhat of an uncomfortable angle. His lips were just over hers, his fingers tracing that hook in the back. "We're not equals, Marguerite. For this weekend, I'm your Master."

The catch released and the bra loosened. He shifted his grip, took the straps just off her shoulders and then tugged downward, bringing the bra into a roll of cloth just under her now bare breasts. It was a dishabille pose, her hair on her shoulders, clothes not nearly removed and her upper body tangled in them, giving him easy access and her little freedom of movement. "You'll look at me now, Marguerite."

When she raised her head, her features rigid in protest, he drew back, studied her, his gaze slowly traveling down her throat to the breasts now bare to his gaze. Then he picked up his fork, speared some of the spinach and red lettuce salad. It was cool to her overheated senses when he put it between her trembling lips.

"This is a raspberry vinaigrette dressing. The salad has dried cherries, parmesan, slivered almonds and some other things I think you'll like."

He didn't make her say anything further, simply took his time, examining her body at his leisure as he fed her one bite at a time, moving from the salad to a sweet cornbread, crumbs tumbling down her front. Then back to some more of the soup. Simple, nourishing food of excellent quality that told her Sarah took very good care of him. As her anger ebbed in the quiet, it made her wonder what it would be like, to care for a man like Tyler.

He'd been helping himself to an occasional bite and abruptly she lifted a hand, rubbing a thumb at a corner of his mouth where some of the dressing glistened, a small piece of basil he'd missed. Even as she did it, she felt the constriction of the sleeves of her shirt, the straps of the bra pressing into her upper arms and remembered she wasn't supposed to lift her hands.

But he let her do it, his eyes intent on her. He waited until she was finished, then he took her hand in his. "You need to remember my commands, or I'll have to think up new ones that you can remember better."

Instead of placing her hand back under her thigh, he guided it over the leg, turned it inward, his cupping hers. Sliding her fingers under her body at the juncture of her legs, he made the heel of her hand press her clit. The pressure tightened her thighs causing her to exhale sharply, an unfamiliar sensation springing just above and beneath her touch. She forced herself to keep her hips still.

"Full enough?"

She nodded.

"Good. I'm in the mood for dessert. Keep your hand where it is." He put down the spoon and cupped her bare breasts, inserting the one hand in between her side and the arm she had holding herself. He weighed the curves in his palms, kneaded. She shuddered as his thumbs brushed over her nipples and they drew tighter under his touch. His eyes flared with desire but his tone stayed mild, as if they were in an elegant restaurant.

"Be still, let me touch you. You should be open to my desire to caress you at any time. At this dinner table, in the garden, in the bedroom, everywhere I command."

She worked so hard to keep everything under control inside her but here was need rolling up and over her, tumbling her like an ocean wave, pounding upon her. Anxiety rushed in, the inability to breathe. Only moments ago, he'd been prying into her life as if he had every right to her secrets. Now she was sitting here yearning for more of him.

She lunged back, as far away from his touch as her limited position allowed, her hand closing into a fist on the handle of the fork. Gasped as his much larger hand clamped down over it, held her there. She could not move her hand, his strength literally pinning it to the table, holding her arm so it immobilized the rest of her. The tension of muscle in his thigh against her hip told her he was more than ready to combat any other movements.

"Breathe, angel," he said. "Breathe. Look at me. *Look at me.*"

He snapped the command apparently to jerk her attention to him. Once he had it, his voice immediately softened. "Let go of the fork. Focus on my voice, my commands. That's the only responsibility you have, remember? To obey my commands."

Her breath rasped out of her. When her hand tightened on the fork, the strength of his grip increased, not hurting her but making it clear she would not move that hand if he didn't want her to do so. "You let go of that fork, turn your hand over and lace your fingers with mine. Or else we'll go directly to the spanking lesson."

Didn't he understand? He was acting like this was normal, when she was so close to everything being white noise, inside and out, a void of nothing, a buzzing that would drive her insane.

"Breathe." His other hand held her opposite arm to her side but now his hold eased, his amber eyes intent on her face

131

as he watched her reactions closely. "I know violence rides very close beneath your civilized veneer. Too close. I know that the tea ceremony and the careful rituals at The Zone all help to keep it leashed, but it doesn't take that much to snap that leash, does it? You can run wild with me, let it all out. I can handle you. But you won't use it to drive me away. Let go of the fork and hold my hand. Breathe. Deep breath."

It was coming easier now, the oxygen in and out of her lungs, the prickling heat of the rage no longer irritating her to the point of insanity. It was because of his voice. She was holding on to it, using its rich tone to steady herself, its mixture of implacable demand and soothing calm.

"Tyler." She closed her eyes. "Talk some more. Please."

He gave himself a moment just to look at her, his ice queen. So somber and tense, believing this was something she had to survive and tolerate instead of experiencing. Savoring.

He wanted to do several things. He wanted her to trust him enough that he could curl her up in his arms, take her to a quiet, dark room and simply hold her until the nervous vibration of her limbs and the sick panic in her eyes were gone and no longer tearing at his heart. But to do that, he had to get her to believe he could protect her from her fears.

"I've got a better idea."

He released her hand and her arm and put his hands back inside the shirt, around her rib cage. Placing his mouth over her left nipple, he drew her in, suckling, moving his arms all the way around her to bring her to the end of the chair such that his knee came to rest against her mons.

Her fingers on the outside hand clutched at air then latched on to his thigh, her back arching as his grip increased, holding her to him, allowing him to nurse her sweet taste. He'd never felt skin so smooth. The nipple in his mouth had an exotic flavor, the tight point as aroused as he could wish.

She was making silent little puffs of air through her nose as if fighting her vocal cords, forbidding them response. Her body was a rubber band drawn to maximum stress beneath his touch. Rocking his foot, he rubbed the bones of his kneecap up and down her clit. Slow strokes, and imagined his tongue doing the same. He promised himself he'd taste her there before the weekend was done, see if this same flavor was between her legs or if it was something even sweeter. He nipped her with his teeth and she gasped, her hand rising to grip his hair. Lowering his hand, he unhooked the opening of her slacks and pushed down the zipper, moving inside and searching past the wrinkled fabric of her tucked shirt to find the lace and silk of her panties.

Neither boxers nor briefs then. Despite her frantic tugging on his hair, part uncontrolled passion and part denial of what he was doing, he slid two fingers into her heat. His thumb worked her clit in circles as he continued to keep her trapped with one arm around her back, his mouth on her breast. When he ran his tongue in between them and moved to the other one, he saw in the corner of his eye that she was staring with glazed eyes at the distended nipple wet from his mouth. Her hips were making tiny jerks against his hand, and he heard her voice, tiny, breathless noises, a word. "No...no...no..."

"Yes." He growled it against her flesh, maddened by her resistance, knowing she was responding to him as he'd never seen her respond to anyone. He would have all of it, all of her. He began to move his fingers inside her, teasing the silken walls, keeping up his massage on her clit. Her body gathered. Something in her eyes said she couldn't go over, was too terrified of where he was pushing her. Then she released the fork with a clang of metal against the table and grabbed his upper arm, her fingers digging into him.

He made his decision and broke her rule. Letting go of her breast, he covered her mouth with his, making that ultimate connection to drive her to climax. Rising up so he was half over her, he pushed her back in the chair so it was on two legs. Her hands clung to his shirt at his waist just above his jeans as he felt the soft slippery bud of flesh quiver, harden, heat beneath his touch.

"Come for me, Marguerite," he whispered roughly.

There was nothing easy about it. She reacted as if her mind was fighting every wave but the body would not be denied. She bucked, small movements on the chair, her grip slipping to his thighs, clutching at his hips as the orgasm took her so violently that she broke free of his mouth. When she tucked her head under his chin a small moan came out of her. She pressed against his chest, holding back the sound as she jerked, her breath shallow and fast.

It reminded him of the aftermath of a seizure, the disorientation, the twitching of the limbs. A moment of unease gripped him, making him wonder if he was in over his head after all.

Then he remembered his words to Violet. Something or someone had made Marguerite into this. But he believed that her strength and the intriguing combination of items she'd become were in spite of those circumstances, not just because of them.

He could handle this. They both could. Because at least for this weekend she was his. And he wasn't going to let anything happen to her.

Chapter Seven

ℰ◑

Before she could recover her wits and try to re-weld her considerable shields in place, he bent and lifted her up in his arms, guiding her arm so it was around his neck. Her other hand stayed curled in his shirt front as he lifted her, turned and moved out of the living area toward the wide staircase to the second landing.

"What are you doing? Why are you—"

"Carrying you."

"Put me down." Her voice was weak, her body still moving with sexy convulsive shudders that made his cock even harder.

"That's 'Put me down, Master', and it should have a please at the front and a question mark at the end."

Marguerite ground her teeth. "Would you please put me down?"

"No. Just hold on."

She tightened her grip but realized immediately she was quite safe. She'd never thought of herself as a woman who could be carried, because of her height and just... Well, because it had never occurred to her. Since he wouldn't release her she was forced to experience being held in a man's arms, a man apparently strong and balanced enough to carry her up the stairs two at a time with nary a break in pace. It put her body in close proximity to his, of course. Her arm around his neck, her side pressed against him and the cloth of her open shirt crumpled in between. Her breasts were still bare, such that he was indulging himself in a thorough study of their liberal movements caused by his strides.

"You should keep your eyes on the road," she said, noting how far up the stairs they were.

"Marguerite, in another minute, I'm going to gag you."

"I thought we'd already covered restraints."

"First off, there may be overlap in the requirements that will bring restraints into play again. Second, a gag is not a restraint. It's a life-saving device to keep me from strangling you. Hush now."

"My suitcase—"

"Robert put it in our room."

"Our room. What—" She closed her eyes at his look. Sucking in a deep breath, she made a concentrated effort to try and conform to the rules. "May I ask a question?"

"You may."

"Why would we be sharing a bedroom?"

"You know the answer to that. Being a sub is about being available to your Master's desires at all times."

She would be sharing the same room with him, possibly the same bed. And while she'd laid down the rule of no sex, how could she have anticipated or even framed a rule of "no intimacy"? She would have been better off allowing sex and then perhaps he wouldn't have put so much effort into the other. Or perhaps the best way to have avoided the trap was not to have faced the hunter at all.

He took her into a bathroom large enough to be a master bedroom. With its separate sauna and hot tub it reminded her of the kind of bathhouse the Romans might have favored. Towels stacked next to a tray covered by a hand towel drew her attention to a shallow square tub filled with steaming water about three feet deep. He lowered her to her feet as effortlessly as he had lifted her and she found she needed to hold on to him a moment to steady herself, the aftereffects of the orgasm still affecting her.

"I'm going to undress you and lay you in that pool, massage your muscles with the jets." He drew her forward and uncovered the tray, revealing a gleaming line of shaving implements, lotions and creams. "And when you're lying there relaxed, I'll spread your legs and shave your pussy. Make it smooth for my touch. Preparing and handling a sub's body intimately is a critical part of being a submissive and a pleasure to a Master."

He was sure she had no idea she'd gone as white as a sheet. Calling on the streak of ruthlessness that he'd employed before in the face of a sub's fear, he used it now with calculated, benevolent intent. Knowing the woman in his bathroom was off balance because the world she'd known was tilting on its axis, he was determined to have her tumble safely into his hands.

"Think about your subs. Those preparations you've chosen to do yourself. Understanding what they were feeling as they submitted to your touch, knowing everything you did to them was your Will. Because it brought you pleasure and them pleasure as well. All right?"

She nodded, a bare movement, her gaze on something distant. Using a finger under her chin, he lifted her face. "Unlike some Masters, Marguerite, remember, I want you to always look at me when I speak at you."

When she raised her lashes, those clear pale eyes focused on his. His heart lurched at the visible attempt to keep panic under wraps. This was more than a Domme wary or even anxious about losing control. From her violent reaction at the table, he knew it sincerely frightened her.

Taking both of her hands, he held them, encasing ice in warmth. Letting her feel the pressure of his fingers. "I'm going to undress you now. You'll stay still, only moving when I tell you that you have permission to move. Tell me you understand."

She nodded again, a quick jerk.

When he unbuttoned her cuffs and took the shirt off then the bra, Marguerite couldn't help but notice the gentle strength of his hands. She often shied away from being touched by adults, though she could manage the casual cordial touches that typified Southern relations in her tearoom with clients like Mrs. Allen. The few times a man had touched her she'd been neutral about it, uncertain or decidedly uncomfortable. This felt different, this slow glide of skin over skin, again that heat sinking into her, the power that could take her over, force her physically to do what she didn't think she wanted to do.

Her unfastened trousers were low on her hips and he slipped those down her legs, circling her hips with one arm to steady her, his palm comfortably braced on her buttock as he removed her shoes.

While she did prepare her subs herself to a certain extent, she knew that he was aware she mainly focused on restraints. This intimacy she did not do. She usually had her subs undress themselves if they were not already restrained but oddly it did not seem servile for him to be attending to it. It felt like he'd taken the reins from her and was handling everything. Keeping it personal.

When he took her slacks over her feet she had nowhere but his shoulders to place her hands for balance, so she cupped one palm over the solid bone and muscle, feeling the fabric of his shirt, the shift of his body as he removed her panties. His thumbs slid intimately into the crease between thigh and pubis, making her feel the slick moisture there because of the startling climax he had pulled from her body. It wouldn't happen again. He'd caught her off guard. Her experiencing sexual pleasure wasn't one of the requirements and she needed to exercise better control. He probably thought her a poor Mistress, so quickly gotten off.

Why did she care what he thought? And why was she vacillating between professional pride and female vulnerability?

"You're thinking so hard there's smoke coming out of your ears." He rubbed his thumb over her clit, making her gasp. "You're still swollen there. You'll arouse again in no time. You're so beautiful, angel."

She blinked, surprised. She hadn't anticipated romance but it was in his face and voice as he looked at her. The sternness of a Master was in the set of his jaw and eyes, the resolution. That, along with the proprietary gaze he directed over her body created resentment but she knew that was knee-jerk and likely based on fear. Below that was something else, something that left her a little breathless and weak-kneed, an altogether perplexing reaction for her.

His gaze descended, lingered on the ragged scar just below her knee, an oblong, rough-edged mark.

"Looks like a bone came through there." He went lower, to the second one at her shin. "And there." His fingers touched it. "Part your thighs for me."

Determined not to hesitate, she took one step out, as rigid as a soldier. But it seemed her muscles could not help tensing as his touch followed the inside line of her thigh. She had to will herself not to clamp her thighs shut. "Clasp your hands behind your back, Marguerite."

The classic sub pose, allowing the Master unimpeded access to touch anything he wished. Legs spread, arms self-restrained and out of the way. His thumb and forefinger gently pinched her clit again, then he combed through the soft down of clipped hair over her pussy, his attention traveling up to her breasts, now tilted up from his ordered pose.

"You'll be lovely shaved."

"Why is it that men like a woman's pussy so bare?"

"To see it better, of course. And because a woman reacts so much more intensely when the skin is exposed to the least amount of friction. You keep yours nicely trimmed, though. Why do you, since you rarely take your clothes off at The Zone?"

"I…I like the way it feels. Shorter."

"Hmm. Well, it's about to be not only short but gone." When he pressed a control, she watched amazed as a stone square slab rose up in the center of the bathing pool until it was about six inches from the surface of the water. There were eye bolts embedded along the sides. Then he drew a full head mask from between two of the bathing towels. The mask only had one opening, for the mouth.

"When I lay you down on that tablet, I'll put this on you and bind your legs, arms and upper torso securely using those bolts." His voice was mild, inexorable, his eyes pinning her in place. "Once I have you immobilized with the mask on, I'll tilt the stone tablet so your head and upper body just past the breasts will be below the surface of the water. Your hips, pussy and ass will be just above it, elevated so I can do a better job of removing the hair." He picked up a soft rubber tube and mouthpiece. "This will allow you to breathe."

She stared at him. "Well, I guess when I said do it all at once…" She broke off, took a step back. Then another. "I… No. Please don't make me do this." Her fingers curled into fists, ready to fight, to claw, to do whatever needed to be done.

He sat down, a hip on the edge of the bathing pool, studied her with an expression that was far too compassionate. "You're not a prisoner here."

"Yes, I am. Because I know I have to do this as long as you're asking it. But if you don't ask, I don't have to." *I won't have failed. I'm not a coward.*

He nodded. "I can see how you'd see it that way. But Marguerite, listen to me. I know how hard this is for you. It seems daunting, terrible. But remember what we talked about earlier, what this whole weekend is about?"

"Letting go of control."

"Yes. But more importantly it's about trust. I have to keep reminding you of that. Learning that you can trust your Master. Can you trust me?"

She opened her hands, drew in a breath. He waited on her. Gave her the time and space to pull it all back together, steady herself. At length, she lifted her gaze to his.

"I want to."

"All right, then." Tyler resisted the overwhelming urge to draw her into his arms, hold her close until she realized she didn't always have to manage her fear alone. "I'm going to do a little more explaining. I didn't choose this idly, or to make you panic. The whole process I described centers you on just one sensation. Physical touch. You're aware of your total helplessness. The only thing that tells you what's happening is my touch on your body. And gradually your thoughts will float away and there will only be sensation. When that happens, your fear will float away. You'll start to feel pleasure in that stillness. 'God is in the silence'," he reminded her. "It was your scroll that made me think of it."

"In the empty space," she murmured.

"You can do this, because you aren't doing it alone. I won't leave you for a second. You'll feel no pain. You'll sense nothing but my hands on you, your Master's hands your only focus."

She closed her eyes so she could say it, a child's question. "You won't leave me there?"

"You have my word, angel." He touched her mouth with his fingers and she opened her eyes to find him in front of her. "I won't be more than two feet from you at any time. I swear."

"You're not doing the things I expected. Making me call you Master, get on my knees and suck your cock."

He winced. "Is that how you do it with your subs? Just strip, let me tie you up and I'll torment you until I get you off?"

She looked startled, then inclined her head. "Touché."

"That said, with male subs it is likely more physical," he acknowledged. "What they want is simpler. They don't necessarily play a lot of games with themselves about sex.

Women are more emotionally complex. Sometimes they don't know what it is they want until they feel it, and it can change from session to session." He smiled. "It makes being a heterosexual Master very challenging.

"There's a time and a place for passion, the rise of possession in its rougher forms. But a submissive's surrender is a sweet, sweet gift. And perhaps a male sub comes to it in a more primal state. Most Masters enjoy the process of wooing, of winning that gift. And every woman is different."

"You must think I'm incredibly foolish and weak."

"Anything but." And he said it with an instant fierceness that warmed the chill inside her. "Marguerite, most Masters and Mistresses face this training with trepidation. They slog through, maybe enjoy some aspects of it, but they're always uncomfortable with giving up their control. You're obviously terrified at a bone-deep, phobic level. And yet here you are, doing it anyway. In my book, that's damn brave. And your opening up to me specifically means a great deal. Come on then." He took one of her cold hands in his. "It will be all right."

Such a simple reassurance but one she held to as he guided her to the side of the tub and picked up the head mask. "Lift your arms and twist your hair up so it will be tucked in and won't get wet."

He reached out as she complied, ran a hand down her side, over her hip. "You're lovely, Marguerite. I'm hard just looking at you, just breathing in your scent. Put your arms at your sides now."

It was silly but the sensual compliment did reassure her, warm her. He eased the hood down over her head, laced it securely so she felt the restriction on her neck, the sides of her head, nose and ears. Darkness descended and noise became muffled but discernible, which she knew would end when he had her head under the water.

"Tyler?"

"I'm here. Stand where you are and don't move. I'm sitting on the edge of the tub, just looking at you. Your breasts, the nipples drawn up hard and firm. Your soft cunt, long legs. Those pink lips of your mouth and your sex, making me thinking of stretching either or both with my cock. You are the most beautiful creature I've ever seen."

He caressed her pussy and she gasped at the surprise of not hearing or seeing him coming. And at the fact that his words had made her wet again, despite her trepidation.

"Tyler. I can't handle…hands in the dark."

Taking both of her hands, Tyler let her feel his grip, warm and sure. "They're my hands. Me. Only me. And it won't be dark for long, I promise. Trust me."

Carefully, as he would guide a wild animal, he brought her to the side of the tub.

The paleness of her skin, the long legs, the faint tremor through her breasts as she moved and an ass that he could pet and stroke forever until she was writhing with the stimulus. It all had him suppressing a groan. He wanted to bury himself in her wet heat, again and again. He'd like to spend a week on each feature. He wanted to devour her whole, now.

To rein in his passion, to serve her best, he turned her so her back was facing him. So he could see more clearly the marks she hadn't wanted him to see or ask about. The marks he'd felt when he removed her shirt. Small circles, two lines of them going up either side of her spinal column. At her shoulder blades they arced out and curled over and under like a hideous Art Deco rendering of angel wings.

Perhaps another person would have thought, based on her performance with Brendan, that she liked ritual scarification. So much that she would subject herself to well over sixty separate burns. But Tyler knew what he was looking at, understood it now because of her reluctant admission. *I can't handle hands…in the dark.* And because he knew what a cigarette burn looked like.

143

Submissives often dealt with a lot of emotional baggage during the first rough steps of learning to relinquish control as they craved to do. At some point in her life, she'd had control wrested from her, repeatedly.

And she wondered if he thought her foolish and weak? Her courage humbled him beyond words, as did the faith she didn't even realize she'd offered him by choosing him to fulfill this requirement.

It looked like the pattern wasn't finished. While balanced, it was obvious the inflictor had spaced the burns so the design would fill in over time.

"You said you wouldn't ask." Her voice came into the pregnant silence.

"I haven't. Just tell me one thing. Is the son of a bitch dead?"

Her body tensed and he ran his hands up her arms, gentling her. "Don't answer, sweetheart. I promised no questions. I withdraw it." But he'd make it his business to find out, to make sure whoever had done this to her was no longer a threat. He would prove himself worthy of her faith.

"I could just be into burns."

"If that were true, you would shiver with pleasure when I touch you there. Instead you go cold and still, like a corpse."

His arm went around her back and under her knees. He lifted her, setting her down on the marble surface of the square center of the pool. "That stream you're feeling is warm water flowing over the marble from small openings all along the edges." Easing her back, he laid her head down and straightened her arms.

"Hold on to these." He threaded her fingers beneath a metal bar embedded at the left and right corners just above her head so her arms were stretched out to either side, at an angle just above the height of her shoulders.

Marguerite felt the cuffs come down, snap into place over her wrists and was glad for the bars to curl her hands around.

144

"I'm here, Marguerite. Don't forget that." His hands were on her legs now, spreading her thighs about two feet apart. Then the thigh restraints were locked down. Next came a band beneath her breasts, which pushed them up. He added a restraint above her breasts, compressing them. Another strap tightened securely at the waist. Her ankles were also cuffed down and now she had no mobility except her head. Almost as soon as she had the thought, she felt his hands at her neck. He buckled a strap loosely around it and then apparently clipped it to two restraining hooks on either side. He performed the same process across her forehead. Now she could no longer lift her head.

"Tyler..." Her breath was moist against the edges of the mouth opening of the mask.

His hand lowered to toy with her right breast, caress the nipple, making her want to squirm against...something. But her legs were spread. The only thing touching them was air.

"Tyler."

"Yes, Marguerite." The voice of a Master, implacable, aroused.

"You didn't say anything about..." She stopped, started over. "Why did you restrain my head?"

"Because I intend to pleasure you often while you're being shaved. When you go under water, you'll be holding a tube in your mouth for air. If you should turn your head from side to side you might drop it or dip it in the water. The fit of the mask keeps the water from coming in and getting up your nose if you're relatively still. I'm going to start lowering your upper body. Your hips will elevate as your head goes underwater. You won't be able to hear me but just remember to breathe through your mouth. If you're in distress, I have a control that will release all restraints simultaneously and bring the tablet up. Do you understand?"

"Yes." She wondered if she was ever going to be able to stop trembling.

He bent, placed his lips on her bare abdomen just below the point of her rib cage. He lingered there, stimulating the area with his lips and tongue. When he rubbed his cheek against her, she found the gesture reassuring.

He moved closer to her head and his jeans brushed against her fingertips. When he laid his hand over hers and pressed the backs of her fingers against him, she felt his hard cock beneath the denim. "That's what looking at you naked and spread like this does to me."

She straightened her fingertips, felt the ridge of his head, prominent against the fabric. She could do this. She would. And with an unexpected feeling she refused to define as guilt or confusion, she realized that she could do it only because he was the one here, the one doing it.

"When your head first goes under you may feel a moment of claustrophobia. Just take deep, slow breaths through the tube. It's important that you obey me in this, obey me in all things now. You'll focus all your attention on my touch. There will be nothing but my hands in your awareness. No fear."

"How do I tell you if something is wrong, if I need to stop?"

"I'll be watching you very closely." Tyler knew a safe word or gesture would do her no good at this juncture because everything was panicking her. He gazed at her body, vibrating with hyper-excited nerves. Her lips, the only visible feature of her face, repeatedly pressing together, moistening. Her arms, restrained out so he had access to the beautiful curves of her breasts rising above the fragile network of ribs, her legs spread open. He wondered what it would be like to keep her this way forever, at a level of arousal that would make her come again and again. Leave all her fears and worries behind. It was the first time in a long time that he'd had to fight so hard against a desire to keep the woman who had agreed to submit to him. He wasn't sure if he completely had her agreement but he was going to do his best in this session to convince her that forever could be a very pleasurable word.

"Open your mouth."

He inserted the mouthpiece of the air tube in between her teeth. "Bite down. Not too hard. You just need to hold it a moment." He buckled the elastic band around her head. Her chest was rising and falling more rapidly now, he saw. He heard the rasping sound of air coming in and out of the tube.

It was an advanced level for anyone, not just a person who resisted loss of control to the degree she did. He didn't know what instinct was driving him to push her into such an extreme sensory deprivation session so quickly, except that he'd told her the truth. That, perversely, the experience could help calm a nervous sub once she was immersed in the stillness of the water. However, if he didn't get her there soon, she might genuinely panic and his heart wouldn't hold out against her distress.

He also knew if he didn't start shaving her soon, change *his* focus, he was going to be eating her pussy until her breath became downright asthmatic, her teeth biting into the hard rubber of the tube like a rabid dog, her silken muscles rippling along his thrusting tongue. What he really wanted was to take his trousers down and drive into her, ignore the rules. He pressed the controls.

The upper part of the tablet began to sink into the floor, taking her body down, down. The water rose to her ears, the side of her face under the mask. He watched her muscles tighten in panic, then she was immersed. He forced himself to keep her going until her body was at a forty-five degree angle and about five inches of the tube was visible. The water wavered over her, creating a beautiful mermaid image before his eyes. Her lips pressed hard on the tube but he knew she'd ease up when she realized that the straps would hold it in place without her tiring her jaw.

When he pressed another control, the section beneath her calves began to descend, a separate jointed piece of the tablet.

It gave him the ability to draw a tall stool into the shallow water in the channel below her feet, move between her spread legs to her knees and study the delectable pussy completely available to him. It also gave him a clear view of her sloped out beneath him. He turned on the audio system of the room and the soft notes of *Claire de Lune* began as he picked up his razor and the apple-scented skin gel he'd chosen. He hoped it suited her tastes, as much as her tea choice had suited his.

Chapter Eight

&

Silence. As the water caressed her lips, clasped around the tube, as it moved between the spaces of her fingers, she felt the silence descend. Where was he? He said his touch would be there. In this world, five seconds could become a lifetime. The panic was immediate, seizing up her throat. She needed his touch, needed it now. She'd never done this level of sensory deprivation with a submissive. While all good Masters and Mistresses provided pleasure to the sub, it was a balance; the desire of the sub for pain or submission balanced the Dominant's need to dominate, to test the levels of submission. Tyler's need was apparently for total raw vulnerability.

She wanted this to stop. Couldn't do this. Where *was* he?

He'd told her to focus on touch and what else? She strained against the bonds, all the cool rationality, the total control exercised by her as a Mistress fleeing before the power of the terrifying anxiety. Was he playing with her?

She realized then how much her subs had given her. She didn't think of herself as a coward but would she ever willingly have given up control as Brendan had done had she not met Tyler? Had she not had The Zone requirement, she corrected herself. But the correction was an evasion of the truth her mind had stated baldly. She would not have done this with any other Master.

Please touch me. God, now. I'm frightened.

Her breath expulsed on a near sob as he touched her thigh. Stroked. Drew a... He drew a heart. Once, twice and then again. Then wrote, one letter at a time, big unmistakable. Upon her flesh. B...R...E...A...T...H...E.

Breathe. That was what he had told her to do. Breathe.

149

Some of the panic receded. She took the deep breath and recovered enough to draw in the second one more slowly, then another. His thumbs were passing over her clit now, touching her hair. He was combing the short hair, being infinitely careful, making sure he did not snag her in any way. She wasn't in a tomb. It was a womb and he was caring for her. He was here. He said he wouldn't leave her. He promised.

But she found she still needed to feel his touch every second, her mind freezing up again in the several seconds it withdrew and then came back. Heat, shaving lotion being applied. Spread out on his palms, obviously warmed between them before he applied it upon her. His fingers spreading it over her mons, her labia and even under her, parting her upraised buttocks, the pussy hair that grew back in the area of the anus.

As he touched her in what should have been a functional manner, handling her pussy as if he had every right to groom it, the anxiety coil in her stomach was twisting, shifting. Changing. She realized her breath was becoming shallow now from arousal. The moment she had the thought, he drew the heart again. She put it together, that it was a quick symbol to remind her to keep breathing deeply, simply. She should know all this. She should be totally in control of this situation. All of it, her emotions, her reactions. She'd been a Mistress forever. There were several other parts of her life where breathing, focusing on details in extreme circumstances and keeping one's head was crucial. She also ran a business, for heaven's sake. Why was this throwing her for such a loop?

Thought fled as his breath touched her. When she realized his lips were close to her cunt, her thigh muscles reacted like a drawn bow, straining outward, a futile effort because of her restraints. What was he doing to her?

He pressed his lips to the inside of her thigh, lower down, and licked her. A tiny bite of teeth. Another drawn heart, this time with his tongue.

Breathe in, breathe out. His hand rested on her cream-coated pussy, warning her before she felt the slick glide of a razor. When he shifted his hand so it was on her thigh, he inserted a thumb between her leg and her sex to steady his strokes. All she could think about was that thumb. He shifted it over her folds to hold them closed, increasing sensation as he navigated the razor down the side of the labia just above the tender pocket between thigh and hip. Her stomach muscles quivered. Trying to lick her lips, she licked the tube inside the mouthpiece. That made her think about tasting him. Sucking in another breath, she quelled the absurd urge to nip and suckle the thing in her mouth. The oral craving rose in her so strong and immediate it brought to mind his hard cock and one of the most potent acts a submissive could perform for a male Dom.

Was this what being treated like a sub made even a Domme feel when she was subjected to it? Or was it just Tyler and the unique chemistry they seemed to have?

She wanted to examine it further but the pulsing demand beneath his fingertips was distracting her. She meditated, practiced yoga. She knew what it was to still everything in the mind but she'd never experienced this, a silence so complete that she only had one focus beyond her jumbled thoughts and that one focus was taking even those away.

She arched as his thumb shifted, bearing down again on the outer lips to more smoothly shave a straight line from the mons down into that area. As he did so, turning his hand, he slid his fore and middle fingers partly inside her. The thumb shifted to her clit. And though the water provided lubrication, she knew she was slick with heat for him.

God, how could she breathe through this? His fingers eased slowly deeper, the thumb pushing up, applying simple, inexorable pleasure. She felt the heavy pulse of blood in that area through the pressure of his finger. Lifting her hips because she couldn't help herself, she moved into the touch as much as her bonds would allow.

He was right. She unconsciously tried to turn her head, allow that part of her to thrash, but the forehead and neck strap kept her fast. She gasped through the tube, her hands clenching on the handles he'd told her to grip before he cuffed her wrists to the marble.

Tyler watched her, his mermaid, as she responded to his touch, her cunt muscles tightening on his fingers, wanting more. He understood the feeling painfully well. She arched, her ribs smooth ripples along her sides as she fought the restraints. Her lips were working behind the mouthpiece, biting down, if her tense jaw was any indication, displaying an oral demand his cock was throbbing to appease.

Not yet. *Not yet.* He employed some of the same deep breathing techniques he'd urged upon her, knowing the rewards for waiting. As a Mistress, she knew them, too, but he understood that she was discovering one of the amazing pleasures of submitting. With nothing required of her but the Master's Will, inhibiting her desires outside the requirements of his commands was not necessary. He'd thought if he restrained her, deprived her of most of her sensory ability, she could fall into that never-ending playground of sensations and instead of thinking about the boundaries, she would run from playset to playset. He'd succeeded and Christ, she was killing him.

She was soaked. He could tell the difference between the water's light touch and the heavy slickness from her body. He looked at his palm, saw her fluid had trickled down into the shallow bowl of it. But her chest was expanding and releasing too quickly now, the air sighing out of the tube in a way that easily brought to him the vision of her lying on his bed, writhing against him and moaning her pleasure as he brought her to peak, again and again.

He'd ordered her verbally last time. This time he didn't give her the chance to think or resist. Stroking his thumb back and forth across the distended clit, he found her sweet spot inside with his fingers and laid the finger of his other hand against the opening of her anus, accessible to him from her position, just teasing the rim.

The water rolled as she lunged up against her restraints. Her forehead pressed hard against the strap, tighter than the one on her throat so at this type of moment the pressure on her throat would not be hazardous. The rasping in the tube became a guttural sound, somewhere between a wheezing sob and a breathy scream. He closed his eyes, reveling fiercely in it. In feeling her pussy ripple and contract in a long, hard orgasm that he'd made her helpless to deny this time. Her breasts were tight points even as he worked her through the after-shudders. When he slowly, reluctantly withdrew his fingers, he reached for another way to keep her mind focused on only one thing. His Will, and the pleasure it could bring her.

Standing, he trailed his fingers down her belly into the water and cupped the left breast, still rising and falling rapidly from her exertions. Fitting the rubber sides of the clamp around her hard nipple, he followed her movements to tighten the screw. He stopped when he felt her tense, then let it back out one adjustment. He wanted her to wear them for a while and feel their pleasurable discomfort, but not slide into pain. He moved across, did the other one and then let the heavy chain that attached the two float down and rest in a crescent along her upper abdomen.

Marguerite could not keep up with each new sensation. Her body was still throbbing from the second orgasm he'd given her in less than an hour. When those hands drifted up her rib cage, bringing the touch of a foreign item, she had a moment of trepidation. Then reaction shot from the compression of her nipple straight into her lower belly, coiling together with the aftermath to keep her in a state of wanting.

What are you doing to me? She'd been thankful for the strap holding the breathing tube in her mouth, for she couldn't possibly have held on to it during the soaring pinnacle he'd just sent her tumbling over.

Now his hands never left her, one on her at all times. She caught a breath in her throat as he slid something thick and short into her pussy, something that had a clit stimulator. The waterproof vibrator immediately pulsed on her clit at low setting, causing her to squirm as the extra-sensitive tissues were stimulated further. No, she couldn't... It didn't feel... It was uncomfortable so soon after the orgasm but a pleasurable response clutched in her lower belly. Her restraints only intensified it, because between that and the thigh straps she could only twitch in small movements against it.

The razor was back, working on the left side of her pussy. She gnawed on the mouth tube, trying to breathe, trying to calm herself down, despite the steady pulse of sensation against her clit.

She couldn't control anything. Though she knew that was the point, she hadn't expected this. This disintegration of her mind into a million bubbles of floating torment where all she could think about was his touch, what he would do to her next.

She screamed as he bumped up the setting abruptly to maximum. No, no, no... It was too much sensation, too much. It hurt, it didn't hurt, it was just too much, taking her clit up to a paralyzed, pre-orgasmic state where it could not go further, could only do its best to withstand the battering staccato vibrations. Too fast to let her go over, too much stimulus not to. As she hung on that precipice, her body heaved against unrelenting bonds.

Then, unbelievably, another orgasm ripped through her body, too ruthless to be called pleasurable but underscoring a point she understood as clearly as if he'd spoken it. He'd take her up and over whenever he wished, until she was exhausted and could not think beyond the next wave of desire.

When Tyler gradually lowered the small vibrator's setting, he took careful notice of her spasmodic shudders. Her body was reacting to the stimulus but was otherwise nearing lethargy, worn down by the physical and mental stress of their evening together. It was time to put his baby down for a nap.

It was going to be hell to lie next to her, knowing there was no relief in sight for him. He had no intention of breaking her rule about sex, though it was obvious he could do it easily. He'd mowed over her restraint about kissing as if it had never been but he wouldn't do so again. He intended to hear the sweet sound of her begging to break all her rules before the weekend was over.

He'd caught her off guard, taking her where she didn't expect to go. Once she had time to think, she would re-marshal her defenses and make it that much harder for him. And he was going to let her do it, because he was going to prove no matter how thick the walls she built, he could shatter them.

* * * * *

It took twenty minutes of meticulous care to shave her completely. When he was done he eased out the vibrator, wet with her post-come honey as well as the arousal the continuing stimulation had coaxed from her. He rubbed her skin down with benzocaine gel and a lotion with the same light apple scent. He liked massaging her soft, smooth skin, looking at her nipples large and aroused in the nipple clamps. Occasionally he tugged on the chain, felt her pussy contract beneath his thumb and nodded, satisfied she had become thoroughly aroused again despite her exhaustion.

At length he pressed the controls, keeping his hand on her as the marble slab began to come up, taking her back to a level spread-eagle position. Removing the strap across her forehead, he took the mouthpiece from her lips, resisting the urge to suck the beads of water from around them. Then he unlaced the head mask, taking it off, smoothing out her hair as her pale eyes focused, sought him.

Marguerite was hungry for the sight of him. She was glad for the restraints that remained so she didn't do something ridiculous. It was odd, but the silence of the water had come above the waterline with her, so all they did for a few minutes was look at each other, his hand caressing her hair, her temple. She felt soothed, quieted by the touch. She didn't feel a need to do anything at the moment but look at him, and it seemed he was indulging in the same activity. Eventually he pressed a control. True to his word all the restraints released at once with the exception of the adjustable straps at her throat and breasts. Those he released himself, his fingers grazing her sensitive skin. She shuddered as he unbuckled the strap around her throat. His hands stilled momentarily, his eyes studying her. Then he finished removing it without comment and set it aside.

"Stay where you are." He picked up a towel and began to dry her, starting at her feet and working up, patting her thighs, her smooth, silky cunt. He took her hand, laid it there. "Do you like the way that feels?"

She did, because he had done it and because it obviously gave him pleasure. Her fingers began to inch away but he caught them, held them on herself. "How often do you touch yourself, Marguerite?"

"I don't."

"A toy, then."

She shook her head.

"You never pleasure yourself alone? Not with a toy or your fingers?"

She could answer the second question truthfully, so she shook her head.

His eyes crinkled with humor but there was something more serious there. "If I had a cunt that beautiful, I'd touch it all the time."

"Well." She wasn't sure what to say to that. "I suppose that might drive away my customer base."

"So it might. But you might get some new customers."

Her gaze flitted down, rested on the very prominent cock pressing against his jeans.

"You can touch me, Marguerite."

She didn't need to be told twice, reaching out to rub her palm over the solid heat of him. When his hand became a fist in her hair, she heard him exhale sharply.

"I want my cock in that hot, wet mouth of yours, Marguerite."

She wanted that, too. What's more, she wanted to be on her knees doing it. She sat up, swinging her legs to the side away from him, her world spinning both figuratively and in reality as the disorientation of her previous position descended on her. She felt his hands on her shoulders, steadying her.

"Easy," he said. "Easy now."

None of this was easy. She'd been here less than a handful of hours and her emotions felt battered. Her body was not nearly sated, though she'd had more orgasms in this short time than she'd had in weeks.

"Come on." When he threaded her arms into a satin robe, the silken fabric brushed her clamped nipples, making her pussy moisten further with need. Would this new level of wanting he'd unleashed in her ever stop?

He guided her into an adjoining bedroom that was even larger than the bathroom. Decorated like a queen's sanctum, it had a canopy bed so high it required a velvet-cushioned set of stairs for it. A set of comfortable chairs were arranged next to a fainting couch. The arched floor-to-ceiling windows with their tapestry hangings gave the impression of a royal's chambers.

This was obviously where he spent his nights with his submissives. She was sure that the mahogany lingerie chest and dresser held a wealth of sensual aids to make those nights memorable ones for the woman in question. It didn't please her. She balked at the door.

"This isn't your room."

"No. This is our room. The room I share with a guest who honors me enough to let me share it with her."

She wanted to pull away, back into the bathroom and stay there, not bring her skin into contact with things other women who had pleasured him had touched.

But this was training. This was not supposed to be personal. She wasn't his lover or girlfriend. She was having such difficulty holding on to rationality, this was one thing she could and would stay reasonable about. She stepped into the room, knowing her posture was too stiff. "All right."

He studied her a long moment before speaking again. "Do you sleep on your stomach?"

She nodded. The king-sized bed, with comforter and pillows, looked like the most comfortable of nests. He probably shared it with women every other night.

"I'll give you five minutes in the bathroom." He opened the front of her robe, removed the nipple clamps, causing her to sway as he massaged her. "We'll put these on in the morning."

When she returned, soft lamp light filtered through the room and she noticed the fragrance of fresh flowers. A bowl of cuttings from the ginger plants was on the nightstand. Her legs were trembling as she crossed the room to him.

"Up you go." Apparently noticing, he took her hand to guide her up the steps onto the bed. She curled her bare toes into the velvet cushioning. Before she lay down, he stopped her, slipped the robe off her shoulders. When he settled her on her stomach, his hands glided along her back, the curves of her buttocks. She closed her eyes, then immediately opened them as she felt a soft touch at her wrist. Snapping a fleece-lined cuff there, he threaded the tether attached to it through the bedrails and out the other side of spindles farther down the bed. When he secured the other wrist with a matching cuff, she could bend her arms or straighten them a modest amount but not enough to free them.

"Tyler..."

His hands efficiently arranged her legs, spreading them, restraining them in the same types of cuffs, only these he drew taut so she was helplessly exposed again. He further raised her trepidation by slipping a soft blindfold over her eyes.

Tyler turned on the heating element in the pillow topper so she'd be warm without covers and then trailed his fingers down the slope of her spine, down the crevice of her buttocks, probing her where so many emotional secrets were held. He brushed a hand over her lips under the blindfold, knowing the lack of sight, just like in the tub, would increase the sensitivity of her mouth.

"No kissing," she managed.

"Not unless you beg me," he agreed in a husky tone.

He put a knee on the end of the bed and Marguerite felt the mattress depress under his weight. Had a moment to wonder what he was doing.

Oh, God. His mouth settled over her newly shaved pussy, his nose tickling in between the smooth cleft of her buttocks as he began to lick her cunt, tiny incremental touches of his tongue, his breath hot on her flesh, teeth nipping.

Time began to have no meaning. When she was in the bathroom, she'd told herself that she could and would withhold the next orgasm he tried to wring out of her. But he didn't rush, seeming to enjoy having her pussy available to him, teasing it to raging heat then easing back, keeping her jerking and gasping with the tiny kisses and explorations of his far too clever tongue. Her buttocks writhed against his jaw as she tried to press down, get away from the inexorable demand. He simply scooped his hands under her thighs, lifted her up against her restraints and easily held her struggling hips, using her movement against her, creating more friction. His tongue slid down her clit with the lingering touch of a boy enjoying a creamsicle on a hot day. One savory lick at a time, a little sucking to keep the cream from dripping off the bottom. Then, giving in to temptation, a whole covering of his mouth over the treat, teeth nipping at the edges, tongue swirling.

As she squirmed, her sensitized nipples rubbed against the bed. She couldn't keep doing this. There was no way... How could he be drawing out of her what no sub could? Pleasure was a measured response, more intensely felt if severely restrained, allowing almost a spiritual clarity in denial. This was its opposite but somehow it was the same, the confusing chaos of sensation and color taking her far past rational thought to a place where thought and even spiritual enlightenment were not necessary. It was the childlike joy and wonder of Eden, simply felt, accepted. Only she couldn't accept this. She began to fight the bonds uselessly, pulling against the iron headboard, trying harder to break free of his grasp.

His response was to lift her higher, the full several inches the tether allowed, letting her feel the restriction of the bonds more keenly. His one hand came under her, manipulating her pussy with devilishly knowledgeable fingers while his mouth went between her cheeks, tracing her rim, unleashing an incredible euphoria of *feeling*, everything from terror to ecstasy.

And so it went on. It was the most merciless punishment she'd ever witnessed as a Mistress. The clock on the nightstand ticked on and on as he brought her up to a pinnacle with a mouth and tongue that never seemed to tire of eating out her pussy, of playing with her anus, of making her ass and quivering thighs tender with short bites that she suspected were leaving light marks on her skin. Again and again she almost came, but he'd pull back. He brought a bucket of ice to the bed. At times he would clamp a handful of it down on her nearly climaxing clit, numbing the reaction, drawing it back. One, two, three...seven times. On the seventh time, tears were running down her face from the frustration, her body all fire. She was coming no matter what, damn him. He couldn't take away the choice. But then she gasped as his fingers opened her and he began to gently insert round balls of ice in her cunt. Two, three of them. And then, though she writhed and screamed, he did the same to her anus. Putting the ice balls in his mouth first to suck off the potentially rough outer coating, he made them clear and slick before he inserted them, the cold instantly burning. When he finally put his hot mouth over her pussy, heat and cold warred at cross purposes.

She couldn't do anything. Every touch brought forth a cry from her lips. She was beyond the ability to form words which was a blessing, because she would have begged without shame for the climax he was holding just above her head, daring her to ask for it. And she understood that was the purpose, with the clarity that such incredible torture was bringing to her.

He'd told her he would teach her about the nature of a submissive but he was also teaching her how to be submissive to *him*. That wasn't a newsflash to her, but to take her rushing down a slippery slope to it so quickly… She couldn't resist at this moment, couldn't even think. All she wanted was to come, to have him make her come. Every wiggle made the ice melting in her body drive her higher, wilder with no relief. He let her thrash now, caught between unbelievable discomfort and pleasure at once, the cold searing her, demanding her compliance.

She'd said no sex. She didn't care if he broke the rule, she just needed the craven want to stop. Oh God, how could something hurt so much and feel so good? Her cunt aching from cold, screaming for his heat, she wanted his mouth even deeper.

Then she heard him unfasten his jeans, the zipper coming down. He straddled her hips, his thighs pressing on either side of her.

The wet tip of his cock trailed down one quivering buttock then the other, then up the crease in the center, teasing her entrance where water from the melting ice was dampening her, trickling down to the folds of her pussy to join the water pooling beneath her there.

He shifted, moved and she felt him applying a lubricant along the inside of her cheeks. Not the rectum itself but the inside crescents of her buttocks. As she grasped what he was about, he took hold of her ass and started to rub his long, very thick length up and down between them, holding her tight around his pumping cock, increasing the incredible sensation of the ice inside her opening. She moaned, guttural noises she couldn't stop as he used her body as a Master would to achieve his pleasure. While denying her because of her disobedience, her resistance. She was a Mistress, damn it. It was hard for her even to pretend to do this. He knew that. So why was he asking so much of her? And why did she want so much to give him what he asked?

It had been nearly ninety minutes since he'd laid her down here. She felt like her entire body had shattered into individual atoms of screaming need. She'd become a swarm, a cloud of energy with no real substance or form.

How many of her subs had cursed her and begged in the same fervent thought, the way she was cursing him and begging now?

His breath grew harsh in his throat, the clutch of his fingers becoming nearly bruising. Catching hold of her hair, he swept it to her right along the pillow, baring her nape. Letting go of her ass to brace himself with an arm on the mattress, he began to come, his thighs tightening against the outside of her hips.

As he spurted onto her, she felt the hot seed coat her back, the sensitive inside of her shoulder blades, spilling over her scars. Something broke in the shadows of her soul as she understood what he was doing. Marking her as his. Sending a message to the deepest part of her psyche, the part that thought she would never be safe, never be able to elevate herself above the dark level of her nightmares no matter how high she climbed. He was here, guarding the passageways. He knew where she was, could find her anywhere. He knew her.

Her body quivered, wanting so much to accept it, yet overwhelmed by it.

"Please." She managed it, though fear clutched at the word as it emerged from her raw throat. "Please let me come."

The tip of his cock trailed down her ass and then his head was between her legs, his hands on her thighs, forcing them more widely apart. Lifting her as his tongue thrust in, he brought heat among the remains of the ice, stroked her passageway and brought it back to warm life. The five o'clock shadow of his beard scraped her clit, her thighs.

Finally, he let her go over.

The orgasm grabbed her body in hands as ruthlessly pleasurable as his. Her abused throat could not stop what went beyond a scream and into the realm of a tearing wound. Body thrashing wildly, hands pulling at her bonds, she sank her teeth into the mattress. She thrust against his mouth over and over until her body simply gave out, the muscles no longer able to do anything but twitch. Small, painful whimpers came from her throat as the pleasure kept whirling through her.

He kept his mouth working her long after she was done and had become so sensitive she was jerking in convulsions against his touch. It told her more adamantly than words that he was making sure he'd driven the lesson home.

Whatever reality existed for her when Sunday came around, he'd taught her in less than an evening that he had the upper hand. That he could Master her.

* * * * *

At last he rose, stood by the bed. Vaguely she registered the fact that he was pulling a towel from the dresser drawer.

"Ty..." She stopped, cleared the residual lust out of her voice that made it sound so husky and intimate. "Tyler?"

"Yes, baby?" He knelt next to the bed so she could see his face, the stern set of his mouth, the gentle look in his eyes. No one could be as gentle as a powerful man. Or as ruthless. He was both sides of that coin, cloaking one in the guise of the other, changing back and forth and making her crave both.

"Will you…leave it?"

She could barely form words, so exhausted that the energy to move her lips was an effort. She wanted his mark on her, wanted to feel it dry on her skin, smell the heavy scent of him.

The immediate burn of hot possessiveness in his eyes told her she'd pleased him immeasurably. She didn't want to feel the new flood of aroused reaction in her body that came as an involuntary response to it.

"All right. Sleep, Marguerite. Close your eyes."

Relieved to finally escape that direct, all-too-knowing stare, she closed her eyes.

"I want you to answer me a question before you slide off into dreams." His voice was a murmur. A lullaby. "And answer it without thinking it through. What is it about BDSM that attracts you so?"

The question rolled around her mind as if on clouds. The answer came slowly, dreamily. "People are…themselves, their real selves in sex. Particularly BDSM. Can't hide evil, good…weakness or strength. When you strip a sub down, you know who they are. They can try but they can't hide it—not if the top is good. It all comes out…"

"Good answer." She felt his lips brush her nose, her closed eyes. "Sweet dreams, princess."

"H've…you ever called someone else that?"

Another pause. "Yes. But I've never called anyone angel."

"'S okay." And then she was lost in those clouds, somehow knowing he was around her, watching over her so she didn't have to dream.

Chapter Nine

✿

That sense of reassurance was the thought that first hit her when she woke. In the manner of coping she'd used for a long time, she turned it around. This whole weekend was about suspending her natural reality. She'd been reluctant to do so and yes, Tyler had masterfully, no pun intended, made her accept it. She'd known he was a powerful Master, capable of taking over a sub's will. Well, perhaps most women's wills, bringing them to higher pinnacles of pleasure than they otherwise ever would know. Kudos to him for that.

Why not enjoy the benefits of being his "play" sub for a weekend? When it was over, she would reflect on it as a truly enlightening experience that would help her achieve a deeper connection with her own submissives. As he'd said.

She was untied. Someone had cared for her, cleaned between her legs, cleaned the evidence of his desire off her back and buttocks at last. She'd been so exhausted she'd slept right through it. She, who was hyperaware of the casual brush of a passerby on the street, had slept through him intimately touching her. For she was certain Tyler would entrust her care to no one else.

She rose slowly, her muscles aching, and managed to get her feet angled toward the floor, her head in the upright position. Though sore, she felt alive, energized, aware of her surroundings and his scent. Not allowing herself to think about the compulsion, she leaned back, her hand finding his pillow. Hesitating only a moment, she brought it to her face and inhaled. He'd slept with her, she remembered. Waking up in the middle of the night, she'd felt his body against the side of hers, his arm on her waist, palm on her hip, idly stroking her buttock, his breathing even, deep.

Appalled at the fact she was lingering over memories of him, she dropped the pillow and noticed the chair set up near the bed. The robe she'd worn was draped over it. On the pool of silk in the seat were the nipple clamps, a brush and a note.

Leave your hair down. Put on the clamps and adjust them the way I had them, one turn before they're too tight. Wear the robe or not. Your choice.

And under those last two words he'd drawn a small likeness of a cartoon devil grinning at her.

Moving into the hallway a few minutes later wearing the robe, she took in some of the details she'd missed the previous night. The eclectic though sparse style of his home reflected that he chose only things that interested him. Intriguing, individualistic pieces lined the walls, drawing her attention as she made her way down the landing and out onto the open stairwell. A bronze sculpture of a dancer had been placed on a pedestal. A landscape painting, showing a sailboat tacking off a rocky shore, was under a small spotlight mounted on the hallway wall. A trio of photographs showing her scenes of third-world children with simple pure smiles and mountain vistas in the background, was at the top of the stairs.

As she looked over the railing, she noted that the living room designed for male comfort with its sectional sofa and widescreen television had colorful area rugs that looked handwoven. Probably from some lovely South American village where the women who had made them couldn't imagine what a widescreen television was, let alone that their handiwork would soften a room with one in it.

But it was as she walked down the staircase that she found the pieces that gave her a more personal glimpse of the man. There was a black and white photograph of Leila, one of the submissives who frequented The Zone and who had been an item with Tyler at one time. In this photo, the woman was sitting at a vanity completely naked. Her back was to the camera, her hands bound behind her back, her eyes studying the photographer by reflection in the mirror. Though he had taken the photo at an angle, standing clear of the shot so as not to mar its perfection, it was obvious from the avid look in her eyes, mixed with a quiet joy and tranquility at being where she was, who it was who took the picture.

Down another few steps were the family shots. Tyler's parents probably, an old black and white of their wedding as they stepped out into a new life together, rice scattered over their head and shoulders. It was positioned diagonally with a more recent photo of the couple. She saw Tyler's bone structure and height in his father, his complexion and nose in his mother. Some of his implacability was in his mother's face, his tender side in his father's.

If she was right about the way he did his decorating, these photos all had significance, important memories or relationships stored behind each one. Nothing in this house had been randomly chosen. And that, she realized, included her.

When she heard the sound of a pot clanging into a sink, she drew in a breath. Her nipples tingled in the grip of the clamps, reacting to the evidence of his close presence. Bemused, she continued down the stairs, though she trailed her fingers over the pictures as if she were absorbing his life through her touch.

Stepping into the kitchen, she found Sarah absent and Tyler her chef for the morning meal. He wore a pair of drawstring cotton pants, a natural undyed fabric that was long enough that the back cuffs were worn from his bare heels stepping on them. He wasn't wearing a shirt and he'd not yet shaved. The muscles along his back shifted with smooth grace as he moved around the kitchen. Unlike most of her subs, Tyler had a light mat of silky dark hair over a powerful chest and sectioned stomach muscles. She liked the definition there, a man who kept himself in good shape.

Desire didn't rise, it roared up through her as if it had not been sated again and again less than a few hours before. She wasn't going to be the way she was yesterday, immature and embarrassingly intimidated in the face of their undeniable attraction. She'd given herself permission to indulge it, contingent upon her belief that she could enjoy this reality without censure for two days. So she found herself moving into the kitchen, only one thought in her mind.

He turned at her approach. Whatever he had parted his lips to say never came forth as his gaze registered her expression. When she reached for his waistband, he caught her hands in a firm grip, causing her to stumble mentally.

"Do you want my cock, Marguerite?"

His eyes were vibrantly gold, filled with her, helping her find herself again.

Nodding, she shifted her gaze away, remembered and brought it back just before he brought his hand to her chin to make her meet his eyes. And then she did what her mind told her unbelievably that she wanted to do. Keeping her eyes on his, she sank to her knees, the silk pooling around her like a queen's mantle.

"Open your robe, Marguerite. Take it off your shoulders."

He would have her serve him naked, as a slave would.

Even knowing that, she slipped the belt free without protest and let the robe fall behind her. She moved her attention now to his hands as they went to his waistband. Loosening the drawstring, he let the pants fall, showing her at close range a cock that was already becoming erect despite the fact she'd stepped into the kitchen less than a minute ago. She was actually salivating, and it wasn't for the breakfast he was cooking.

Reaching down, he used the nipple chain to tug her off her heels onto her knees. He dropped the chain over the top of his cock and curled one of her hands around the base, which served the purpose of keeping the chain anchored there.

"Suck me, Marguerite. Suck me hard."

He was a big man all over. She reveled in the need to stretch her lips to work her way down to where her hand held him. She made a noise of pleasure as she took him in, her whole body reorienting her to the position, the moment.

At the first touch of her mouth, he let out a feral growl. Wrapping his fingers in her hair to better control her movements on him, he held her there, aiding her greedy sucking and licking of the hard organ in her mouth. She liked the salty taste of him. The nails of her free hand curled into his upper thigh, marking him.

"That's right," he said, his voice low, dangerous to her sanity. "Dig your claws into me, angel."

As he drove her up and down on his shaft, the nipple chain drew taut, tugged and released, creating an excruciating sensation that built in her chest and belly. With him keeping her on her knees off her heels, there was no friction or relief for her pussy. Every stroke of her mouth on him felt like a stroke deep in her mind.

She'd never felt so single-minded, so untroubled by anything else in her world. His heat was in her pores, her mouth, her nose. She realized she was making animal noises of need as she went down on him, her hair brushing her back, his harsh breaths the most beautiful song she'd ever heard. She wanted to be closer. Hoping he wouldn't deny her, she moved that free hand up his leg and around to his buttock to find hard, flexing muscle. The movement changed her angle so he was driving more deeply into the back of her throat. The jerk on the nipple clamps grew more insistent. Her eyes watered, her lungs burned for air but she didn't care. She used her teeth, scraping him, her nails now digging into his buttocks, her other hand stroking him, her thumb rubbing his silky underside.

His voice was strained. "Take me into you, Marguerite."

His hand convulsed in her hair and then he was pumping hard into her mouth, yanking on her nipples with the force. Pain and pleasure came together as he jetted, spraying the back of her throat with liquid heat. She worked him with her mouth, growling, only gagging once as he plunged so deeply into her. He kept going and she wanted him to, wanted his desire to override all else.

When he finished, he was still hard and she didn't want to let go. She slowly took her mouth off him. Rubbing her cheek along his length, she felt the sturdy wetness of him, the life pulsing beneath her face. What would it be like to have that pulsing inside her, ramming into her pussy with his overwhelming strength?

"Angel." Reaching down for her, he brought her to her feet. Before she knew what he was about he'd lifted her, set her bare bottom on his kitchen counter, leaving the robe on the floor. He readjusted his pants and took a warm washcloth from the sink to wipe her tears, her running nose and the remnants of his come from her lips and chin. "You keep this up and I'm never going to let you go."

She told herself it was just the mood of the moment, but why did it feel so inviting, the idea of staying in this world forever and never having to face her reality again?

Stop it, Marguerite. Don't make it more than it is.

But it made her tremble, the way he could hold her on her knees and make her service his cock, and a moment later he stood between her knees wiping her face and caring for her as tenderly as a woman could wish. She'd never allowed herself to experience a lover's powerful passion or tender nurturing. Both held equal dangers for her.

"Come here." He scooted her off the counter into his arms, further turning her world upside down by holding her in his embrace. A hug. He was hugging her, holding her naked body close to his nearly naked one, her head tucked under his chin. She raised her own hands, skimming over his buttocks and the small of his back, holding him as well.

"You hungry?" It was a soft murmur against her hair.

She smiled, despite herself. He felt it, chuckled. "Well, we satisfied that appetite already. I'm thinking we need to get something else in your stomach." He released her to pick up her robe, put it back on her. When he re-belted it, he arranged the sides deliberately so the chain was revealed, as well as the curves of her breasts almost to the nipples. "God, you are a beautiful woman, Marguerite. You're wet for me. I can smell it. Tell me you are."

Her lashes lifted, eyes dwelling on that ruthlessly sensual mouth a moment before rising to meet his gaze. "Yes."

"Good. I like keeping you that way. Go sit at the table and I'll bring you some breakfast."

She stopped beside the small bistro, noted the lovely blue and rust mosaic tile design on it now that the tablecloth and candles had been removed. The early morning sun coming through the surrounding windows made the tiles gleam, bathed the area in sunshine. "So, do you keep pictures of the others around, or just Leila?"

There was a pause. "I have pictures of some of the others."

"Are they trophies? Will you have a special photo of me?"

Tyler met her challenging gaze and thought her moods were as mercurial as the sunlight haloing her pale hair. "If you're trying to bait me, angel, I'd rethink that course."

"I'm not afraid of you. I'm not afraid of anything."

"Yes, you are, on both counts. You're afraid of everything. In England there are castles with stone walls that go up over a hundred feet, built during a time when it was the strength of your fortress that won battles. Each time I look at you, I marvel at the feat of organic engineering that's allowed you to create such a fortification within a perfect composition of female flesh."

"How do you do that?"

He sprinkled chopped tomatoes over the omelets he'd placed on plates and carefully arranged a sprig of greenery alongside. "Do what?"

"Compose words in the air like you would on paper. It's remarkable." She looked back out at the landscaped grounds, the live oaks beyond them framing the view of the water.

He could have demanded that she look at him but chose not to at this moment. Instead he brought her breakfast. Let her sit with her head tilted at that angle, the lips that had so cleverly brought him to a ripping climax simply sipping juice now. It made him hard again, knowing that his taste was still in her mouth. Thinking about how she had walked into the kitchen with that hunger in her eyes, her desire to take him down her throat so obvious.

Her emotional and physical reactions were all over the map right now. She'd probably figured a way to rationalize her reaction, chalking it up to a temporary insanity that would retreat into nonexistence the moment she drove back down his driveway. If that was the case, he was going to have to make damn sure the experience was impossible to confine to this weekend.

"*Are* they trophies?"

The question was so soft, he almost missed it. Tyler tenderly cupped her face, brought those unsettling blue eyes back to his face. "No, angel."

"Don't... Why do you call me that?"

"Because." He leaned forward, his hand slipping up her back to unerringly trace the scar tissue of the design burned there, now concealed under the robe. "Someone drew you wings a long time ago and you've been trying to decide whether to fly away ever since." His hand moved to her waist, up to cup her breast, his thumb toying idly with the nipple chain. "And because when I look at you, I think you're a gift from God."

Before she could think too much about either explanation, Tyler directed her attention to her plate.

"Go ahead and eat. We're going to do a few less intense things this morning. At least that was my plan until you came in with other ideas."

"I don't know why I did that." She stared at her food, a flush rising on her cheeks.

"I do." He put a fork in her hand, got his own plate and joined her at the table.

He enjoyed the way she examined the veggie protein links, picked one up, sniffed, raised her brows.

"Mac turned me on to them. You know, Violet's Mac?"

"He's a vegetarian? He looks like he eats raw meat for breakfast."

Tyler grinned. "That's an understatement. But yes, he's a vegetarian. I'm suffering from the typical high cholesterol of too much good living, so he's been giving me some tips."

She ran an appraising eye over him, a Mistress's look, so much a part of her she was probably unaware of it, or how it made his blood heat. "You don't look like a person with high cholesterol."

At the sudden flare of desire in his eyes, Marguerite quickly lowered her attention to her breakfast. Whole wheat toast spread with fresh blackberry preserves, a vegetable omelet sprinkled with Gouda cheese and cut tomatoes, three wedges of pink grapefruit arranged in a fan shape alongside and the protein links. He'd put it all on an aquamarine plate sitting on a linen placemat. A tiny bundle of wildflowers in a small water glass was the table centerpiece. Simple, pretty, everything placed for maximum aesthetic effect. She wondered if it came naturally to him or if it had been an attempt to please her. Both possibilities made an impression and she wanted to look at him again, so she raised her lashes to do just that.

He was leaned back in the chair in the casual posture he seemed to favor, his leg straightened out so it flanked her, the other crooked. It drew her eyes to the part of him that she'd so recently had in her mouth, a nice curve of testicles, a cock of impressive shape and size. The view stayed as pleasing as her gaze rose, covering the well muscled chest and abdomen, the dark hair of his head gleaming with threads of silver at the temples. Those broad shoulders, long arms, the capable fingers holding the coffee cup to his lips, taking a sip as he watched her watching him. The shadow of a beard.

She'd had some beautiful men at her mercy and she'd appreciated that beauty. Their smooth muscles and unscarred bodies, most not yet showing any of the effects of age and experience. But she couldn't tear her gaze away from Tyler's. He had scars. Such as the one on his chest, a jagged cut near his abdomen. Another round scar just over his right pectoral. His hand rested on the table next to his plate, and now she tapped her finger on a small half-inch white ridge on one knuckle. "Where did you get that?"

"You just looked at every scar on me. If you ask about the one most likely to be a childhood scar, how am I going to impress you?"

She cocked her head. "Do you want to impress me?"

She had trouble swallowing her mouthful of eggs at the flash of teeth, at what a true, boyishly mischievous expression did to that face.

"I think I'm succeeding." He ran a finger down her wrist, with a raised brow to tell her he registered her increased pulse. "You know why you're fascinated with me, when you've had so many pretty boys at your beck and call? Because you've never trusted yourself with a man."

She withdrew her hand, lifted her cup of juice. "That's a very arrogant statement, assuming a great deal about me you don't know."

He circled her wrist with his hand when she put the cup back down, drawing her hand back out to the center of the table. "I'm a very arrogant man," he agreed. "Why don't you tell me more about yourself, then, so I don't make assumptions?"

"I'm eating."

"So talk and eat. Have you thought about why you begged me to touch you earlier? In your own sessions, you don't seem to think a sub needs to touch you to experience the fullest pleasure."

When she pulled against him, he simply tightened his grip, holding her fast.

"I didn't beg," she said. *Not exactly.* "But even if I did, that's part of what it's about. Denial increases pleasure and in order for denial to work that way, you have to be aroused to desperately want what you're being denied."

"So if I'd been a better Master, I would have denied you."

She gave him a sweet look. "That's up to you. I would never presume to tell a Master what to do."

"Smartass." His teasing surprised her but then her tartness vanished as he leaned forward. Despite herself, her gaze was drawn to his mouth. To its inexorable progress toward her, until it hovered just above her lips. She couldn't form the words to remind herself of her rule, let alone him.

"Anticipation is not a bad thing." His breath caressed her lips. "But a memory keeps you warmer longer."

He sat back, just as slowly. From his satisfied gaze, she realized she'd parted her lips in anticipation. She pressed them together, closed her fingers into a fist by the placemat, trying to tamp down the annoyance that he could pull this from her so easily. Anger that came from his manipulation, his ridicule of her resolve.

"Tell me why you didn't touch Brendan after you finished branding him. I could tell you wanted to."

"I can't tell you that."

"Yes, you can. Marguerite, the way you feel inside about things isn't a matter of national security. Just tell me. Why are you so afraid of emotional intimacy with your subs, angel? That's where you can find the real Nirvana."

"Why don't you answer the fucking question about your hand first?"

Tyler's gaze snapped to her face. Not by any vocal inflection did she indicate the heat behind the crudity she'd injected into the sentence, but her eyes were hard and bright, the set of her shoulders tense, danger signs he was beginning to recognize. He'd pressed on a nerve. Casually, he laid his hand down on her forearm, tightened his grip when she began to draw back, held her there, felt the heat spread under his palm.

"I was in a knife fight," he said mildly. "My opponent swung wild, I had my hand up, he clipped my knuckle, took a flap of skin off. Didn't have time to treat it for several days, so it didn't heal very pretty. Why do you avoid intimacy with your subs?"

"I'm not looking for that. I don't crave that."

"Don't you? What's so bad about it?"

She stood up, her hand still in his grasp, so she pulled against him. "You promised I could have my two hours for tea. I want it now."

"Sit down, Marguerite." When she didn't move, he reached up, feathered a hand on her face. "Please sit down."

"We covered this last night. Don't play me, Tyler. I'm not a submissive you have to crack open to teach her to find fulfillment under your Will."

"Aren't you?" He saw the shock course over her features, a remarkable tremor. She firmed her jaw.

"You know why I prefer boys to men? Because boys haven't learned to be bastards who take and take, who think they have a right to your secrets. They're just grateful for what you can give them. Let go of me." She snarled it this time and raised her other hand. He caught it, neatly twisted and tumbled her into his lap in the chair, her arms crossed over her chest, his arms bound around her.

"Let go of me."

"Tell me why you wouldn't touch Brendan."

"You son of a bitch, I want you to let me go." She struggled, kicked out at air, loosening the robe so it fell off her shoulder.

"Answer the question."

When she tried to bite his arm, he caught her hair in his hand, his grip unshakable, stilling her. "I won't hurt you, Marguerite. You can have as many tantrums as you want. In your own words—answer the fucking question."

"Why can't you leave anything alone? What do you want?"

"I want an answer to the question, that's all, angel. A Master asks a sub a question, she's expected to answer."

The training. This was supposed to be about the training. He was remembering it but she couldn't even figure out what her purpose for being here was anymore.

Marguerite closed her eyes, a shudder running through her. "Please let me go. Please."

"Just say the words. They're there, on the tip of your tongue. You know the answer."

"I can't hold him." She forced it out of a raw throat.

"Why?" He asked it after a quiet moment, his breath close to her ear. Somehow his grip had eased her back, so instead of being rigid against his embrace she was sinking into it, into the curve of his body, how they had spooned together through the night. "What's wrong with holding a man in your arms, Marguerite?"

"Because once I start touching them, holding them, I won't stop, they'll end up holding me. They'll take. I can't let them take..."

"Ssshhh..." He let go of her wrists, pressed one hand to the side of her face, shifted her so her body was turned, cradled in his lap. He urged her head down on his shoulder, stroked her hair, ran his fingers soothingly up and down her sternum, revealed by the open robe. When his fingers brushed the nipple clamp of the right breast, she winced. He stilled, registering that he'd felt the reaction. Pressing carefully around each one, he released the clamps. She drew in a breath at the rush of tingling pain.

"You did it too tight, baby." He bent his head. Brushing the robe out of his way, he covered her right nipple with his mouth. Cupping her breast in his hand to increase the sensation, his fingers traced idle circles on her flesh as he suckled her with soothing pressure. His other arm held her body close, his forearm warm against her back.

Marguerite closed her eyes. Her hand found its way to his head, threaded through his short hair, stroked it. He held all of her easily, the same way he'd carried her and overpowered her just now. The devastating tenderness he was lavishing on her breasts, soothing her sore nipples, drained her protective anger away, left her with no desire but to be quietly there, docile. Raising his head at last, he brushed his lips along her chin. "When they go back on, I'll do it. I won't let you hurt yourself, Marguerite. It's a Master's job to take care of you, protect you. Now, is this so bad? Being held?"

Yes. Because it makes things break inside. His tenderness was like a single operatic note, shattering the delicate stems of wineglasses.

"Relax." He kept her in the span of his arm but adjusted himself back alongside the table so he could pick up his fork, scoop up some egg and bring it to her lips. "Take a bite. I rarely slave over a stove and I want my efforts on behalf of a beautiful woman to be appreciated."

"This is...difficult." She took a deep breath, thinking that was the understatement of the world, the way he was keeping her rolling over from one emotion to another. Automatically she opened her mouth, took the bite, chewed, swallowed.

"A Master doesn't just take, Marguerite. He gives, too. Care as well as pleasure. I like holding you like this. Not just because I like the way your ass feels rubbing against my cock." He smiled that quick smile. "But because I like holding you in my arms, feeling you relax. Which, though you haven't done that yet, you're more relaxed than you were."

"Are you instructing me?" She sounded cranky, even to herself.

"Maybe I'm reassuring you that this is normal. The way you're feeling. And I won't abuse your trust. Whatever you need to be or do to get through this, to figure it out, I won't shake off and I won't judge you or share with others what happened here."

"You like it when a woman bares the darkest parts of her soul to you? So you can have power over her?"

"I like it when she gives me the gift of her trust. When a woman like you eventually does that, I know I've earned it. The power comes from giving a woman pleasure, watching her become helpless to me, hearing her beg for more." His eyes lingered on her in a way that made her feel anything but annoyed, but she tried to hang onto it anyway.

"But why do you want her trust? What do you want to do with it?"

"If not abuse it?" He tightened his grip on her when she tensed. "Sshhh. Be still. That's the only reason you can think of for a man to want a woman's trust? So he can take advantage of her? Marguerite, think about why you do what you do at The Zone. What is that about? What did you tell me?"

She refused to answer, staring out the window. Rather than press her to look at him, he reminded her of her own words. "Everybody tries to make a connection to someone else. And I don't mean acquaintances, friends. We look for a connection to a soul."

179

He ran his fingers through her hair, tangling there idly. "Good friends, lovers, subs, even sometimes with family… We enjoy time with them but usually move on after a while. But when we find that one person whose heart we want to win, we'll pledge everything we are or ever will be to get it."

"Sounds like a marvelous fantasy. An adult fairy tale."

"Sounds like hard work, the kind of hard work for which the reward is ten times worth the effort."

Her radar picked up something different in his tone. Her gaze flitted up to his face. This time she was intrigued to see *his* eyes turn away from direct contact with hers. "I think you relax more when you argue with me," he said abruptly. "You're not sitting like you've got a flagpole up your backside any more."

She was in fact sitting quite comfortably now. While he was talking, she'd settled in, so her arm was threaded under his, touching his waist through the slat of the chair, her fingers hooked loosely in his waistband. His body was strong and solid beneath her, the bare muscle of his stomach pressed against her silk-clad hip.

"Do you usually spout this much bullshit to your subs?"

She wanted to pursue those shadows she'd seen in his eyes but they were gone as if they'd never been there, the moment lost.

He laughed, apparently enjoying her peevishness. "Yes. They're naïve and impressionable, fawning on my every word. Do you play tennis?"

She blinked. "Yes."

"Are you good?"

"Yes."

His smile broadened. "Good. It's time to exercise, loosen up the muscles I abused last night. There's a tennis outfit in our room. Skirt and sports bra, socks and tennis shoes, your size. That's all I want you wearing. No panties."

He boosted her out of his lap, stood with her, his hand caressing her hip.

"How about you?" she asked. "Don't I get a preference of what you wear?"

He touched her bottom lip. "I'm pleased my slave has a preference. Tell me what you would like for me to wear and I'll consider it."

She was used to telling subs how to dress, so the reminder that she didn't have that status this weekend set her back on her heels. She did like looking at him, though. She wanted to deny it. Instead she watched in amazement as her fingers took it upon themselves to reach out toward his bare chest.

Perhaps because he knew how astounding a thing it was for her to want to reach out, he didn't stop her and demand that she ask to touch him first as she knew a Dom had the right to do. As he'd done when she first came into the kitchen. A wealth of spontaneous physical responses were apparently unleashed in her where he was concerned. She laid her fingertips over his pectoral, moved over the soft hair, fingered the nipple as she felt his eyes on her face, his body hot under her touch.

"Keep doing that, angel, and I'll have you down on your knees again." Sensual promise gave his voice a husky tone.

She kept doing it. "Shorts. Just shorts. Please."

Chapter Ten

ဢ

He had a selection of racquets. Choosing an oversized Prince, she tested the strings to make sure it would perform up to her standards. It surprised her, his decision to do this instead of taking her to some dungeon he had hidden on his sprawling estate and spending the day at the same intensity level as last night. She wasn't ungrateful, since her system appeared to be working on overload now.

The sports bra was white, as was the skirt. Being a tennis skirt, it just made it past the cheeks of her ass. Maybe he thought it would distract her. He was in for a surprise. When it came to winning, her focus was absolute.

When she stepped out of the room into the hallway, she found Sarah waiting for her. His house staff person looked in her fifties, with remarkably blonde hair tied back from her shoulders. She had hazel eyes and small interlocking silver heart earrings dangling from her lobes. A wedding band with a modest setting and a diamond anniversary band rested on a finger that, like the rest of her knuckles, displayed the swellings of early arthritis. Wearing a comfortable cotton blouse that rested at the swell of her hips over a neat pair of jeans, she appeared prepared to clean and cook, or step in as an appropriately casual hostess. The blouse was hand-embroidered with a floral design on the tips of the collar.

"Ma'am, Mr. Winterman asked me to show you the way to the tennis courts. He apologizes. He received a phone call in his office and had to take it."

Which explained the surprise of his sudden absence, when he hadn't given her room to breathe since she'd arrived.

"Tell him to take as long as he likes." Then, on a sudden impulse, she asked, "May I see his room?"

When the woman hesitated, Marguerite put out a hand, summoning her most practiced proprietress smile. "With you, of course. The house is so beautifully decorated, I just want to see the pieces he's placed in his own space. And since I have a few moments before he can join me..."

"Of course. I'm sure that would be fine." Reassured, the housekeeper changed direction, took her down the hall and across the landing. Outside the windows the sun was sparkling on the Gulf, the live oaks on the lawn framing it with imbalanced perfection, their gnarled branches shadowing a garden bench, a hammock. Marguerite glanced off the other side of the landing, toward the front entranceway, and saw a ficus tree adorned with fairy lights she hadn't noticed coming in the night before. There appeared to be a glittering of glass ornaments on it.

"Did...Tyler do that?"

"No, of course not." Sarah chuckled. "Everyone wonders about that because it doesn't really match the rest of the house decor, does it? That was done by my grandchildren. Mr. Winterman let them come out for the day when they visited on Christmas break this year. They wanted to decorate it with some cheap little crystal ornaments we found in one of the storage sheds and a string or two of Christmas lights. I was going to take it down after they left, for I certainly didn't think it matched all these pieces Mr. Winterman has so carefully chosen but he told me to leave it. That he liked it. And then informed me that he'd recently read in a *Woman's Day* article that such things were very fashionable, particularly when concerned with 'decorating on a dime'."

Marguerite was amused at the woman's impression of Tyler's masculine voice. "So do you ever get the urge to slap him?"

"Constantly. Almost as much as I get the urge to mother him. I suppose they go hand in hand." Sarah beamed.

183

"Sometimes I come upon him here first thing in the morning. He'll have his coffee and be sitting on the landing in his pajamas, his feet between the railings dangling down like a little boy's while he watches the sun come up. Of course, once you get above those feet nothing else reminds you of a little boy." She gave Marguerite a mischievous glance that made Marguerite bite her lips against a smile. 'Good morning, Sarah,' he'll say with a smile, as if it's the most normal thing in the world for him to be sitting there. Then again it'd be almost a sin to have that view in the morning and not take time to pay tribute to it."

"You're obviously fond of him."

"He's a gentleman, in a world where they're hard to come by. Both meanings, you know. Gentleman and gentle man. Like my Robert." Sarah pushed open a door. "This is his room, Miss Perruquet. I'm sorry but I do feel like I should stay."

"I enjoy your company," Marguerite reassured her, stepping in and appreciating the woman's sense of responsibility, her protectiveness. It was a rare commodity and one of the many reasons she valued Chloe and Gen so much.

Yes. This was his room. It was not just the simple, mission style bed of polished dark wood and matching armoire that looked as if it contained an entertainment center behind its doors. It was the more personal items her sharp eyes caught here that she'd missed in the other room. Several scripts piled on the bureau for review. Receipts from his wallet. A photograph showing a ballerina bent over in a graceful pose, accepting a bouquet of roses from the orchestra maestro while she was on stage.

"Who is the dancer?"

"Mr. Winterman's wife."

Marguerite turned from the photograph, startled, and the housekeeper blanched, realizing the source of her consternation. "Oh, no, not his current wife. She's his ex-wife.

Somewhat. Oh, dear, I'm not sure if that's the right description."

"Somewhat?" Then Marguerite saw a small heart-shaped box next to the picture. Through the crystal top, she could see three rings, the man's lying diagonally on top of the woman's wedding set, linking them.

"I shouldn't have brought you in here. I'm so sorry, Miss Perruquet. I..."

"You haven't abused his trust," Marguerite said firmly, facing her. "I won't abuse the knowledge, but if you don't feel it would jeopardize your position I would like to know what 'somewhat' means."

Sarah pursed her lips, apparently mulling it over, and Marguerite gave her the time to do so with the patience that many a sub had both cursed and blessed her for.

At last, she spoke. "All right. I'll tell you. For the same reason I agreed to bring you here in the first place. Mr. Winterman gave us very specific instructions on Friday morning. He told me, 'Anything she asks for, other than to leave—'" a smile touched her lips, "'she's to have.' He's different about you."

Marguerite tried to appear unaffected by that knowledge. "I'm sure Tyler often offers his hospitality to women."

"His hospitality, but not that. Not an open door." She shook her head. "I've raised my children, I have a husband. No matter the things that go on in this house, certain things remain the same. I know when a man is trying especially hard to make an impression on a woman. And I know enough about Mr. Winterman to know if he's trying so hard for you, then you must be extraordinary."

"Now *that* I don't think he'd appreciate you telling me."

"Perhaps not." Sarah nodded. "But he's got so much charm, I thought you might appreciate having an edge on him."

It startled a wave of amusement out of Marguerite. "I appreciate every weapon I can get," she agreed. "His wife?"

"Oh." The light went out of the housekeeper's eyes and she looked toward the picture. A frown marred her brow and she stepped past Marguerite to straighten the runner on the dresser that Tyler had apparently knocked off kilter when he laid the stack of scripts there. "Mr. Winterman's wife was a dancer, an extraordinary one. European. Very...fragile. Temperamental. All the things you've heard about prima ballerinas—with her, they were true. But she loved him so much, depended on him so much. He..." She paused, as if reconsidering her decision to speak.

"He..." Marguerite prompted. She knew she was prying, encouraging the woman when she shouldn't, but in the past twelve hours Tyler had spun her on her axis. It seemed she'd been in retreat mode the whole time. She wanted to know more about him. While she knew the hazards of that desire, she was too far into the danger zone now to back away from a little additional knowledge. And while she could rationalize and tell herself it was to increase her arsenal of defenses, she wanted to know *him*. Those shadows in his eyes at breakfast had bothered her.

Sarah folded her hands before her. "He wasn't always in the career field he's in now. He worked for the government. He left active duty some time ago, though I think he still does some work for them occasionally, mostly out of Washington. When he worked for them full time, he was assigned to Panama during that terrible time with Noriega. He was also involved in the Gulf War. When he came back from those conflicts, something had happened. You could tell from his eyes he saw things the rest of us didn't ever want to see. I thank God for men and women like him who are willing to see it and take care of it so the rest of us don't have to do so. But a part of him was shattered. He needed...he needed a woman's understanding and love, because he was in a very bad place in his heart. And she had always depended on him emotionally."

The housekeeper's glance shifted away briefly. "They had the type of relationship you often see in this house."

A submissive. Of course. So Tyler's Dominant side had been a part of him so long it had even been part of his marriage.

"She didn't know how to help him, couldn't even understand it." Sarah shook her head. "It broke my heart to watch them. She thought that he should just be able to be home, watch her dance and that would make his heart happy again. Two years later she left him, confused. He let her go, too heartsick to help her find him again because he couldn't find himself. As I said, she was a fragile creature. It took him about eighteen months after that, after she went back to Europe, but he straightened things out for himself and went after her."

"They never..."

"No." Sarah stroked a hand over the bed, as if she touched the man who slept there, her hazel eyes sad, loving. "He never divorced her, you see. And she never asked for one. But before he could reconcile with her, she killed herself. Right after a stunning performance of *Swan Lake* where the troupe was called back for five curtain calls. They said it was the most poignant dancing she'd ever done. When her Odette died, there wasn't a dry eye in the entire theater."

"Dear Goddess." The words were spoken before Marguerite could think to hold them back. "Tyler... What did he do?"

"He buried her, mourned her and picked up the pieces. I thought for a while he'd never reach out to a woman again. But after about three years he started having lady guests."

"Like Leila."

The housekeeper didn't look surprised that she knew about Leila. But if Tyler held D/s parties here regularly, there probably wasn't much about Tyler's current or past relationships that startled her. Yet she had called Tyler a gentleman and meant it. Which meant Sarah was an extraordinary housekeeper. Or she worked for an extraordinary man, a sly whisper from her subconscious that Marguerite chose to ignore.

"Miss Leila was a good thing for his heart. She laughs so easily and enjoys the types of things Mr. Winterman enjoys." Again that tactful wording. "She was a strong woman. I guess..." a faint blush tinged her cheeks. "I thought all women who did that type of thing were like Mrs. Winterman. Somewhat dependent, needy. I realized then that it was just a part of Mrs. Winterman.

"We all have our ghosts that haunt us." Her gaze went to another photograph, this one on the wall. It was a photo from what Marguerite now guessed was Panama. A soldier surrounded by children, reaching up for candy. "Sometimes when I come in and see him sitting on that landing, I know he's been sitting there half the night, watching the water, waiting for the sun come up. He's managed to heal himself, but it was a near thing. He put the pieces back together by himself. And most people couldn't have done that."

After a moment of silence between the two women, Marguerite spoke. "No, they couldn't. Thank you, Sarah. I appreciate your honesty. And I promise, regardless of what Tyler and I inflict on each other, I'll try not to use the things you've told me to hurt him."

Sarah gestured, letting Marguerite precede her from the room. As she closed the door, she paused with her hand on the knob. "Miss Perruquet, regardless of the instructions Mr. Winterman left me, I didn't plan to tell you such personal things about him."

"So why did you?"

"I'm not sure." The housekeeper considered Marguerite. Marguerite was thankful she kept her eyes on her face, not on the rather revealing outfit. "I just felt it was the right thing to do."

After that surprising statement Sarah led Marguerite out of the room, down the stairs and back through the kitchen. "The tennis courts are out this entrance. Just follow the path through the gardens and you'll see them below the pool house. Mr. Winterman also told me to give you this note to take with you." She handed Marguerite a folded piece of heavy, cream-colored stationery from the kitchen table. "He said to read it when you reached the orchid area. You'll recognize it. There's a small greenhouse for the more exotic ones. He has the hardier species planted in a bed just beside it. You'll also find a statue of Aphrodite there and a fountain pool with koi fish. Now, you and Mr. Winterman be sure to come back in for lunch soon. I'm making up chocolate chip cookies for dessert and snacks. You'll know they're ready because you can smell them all the way into the gardens. It usually brings Robert in, no matter how far afield he's wandered."

Marguerite nodded, not sure whether to be amused or disturbed at the dichotomy, a motherly admonishment offered as she stepped out in a tennis outfit that hardly covered her bare ass.

The gardens were Southern landscaping at its finest, foliage arranged in artful wild clusters of white and deep fuchsia azaleas, oleanders, ginger plants with salmon-colored, pink and yellow fragrant blossoms. Everything carefully planted and arranged to look natural and yet not cluttered. And throughout the garden was one of the most amazing collections of bronze statuary she'd ever seen. A lone soldier. A dog lying down, asleep. Dancers. So many dancers, slender bodies reaching, stretching, appearing as if they danced for the joy of the sun-drenched day and the flowers around them.

The care lavished on his property, not as an absent landlord throwing around money but as a man who enjoyed living here, who desired and perhaps needed a sanctuary more than most, was obvious. She pictured him sitting on the bench she sank down on now, a book in hand, studying his orchids, opening up the top of the greenhouse to sift their soil in his hands or bending to examine the ones in the outdoor bed. It would all seem like a Cary Grant cliché except she'd already seen the shift of the waters, the flashes of temperament, wells of sorrow, glints of humor sparkling.

The bench was in the shadow of a life-sized bronze statue of Aphrodite as Sarah had noted, ruling in queenly serenity over a pool sprinkled with floating lilies and containing gold and silver koi. After a moment of study, Marguerite opened her note. He'd scented the paper with orange peel fragrance and done the script in calligraphy. The note had been sealed with a brown wax like chocolate. Lifting it to her nose, she confirmed that it smelled like chocolate. The stem of a tiny lavender wildflower had been captured in the wax, a flower from breakfast. She shook her head, thinking a man this practiced in seduction should be labeled a dangerous weapon to protect any woman within twenty yards of him.

I can see you from my office. Put your hand beneath your skirt and play with your pussy for me. Distract me enough and you may have half a chance of scoring one game on me.

She glanced toward the house and saw that the gardenias to her right shielded her from the house's first-level windows. So Tyler was on the second level. From the sun's angle, she couldn't see him. The light reflected against the glass, making them into mirrors.

One game? She was going to trounce him in straight sets, let punishing him on the courts be her outlet for the tension of the whole past week. A tension that strangely felt not so near at hand as she sat within his carefully cultivated gardens. His native orchids were graceful ladies within ten feet of her. With petals of so many shapes and colors, yellow, pink, purple, white, as delicate as thin paper, they fluttered from the wind stirred by the fountain of water that emerged from the platform under Aphrodite's bare feet.

Putting her tennis racquet to the side, she tentatively opened her legs. She'd run her hands over her body before to titillate a sub and done some things for herself at home. Just not…this.

Concentrating, she summoned an image. Tyler, standing in the kitchen in the loose cotton pants, low on his hips. The firm mouth, which she'd felt taking control of her clit before she'd been lost to dreams. His long-fingered hand lying next to his plate, his gold watch against his tanned skin.

Her fingers crept between her legs, stroked. Her clit responded eagerly, startling her. She widened her legs farther, just a bit. Even so, the short pleated skirt would now give a clear view to anyone approaching her.

Tyler at The Zone, his lips beneath her ear. His hands on her breasts, tugging the nipple chain ruthlessly. Her fingers played among petals of flesh that were getting slick with dew. She unfolded, straightening out on the bench, her head resting on the back as she imagined welcoming Tyler in between her thighs. Wrapping her legs around his muscular hips, clutching his neck, biting into his shoulder as he thrust into her. Just imagining it made her pussy ripple, weep and spasm for what she could not have. What she was denying herself. Her other hand moved up her stomach, over the tight fit of the sports bra to her right nipple. Found it aching for the pinch of her fingertips. She remembered his words about a woman's breasts and thought he might be right. She was wanton, drunk on sun and the smell of flowers, her body dancing like the bronze statues, celebrating the feeling of life and desire surging through her.

Her position had moved her forward so the skirt was rucked up, her bare ass on the bench's smooth surface. Feeling the hardness, she thought it was like the unyielding line of his jaw, his tough body as he demanded things from her she was terrified to give.

When she opened her eyes he was standing there, wearing just the shorts. A muscular god, as bronze and perfect as any of the artwork. But alive, so charged with energy that the electric static of it buzzed off her skin.

He'll take me down to the ground now, she thought, looking at his aroused features. *Fuck me whether I want him to or not. He won't give a damn about the rules.* And she would let him, because her body would go where her heart could not. And it would shatter her.

She scrambled up, pulling the skirt down, her cheeks flushed. All of her flushed.

"Did I say stop?" He lifted a brow. She shook her head but didn't move. "You asked to see my room," he commented after a moment of silence.

"I did. I wanted…" She didn't want Sarah in trouble, so she made herself say it. "I wanted to know more about who you are, Tyler."

He seemed to consider that, inclined his head. "Then I'm flattered."

"Your room. You don't usually sleep with your subs."

"No."

"Why?" *And why me?*

His attention moved briefly to the fountain, again that odd evasion. "Last night was different. I usually don't sleep easy, angel. It's more courteous to let the lady in question have a good night's sleep. How about you?"

She shook her head. "I don't sleep with anyone."

Until you. For she'd wanted him there last night, clutched to her in her dreams as she'd been unable to do with her restrained arms.

His gaze lowered. "Lift the front of your skirt."

As she obeyed, he walked toward her, taking his time, appraising her. When he reached her, he put one hand at her bare waist, his other moving between her legs. Her free hand caught onto his shoulder as a ripple of reaction unbalanced her, her lips parting in surprise at how strong the instant surge of arousal was. Already somewhat slippery just from the act of having his hand on her hip, knowing she was bare beneath the clothes, his touch brought forth enough liquid heat that he made a guttural noise of approval. No matter what the terms of this weekend, at the moment, she felt like she belonged to Tyler Winterman. Underneath his much too knowledgeable attention, his sure fingers, the sense of powerful sexual male was too all-encompassing to deny. Her instincts overwhelmed rationality. And with the sun warming her back, his hands caressing between her legs, she couldn't find it in her to panic or rebel.

"I don't mind you looking in my room. But I didn't tell you to stop touching yourself. You should have waited for my permission."

"I'm sorry." But she wasn't.

Taking his hand away, he guided her to the edge of the garden, ducking under the waterfall of blossoms of a weeping cherry, a curtain of white touched with pink. "Put your hands on the trunk, your back facing me." At her hesitation, he reached out, touched her cheek. "I'm going to spank you. Just as a reminder of whose Will you obey. With my hand. I will never use anything else to strike you, and your beautiful ass will be the only place I do so."

"I didn't ask for that restriction."

"No, you didn't. But pain isn't my way of Mastery over women." His gaze coursed over her, the sternness in his voice modulated by a devastating tenderness. "And just the suggestion of it has you trembling."

"I am not." Her voice broke.

He took her arm, turned her toward the tree. "Palms on the trunk, angel. Let's check off another box on that sheet of yours."

She obeyed at that, reluctantly, her breath catching in her throat, caught on something there she couldn't swallow past. Her fingers dug into the rough bark. He was subjecting her to the easiest type of punishment to take. He could have taunted her for being apprehensive about something that was nowhere near as severe as what she'd doled out to her own subs, but he didn't. Partly because they both knew it wasn't about pain. He knew the very act was pushing enough of her panic buttons.

His hands slid down her back, pushing her forward. His other palm on her stomach beneath the skirt brought her out so her arms had to stretch to keep her palms flat on the tree as he directed.

"Lift on your toes, Marguerite. High as you can get."

She did and felt air as he lifted the back panel of the skirt. He tucked the edge in her waistband, getting it out of the way. Moving his palm on her belly so his two fingers were low enough that they rested on her clit, he massaged her there as she quivered on her toes, her legs spread open. Her body was beginning to ripple with overwhelming desire even as the coldness in the pit of her belly dug its claws into her vital organs.

The flat of his hand struck the bare curve of her buttock, the most fleshy part so it wobbled, sending frissons of sensation across the whole area. It didn't really hurt but of course that wasn't what she had feared about it. He did it again and changed sides, striking her across both buttocks.

The icy ball dissipated under the clever manipulation of his fingers on her clit as he did his spanking. The strain on her back tendons increased as she tried to stay up on her toes for him. Urgent arousal unsated from this morning was grasping her, a need to come all over those fingers that somehow knew her body. She wanted to take the hand striking her, suck and bite at the flesh that was creating a stinging sensation across hers.

He hadn't given her time to get too panic-stricken over it, springing it on her as he did, but he'd also taken the time to explain and reassure her in an odd way. And now, what she never would have expected, the stinging slaps were arousing a reaction of genuine, strong lust with the most shameless desire to lift her hips up further to his touch. It happened to her subs of course but she'd not expected it in herself. The bark bit into her fingers as she curled into it.

He stopped, rubbed his hand in slow circles, kneading her buttock, his fingers tracing her wet labia and clit. "Don't come, angel. You don't have permission to come."

"What if I do anyway..." A breath rasped out of her as he pinched her gently. "By accident?"

"I'll just have to tie you back down on the bed like I did last night and tease you for hours, not letting you come until you're screaming for it. Do you want to come for me?"

She could not answer such a question. She couldn't shake the feeling that this wasn't a game or just a weekend, that the control of a lifetime was slipping away before her eyes. Before his eyes.

His fingers sank deep into her and she moaned. "You'll answer me, Marguerite." His thumb passed over her clit and she couldn't help it. The shudders started coming from deep within her, a place she couldn't control.

"I'm sorry...I can't..." Her voice rose in desperation.

"Come for me. Now." One of his other fingers pressed against the rim of her anus, penetrated, just the tip.

She held on to the tree, her fingers scrabbling for purchase as her hips wantonly rocked against the pumping of his fingers, the working of her clit. It wasn't enough. She wanted him inside her. Her nipples ached for his mouth against the restriction of the sports bra. The pleated edges of the skirt whispered against her thighs in front as he kept it pushed up her back, exposing her to him.

Her legs were quivering at the exertion of staying on her toes. When the hardest wave hit, her balance went, the ankle weakened from the mugger's attack giving way. In an instant he had her around the waist, his body hard against hers, his hand still insinuated between them to draw out her climax. She writhed and cried out, feeling the heat of his body, the massive size of his cock against her ass and wanted it. Just wanted it. She bit her tongue to keep from saying so and tasted blood in her mouth.

When the reaction finally ebbed to the point some sanity returned, he had her leaning full against the tree, his body pressed against hers, holding her up. Guiding her, he moved her back to the bench, eased her to a sitting position. It was then she raised her disoriented gaze to Aphrodite and noticed an important detail she'd missed.

The beautifully sculpted goddess was wearing a collar, connected with delicately wrought chains sculpted in the metal to manacles around her wrists. Her fingers twined in the strands of her hair and played over her sex. Not hiding it as Marguerite had assumed at first glance, but stimulating herself.

What she'd thought at a distance was simply a reproduction of Greek statuary was an original interpretation. Her mouth was open as if gasping her pleasure, her lips in a pleased smile. Marguerite recognized the style.

"The artist for The Zone must be a personal friend," she said, trying to regain some sense of herself.

"He is. And can you imagine anything more explosive to a man's fantasies than to have the honor of mastering a Goddess, bringing her pleasure, bringing her ecstasy after ecstasy until she might willingly become yours forever?"

"I think you better watch out for lightning strikes. You might make that particular Goddess angry."

He went on to one knee by her, pushing her legs apart and putting his hands on her waist, drawing her to the edge of the bench so her throbbing center pressed against his hard abdomen. "Put your arms around my shoulders."

He tightened his hold so she had no option but the one that offered itself, to lay her head on his shoulder as he held her in the close embrace that shattered her, made tears rise in her throat. He kissed the side of her head, his lips gentle on her hair. "I worship this particular Goddess. There's nothing she could ask that I wouldn't do for her. I'd be devoted to her forever, never worshipping any other."

"Tyler—" She squeezed her eyes shut and gripped him more fiercely with her arms, though she told herself not to do so. There was the urge to do the same with her legs, hold on to him with both the fervency of a lover and the neediness of a child. "Please don't do this to me. You know this is just the false intimacy of sex, the way it makes you believe things you shouldn't."

"But it's never affected you that way before, has it?" He rubbed his cheek against her. Sitting back on his heels, he rose, drawing her to her feet. Backed her into the tree again and kept her close enough that she was still leaning into him, so she wasn't completely bereft of his presence. "You smell like... What is that?"

"Tea tree," she managed. "Scented with—"

"Jasmine. Just the faintest whiff, like the call of the Grail to a knight's heart."

Wooing a woman with poetry should have lost its effectiveness with the jaded cynicism that had infused the latter half of the twentieth century. But here in his garden with the willingly bound and pleasured Aphrodite looking over them, it was as if that time of bards had never left, the modern world merely a stray bit of garbage that had been pushed away to reveal the world Tyler had created for her.

His hand came to her face and she smelled the scent of her climax on his skin.

"Take my fingers into your mouth, Marguerite. Suck on them."

She did, tasting herself now, feeling him grow impossibly thicker and harder against her.

When he withdrew, she struggled to get some type of a grip on the situation. "You really are insufferable. You must know that."

197

His eyes coursed over her hard nipples appreciatively, pressing against the thin stretch fabric of the sports bra. With the flat of his hand against her lower back, he lifted her so her clit was pressed against his arousal. She uttered a cry of pleasure as a hard aftershock tightened her body against him and he sandwiched her against the tree.

"You've got plenty more of me to suffer before Sunday, angel. Tell me you want me to fuck you. I want to hear it from those beautiful lips, those lips that have sucked my cock but not given me one free kiss. Let me inside you."

It would be so easy. She could claim it was just part of the weekend but he'd know it wasn't. It was a line she just couldn't cross. As long as kissing on the mouth and sex were not part of it, she could keep this in perspective, make it work. But all those rationales were drowned by the scream of her body for his.

"No." She turned her head away, pressing into his shoulder. "No."

He put his forehead against her temple, let out a sigh that passed warm air over her cheek. "All right, then," he said at last, quietly. She felt the tension of his body, a mirror of the conflict in her own. "Then we'll just have to do something else." He eased back from her, put her tennis racquet in her hand. "Since I'm going to whip your ass in tennis, I guess I'll give you a chance to beat me to the court. And before you say I have the advantage in a foot race because you just had an orgasm, let me note my handicap is significantly larger." He glanced down at himself, pointedly.

Marguerite told herself there was no way he could take her from intense passion to humor in the blink of an eye.

"That doesn't look like much of a hardship to me," she scoffed.

Putting both of her hands on his shoulders, she shoved, knocking him off balance with the unexpected move.

Springing away from the tree, she dashed down the path, headed for the tennis courts.

"You little—" She was less than ten feet away when he recovered. She snorted, lengthened her strides.

Fun. Had she ever had fun with a lover? For that matter, had she ever had a lover? Someone who flirted with her, listened to her, talked to her about himself, took her out to dinner, went driving with her? Went to a movie?

She redoubled her efforts, running from the desire as much as from him. Gauging the hedge before her, she leaped, rather than zigzagging to stay on the path as she was sure he expected. It was a smooth hurdler's jump, a shortcut, one which she hoped wouldn't encounter any prize flowerbeds. She was determined to win at least one competition with him. Two, because she was going to trounce him at tennis.

The ankle held up, which pleased her after the strain at the oak tree. But a glance to the right showed her he was closing the distance, taking an opposite path, for he knew some of the cut-throughs she didn't. He ran like a tiger in truth. Full out, fast, telling her that he'd be a tough opponent on the court if he could match skill with speed. It made her look forward to the match. It also made it hard to tear her gaze from the movement of the muscles of his upper body, bared by her request.

They burst out of the garden about twenty feet apart, her slightly ahead. She lengthened her stride, calling on high school track team experience and her daily exercise regimen. She was discovering that Tyler kept himself in shape. In a moment he had her by a length. She fought and got it back, but she couldn't get ahead of him matching leg to longer leg. They hit the chain link fence surrounding the court together, both breathing hard, his eyes dancing. From his pleased reaction she suspected she had a matching expression.

"Come here." He put his arm around her waist and drew her to him, brushing his lips over hers. Just a quick meeting of mouths, almost chaste, except the very light quality of the touch made heat pool in her lower body. She suspected her insides were starting to resemble the hot springs of an underground cavern.

"You're not supposed to do that," she complained but she didn't move back. Her hands had somehow settled on his chest and his heart hammering beneath her touch. Her finger was so close to a flat nipple she itched to tease it. Pinch, scrape her nails across it.

He kept his hands on her hips and laughed. She thought that there were few sounds quite as sexy as a man's laughter infused with such sensual promise. He drew two Velcro straps from his pocket, making her tense but then he surprised her by using them to pull her hair up in a ponytail, double wrapping it firmly.

"I have other uses planned for those but I don't want you claiming your hair got in your way." His fingers drifted down over the scallops of her ears, rested on the sides of her neck. He held her that way, his expression becoming serious as he studied her for several moments.

"You would look beautiful in my collar, Marguerite. Naked except for that."

She raised a brow, trying not to show how his hands resting there unsettled her, though all her senses had gone on high alert. "Maybe you would, too."

"You'd have to get it on me, angel." His gaze lowered to her throat. "A double helix of seed pearls, every third or fourth set of pearls interrupted by a silver icicle. The main pendant would be stylized, the impression of an angel's head and wings, the wings serrated delicately like the icicles. When you turn your head, the icicles would make tiny pricks into your delicate skin, sensitizing it and keeping it aware of my claim when you moved."

She brought her gaze deliberately to his throat, determined not to appear ruffled by the detailed description, the intent heat of his eyes. The paralyzing sensation of his touch. Though she just had to hope he'd think her voice was breathless from the run only.

"For you, I'm seeing one of those chokers with long sharp prongs on the inside. The kind the pet stores sell for overenthusiastic Labradors."

His eyes sparkled, appreciating her. "Just so long as it's not one of those pink vinyl collars with rhinestones for poodles. Ready to get your ass kicked?"

"The only way you're winning this match is if you make it a command. *Master*." She added it sweetly.

Grinning, he held open the gate and she preceded him onto the court. "Bullshit. You wouldn't obey me anyway." He inserted the edge of the tennis racquet under her skirt, flipping it up as she propped up her tennis shoe on the bench to tighten the laces. Narrowing her eyes at him, she adjusted her hips so she was out of range from where he leaned negligently on the fence. "Of course, if I did order you to lose and then let you win, I could punish you for disobeying. Then we'd both win."

He shifted closer, let his racquet drift up her calf, turned it so it got caught between her thighs when she tried to move.

"That gorgeous ass of yours was lifting to meet my hand when I stopped, Marguerite." His voice was soft, his eyes drifting over the pulse in her throat, reminding her too clearly of what his hand had felt like there.

"Distraction is not going to work," she said, trying for a haughty tone. She held out her hand. "Balls."

She winced at his burst of laughter. "And why do you get the serve advantage?" he demanded.

"Because I'm a guest and according to your housekeeper you're a gentleman. Though I've seen no proof of it."

With a wicked look, he laid the tennis balls in her hand. "Warm up?" she asked.

"Sure. Let's take about five minutes."

Though Tyler was certain he was warmer than he'd ever been, every organ and muscle of his body revved for action. And she was making it far, far worse. Having brought her to climax several times now, he saw no sign that her response was in any way sated. It was as if her body was starved for sexual fulfillment, while his cock was staying in a state of painful rigidity. He had worked it down during their banter but the Florida heat and their impromptu race had already dampened the skin beneath the sports bra. He could see her nipples peaking hard and aroused against the stretch fabric. And when they started volleying for the warm-up, each spin on her toe or jog to return a ball gave him a flash of bare pussy or ass that was going to have him calling paramedics.

No, doctor, I'm not on Viagra, but I've had a nonstop hard-on for forty-eight hours, thanks to my angel.

His angel. It wasn't just the scars on her back, so obviously designed to mock one. Her profile as she looked over her shoulder, her white spill of hair. Her elegant bearing. It made it so obvious, the likeness to myth, art and imagination.

The night the mugger had attacked her, he'd seen her fight with all the fury of an avenging warrior. Then there had been her forgiveness, offered along with the money and the advice that likely wouldn't be heeded, because that was the kind of world they lived in.

She was so many things, always surprising him, like now. Definitely an athlete, she didn't play like a girl. Her return strokes were powerful, controlled, the lean muscles of her upper body showing that Marguerite Perruquet took care of herself very well. He wondered where she worked out and had a very disturbing image of her doing bench and shoulder presses. It made him miss a relatively easy cross court. Thank God it was only a warm-up.

"You ready?" she called out. Her color was up and there was a light, challenging curve on those lips that never did seem comfortable with a full smile. As he suspected, the simple physical exertion without the emotional pummeling that seemed to go hand in hand with sexual expression for her was doing her good. It would make her more relaxed for what he had planned for her later.

"Ready," he responded.

"First set, first game, first point, love-love."

She threw the ball up and her body poised, frozen in a split second of motion, arm pointed up toward the ball, racquet back, back arched, the line of her throat perfect. If he could have frozen the moment, she would have been Athena with her bow and arrows, her sleek hunting hounds clustered around her bare calves. He was beginning to wonder if she had any moment, any movement, that wasn't sheer aesthetic perfection.

Once at his dentist's office, there'd been a woman sharing the waiting room with him. She'd been fascinated by the Siamese fighting fish gliding lazily in an aquarium there.

"You seem very interested in him," he'd said.

"Because he's always beautiful," the woman had responded instantly. "The way he moves, sudden charging bursts or gliding like this. And all the marvelous colors of his body. He knows he's beautiful. He's so comfortable with it, he's as near perfection as one of God's creatures can be."

That woman had been Leila, the first time he'd met her. Her words now filled his mind as Marguerite's presence filled his eyes and heart, giving him a strangely tranquil moment where he realized he could easily spend eternity just watching her.

When the ball sizzled just inside the center line, he didn't even make it to the balls of his feet.

Marguerite gave him a look of pure feline satisfaction and moved to the left side. "Fifteen-love. This is going to be too easy."

He bared his teeth at her, took a ready stance. "That's what you think, angel. Just building your confidence."

Her eyes gleamed in response as she served the second point.

The sun climbed into the sky as they worked their way through the first set. She had great ball placement control and strength behind her strokes. So did he. He could knock her back with lobs but quickly realized she was deadly at the net, never flinching to throw herself out to return a ball and drop it over. She was faster on her feet but he had more power. As a result, the intention of two of three best sets diminished for them both as they fought for every point of the first set, never holding more than a one game lead until they were up 6-5, with him leading. Then she won the game point, taking them to a tie-breaker.

It was marvelously arousing, Marguerite thought. She'd never experienced a demand on her senses from two such equally strong compulsions. Determined to win, she was nevertheless undeniably affected by the way his body moved, the thigh muscles bunching, stretching as he pivoted and charged. His bare chest glistening with heat and the ripple — and ripple was exactly right term for it — of shoulder, oblique and biceps muscles when he drove a shot down the line.

While their focus was absolute when the ball was in play, they baited each other verbally between points, the sexual tension never abating. She started making a habit of bending to pick up a ball rather than using the side of her foot and racquet to pull it up into the air. It wasn't exactly to distract him, because she liked the idea that she was holding her own against his best game. But she did want to see if she *could* distract him. She wanted him to ache the way she was aching, seeing his body move, sweat, stretch.

At one point, while he was retrieving one of her balls, she bent to flex her calf, to stretch out her hamstrings, something often done during a tough game, only this time she did it with slow deliberation, at a very slight angle to Tyler, so he had an unimpeded view of her ass and pussy. Then she straightened, strolled to the sidelines and got a drink of water from the cooler. When she glanced at him, she found he was leaning on the back fence in the shade of the screen cloth, his gaze as predatory as a hawk's. His body still, waiting. Feeling inexplicably wicked, wanting to taunt, she pulled the sports bra up, exposing her breasts and poured the remainder of the icy water over them, cooling her down with gasping pleasure in the humidity. She slicked the water over the curves, her nipples now puckered from the cold. When she lowered the band back below her breasts, the fabric stuck, transparent, the dark areolas clearly visible.

He still hadn't moved. She sauntered slowly back to the line, bent one more time, this time to retie her shoe. The flexibility she'd earned from yoga served her now as she brought her chest practically to her kneecap, suggesting the sexual possibilities. This time she heard a muttered oath, coupled with a chuckle.

She'd never indulged or enjoyed the art of flirting but her blood was high from the competition, everything charged up and ready to do battle on this more playful field. It was obvious from the fit of those wonderful shorts that he was aroused. And yet he just watched from that fence. Letting her display herself to him as if he'd commanded it rather than her choosing to tease him.

The startling thought sobered her. She straightened, taking the line. Cleared her voice. "First point of the tie breaker."

He nodded, came to his line. "Marguerite?"

"Yes?"

"Every time you go after a ball from here forward, you'll bend to pick it up and do it as you just did so I can see your cunt fully. You understand me?"

"I don't intend to be chasing any balls on this side."

He showed his teeth. "Serve."

She sent a serve down the outside line to his forearm. Spinning on the balls of his feet, he delivered a cross court back that skimmed just over the net at a tight angle impossible to reach in time. "My serve. Let me have the balls, angel."

"I have two." When she started to bounce them across, he shook his head.

"I want that one in the corner," he explained. "You'll spread your legs wide when you go down for it. Then bring them all up here to the net and hand them to me."

His gaze was unreadable. As she turned she felt moisture trickle down her thigh. And unless she wanted to lie to herself, she knew it wasn't perspiration making her thighs slick.

She got to the ball in the corner, bent all the way down, spreading her feet apart as he required, displaying herself for him, feeling his gaze like a lick of heat in her pussy. Rising, she turned and approached the net, trying to make her strides matter-of-fact. She had a difficult time meeting his eyes, for the first time not because of her habitual avoidance of it but because his intensity was overwhelming her.

"Marguerite, you know the rules. Look at me."

She brought her chin up, dragged her gaze to his face. Setting his racquet down, he propped it against the netting. He put both hands to her neckline, ignoring the balls she carried in both hands. She realized he was holding something in his other hand. "Don't move," he warned.

It was a small pocketknife, precisely sharp. As she stood there, motionless at his command, he etched a cut in the fabric of the sports bra. All the way around one nipple, then back to the other and under, so that an oblong piece of fabric fell loose. The garment still supported her but now the compressed inside curves of her breasts and her jutting nipples were visible.

"The next two points are mine, I believe." He took the balls and brushed the soft plush of them over her exposed breasts. Marguerite bit her lip, holding back a breath of reaction but his sharp eyes caught it. He made the pass again, even more slowly, so that she swayed into the touch.

"The next two *serves* are yours," she managed. "Not necessarily the next two points."

His gaze went down. "Trust me, angel. Those two points are all mine."

She sniffed, despite the flush of heat that spread over her skin beneath his gaze. "Juvenile. I'm not intimidated by you. You shouldn't be able to play tennis worth a damn at this point." She shifted her gaze deliberately to the shorts. "Men don't multitask."

"Angel, men can multitask. When it's important."

He smiled that infuriating smile and she pivoted on her foot, went back to the line, her flesh wobbling erotically as she moved into position, turned. When he served, she knew her nipples, her breasts, would be on display for him. As all of her was, as was appropriate for sub training, which she'd somehow forgotten all about for the past hour or so. The cuff of her sock was getting damp from the flow of arousal down her leg.

He served, hard. She went after it, just tipped it over the net, out of necessity rather than a plan. He put on a burst of speed, scooped it up, lobbed high as she was trying to come to the net. She backpeddled to the back line, got to it, swung, brought it back to him at the net, trying to get it past him, but she hadn't had enough time to position it. He slammed it down the sideline on the opposite side of the court from her.

Even aroused, she was sure she could focus as well as he could. But despite that he won point after point, making it up to 6-0 so he was serving for match point. She was breathing heavily, not so much from physical exertion, though there was that. Her thoughts were whirling. His gaze locked with hers between every point, the heat building, so that with each volley the air seemed to get thicker between them. As if with each point he was somehow backing her into a corner. He single faulted on each of the tie-breaking point serves so she had to go and bend for the ball as he had commanded. But he hadn't single faulted once during any other game he'd served during the set. And, emphasizing that the strategy was deliberate, he delivered a sizzling second serve each time.

He wasn't going to win this match. All she had to do was get eight consecutive points. He had managed six, why couldn't she manage seven? She rolled on the balls of her feet, bounced to keep herself ready, knowing it would also create a highly distracting effect for his focus. Or spur him further toward a direction she could feel coming like an impending storm. Perspiration rolled between her breasts. She moistened her lips. Watching. Waiting.

Tyler threw the ball up high. It came down and he served. The ball hit with a hard *plock*.

She never moved. Never had the opportunity to move. It aced her perfectly, landed in the outside corner of the serve area and banged against the gate with a resounding clang.

He dropped his racquet. "Point, set, match. Come here, Marguerite."

She wasn't afraid of him. She was afraid of herself. She bolted, dropping her own racquet, not even sure where she was headed. She knew she wasn't leaving, just delaying the inevitable, what her own body was screaming—no, begging— for.

He caught her in the garden. Just like the tennis match at the end, this time there was no equally matched contest. He had the strength, speed and intent of a predator and she was the prey, thoughts jumbled by panic. The moment he touched her, seized her around the waist and brought her to the ground, her body reacted, screamed one word. *Yes.*

They tumbled. When they stopped, she was on her back and he was lying on top of her, that long, hard body interposed between her thighs, his intent pressed firmly against her.

"No..." It was a bare whisper.

"You've lost the right to no, Marguerite," he growled. His fingers curved into her scalp, holding her head still and making her stare up into the truth.

"One word from you, relaxing the rules of the weekend and I'd have taken you in a heartbeat. You couldn't do that, so you cheated. You know that political correctness means nothing to a Master like me. I take my cues from your actions, not your lips, listening for an entirely different set of signals, like this." His hand dropped, probing the wetness between her legs. "It'll be the last time you force my hand so you don't have to go through the formality of submitting. No more cheating."

"No." She tried to fight him but he had her firmly pinned and the movements just dragged her hard nipples across his hair-roughened chest, arousing her and inflaming him further.

His hand moved around and cupped her ass under the skirt, her sweat-dampened buttocks. It felt so good she couldn't stop herself from arching her back, offering herself up in an invitation he wasn't requesting. He was taking, just as he had said. His mouth came down on her nipple, suckling urgently. She cried out, she who always chose to take her pleasure in silence. Her whole body was screaming, out of control, so why not her voice? His other fingers dipped back into her pussy, found it wet and moved to find the track down her thigh where her arousal had run again and again during their match. Then his lubricated finger entered her backside, making her twist and moan as he suckled, pressed himself firmly against her. It was rough, frightening. She didn't know if she was enjoying it or being shattered into fragments. She didn't allow herself this type of pleasure, but he hadn't asked for her permission. And her body trembled, her mind shying from the realization that she hadn't wanted him to.

"When was the last time a man fucked you?" He demanded the answer in a whisper against her ear. "Fucked your ass and that sweet pussy with his cock?" His fingers teased both openings so that she could barely get out a word of response.

"Not...in a...oh, God. In...a...long time. Please don't. I can't take this."

Her hands were up at her face, covering it, her fingers in claws. Tyler felt her quaking, fighting. Catching her wrists, he brought them down, loosened the Velcro straps from her hair and used them to strap one wrist to each of her thighs, holding her arms immobile at her sides. He'd intended to use them later in one of his shade gardens. Have her lie on a blanket bound this way while he sprinkled rose petals on her naked body, kissed her, read a book, just enjoying having her laid out before him, accessible to his hand and tongue. But his body had only one thing in mind now. Possession.

"Tyler —"

"Master," he snapped. She shook her head, in denial or sensual thrashing he could not tell. Returning to the tight rim of her ass, he worked her there, sensing the release of inhibitions. Her hips were rocking up, her pussy so wet the bare smooth lips he had shaved were glistening. He took a condom out of his pocket, leaning on his hip, which put him close to her bound hand. Her fingers seized it, scraping him, crushing the package in the ball of her fist.

"No." Tears were squeezing out her eyes. "Nothing between us. Please." Her eyes closed and her body went still, waiting.

He'd been prepared for another refusal. Her words stunned him to the core.

When she'd run, the instinct of the wolf had kicked in and he'd chased, determined to run her to ground. But the tears and the sudden frozen rigidity of her body told him she was moving into the mode she'd been in at the beginning. Her body wanted this so much it was screaming for it but her mind was going to force her to endure it only, rather than embrace it. To make it easier to walk away.

Her eyes opened when he released the straps. He caught her wrists in gentle hands. Sitting on his heels, he lifted her, brought her up so she was sitting astride him, his arms curled around her waist and hips. He stroked the long line of her spine, slick with the damp perspiration collected there. Her hands were still in nervous balls, resting uneasily on his shoulders. Pressing his face between her breasts, he kissed the valley there. Nuzzled her with his tongue, playfully brushed the pale curves with his jaw. The fists unfolded, rested on his shoulders. He unzipped the skirt, took it up her waist and over her rib cage, gathering up the hem of the tattered sports bra.

"Lift your arms, angel."

He removed all her clothes. When he worked off her shoes and socks, he made her lean against his shoulder, held her around the waist with one arm while he took them off, then returned her to the same position. Now she was clasped in his arms in simple, pure nudity. He went back to nuzzling her breasts. "Touch me, Marguerite. Touch me the way you'd like to."

It felt...different to be sitting on him this way, clasped in his arms, in his lap. He was cruising up over the curve of her breasts, his touch and his kisses so achingly tender that she was torn between a heavy wave of lust and helpless immobility that kept her almost limp in his embrace. A moment ago, she'd steeled herself for the moment she could no longer resist, but for some reason he'd withdrawn, taken her to this devastating point instead.

One of her hands moved to the side of his head, her thumb brushing his ear, the soft ends of his hair just over it. She registered bone structure, the roughness of his jaw. Though clean-shaven, she felt the prick of the five o'clock shadow to come. Under her other hand she felt muscle, more sleek skin, damp like her own from the sweat of the match. Her head fell back as he began to work his way up her jugular. Her hips moved, a stroke of need against his hard cock. His fingers tangled in her hair, and though she felt his desire to sink his hands in, pull and hold her head back, her throat exposed to him, he didn't. His touch remained insistent but gentle as he turned every nerve ending from fear and resistance into arousal. The fear was slipping away from her, beyond where she could reach for it to shield herself.

"Are you protected from pregnancy, angel?" His voice was soft. "There are certain choices that I'll never take from you."

She wouldn't survive this, she knew. The demons that were going to be unleashed from their lovemaking would surround her, take her over. Not today, not even tomorrow, but the moment she left they would be waiting at the end of Tyler's driveway. Could she survive hell again?

"Tyler…"

Perhaps it was the way she said it, in a voice that might have been the wind itself. Regardless, he raised his mouth from her. "Yes, angel?"

"You're right, I teased you." She swallowed, made herself meet his shrewd gaze. "And maybe everything you just said is true…but I'm asking you."

Begging you. But she couldn't say that. "I'm not ready for this. I know…it would be easy to keep going…"

I can't say no to you. I need you to say it. But she definitely wasn't going to say that out loud.

He studied her for a long minute. "Do you like the way this feels?" He indicated their position, with her so securely cradled in his arms, straddling his lap.

"Yes." She was lost in his golden brown irises.

"I like it, too." He tugged on her hair, caressing the small of her back. "You play a hell of a tennis game, by the way."

"You slaughtered me at the end." Some of her worry slipped away as the tension of the moment eased, as they pulled back from that dangerous edge.

"Only because I took away your focus. I didn't give you any points, Marguerite. I promise. There are games I'll let you win..." His gaze grew more serious. "But very few."

He shifted, came up to his knees and laid her down on her back again. Leaning over her for a moment, he stroked her hair, fanning it out on the soft grass around her. She kept her hands at his shoulders and neck, even let herself stroke a finger over his firm lips, feeling safe in the quiet moment to do so. He kissed it, took it into his mouth, nipped.

"Do you have any clue how beautiful you are?"

Tyler wondered if she knew that he meant more than the way she fixed her hair, or how she did her makeup or kept herself in shape. He meant the total appealing complexity of her. She'd played a sub's game with him at the court, though she didn't realize it. But when it came down to it, she chose honesty, trusting him to understand. Trusting him not to push when a mere breath could have had his cock inside her. It was the first time she'd trusted him, and he'd recognized it. It had helped him overcome the roar of his own hormones and desire for Dominance to honor it as the gift it was. And now he intended to thank her in a way that would make the moment memorable.

"Marguerite." Lying down on one hip beside her, he propped his head on his palm. "Give me your hand."

When she did, he guided it to her mound, molding her fingers over her clit. "I want you to finish what I had you start earlier. I want you to make yourself come while I watch."

He kept his hand on her wrist, anticipating her attempt to withdraw. "I've told you... I've never done that."

"You'll do it now. Just let your body guide you."

"What are you going to be doing?"

"Watching you. Getting...or rather, staying, rock-hard while the scent of your aroused cunt fills my nose and your breathing gets even more erratic. While your body begins to squirm, your ass getting grass stains as you rub it into the ground, trying to pump your fingers like you would want my cock to move in you."

"I don't—"

"Here." His fingers straightened, lying between the spaces of hers. Just like the dance at The Zone, he began to guide her, making her rub her clit in slow, dragging circles while he pressed down on the digits, adding pressure. His other fingers caressed the outside of her labia, her thighs, the spaces between.

The feel of his fingers with hers made it that much more powerful in her mind. Her hips pressed down, her back arched as he had predicted. He watched her with those intent eyes as he withdrew his touch, caressed her hip. "Keep going, Marguerite. I want to see you come. And I don't mind if you go slow." He gave her a wicked look. "Seeing you spread out here, baring yourself to pleasure at my command, there's no reason to rush. How does your pussy feel? Look at me," he reproved as she tried to look away, as she parted her lips. "You keep doing that and you'll earn yourself another punishment. I like watching your eyes get glazed with desire as they are now. Answer the question."

"W-wet."

"Hmm. And what else?"

"It's warm." She drew in a ragged breath as her fingers feathered on her clit, learning that a light, fluttery touch could make her squirm, a rubbing stroke could make her insides turn into a whirlpool of rich molasses. The two methods applied together could whip it into a thicker, turbulent froth. "The skin there is…soft, slick."

"Keep going." He dipped a hand beneath her working fingers, brought back a finger damp with her juices, tasted it. "Open up."

She opened her mouth and he put the same finger in her mouth. She startled herself by sucking greedily, tasting herself, tasting him.

"And how do you taste?"

"It's not really describable. Like me but muskier. Thicker."

"The scent of your sex could turn any man into a rabid dog." He nodded. "I would start every day with my face in your cunt, eating you out, scraping that sweet clit with my teeth."

She gasped, her hips working harder, her head coming off the ground. Her back was curving as she shamelessly, intentionally displayed the taut points of her nipples to him. Why wouldn't he touch her?

"You'll come for me before I touch you again, Marguerite," he said, as if reading her mind. "But I expect you to ask permission before you do it. A sub never comes without her Master's express permission."

Why was she continuing to be surprised that he could do this to her? Perhaps because no man's touch ever had. She couldn't possibly ask his permission and he'd insist, but oh…her body was so hungry, so ravenous. She watched his face, the elegant, lean body, the gleaming muscle. The tight bulge at the crotch of his shorts, the columns of his thighs, one propped up in a vee to brace his body. When she'd been on his lap that scent of his, the heat of his embrace, had been the closest thing to safety she'd ever felt. Sanctuary had always meant a place for the mind and soul to be at rest, not to experience this wild spiraling.

"God, your nipples are so swollen."

"Touch them…" She wanted it to sound forceful, to compel him, but it came out like a plea even to her own ears.

"Come for me and then I'll touch them. I'll suck on your pretty tits and leave teeth marks on them, branding you as mine. You're mine, angel, you know you are. You want me to fuck your cunt, your ass, stretch your mouth, take you again and again until you can't walk, until you can't remember anything but wanting to please me with your cries when you come. Do you have something to ask me? You come without permission and you will be very, very sorry. Ask."

The words were so difficult it felt like they were ripping the lining of her throat. But there was something ripping low in her belly that needed out more than her pride.

"May I come?"

He waited a solid ten seconds, his eyes glittering upon her, his mouth set and firm. "Please..." she gasped, feeling the orgasm start to take her.

"Come for me, Marguerite." And he laid his hand over the top of her furiously working one.

The strength of his touch, the shock of it, exploded through her. Fire surged through her blood, tightening every nerve ending so she bowed up even more. He went down, biting her right breast. Seizing her left arm before it could rise up, he held it down above her head as she bucked and screamed. The climax tore through her, destroying another barrier she thought she'd managed to put up against him. Her fingers slid deep into herself, pushed in with his. The fullness of it made her scream into a guttural groan as she worked her hips hard against the thickness. She wished it was him, wished her body was covered by his, that he'd opened her and taken away every choice. Been cruel and given her bliss, however fleeting it would be before the darkness would claim her. His lips and teeth tugged at her nipple, and long after the climax reached its crest she continued to mewl and writhe against his touch, aftershocks shuddering back and forth between their fingers and her nipple, the heat of his mouth. He did not withdraw when even that died away, suckling her, massaging her overly sensitive clit.

When she would have shifted, he shook his head. "Be still, Marguerite." The powerful male desire in his eyes as he lifted his head held her in place as much as the command. "I want to play with your beautiful tits, your wet cunt and have you understand that it's my right to do so as long as I wish, even if you get aroused and come again."

"A fate worse than death," she said, her voice breathy. He smiled as he bent and pressed his lips against her nipple again.

"I thought you would feel that way."

Chapter Eleven

ဢ

He concluded his foreplay fifteen minutes later, strategically when her body was starting to rouse to his touch. He wanted her panting and wanting so her mind couldn't interfere with the pleasure he could give her. It was obvious that rousing to a man's touch was new to her but he knew her to be disciplined enough to relegate it to a mere physical issue. He wanted to keep her emotions involved.

When she started to reach for her clothes, he shook his head. "Carry them."

"But Sarah...Robert."

"They know my house, my ways. And that's another requirement met, submitting to my demands in front of others, isn't it?"

"Are you trying to humiliate me?"

"Think, Marguerite. Are you trying to humiliate a sub when you strip him and open up the glass screen?"

She clutched the clothes, her brow furrowing, telling him that even when she was defensive she never let her pride keep her from thinking.

"I'm not sure. I...go on instinct most of the time. It's more feeling than thought to me, Tyler. I don't analyze it. I'm listening to something beyond voice."

"Let me take those." He removed the clothes from her grip, laid them neatly on the bench with her shoes and socks for later retrieval. "You'll just hold them in front of you like a shield. The point is not humiliation, angel, not with me. It's about your pleasure."

"And you get nothing out of it."

218

"It's not a war, Marguerite. Getting a slave to capitulate to her own pleasure, accepting that she desires to be Dominated, welcomes and embraces it, is the goal for both of us. And sometimes, for a very lucky Master, a sub feels that way only about a particular Dom. Now, enough questions." He took her hand, tucked it securely in his elbow and led her back toward the house. "I believe it's time for you to have your tea. Which means reluctantly I'm going to let you go put something comfortable on once we're in the house and leave you alone for your two hours. After that, I'll come get you and take you for a picnic lunch."

It surprised her that he was going to give her space when he'd implied that he would join her for her tea times. But her surprise at that was not as strong as the unexpected feeling of disappointment, indicating that she didn't necessarily want to be without his company.

She kept her tone and expression neutral. "All this and picnic lunches, too," she observed.

"We're a full-service BDSM bed and breakfast."

As if arranged, they passed Robert in the garden, lean and tan from gardening, his face weathered and handsome with a depth of character that told Marguerite that Sarah's affection for him was well-founded. He did give her body an appreciative look with discreet courtesy as she passed him in profile, so that she felt his eyes linger on her buttocks, the movement of her breasts as they turned on the path. And of course, they found Sarah in the kitchen finishing up the preparations for their midday meal, the predicted aroma of cookies in the air.

Being naked in front of them made Marguerite vastly uncomfortable, Robert particularly, but another unexpected thought crept unbidden into her mind, keeping her steps even and measured as she passed them both. *I belong to Tyler. I'm safe.*

At least for this weekend.

She made herself add the last, well aware it was a conscious effort to do so, whereas the first part of the thought had simply appeared in her mind like a child's truth.

Tyler felt some of the tension go out of her as they moved deeper into the sanctuary of the house, out of Sarah and Robert's presence. Taking her hand, he laced his fingers in hers to reassure her. He'd felt an unusual compulsion to shield her with his body when he passed Robert, something he'd never felt with his submissives before. He mused on it as they made their way to the stairs.

He'd seen her start to gather her reserve around her the moment he indicated he was going to give her the time she demanded and cursed himself for a fool. He should spend that time with her. Even if the tea time could not involve D/s play, he knew it wasn't advisable to give her breathing space for the objective he was trying to reach.

But he also knew he had to do something to burn off the physical hunger in himself. As well as the emotional hunger that he didn't want to explore too deeply. He'd never had such an ache. It was time to bite the bullet, literally. Sweat it out and take the risk of leaving her side before he did something that would destroy her trust.

Patience. It had always served him well as a Master and he needed to embrace it now. Though he felt more like choking than embracing it.

* * * * *

Before an hour had passed, she found herself restless. Sarah had laid out the Japanese boxwood tea set she'd brought and prepared the Assam tea perfectly without any instruction. Marguerite considered stealing her away from Tyler, though she suspected she'd have to mortgage the café to afford the salary Tyler likely paid her. When she tasted one of the cookies Sarah had left on a plate, Marguerite decided she'd be worth whatever it might cost.

"Miss Perruquet, is the tea not to your liking?" Sarah, as if she had been imbued with special culinary empath skills, stepped into the bistro nook which was right off the kitchen area.

"It's perfect." Marguerite nodded courteously.

"Well, then..." The housekeeper studied her, her expression carefully neutral. "If you'd like, Mr. Winterman is in the range room."

"Range room?"

She nodded. "Downstairs. We have an underground level. One part of it..." She pursed her lips. "It used to be for entertaining guests, but after the unpleasantness with Violet and Mac and that terrible woman, he had it converted to a workout area and indoor shooting range."

That was interesting, for Tyler's parties in his dungeon had been the stuff of legend. But Marguerite understood. The bust that had taken down the S&M Killer had happened at Tyler's home and almost resulted in the death of Mac Nighthorse as well as Violet. It moved her to know he wouldn't countenance using the room again for D/s play. Not when it had been used to serve a horrible, twisted version of the sexual lifestyle he approached like an art form.

"Yes." She'd take the opening to see more of the man than he was choosing to reveal. He'd said he would come and get her in two hours, fully anticipating she wouldn't seek him out. Perhaps the error in judgment on his part would give her a tactical advantage.

Sarah, oblivious, was more than willing to show her the entrance to the basement. She handed Marguerite ear protection before she opened the door. "Just go right down. There's a glass wall where you'll be able to see him and a buzzer for the door into the shooting area. You'll need to press that first for him to let you in. Mr. Winterman is very particular about safety with respect to his guns."

The man had guns, plural. That was alarming. Marguerite nodded, started down the stairs.

She heard the muffled report of a weapon. When she turned the corner, she was in a small room similar to a police anteroom where cops could watch a suspect be grilled behind two-way glass, except this appeared to simply be a normal clear window of bulletproof glass The room in which Tyler was practicing was not small at all. There were targets set up and an obstacle course which he was working now.

He'd put on a T-shirt over his shorts but he was obviously pushing himself hard. The cotton was wet, clinging to his upper body.

He advanced, firing the gun and spun as a mechanized target swung toward him. Knocking it down, he did a roll across the ground, fired, rolled back behind a barrel, fired again. This time the shot went through a six-inch ring mounted on a pole and hit the target just beyond it, a metal circle that clanged at the impact and spun wildly. Back, forth, back, forth, he went from one obstacle to another, shooting now from his stomach flat on the floor, then back to his feet to fire again while running forward. He leaped over a wooden bar... No, *onto* it, going to a crouch, firing left then right, his feet balanced on no more than a three-inch span of wood as he punched through two cardboard targets. For the most part, she noted he was hitting every man-shaped slab in the chest area. One or two he took through the forehead.

She knew he was in good shape but had not realized how supremely fit he was. She blessed the gods above when he laid down the gun and removed his eye and ear protection to impatiently strip off the shirt, using it to mop up the sweat on his chest and the back of his neck. Tossing the shirt over a wooden target, he put the glasses and headgear back on.

She saw a workout room to his left behind another sheet of bulletproof glass but she wasn't looking at a man who used those weights to build up his muscles for show. He was staying in a state of military preparedness. Whether with intent or by habit, she didn't know but she couldn't say she wasn't impressed. Her pounding heart as well as the slight perspiration in her palms betrayed her reaction. It was like watching a wild animal. So incredibly fit and graceful one almost forgot the animal's purpose was savagery.

He finished loading a clip, locked it back in, worked his way through the same course, moving backward this time. When he was done, he stood with his back to her, breathing hard. She watched perspiration roll down his nape and the center of his back. The moisture was stopped by the waistband of the shorts in a way her gaze wasn't. She continued to let it travel down the curve of his ass, the long lines of his thighs. What would it be like to steal up behind him, kiss between his shoulder blades, taste the salt of him? Need was wound tightly in her. She knew that her intent to come down here and catch him unaware had created as much of a handicap for her as she'd intended for him.

He turned then, as if he sensed her. Met her gaze in the glass. His surprise turned to something else. Wariness. He really hadn't meant her to come here. She straightened, walked deliberately to the door and pressed the buzzer, cocked a brow at him.

It took him a moment but then he moved. Opening the door, he leaned on it, not necessarily an inviting pose. The draft brought her the sharp smell of gunpowder, of sweaty male.

"I thought your tea time was two hours. I intended to take a shower before coming to collect you."

"You intended that I wouldn't see this."

She took an assertive step into the room with a casualness she didn't feel. He drew back abruptly, avoiding any unintentional brushing of their bodies, surprising her. The evidence of the violence he'd exhibited lingered in her mind, stirring up more questions than she wanted to have. Stopping before a target, she reached up and touched the holes in the center of the silhouette's torso. After a thoughtful moment, she removed her ear protection and laid it down.

"Who did you work for in the government? And don't come back with some diversionary quip like 'I could tell you but I'd have to kill you'."

He winced. "I'd never do that. For one thing, it's been overdone." He put the gun down on the counter in front of the glass viewing screen, next to an open gun case and four cardboard boxes of bullets, two of which were empty. "The CIA. I was a field agent. I did script writing for the erotic film industry off and on for most of that. A talent that, thanks to my college friendship with Michael Atlas and our mutual interest in seeing erotic film separate itself from porn, resulted in a fairly successful side business that helped maintain my cover. And I came from a great deal of family money, so finances have never been a problem."

It didn't surprise her, for the man's style and mannerisms had always fairly screamed Georgia old money. "So did you retire early or late for the type of work you did for the CIA?"

His gaze shifted to hers. "What are you fishing for, Marguerite? These are waters you don't want to be in."

"Why?" She faced him. "It's okay for you to drown me in my memories but I can't even put a toe in to stir your waters?"

"You stir me up plenty, angel." He unloaded the clips and she noted there were two guns sitting on the platform, one much larger than the other. "Why don't you ask me the moronic question everyone feels compelled to ask?"

"Did you kill people? I know you did. I can see it in your eyes. I didn't recognize it for what it was until Sarah told me about your job."

He raised his head, locked gazes with her. As she looked into his eyes, she wondered herself at what she was trying to accomplish here. He had unsettled her, so there was some *quid pro quo* going on. But this was more. She wanted his shadows.

Perhaps she not only wanted more of him, she wanted all. It was a compulsion no true Mistress could resist.

"How did it feel?"

From another person, Tyler would have considered the question vulgar curiosity and met it with the cutting disdain it warranted. But Marguerite Perruquet didn't ask idle questions.

"I can't tell you that. But not because I'm not willing to tell you." He looked down at the guns. A Desert Eagle and a Sig Sauer nine millimeter, and he'd killed with both of them. "When you take a man's life that's between you, God and that man's soul. It's a personal conversation you work out your entire life. I can't talk about it because there are no words for it."

"There are some things there are just no words to describe and understand." She nodded, simple understanding in her eyes that eased the tension in him. It also raised his curiosity, but she went on. "I'd like to ask you one more question."

"I don't know how to say no to you, Marguerite."

"That's not true," she responded. "You didn't want me to know about this, see it. You hold a large part of yourself back and I'd like to know why." She raised a hand. "But now's the wrong time. I know that. My question is different. How did you get into D/s, Tyler?"

He could not conceal his relief and he knew by showing it he'd just given her a tactical advantage, provided a doorway to his own vulnerabilities. There was too much raw expression lingering in this room to prevent it, which was the reason he hadn't wanted her here. But she was here now and she deserved her answers.

"In this country, men have to be very careful about exploring their Dominant side." He shrugged. "It wasn't until I spent time in Asia and South America that I got into venues where I realized it fully in myself. Where men could be alpha, Dominant and it wasn't considered a taboo."

He reached out now, deliberately, brushed her hair over her shoulder. Ran his thumb along her collarbone, studying that part of her, making Marguerite's breath hold in her throat at the sensual scrutiny. The lingering residue of gunpowder burned her nostrils.

"To restrain a woman, bring her to pleasure over and over, see her obeying my commands, spreading her legs when I order her to do so..." He shook his head. "It's not something I can explain."

"Maybe it's beyond us as Master and Mistress to explain or understand it. We just know."

He held her gaze a long moment. "Yes. We do."

"Was it that way with your wife?"

"Don't do that." His grip tightened on her shoulder close to her neck. Marguerite swallowed at the dangerous flash in his eyes, the instant reaction of her body to his strength at that vulnerable part of her.

She might not know the specific details of his life but she understood the degrees of experience that had created that pattern of shadows. Knew there were likely as many rooms of dark to balance the light in his heart as there were in hers. And from Sarah she knew that at one time it had all gone dark, all the lights shattered. He'd had to stumble around in the dark, scream his fear amid that void. Then pull himself together and find a way to start relighting enough rooms to go on, to make his heart function again. She'd known it the first time she'd looked into his eyes, felt it in his touch. And perhaps that was one of the strongest bonds that connected them.

But she couldn't go into that room in his soul without agreeing to let him into hers. So she dropped it. "I apologize. Thank you for giving me that much."

His grip eased, his thumb rubbing the line of her shoulder, his gaze focused but not seeing her. He was seeing other things, things she'd stirred. Ashamed of herself, she raised a hand and put it over his to draw his gaze back to her face.

He had a way of forcing himself into the rooms of her soul without her permission. She wondered if she could set up one of those buzzer systems like he had for this room, where entry was not possible through the steel-reinforced door unless the person inside let them in. But when he displayed a moment of complex vulnerability such as he'd just given her, she knew any such defense would be useless. Locks did not work if the person on the other side was compelled by her own heart to open the door herself and let him in.

"Will you show me how to shoot the bigger gun?"

The shift of subject was intentional, to take them back to safe ground. He was still for a moment, watching, gauging. She waited, tense until a smile touched his mouth.

"Absolutely. Though I'm sure I'll regret it."

Chapter Twelve

ഇ

Once they went upstairs, Tyler left her to take a quick shower in his room and let her pack up her tea set. When they reunited in the kitchen area, he found Sarah had finished preparing their lunch. The clean smell of pickles and mustard drew his gaze to the deviled eggs contained in a wicker basket on the table.

Marguerite stood by the table in a light cotton dress. Tyler stopped for a moment in the doorway, looking at the way the light from the window filtered through, outlining her body. She turned at the noise of his approach.

"Where are we going now?" she asked.

"A surprise." He cocked his head. "Take off the dress. I want you naked."

Marguerite saw Sarah through the open archway to the kitchen. The housekeeper's fingers paused briefly over her task, but then she kept on slicing vegetables, keeping her attention on the counter.

"Marguerite." His voice was a low caress. "Obey me."

Marguerite untied and lifted the dress over her head, feeling cool air touch her skin. She hoped Tyler would take them out of the kitchen before Sarah had to turn. He seemed in no hurry though, his gaze coursing over her slowly. She wondered if he was deliberately putting her in an uncomfortable position to regain some of the control he'd lost with her unexpected invasion into the range area. The satisfaction she should have felt at that idea held little staying power, however. As she stood before him naked, feeling his gaze caress her, her body responded, moistened. Her back instinctively straightened, displaying herself to him, her chin lifted in challenge.

Even if his motives were petty, after a few charged moments she was certain physical desire had taken the upper hand for both of them. Her nerves vibrated as if he were stroking her. Her gaze swept down over his erection pressed against the jeans, clearly revealed because he wore a golf shirt tucked into them. Drifting from that pleasing sight to his hand hooked in his pocket, her eyes dwelled on the rough knuckles, the lean forearm. It made her remember how his hand had held the gun. The strength and steadiness.

He stepped forward at last, clearing his throat gruffly. Picking up the basket, he took her arm. "Come with me before I fuck you right here," he muttered.

The west wing of the house had a solarium that exited into a very private garden surrounded by hedges and wrought iron. A bed of green grass surrounded a smaller wishing pool. The centerpiece of this one was a Chinese goddess, water spilling out of a vase in her hands. Bright pennies glowed in the bottom of the pool and Marguerite saw there was a small complement of uncast coins in a shallow earthen bowl on the stone ledge.

"Is that a reproduction?"

"No, she's from the eighteenth century, Lamaistic period. I like some of the other depictions of her as well, but bronze is my preference for gardens." He spread out the blanket. "I thought this was an appropriate place to bring you, based on her story."

"There are a lot of stories about Qwan Yin."

"Yes, but I have my favorite. Would you like to hear it?"

After a moment, she nodded and his eyes warmed on her, making some of the earlier tension ease. "Qwan Yin was a devout Buddhist in her human form, one who demonstrated great sacrifice and boundless love during her life. There was no question she'd earned the right to enter Paradise when she died. But just as she was about to enter the gates, she heard a cry of anguish from the earth below. Unable to bear the thought of not answering that cry, she turned away from Nirvana and found immortality instead as the Goddess of Mercy."

"I don't think my subs think of me that way."

"I think you'd be surprised. Mercy has many forms." He eased her down into a sitting position on the blanket, putting the basket in between them.

"No way out." She gestured to the fence that had no gate.

"And why would I want a way out?" He unpacked the basket. "Food, sunshine and a naked woman for company. Beauty in every direction I look." Though she noted he didn't seem inclined to look anywhere but at her.

"Maybe I was thinking your guest would need an escape route."

"Nonsense. All women desire to be in my company." He winked at her, though she still noted a bit of strain around his mouth, keeping him from a true smile. "I'm charming. And if that's not true, at least I'm filthy rich."

She choked on the bite of egg he put between her lips. She managed to swallow, wiped her lips as delicately as possible with her fingers. He didn't offer a napkin, apparently preferring to watch the way she removed it with her own hand. "I can't decide if you're just completely self-aware, or an arrogant bastard, or both."

"Does it matter? I want you to lie on your back, angel. Look up at the clouds."

Once she was settled, this time he put the entire half-egg on her tongue, making it an awkward moment to chew and swallow without getting yellow yolk around her mouth. He collected the excess with his fingertips and inserted them between her lips so she could lick the rest off.

"What's the verdict?"

"Delicious." Cicadas were singing their rasping song as the day's heat soaked into her skin, joining the heat spiraling up from her insides. She wanted to reach up, thread her fingers through his hair, draw his lips down to hers where she lay on the blanket. Her eyes lingered on his mouth. When recognition of what she was doing darkened his gaze, she tore hers away.

"Exactly my thought." This time he took the deviled egg, turned it upside down and spread the filling over her clit and pussy lips. She squirmed at the cold but then he distracted her by moving down to the end of the blanket. Lifting her legs onto his shoulders to pull her hips up to him, he sat on his heels and began to eat the filling. Rather than trying to stroke her the way that would arouse her using the egg as the excuse, he used her pussy very functionally as his plate, methodically sucking and eating each portion of the filling, licking where needed to get all of it. Her hands and arms lay loosely above her head, the only place for them. She closed her eyes, immersed in the feel of his mouth on her, his utilitarian use of her body. His to do with as he wished. For some reason the thought of that alone could shoot her up a spiral of hard, unrelenting arousal.

He ate his salad on her stomach, drizzling the dressing over the spinach leaves. He gave her bites of it, getting the greenery on his fork with modest pricks that made tiny imprints in her skin. Then he split a sandwich with her, making her eat it from his hand as he watched every movement of her body, the liquid arousal on her thighs, the heightened pulse, the parted lips.

Objectively as a Mistress, she realized he was training her quite effectively to reach full arousal quickly and then stay there, so that she could think of nothing but the demand of her own body, the desire to have him fulfill it. To fulfill him. So it seemed the most natural thing in the world when a crust of bread fell to lift it toward his mouth, wanting to feed him. Serve him.

His eyes were molten gold on hers as he took it, sucking on her fingers while her body trembled, caught in the charged silence.

"Would you take off your shirt?"

She barely recognized her own voice. He nodded, stripped it off, then leaned forward over her, one hand on the opposite side of her shoulder, then the other, bracketing her. Slowly, slowly he moved on top of her, settling his thighs in between her spread ones with a nudge to accommodate himself. His hips were against hers, his bare stomach touching her quivering one, his chest on her bare breasts. He bore his weight on his arms so as not to crush her, going to one elbow to stroke her face with one hand, touch her lips.

"Ask me to kiss you. Marguerite." Her lips parted involuntarily but her lashes fluttered closed. "Look at me."

"Just..." Why wouldn't he just overwhelm her and do it? Do what it was so obvious she was aching to have him do?

"There are limits, angel." His voice had gotten low, a dangerous rumble.

"Yes." She opened her eyes. "There are. And you keep pushing them. This isn't about you and me. I'm not stupid, or gullible. I know you don't push this hard and personally with another Domme under training."

"No, you're not stupid," he agreed. "You knew it would be about more than that between you and me. Yet you chose me. So just say it. I know you want me to kiss you."

She shook her head, not meaning no, meaning something else that was welling up in her, that his constant barrage on her body was drawing forth from her.

"Damn it—"

"Just *stop* asking," she burst out. "Just take. Please...just take over. I can't...give. You just have to take what you want."

Tyler stared down at her a full ten seconds, felt her heart pounding beneath his, the taut urgency of her hips pushing against him. He lowered his lips to a fraction above her mouth and she didn't move, her eyes staring into his, pleading in a way her voice could not. She couldn't ask but it was obvious how much she wanted. And he could deny her nothing, whether she realized it or not.

"You never answered me, about pregnancy."

"I'm safe. And I can't have children."

He saw a wealth of memory and pain behind the simple statement but he could tell she didn't want this moment to be about that. He capitulated, plunged, covering her mouth with his, swallowing the near sob of relief she made as he fisted his hands in her hair roughly. Taking over, he scraped at her with his teeth, stroking her tongue with his, cognizant of her body rubbing against him, her pussy so wet he could feel it through his jeans, making him lose his mind and restraint.

Her hands were on his head, his neck, digging into his shoulders, his back. He didn't want to pull back but he did, catching up one of her hands and putting a kiss on her palm before he stood up to remove the jeans. He stripped while standing between her open legs, tall above her. He looked down at her clear pale eyes fastened on his every movement, her hair spread out on the ground around her, the moonlight color gleaming silver in its marriage with the sunlight.

"Put your arms back above your head," he said roughly. "Leave them there."

He wanted her lying beneath him, completely his for the taking. But she didn't move, just trembled and looked at him with those hungry eyes. In them, he saw a combination of desire and fragility so powerful he wondered if he could ever get enough of her or let her leave the house. He was overwhelmed with a desire to fuck her senseless and protect her both.

She couldn't say the words but she was able to form them with her lips.

Make me.

It wasn't in her to surrender to a Master, as much as he knew she wanted to surrender to him. But her desire was making them both insane.

He wanted to be gentle with her. He wanted to take her hard. Even knowing that he was going down a path he shouldn't go down, he acted.

She anticipated him, lifting her hand to block him. But as capable as she'd proven herself to be, she was no match for a person with his training. Not combined with his superior strength which, if she'd had any doubts on the difference in their ratios, he ended it in a split second by catching one wrist in either hand, bringing himself down on her. His knee inserted itself between her thighs and, using the bucking of her body, he slid himself into her.

She was so tight that even with her slickness he felt the resistance, the infinitesimal stiffening and then her attempt to compensate and relax after pain had already been inflicted. He stopped, holding her down while her shuddering reaction gripped him, stroked him, made him want to spill himself into her. Instead he eased forward, millimeter by millimeter.

"Just do it," she gasped. "Just fuck me, hard."

He shook his head, bent and brushed a kiss along her clenched jaw. "There's not enough of anything in this world to make me hurt you. We're not going down that road just so you can keep yourself from me. God, you're so lovely. You feel like everything that will ever be good, perfect." He pulled back out, then eased in, slowly. "Ask, angel."

She was panting. "No, not like this. Hard. I don't want it this way."

"One, you don't have a choice. Two, yes, you do want it this way. You're so close to coming your eyes are glazing." His voice dropped, his eyes burning into hers. "You think I don't feel your cunt clamped down on me, rippling? The way your body is moving, tightening, gathering itself?"

"Get off me." She practically snarled it. "I didn't agree to this."

"No. You wanted me to rape you so you could keep me at arm's length." He let go of her wrist, caught her chin and jaw in firm fingers to make her look at him. She began to raise her hand.

"You move that arm, I'll strap you to my bed and prove to you what you really want for the rest of the weekend."

The fingers curled into a fist but it stayed put after an obvious battle with her own will. He moved again, another slow stroke, then another. Changing his grip, he rested his body wholly on hers, pressing her down, lifting his hips. Sliding out, back in, slight adjustments of angle, deep, slow strokes to the hilt each time, stretching her open. He let her feel the press of his body against her opening, his testicles against the crease of her buttocks. Wrapping his fingers in her hair on either side, he held her face still, his forearms against her arms, his thumbs at the corners of her eyes. Making her look at him as his expression became more intent and hers became more panicked.

"You'll come for me now," he whispered, fierce, brutal in his need, his body tense, his muscles hard all along the length of her body as he fought to hold back. "I'm your Master, Marguerite. I am, always have been, always will be. That's what has terrified you from the beginning. I'm the man who's supposed to love you, take care of you, be with you. We knew it the first time we met and you've avoided me ever since. Come for your Master."

He didn't know where the words had come from. But he looked down in her face, felt her body quivering beneath his, so strong and vulnerable at once and knew there was no going back for him.

"It's not all about taking," he said. "It's about giving, too."

Her body arched helplessly against the weight of his, her hips suddenly moving of their own accord. Her head fought his hands as she tried to look away but he was having none of it. Her reaction swept over her face, that wondrous combination of panic at the lack of control and intense sensual pleasure that women felt so deeply. Those silken limbs lifted and clamped over his hips now of their own volition. He gritted his teeth, trying to hold on one more minute, just one more minute...

She screamed, a tearing sound as poignant as a death cry. Her pussy spasmed around him, urging him to spill his seed into her.

"Touch you..." It was almost incoherent but he heard her in his heart and let her go so her arms could wind around him, her face bury into his shoulder and chest. Only then did he let go, closing his arms around her, driving into her again and again with ruthless tenderness, wanting her to be his. His.

She came for a long time, as if a dam had released in her body. Even after the initial deluge the water kept flowing, her mouth making soft cries against his skin with every wave and ripple. Her hands held him close, shaking, desperate. He kept stroking inside her as long as he could, long, dragging movements that made her shudder with every degree of friction in a way that he knew would have him hard again in no time.

But that was the problem. There was no time. He saw it as she laid her head back on the ground at last, looked up at him with eyes that were even now withdrawing from him, seeking escape. Her hands moved wistfully over his shoulders, the slope of his chest, taper of waist, buttocks. But then it seemed her mind reined them in, for she stilled, drew back. "Please...I need to breathe."

He complied, not calculating the mistake of breaking the connection she could not deny. She sat up, rose, not even lifting a self-conscious hand to her hair or to brush grass off herself. It reminded him of how she'd shut herself down right after the mugging, turning to walk to her car as if nothing untoward had just happened. He rolled to his feet, pulling on his jeans, ready to head her off.

"I can't complete the weekend, Tyler. This has gone farther than I wanted it to go."

"Damn it, Marguerite—"

"No, I'm not blaming you for what just happened. I asked you to cross the line. No matter how I asked for it, in what way, I did ask." She shook her head and there was a quality in her eyes, a desperation he could not ignore. Not as a lover, a gentleman or as a friend. He thought himself at least two out of the three when it came to her.

"I've done what I was supposed to do and then some," she said with quiet dignity. "You can't ask more of me. I've got nothing left to give. All right? Please just let me go. We're done."

She stood before him, a remote queen with his semen tricking down her thighs, mixing with her own climax, her eyes somewhat wild, dangerous, belying the even tone of her voice. He read body language well enough to know that this time she meant it. She needed to go and would go unless he used an unacceptable level of force.

Apparently seeing in his face that he understood, she inclined her head.

"I'm going to go in and gather my things. I'll meet you at the car if you want to see me off. If you don't, I'll understand."

She turned and left him, her body moving a little less gracefully than usual, revealing the physical strain he'd put on her in the past two days.

For his own part, he felt as if he'd just witnessed a car collision where the passenger walked away apparently unscathed but with internal injuries she refused to have treated. He had to fight every primitive instinct he had to stop himself from going after her, grabbing her up and imprisoning her in his room until she learned to accept him.

Somehow, as criminal as that sounded, letting her go left him much more uneasy.

* * * * *

Marguerite did not look at herself in the mirror. At first. She gathered her things, put back on the trousers and masculine-style shirt she'd worn, which Sarah had been kind enough to press and bring up for her. When at last she used the mirror to arrange her hair and face, she didn't focus on the expression of the woman reflected there, though she couldn't help but notice the shadows under her eyes like bruises, the taut set of her mouth. She'd survived worse than this. She'd be fine. She applied a little makeup to cover the shadowing, brushed and braided her hair, put on lipstick and adjusted her slim belt around her waist. Shouldering her overnight bag, she took the stairs down to the main level. Through the window view she saw him leaning against her car. He also was dressed in the same clothes in which he'd started the weekend. As if they had just started. Or it had never happened.

But it had. The damp cloth she'd applied between her legs, stirring up his scent, the soreness and searing reaction when she pressed her fingers where his cock had penetrated her, told her that. Even now, seeing him, a knot formed in her throat, her body yearning, wanting him in a way she could not permit herself to want. And there was no way to make him understand it.

Then she noticed the ficus tree in the front entranceway with the fairy lights. As Sarah had noted, the glass ornaments hanging from the branches were inexpensive trinkets, though quite pretty in the way they reflected the tiny lights. Thoughtfully, Marguerite plucked off one figurine that seemed to have the most replicas on the tree and stepped out onto the front porch.

He watched her approach with his serious, unsmiling regard, as if he saw everything she felt on the inside. Maybe if he did, he would understand that he needed to let it go at this.

When she got almost to him, he reached out, took her empty hand.

"Stay with me," he said, making it a soft demand, not a question as he drew her into his arms.

Marguerite pressed her forehead to his chest, closing her eyes tightly.

"No," she whispered. "I can't."

She pulled back, opened her hand. Tyler looked down at the crystal image of a heron she'd taken off the tree.

"It's beautiful," she said. "The long, graceful legs, the tiny head and slender neck, the silver tone of the glass. You look at it and you want to touch it. You can, lightly." Her hand closed over it and his gaze snapped to her face as the glass cracked. "But that's all you can do. Look at it, enjoy its appearance, its performance." She opened her hand, revealed three pieces. "Do more than that and it shatters."

His brow drew together over the welling of blood where the glass had punctured her skin in two places, forming a pool in which the tiny pieces lay, turning them crimson. He turned her hand, made her drop the figure to the dirt and pressed the hem of his shirt into her palm.

"You're not that fragile."

"Yes, I am. I know what I can and can't have to stay the person I need to be. But thank you for this weekend. You're right. It was definitely enlightening." She tried to force a rueful smile to her stiff lips, was unsuccessful under his shrewd regard.

"You're determined to go, so I'll let you go. For now." He looked at her, hard. "I care very much for you, Marguerite, and I respect you tremendously. Do you understand that?"

She swallowed, looked away, then made a conscious effort to look back up at him. "I want to believe that."

"Then do, because it's true," he said bluntly. "You've made this a special weekend for me." He put a hand under her chin, his thumb caressing her lips, his eyes very close to hers.

"I'm going to keep doing my damnedest to win you over but I need you to hear something I'm going to say to you, understand it fully. Are you listening?"

She nodded, just a twitch of movement under his touch.

"You are very important to me. It doesn't matter if you never accept me or what lies between us. If you need me, I'm here for you. Tomorrow, ten years from now, it doesn't matter. And you know me well enough to know I don't make idle declarations of commitment."

No one had ever offered to be her champion. Anything that came out of her lips at this moment would be an artificial gesture with no warmth, just something to cover the fragile condition of her psyche, her rising desire to just get away, to go, to drive, be in motion. She wouldn't insult the gift of his words in that way. But not saying anything would be an insult on its own.

"You don't need to respond," he said quietly, demonstrating his penchant for reading her thoughts. "The offer is there now and forever, whether or not you acknowledge it. But before you go, I'm going to ask you to do one more thing. It's simple and if you do it, I'll consider your mentoring requirement fulfilled."

She suspected his definition of simple and hers were very different, particularly since at the moment it felt like the ground had begun to shake beneath her feet.

"What...request?"

"I want you to ask me to kiss you and mean it, rather than me making you do it. If you do that, I'll let you leave."

There were times that a request could be more potent than a command. Apparently Tyler was intuitive enough to know that, damn him. She inclined her head, feeling like she made the gesture in slow motion, wrapped in air as thick as pillows.

"Tyler, please kiss me." It came out as a whisper of sound.

Bringing his body close up against her, he put his hands on her waist. Moved them around to the vulnerable small of her back to press her breasts to his chest. His lips hovered over hers, his eyes golden lights flickering like the warmth of a welcoming fire, lulling her, hypnotizing her.

"Tyler."

There was no question, just his name, and he seemed to understand that. He closed the distance, settling his lips on hers, the heat of his mouth seducing her to part her lips, welcome him in. Her body melted into his with a sigh that seemed to come from every nerve, every cell, saying this is where she wanted to be, where she wanted to belong.

The kiss might have gone on five minutes or five hours. She lost sense of time, wrapped up in the tenderness of it, so unsettling. It acknowledged the totality of her, of their experience together. Completely shattering the careful illusion she was building that there was nothing hugely personal about this weekend, nothing she couldn't walk away from.

The hand she'd settled uneasily on his chest went up to the open collar of his shirt, feeling his pulse fiercely beating in his throat, the muscles along his jaw shifting as his tongue caressed hers, her mouth, her lips. As her fingers tightened on the back of his neck, the power of his grip increased and a noise escaped her, betraying her desire and longing in that one soft cry. She pulled away.

"Marguerite—"

She shook her head, moved around the back of the car, tossed her bag in the second seat and tucked herself in behind the steering wheel. He stayed where he was though she could feel it emanating from him, all he could and would offer to her. Just like the night at the club. Things that could destroy her and she wouldn't care. But she cared about him, so she turned over the ignition and sped away, not allowing herself one look back.

241

Chapter Thirteen

ॐ

"Mr. Winterman." Sarah had appeared at his elbow. Tyler wasn't sure how long she'd been there. He'd been sitting in the lounger at the pool house since Marguerite left, staring at the pool cleaner making its way back and forth. Apparently he'd been watching it for a long while, because it was full dark. Sarah's face was like a ghost's, the pool lights the only illumination.

"I thought I mentioned—"

"That you didn't want to be disturbed. You didn't want any calls. Yes, you certainly did. But this is the third time Miss Sieman— Mrs. Nighthorse has called. She indicated that if I didn't make you answer she was going to have me arrested for obstruction of an official police investigation."

Tyler lifted a brow, took the phone from her hand. "Pay no attention to her, Sarah. We're outside her jurisdiction and she's just being a pain in the ass." He raised the phone to his ear.

"Didn't you say I was your best friend about twenty-four hours ago?" Violet sounded amused.

"I was feeling sentimental and foolish."

"I'm crushed. What are you doing?"

"Working on a very important production plan for a script I'm investing in."

"That's funny. Sarah said you've been supervising the pool cleaner for the past three hours. Since that's that little bug thing that automatically runs around the pool sucking up algae, I assumed you might have time to talk to me."

Tyler glared at Sarah. "You're fired. All women are a pain in the ass. Tell Robert I'm switching sides. He's looking pretty good in his garden shorts."

Sarah smiled and left him with a pat to his shoulder.

"She calls me Mr. Winterman but she treats me like her son. I'm probably less than ten years younger than she is."

"She called me Mrs. Nighthorse." He could almost see Violet's silly grin.

"You're being a goofy newlywed again. Why are you pestering me?"

"Cop sense. I thought the weekend might be going a little rough, so I wanted to check in. Sarah said Marguerite left early."

"Yeah, well." He watched the pool cleaner make another lap. "I can see the road but there's a force field there I can't get through. And the couple of times I bullied through it, the road changed, went all dark. I feel like I'm missing something. She won't let me in her head, Vi. I got into her body, so to speak."

"So to speak, or actually speak?"

"Briefly, yes. The latter. But I push to a certain point and everything shuts down. I haven't figured out the key. If I'd had more time…"

"You expected to get an invitation into a woman's soul in the course of a weekend?"

"At least a foot in the door."

"Cocky bastard. Tyler, from everything you've told me, there's nothing easy about Marguerite Perruquet. Maybe—and yes, I know you don't want to hear it—you're barking up the wrong tree. You could be wrong. She may not be a switch. And if she isn't, you guys don't suit."

"Damn it, that doesn't matter. That's not the issue." Rising, he went to the end of the pool house seeking air, the salt laden breeze off the Gulf. "I just…"

"You want her." Violet filled in the lingering silence, surprise and understanding in her voice. "You want her so much that being away from her hurts."

"Yes. And if that can happen in a weekend, then I don't think it was unreasonable to think I could get further with her in the same space of time."

"This has been building a while for you and you know it. You've had longer off the starting block than she has. And if you can't have her?"

"You don't feel like this if it's not meant to be."

"It is if she doesn't want it. I know how strong a Master you are, Tyler. Don't push this into dangerous waters."

He stopped, his hand on the door latch. He wanted to deny it but the brief wrestle in the garden flashed through his head. "You warning me as a friend or a cop?"

"Both. The cop who's your friend."

"When she can look me in the eye and say she doesn't want me the same way I want her, then I'll let her go. You should be goddamned proud of me. I let her go today."

Let her go after I messed with her head, left her raw. Yeah, I'm goddamned proud of myself, come to think of it.

"I wouldn't force my attentions on an unwilling woman, Violet."

"I know that. I do. I'm just saying that if she's afraid of her own feelings, she may lash out at you in a variety of ways. And remember I'm in a unique position to have seen that firsthand."

"She's nothing like that." Though he had an immediate vision of the fork in the table, the coarse obscenities that would spill from her elegant lips when she was cornered.

"I hope not. And I trust your judgment but you seem a little messed up on this one."

The one. The only one. He yanked at the door. Snarled.

"What?"

"The damn door won't open." He yanked again and the French door shuddered. "It must be the latch. It must be —" He closed his eyes, counted. "Never mind."

Violet started laughing. "You pulled when you should have pushed, didn't you? Good grief, you are messed up right now."

"Shut up, you little pest." Tyler stopped, his hand still on the doorknob, though he'd stepped outside. "That's it, Violet. That's the key."

"What?"

But he wasn't paying attention. Instead he was listening to the message exploding in his head with the resounding roar of a cannon, a message his gut was saying was right. It shattered the afternoon of foggy frustration and circular arguments he'd been conducting with himself and gave him hope. And possibly a path back into his angel's soul.

"I've got an idea."

* * * * *

Marguerite trolled the dark shadows of The Zone on an exceptionally crowded Saturday night. She usually didn't come here on weekends when it was filled with unknown faces and so much noise. But she wanted the press of bodies, the anonymity, the ability to move like a predator among unsuspecting prey to look for the one who would ease her ache this evening, her frustration.

Her life had been simple, everything on an even keel. So why did she miss him so keenly? Why was every breath difficult, a form of pain that was pleasurable?

"Mistress."

The respectful voice, a familiar one, drew her out of her thoughts. She was passing Brendan, and as she did so, he went to one knee as he always did, bowing his head. On impulse, she let her fingers trail over his bare shoulder, the soft hair just above his ear. His lips brushed her wrist.

She shuddered, remembering Tyler's lips there, his propensity for using the sexual gesture to gauge her pulse, which was nearly always spiking from the moment he touched her.

Several steps past Brendan, intuition pricked the bubble of her absorption. Normally she would have kept going, not acknowledging him further. Instead she turned and looked back.

He was getting to his feet and it was obviously a painful process, his body hunched, his mouth tight and strained. While the brand would still be healing and tender, his awkward movements exceeded what she would have expected in that regard.

A man stood beside him, not offering to help him up, just watching him with a bored, annoyed look. She recognized him as Tim, Brendan's live-in lover, the one who also enjoyed subbing to a Mistress. Once Brendan gained his feet, Tim said something to him, slapped him on the back with cruel playfulness. Brendan cringed at the contact but nodded. Tim sauntered out toward the bar area.

She pivoted, came back. "No." She caught his wrist when he began to kneel again. "Stay standing. What's the matter, Brendan? What's wrong with you?"

"Nothing, Mistress. Just an injury. Hiking." But she was watching his lowered eyes, the way they darted away, the clutch of his fingers pressing against his thigh. He wore a cotton T-shirt tonight, sleeveless and snug along his well-defined upper body but typically he went shirtless, making himself accessible to the touch of the Mistresses who desired to engage him.

She curled her fingers in the shirt at his waist and raised startled eyes when his hand clamped down on her wrist, trying to stop her. Brendan flushed. "My apologies, lady. I just...please..."

"Let go of me."

246

He released her instantly. With a hard, even look, she finished what she started. Raising the hem of the shirt, she worked it up as she stepped around him. He wore a pair of loose jeans that rode low on his hips, again a different choice for him at The Zone, but it was obvious now why he was wearing them.

The brand was infected, the scab torn off, the red edges raw. The center mark, the fleur-de-lis, seeped fluid.

"Please forgive me, Mistress."

Marguerite studied it for a moment and the bowed head of the man who stood still under her touch. She sensed the attention of those immediately around them, a small oasis of tense silence amid a world of noise, flashing light and high energy pulsing in the air.

"Who did this to you, Brendan?"

"Wh-What?"

"You keep trying to dodge my questions or lie to me and you will displease me greatly." The edge to her voice was ice and she didn't hesitate to cut with it.

"Yes, Mistress. You shouldn't concern yourself. I was careless, didn't follow your instructions as I should have."

"On your knees, now."

When he dropped with a painful grunt, she seized a handful of his hair, jerking his head back. Not harming him but putting his mind as well as his body off balance as he tried to hold his weight upright and not fall into her legs.

"You would have followed my instructions to the letter. So once more, Brendan. Who did this to you?" She enunciated each word precisely, clipping it off with sharp teeth. "You're going to say it, because maybe if you say it, you'll realize someone who loves you wouldn't have done this."

During her two-hour sessions she kept her subs safe, gave them pleasure. She'd never thought of them as hers outside those sessions. For the first time in her life, she felt possessiveness sweep over her. She recalled the rage she'd seen in Tyler's eyes the night he pulled the mugger off her. More than just a good man's anger at another man's violence against a woman. The fury of an alpha toward someone who had taken liberties with something that was his to protect.

"Tim, Mistress." His voice was low, broken. "It wasn't... I asked him to help me clean it in the tub. He didn't mean to do it. It was an accident."

"Look at me."

She never asked her subs to look at her, but taking a page out of Tyler's book she made Brendan do it now, tightening her grip on his hair, making him see the anger of a Mistress. The reflection of the truth she was forcing from him.

"Tell me what happened. You can't accidentally pull off a brand scab like this. And if you lie to me once more, I will never look at you again."

Pain lanced through his face. It was remarkable how just seeing it made the same feeling go through her vitals. "Brendan."

"He... We sometimes play at home, Mistress. Soft bondage, to practice for our times here. We both enjoy being a slave, so we take turns with one another. I knew he thought I didn't deserve the honor you'd given me but I didn't think... He handcuffed me, bent me over the tub. I thought he was going to do...something else...and he did...but..." The words tumbled out and then stopped. Though Brendan did not look away from her, his eyes were nearly watering with the effort to face her expression.

"He ripped off the scab while fucking your ass," she said coldly. "While you were bound and couldn't defend yourself."

"He said I should enjoy it, because I could pretend it was you, like when you branded me while inside of me. Only..." He shook his head. "He doesn't mean it, Mistress. He's just troubled. Tim gets so confused about who he is, what he wants. He cried, said he was sorry later."

"Well, that makes it all better, then." If she could have snarled, she would have. She eased her grip on his hair but left her hand on him, keeping him still. "Have you had someone look at that?"

"I tried to clean it myself but perhaps I haven't done a very good job."

The misery on his face told her he'd been too emotionally wound up to give it any attention at all. She put her touch under his elbow, pressured him to his feet.

"Go to the first aid area right now and have Jeremy treat that. He'll tell you how you need to care for it." Even with the situation roiling her, she could not stay immune to the anguish in his eyes. She cupped his jaw. "If you care for it as he says, it should heal just fine. It will keep its shape. If he says you need to go to a minor emergency center, you go. Either way, you'll go home and get some rest. You don't need to be here. You're in no shape to serve a Mistress tonight." *Not emotionally or physically.* She didn't add that, not wanting to twist the knife he had hilt-deep in himself already.

"I've let you down, Mistress."

"Yes, you have. But I'll make you a deal. Next time that son of a bitch tries to hurt you, you knock him on his ass, hurt him right back and I will *consider* forgiving you."

When Brendan looked at her, for just a moment there was something different there, something familiar, something that made her want to bring him into her arms, hold him to her heart, keep him safe forever. She viciously suppressed it. She couldn't keep track of all the ways she was fucked up tonight. Knowing she should follow her own advice and go home, Marguerite stepped back, forced her normal reserve to return to her expression. "Follow my commands, Brendan. Go to Jeremy."

He nodded, moved past her. Even in pain he observed etiquette, making sure his back was not turned to her until he was a proper number of paces away.

Marguerite stood there several moments thinking while the life of The Zone moved on around her. She was not approached. No Dom here tonight was a person who knew her well and subs did not approach a Mistress, particularly one with her presence, though she felt many staying just within summoning distance, hoping. Lifting her gaze, she saw Tim returning with a couple of longnecks. When he saw her, he immediately lowered his long lashes. Showing deference, respect.

She'd just found the perfect sub for her mood.

* * * * *

She chose one of the smaller medieval torture rooms since most of the rooms were already occupied tonight. When he stripped at her command, she saw his physique was similar to Brendan's. Like most men at The Zone who enjoyed the touch of other men and had the income for a gym membership, he stayed in excellent shape.

Shackling him face forward on a vertical rack, she moved to the side table and the tools laid out there. Not sure what she'd intended tonight, she'd only brought a small bag of her own items, so she'd reserved the room with its standard accoutrements. Floggers, paddles, a seven-ring gates of hell cock ring.

As her fingers caressed the gates of hell, she laid her purse on top of the table, retrieved a small box from within it.

Tyler would have been amused, considering her comment about the pronged choke collar. She had something similar in a cock ring, with a second pronged loop attached to it for the testicles. It was a toy she'd used in the past on her subs with a leash. When used correctly, it created anxiety and discomfort. But for a submissive who liked to play on the edge, it could make him even harder. Fortunately, it was one of the few items she'd brought tonight.

Turning, she found Tim already erect and his eyes down, the obedient submissive.

"So will you please me as much as Brendan, Tim?"

"More, Mistress. You won't even remember his name."

"Hmm." She put the cock choker on him, adjusted the lower loop around the testicles, the prongs digging in. Then she put the rings of the gates of hell over him, one after another, watching his expression as each size went on. His erection, thickening from her touch, quickly increased the constriction. Typically she would have done more to warm him up before dressing his cock in the restraints. Raising the pleasure threshold so the endorphins would balance the pain the rings and prongs caused.

"You're keeping your eyes down. Is that for me, Tim, or to hide who you are?" She pushed on two of the middle rings of the gates of hell, bringing them together, pinching his skin. His breath drew in sharply.

"Mistress, your forgiveness, but that hurts."

"Really? It doesn't hurt me at all." Picking up a ball gag, she caught her finger in the corner of his mouth, wrenched it open in a practiced move that he apparently had not anticipated. Jamming the ball past his teeth, she cinched the gag around his head hard enough to pull the skin back from his mouth, baring his teeth in a grimace.

His eyes flicked up, showing her he was startled, a little afraid. Her lips curved in an expression that no one would have called a smile. "There you are. Think I don't see you, monster? Crouching back there, hiding behind a human façade?"

Reaching down, she closed her hand over the choker and began to squeeze, digging the blunt prongs into his tender genitals. His breath whistled through his nose, a grunt of pain making its way past the gag. A quiver ran through his muscles. She could see all the frantic thoughts behind his eyes.

Wondering if this was part of her act, if he just needed to tough it out.

"How does it feel for someone to hurt you and not give a damn about how you're feeling?"

She stepped closer so her body was pressed against his bare chest, her leg against his thigh, her hand gripping him in a way that looked intimate and pleasurable to the security cameras. "I have the power to do anything I wish to you, Tim," she whispered, her eyes no more than an inch from his, eyes that had fully registered the danger he was in. The quiver had become violent shaking, his hands closing into fists, body straining against restraints that would not give an inch, the body's irrational way of driving up its own panic quotient. "Do you know I could emasculate you with one...good...hard...squeeze?" Her hand tightened incrementally and his eyes widened in terror. "Just pop those balls off and let them roll right across the floor. Grind them under my stiletto while you watch."

She stroked the line of his jaw. His breath was coming so hard through his nose that clear phlegm ran down over the rubber ball, mixing with his saliva. "You can smell fear in sweat," she mused. "And you stink of it, Tim."

He made an incoherent sound as her thumb began to press down on one single prong at the base of his cock.

"I have no tolerance for cruelty committed against an innocent. But cruelty against those who commit the crime...well, that's something else entirely."

She pressed harder against that one prong. His body jerked against the rack, an inarticulate plea coming from behind the gag. She kept her gaze locked on his, making it terrifyingly clear to him she was conscious of his distress and was not going to do anything to alleviate it.

"You know why it stirs a Mistress so when a sub surrenders? You will nod your head, Tim."

He nodded, a quick jerk. Tears of pain ran down his face.

"Because that's the place of stillness for both of us, where it all comes together. Where it all makes sense, where thought simply becomes feeling. It's all about existing in that second, for however long it stretches. Would you like to exist in this second forever?"

He shook his head.

"I'm hurt, Tim. Especially since Brendan said you didn't feel he deserved my attentions. I figured you had something extra special to offer me."

Her grip clamped down on the pronged restraint like the jaws of a pit bull. Her nails dug into his shoulder, cutting into skin.

Tim screamed. His chest expanded, muscles straining against the pain. While he bucked and cried out against the gag she leaned in, nuzzled his throat and the line of his shoulder where the blood welled up from her nail gouging. Twenty seconds later, which she well knew was an eternity for extreme pain, she eased her hold. His head dropped down against the side of hers as he breathed heavily, rasping around the gag, an oddly intimate pose to anyone watching. She put her lips to his ear, making sure her voice hissed like a serpent's tongue.

"This is my practice playground, Tim. When I die, I'll serve as a Mistress in hell, torturing the damned for all eternity. And I'll be waiting especially for you."

She caught his chin, pulled his head up roughly, made him meet her frigid blue eyes.

"You can save your soul by obeying me now. You will move out of Brendan's apartment, leave his life. I don't care if he begs you to stay. You leave and you never contact him again. You don't deserve him. If you ever hurt him again, these past ten minutes will seem like the best memory of your life."

There was a beep as the lock on the door was bypassed and it opened, a two-man security contingent entering. Ryan and Dan, both regular bouncers at the club.

"Mistress, you need to step back from him. Right now."

Their tones were respectful, courteous but their alert stances told her they were trained to move in if she gave them cause.

"Is there a problem here?"

Brendan stepped in behind them as Marguerite moved back from Tim, a calm three steps.

"No sir, but you need to leave this area."

"But that's my roommate. Tim, have you talked the Mistress into going too far with you?"

When Dan turned and looked at him, brow raised, Brendan nodded. "He's a pain junkie. May I go to him, calm him down?"

The man's eyes shifted to Marguerite, who kept her expression blank, unreadable.

"Ma'am, you're aware if you've harmed this man without his consent, you face permanent expulsion from the club and possible criminal charges?"

Dan knew her reputation here. She wasn't going to offer anything about her intentions or motives. She inclined her head, simple acknowledgement.

At a nod from Ryan, Brendan went to Tim and removed the choker and the gates of hell. Putting them to the side, he took Tim's face in his hands, leaned in to murmur reassurances to him.

Tim's expression changed. Marguerite heard six of the words.

"…if you love me at all…"

Then Brendan reached up, removed the gag.

Tim cleared his throat as Brendan solicitously took a towel, wiped his mouth, his nose.

"Sir, are you all right?"

Tim looked from Brendan to Marguerite and back again. Dan proved that he was well worth the money he was paid and no idiot. "Mistress Marguerite, Brendan, you need to step outside and let us talk to this gentleman alone."

Marguerite nodded, picked up the cock choker, slipped it in her bag, put it on her shoulder. Brendan extended a fresh towel to her and put his fingers to his lips, indicating she had something on her mouth. Marguerite pressed her lips together, tasting the metallic flavor of Tim's blood. Turning suddenly on her heel, she spat it in Tim's face, making him flinch and cry out in fear.

"Mistress," Dan snapped as he stepped forward.

She held up a hand. Giving Tim a disdainful look, she strode from the room, aware of Brendan following at a respectful distance as they exited and the security team closed the door.

"He could press charges against you for assault."

"And have to state in court where he was and how it happened? Not likely. Did you call the security team?"

"Mistress," he said, carefully, quietly. "I thought...someone came into the first aid area, told me that Tim had lucked out, that you had picked him up. I thought it might be best if...I just buzzed them from down here, told them there might be a problem. I didn't say who I was, just hung up, so I could intervene the way I did."

For the first time without permission or command, he met her eyes. As he held her gaze, he reached out with the towel and pressed it to her lips. She saw the red stain on the white terrycloth. "You shouldn't have done this," he said.

"He's not permanently damaged. I only broke the skin in one place on his genitals and he'll need some antiseptic for the nail gouges."

"Mistress..." Brendan shook his head. "That's not what I meant. You shouldn't have done this."

255

His knowing eyes elicited a weariness in her from somewhere low in her stomach. She was tired. She wanted to go home.

She wanted Tyler.

"You shouldn't have let him hurt you," she responded.

Before he could reply, the door opened. Dan emerged with Ryan a close step behind.

"Tim is getting his clothes back on. He says he doesn't feel he needs any medical treatment other than some first aid here." Marguerite felt his cool eyes on her face and examined the pattern of the wallpaper just to the right of his ear. "He also says that he asked for the blood play. That it was with his consent. However you're fully aware that blood play is not sanctioned at this club. Special performances including it require management approval. I'll need to report this."

She inclined her head. "I'll accept whatever management decides. I apologize for inconveniencing you and them."

He studied her for a long moment. "I appreciate that," he responded with equally formal courtesy. "And I need to ask that you please leave the club until Mr. Stevens or another member of management contacts you and indicates you may utilize your privileges again."

"But she—"

"That's a reasonable request." Marguerite shot Brendan a quelling look. "If you don't mind, I'll take a moment with Brendan here and leave. Unless you feel I need to be escorted?"

"Yes, Mistress. You will be monitored until you leave the grounds. For your safety as much as anyone else's."

She nodded, not offended. After all, Dan had worked at a maximum-security prison before taking the job at The Zone. He had to have realized she'd been out of control, read it in the unnatural stillness of her body. The fury that was just now beginning to draw back inside her like a deadly sea snake retreating to its lair.

With a measuring look, Dan moved off, headed back up the stairs. She felt Brendan step closer to her, his hand hovering an uncertain moment in her peripheral vision before it dropped to his side without touching her. "Mistress, I'm sorry. I shouldn't have—"

"No, Brendan, you weren't wrong. Turn around and let me see the brand."

"I'm fine." He took her cold hands in his, surprising her. "Stop worrying about me. I'll take care of this." He cocked a brow. "I'm a grown man, Mistress, and I let a lover go too far with me. It's up to me to deal with it. I'm more worried about you."

"No one needs to worry about me." Pulling away, she shouldered the bag. "Thank you for intervening on my behalf, Brendan." She turned away from his concerned and unhappy gaze. "If you hadn't come into the room, I'd probably have gone much farther than I did."

With that, she turned and ascended the stairs, followed closely by a watchful Ryan.

Chapter Fourteen

🙟

She'd planned Natalie Moorefield's birthday tea party down to every detail. For the first part of the week the activity helped calm her, helped her reclaim her routine as she brought all those details together. On Wednesday morning, the date of the party, she ran through the last preparations, checking the table settings, the decorations, the frosted cakes and assortment of cookies that were Natalie's favorites. She'd placed glass bowls of daisies on each table, bright and fresh, the way a little girl's life should be, full of smiles and hopes.

"It must have been quite a weekend. You've had that summer love look off and on all week." Chloe watched her boss step back and judge if the tablecloth at station four was perfectly even on all edges.

"What's a summer love look?"

"That's somewhere between euphoria and abject misery. Panic and happiness. Like your face is about to break out from too much chocolate. You're exhausted and disheveled inside, even if everything is physically in place on the outside. Not sure if you want to laugh or cry, or shut yourself in your room all day with a bathtub and a good showerhead. Plus, you had a whisker burn along your throat."

Marguerite's hand flew to her neck and Chloe grinned. But as she saw misery take precedence in the blue-eyed gaze, she reached out, put a hand on Marguerite's arm. "Hey, I'm sorry. I was just teasing. Was it that gorgeous tiger from last week? He seemed like a good guy—"

"He is. He's a good man." Marguerite nodded, smoothing the tablecloth that Chloe noted had no wrinkles. "For the right woman. That's enough about that, now. Natalie's coming up the walkway. Did you put the little glass fish in the bowls?"

Despite Gen's warning look, Chloe opened her mouth to pursue it further but the front screen door slammed.

"Miss M!" Natalie, looking like a seven-year-old princess in a pink dress with a lace crinoline and pink and white ribbons in her hair, did a spin for Marguerite's benefit. "Look, Miss M! Mommy let me pierce my ears and took me to have a mani...manc... My nails!" She thrust them out, the tiny cuticles covered with a light pink frost of polish. A set of small pink rhinestones glittered at her ears as she turned her head left and right, making the curls bounce.

To the jaded, the cynical, she would look a cliché, a gender-enforced stereotype. To Marguerite, she looked like happiness. She squatted, smoothing the fitted silk of her black cheongsam with its embroidered pattern of silver dragons beneath her hips in order to take the little face in her hands and turn it left and right. "Oh, they're so pretty. And you're so pretty."

"That's you. How come you don't have your ears pierced? You don't even wear jewelry. Most times."

"I'm too much of a scaredy-cat," Marguerite confided, slanting a smile at Natalie's mother. Tina Moorefield was in a pale pink linen dress with a matching ribbon in her fall of chestnut hair. An early thirties bank executive, she looked a bit embarrassed but equally lovely, with a light tinge in her cheeks.

"Natalie said we had to match today."

"Show her your fingers, Mommy."

The mother smiled and dutifully extended her manicured fingers in a matching shade of pink.

"Here comes Ria, Sylvia and Mary!"

"I'm afraid she's been speaking in exclamation mode all day." Tina laughed, watching her only child fly out the front door.

Indeed it seemed the party of eleven little girls all arrived at once, punctually on the heels of the guest of honor. There was a great deal of squealing and giggling as the children compared finery.

"This is wonderful." Tina looked around the room, a mixture of elegance and fantasy. Sheer drapes hung in waves from the ceiling, sewn with silver stars, some of which hung free on threads to turn and throw their sparkle over the three round tables. Each was set for five, the tablecloths strewn with rose petals and sprinkles shaped like stars. The three tea sets Marguerite had chosen to use were floral-pattern English bone china. One with deep pink roses at Natalie's table, one with bluebells and one with yellow daffodils.

"Marguerite, I never realized you would go to so much trouble. This is beyond my wildest dreams. I think I owe you more money."

Marguerite shook her head. "Natalie is compensation enough."

Tina's eyes glowed. "Isn't she something? Some days all I have to do is look at her to know my life's worth something." There was a sudden mist in her eyes. "And to think at one time I thought it would be best if the both of us were dead."

Marguerite reached out, covered her hands with one of hers, squeezed firmly. "None of that, now. That's past."

Tina nodded. "Sorry. You're right. It happens so much less now, but it happens. Perversely, on days when I'm so happy. And it always revolves around her."

The two women watched Natalie and the girls moving from table to table, "helping" Chloe drop the party favors, fish made of colored glass, into the bowls next to the daisies in the center of each table. Each girl had her opinion of where she wanted to sit and what fish should be in her bowl.

A teenage girl came in, carrying a load of presents. She laid them down where Gen directed, then took a self-conscious position against the wall, looking bored. "That's Debra." There was an apology in Tina's voice. "I know you said I needed to bring an additional adult to sit at the third table but my friend called just an hour ago. Her son fell off the swings and needed a few stitches and, well, I brought her teenager, Debra." She nodded at the girl, looking sloppy and out of place at the formal affair in her hip-hugger jeans and crop top. "I honestly don't know how much help she'll be but she's been in trouble a lot, so her mother couldn't leave her at home. Dealing with her at the hospital wasn't an option, so I told her I'd bring her to 'help' me." She waved her hands helplessly. "But don't worry. I can just sit my chair between two tables and watch both..."

"Can I be of assistance?"

Marguerite, startled, turned nearly into Tyler, who apparently had come in through the side porch door. Because she was startled, she took a deep breath as she turned. The aftershave, skin, soap, shampoo...all of him.

Chloe was right. The want and longing, banked up and building since the moment she'd left his house, just flooded out through her, making her feel better and yet far more flustered, all at once. His amber eyes were warm and intent on her, taking in everything about her appearance. He wore slacks and shirt, blazer and a *tie*. She wondered if he had a crystal ball.

"I'll be happy to sit at the third table," he said, his attention moving over the Japanese fashion she'd worn that fitted her body with elegant sensuality. He lifted her limp hand in his, kissed her knuckles. "If Mrs..." He turned his gaze to Tina, lifted a brow, his lips curving in a charming smile.

"Moorefield. Tina Moorefield." Tina found her tongue after only a brief hesitation, which Marguerite admired, since she was still looking for hers. "And it's Ms."

"If Ms. Moorefield doesn't object."

"No...objections. If you're a friend of Marguerite's." Tina added it hastily, apparently just managing to remember that she shouldn't be entrusting her charges to a total stranger.

"Well, that's debatable but I'm sure she'll vouch that I can be trusted with the well-being of a group of little girls."

While destroying the sanity of an adult woman, Marguerite thought, but she pulled it together enough to nod.

"I've been trying to talk Marguerite into performing a Japanese tea ceremony for me but she tells me she reserves it only for her special customers."

"A properly done *chaji* takes four hours."

His teeth flashed at her. "I have the stamina."

Tina stifled a chuckle. Eyes glinting, Tyler inclined his head to her and moved to a wide-eyed Chloe, asking her if she needed any help as if he'd worked there all his life.

"I'd offer to catch you if you need to swoon," Tina said under her breath. "Except my knees went weak watching him kiss *your* hand."

"He is *so* irritating," Marguerite said, trying not to grit her teeth. Tina grinned, as though there was a joke everyone understood but Marguerite did not find the least bit funny.

"Men like that are always a handful. There was a bank president after me for a while. I didn't pursue it. Of course, if he'd been able to do *that* to me..."

"What?"

Tina ran a finger up the gooseflesh that still hadn't settled on Marguerite's skin. "That."

"Excuse me. I just need to go settle some things and then we'll get started." She courteously extricated herself from the amused mother and stepped to Tyler's side, catching his sleeve and drawing him into the kitchen.

"What are you doing here?" She tried to keep her tone even, instead of snapping it out like an accusation. "I thought we were done."

"I have a proposition for you. One I think you'll like. But it can keep until later." He nodded at the swinging door, behind which the chatter of Natalie and her friends continued unabated, covering their conversation. "Let's not keep the birthday girl waiting."

"Have you heard of the phone?"

He gave her an appraising look. "Would you have taken my call?"

His intuition was getting on her nerves. She turned on her heel.

She let out a surprised squeak as his hands caught her waist, pulled her back against him. He bent to her ear, his grip appropriately placed, but her skin heated as if he were touching her in far more intimate places.

"I missed you."

She closed her eyes, knowing he was saying what was resonating in her own heart. "Tyler, I told you I can't do this."

"I don't believe that. And I think you missed me, too."

"I left your house just a few days ago. You're not that impressive."

He smiled against her throat. "You were so tight when I slid into you, angel." He nipped at the skin just below the lobe and her nipples tightened traitorously. "So wet and hot."

"Let go of me, you bully."

He chuckled as she wrested herself away with a well-placed elbow to his ribs.

But as she moved away, his eyes sobered, all teasing humor dying away. He'd gotten the report of what had happened at The Zone, talked to Jeremy about Brendan's visit to the first aid area. It wasn't hard to put it together. He still felt it radiating off her. While he hadn't been there for the incident, it did not make him feel any less responsible.

He'd let her walk away, only concerned about losing ground on the advances he'd made through her shields, not about the vulnerabilities his attack on her walls might have left. He vowed he wouldn't make the same mistake again. First he'd talked with Perry and gotten him to agree to lift the suspension of her member privileges. Then he'd checked in with Gen to find out Marguerite's schedule for the week. He'd intentionally come on this day, to see her in a situation where courtesy demanded that she'd have to give him time to make amends.

When he stepped back out onto the floor, Marguerite had the girls gathering around the sideboard to show them the process of prepping the tea, steeping it, explaining the purpose of the utensils.

"That's a pretty color, Miss M. What color is that?"

"Blue, silly," one of Natalie's friends said, rolling her eyes.

"No, it's a very good question," Marguerite said. "It's cobalt. See this texture? It's called a Cobalt Net because it's a netlike pattern with touches of gold. It's been hand-painted, is made out of porcelain and it came all the way from St. Petersburg. Who knows what country that's in?"

"Russia!" Two girls called out. Marguerite nodded.

"It still looks like blue to me," the child who'd teased Natalie said.

"It is blue, you're correct." Marguerite agreed. "But isn't it wonderful that we have so many wonderful names and variations of one color?"

Marguerite was aware of Tyler, leaning against the wall watching her as she stood among the rapt children, pouring tea, showing them how to use the strainer. She was also aware of Debra, standing off to the side, trying not to look interested, trying to hold on to her petulant apathy.

"Now, you want your teapot to be clay or porcelain, to bring out the best flavor of whatever tea you choose to put in it. If you want to figure out if a teapot has good balance, you fill it seventy-five percent of the way full. About how high is that?"

One of the children nearest her touched the outside of the teapot, about two-thirds up. "Very good. A little higher but that's close. When it's that full, if you lift the teapot and try to pour the water out and it feels a bit unbalanced, it's not a good teapot."

"Oh, Jesus." The teenaged girl rolled her eyes, apparently about to burst with her irritation. "Why is this important? I mean, who the hell cares, really?"

"Debra," Tina began sharply.

"No, it's all right." Marguerite gave Tina a reassuring glance. She finished the pouring, considered the question in silence.

"Are you going to answer?"

"Yes. I like to think things through. While you were rude about it, you've asked a very intelligent, thought-provoking question. I assume you're interested in the answer, so I want to give you a thorough and accurate reply." She registered the girl's surprised expression and cocked her head, giving her a direct glance that Tyler suspected had made grown men drop to their knees in a heartbeat, so he wasn't surprised to see it have a quelling effect on an unhappy teenager. "And please don't curse in here. I don't allow cursing in the tearoom." She sent a significant glance over to Tyler. "Those who do are served a tea of dish soap and water, regardless of the age and size of the offender."

He raised an intrigued brow, a spark of challenge in his eye. She looked away hastily.

"You can't make me not curse."

"No." She faced Debra again, folding her hands in front of her. "You're right. Only you can do that. Only you can impose self-respect and therefore earn the respect of others. Now, you asked the question 'why is this important'?

"Have you ever noticed that children Natalie's age almost never ask that question?" She cast an affectionate look at Natalie, sitting quietly now, listening to every word. "Maybe it's because at this point, everything is new, something to be learned that you didn't know. Your mind is this lovely open meadow, waiting to be populated with blooms of knowledge, in so many shapes and colors."

Her voice was captivating, like a storyteller's. She'd nearly hypnotized Brendan with the modulations of that sultry cadence the night she branded him. Now as Tyler glanced around the room, he saw they were all equally drawn in. Of course as far as he was concerned she could read the phone book and have his complete attention.

"As we get older, I think we forget about that meadow. There are so many flowers, we could live a thousand years and never discover them all." Her eyes became more somber. "Learning something new, unexpected, introduces a new bloom to that garden. Do you ever go into your room and put on your headphones to listen to your music, closing out everything? Parents, even friends?"

She waited until she got a reluctant nod from the girl. Tyler saw from Debra's expression that she was somewhat taken aback to be getting an answer instead of an admonishment. "You may not realize it but you're seeking the silence in your soul, a place where you go to find the best of yourself. Learning a simple and beautiful skill, like choosing a teapot, that's seeking that silence, creating rituals where that silence may be found and nurtured. As long as you have that place, you'll never lose yourself, who you are, what you want. But you have to remember to keep bringing flowers into your meadow, always one at a time, to appreciate each blossom, to honor its contribution to your character. It helps make you into the person you were meant to be."

"But Miss Marguerite, there's a really pretty purple flower in my mother's garden but she says it's a weed."

"So why doesn't she pull it out?" Marguerite asked.

The little girl, a black child with large brown eyes and a wealth of pigtails tied with tiny lavender bows, thought it over. "I dunno—"

"I don't know," Marguerite corrected kindly.

"I don't know," she repeated. "She says it's pretty, though."

"Well, another lesson, then. One person's weed is another's flower." She lifted the teapot, glanced at the older girl. "This may be a weed to one person. That's up to you to decide. But for another, it may be a rare blossom."

"Or a weed you like, like a flower."

Marguerite's lips curved, a soft glow in her face that Tyler felt even in his far corner. He thought that rare smile could be the sunshine in any man's meadow, keeping all the flowers cultivated there blooming year long.

"Precisely. The philosophy of one's life is never a straight line. And sometimes, you can overthink things. When that happens there's only one thing to do. Do you know what that is?"

She winked at Chloe and the hostess went to the private tearoom. Drawing back the curtain, she revealed two open chests overflowing with oversized hats, fat, serpentine boas, faux pearls, costume jewelry and high-heeled shoes, all draped artfully over the chests like a pirate's treasure.

"Shopping."

There was a clamor of cheers and agreement and the girls scrambled toward the chests. Chloe supervised them as Gen began pouring out small portions of tea into the cups on the tables and putting tiny cakes on each pretty plate.

When Debra hesitated, Marguerite beckoned her forward, lifting a hat from the wall near her Victorian-period display. The hat was red felt with black chantilly lace and red roses on the brim, the lace forming a veil down the back. "I think you would look lovely in this. It's an original, as you can see by some of the fading. The lady who first bought it was married young, had three children and died at the age of nineteen, complications to the third birth. Whenever I hold it, I wonder what she might or might not have done if she'd known she was going to die so young. What things would have been the most important to her."

"You sound like you're lecturing."

"No, I'm not. I'm telling you something I've learned. What you do with it is entirely up to you."

She arranged the girl's hair for the hat, using a couple of pins from her own hair, which dropped her braid, pinned in a coil on her neck, down her back. When she was done, from the neck up Debra had gone from a slovenly looking teenager to a lovely young lady, although she seemed a bit baffled.

Marguerite turned her toward the other girls, clustered around the chest. "Now, if you can wade in there, there's a pair of ruby ear clips that look perfect with this hat. But that's just a suggestion. You choose what you like best. I suspect you're a very special young woman, Debra. I hope you'll consider coming to my tearoom again, because I'm glad you're here today."

Tyler watched his angel encourage her forward with a nod. The little girls, many now under the floppy brims of the large reproduction hats piled high with flowers, feathers and other trim work, admired the beautiful hat she was wearing. They teetered around her on high-heeled shoes, surrounding her with the heroine-worship preadolescents had for girls who had achieved double-digits in age.

"She's got a gift, doesn't she?" Tina was sitting within speaking distance at the other table. Tyler courteously came and sat at the adjacent table so he was facing her, since at the moment the proprietress and her staff had everything well in hand, occupied in the small confines of the private tearoom.

"She appears to have so many gifts, I don't believe I'll ever discover them all."

Tina cocked her head, studied him. "If you're the real deal, she needs someone like you."

"And if I'm not?"

"She'll get you out of her life easily enough. But she has friends who will help. She only needs to ask."

The blunt response took him by surprise. He took a second look at Tina Moorefield, seeing a different woman from the one who had blushed at his regard. The set of her mouth also made him notice something else, something that caused his eyes to narrow. He leaned forward, touched Tina's chin, startling her. "Who broke your jaw?"

At her sudden discomfiture, he shook his head. "I apologize. Let me ask it another way. Is he gone? He's not part of your and Natalie's life anymore, correct?"

As Tina looked at his resolute expression, she realized that this man would take steps to rectify that situation if her answer was no. Though she'd seen it too rarely in her life, she recognized the signs of a man who felt it was a male's responsibility to protect women and children, *any* woman or child who needed it, regardless of whether or not he knew her personally.

"He isn't. And I didn't think it showed so much anymore." Her hand almost rose self-consciously to her cheek, then she made herself put it down, meet his questioning gaze.

"It doesn't. You're a lovely woman but I'm familiar with how facial bones mend. I apologize if I upset you."

"No." She shook her head. "At the Helen Center, where I'm a volunteer board member, we do all sorts of outreach programs to teach people that they have to get involved if they think a person is being abused. We tell them that they might be that person's only hope for a decent life, a life without fear."

"That's how you met Marguerite, then."

Tina nodded, assuming from the question that he knew of Marguerite's involvement in the Center. "I don't know what we'd do without her. She's a life sponsor, practically pays most of the utility bills from month to month, renovations, supply needs. If we ever run short on donations to keep the shelter going, we can depend on her to make up the shortfall. She was already involved there when Natalie and I checked in, as victims." Her chin tightened. "I hate that word but that's what we were at that point. Marguerite, the Center, they helped us remember we were more than that." She blinked, waved when he reached for his handkerchief. "No, I'm fine. I keep telling Marguerite I'm going to learn to be as strong as she is. She always tells me it's healthy to cry but I never see her do it. Whatever happened to her to make this such an important cause to her, she must have shed her tears years ago."

The mother's gaze went to her child, who was trying on a hat with a deep purple and blue flower arrangement on top of the black felt. A crescent of netting formed a veil over her eyes, which shone through the gauzy fabric like brown jewels. "When something evil is done to your child, you think the whole world must be evil. Those first nights, when Natalie was in pain and my injuries were too severe for me to hold her, Marguerite would put her in her lap, rock her to sleep, sing to her, tell her she and her Mommy were going to be all right. And she has this voice, when you hear it, you just know you can believe it."

"What did he do to Natalie?" Tyler's eyes shifted to Marguerite as she straightened from arranging Natalie's hat properly. She looked at him, her chin lifted, the cool reserve in place.

"Broke her arm in two places when she tried to stop him from beating me. He twisted it—that was the first break—then he knocked her down and stomped on it with his work boots. That's when I knew I had to do something. I left that night when he was drunk. Thank God he died less than six months later, driving into a tree. I leave flowers there all the time. To thank the tree for killing him."

She shook her head. "God, I'm sorry. You didn't need to hear all that. You just…"

As he turned his head toward her, Tina couldn't finish the thought. *You just have the face of a man who can handle hearing anything. Who would take care of anything.* And she suspected, for all her reserve, that Marguerite could use that. Maybe every superhumanly strong woman could.

"Take your seats, ladies." As she stepped out of the private tearoom, Marguerite noted with some concern the conversation going on between Tina and Tyler. She raised her voice high enough to interrupt it. "If you can be patient another moment or two, we'll talk about the tea ceremony and then start our tea."

The children moved as a herd, swarming around the three tables.

"Miss Marguerite?"

She stopped, her hands on the spindles of her chair. She realized that while she'd accomplished her objective of cutting short the possibility of Tina sharing information about the history of her relationship with Marguerite that Marguerite did not wish Tyler to know, she'd also drawn his attention back to her. She eyed him warily. "Yes, Mr. Winterman?"

"With all due respect, I think you overlooked one very important point of etiquette for a tea party, if a gentleman is present."

It was on the tip of her tongue to indicate that one was not. The message must have clear on her face, for Tina coughed over a laugh. Marguerite schooled her expression to polite impassivity. "And that would be?"

"If a gentleman is in the room, he should assist the ladies into their chairs." And to demonstrate, he stepped to Debra's chair and pulled it out, gesturing to her to take her seat with a flourish. She blushed but complied, sitting down and looking self-conscious but pleased as he brought her up to the table.

"Me, me!" He honored the clamor, repeating the act for each child present, as well as Tina Moorefield when the children demanded she stand back up so he could go through the same ritual. He saved Natalie for nearly last. The birthday girl gave him a beatific smile, spread her skirts out and perched. She'd donned a pair of ruby slippers with two-inch heels and now she hooked them on the top rung of the chair's frame to accommodate herself in the adult-sized chair.

"Miss M, you have to wait, too. He said it's etket. Et..."

"Etiquette."

Marguerite stopped, caught in the act of trying to seat herself before he noted that she was the last one standing. As if he had not been aware of that all along, she reflected, with an irritated glance at his amused expression.

He moved behind her with an exaggerated reproving look that made the little girls giggle and pulled out the chair for her.

Marguerite turned her head toward him in a gracious movement but the look she shot him once she wasn't looking toward the girls was pure venom. He seemed unperturbed, his fingertips caressing her back, the tips of her hair as he guided her into the chair. Marguerite took her seat, felt his warmth and strength behind her as he guided the chair up to the table. "Thank you," she said.

"I know who you think is the prettiest girl here," Natalie announced, pinning him with a knowing look.

Tyler grinned. "That would be the birthday girl, of course."

Natalie shook her head, her curls swinging. "You're just saying that because it's my birthday. You think Miss M is the prettiest, because you're in love with her."

There was a clatter as Marguerite knocked one of her fortunately empty teacups across the table. She grabbed at it but it rolled over the edge, skittering away as if possessed. Before she blinked, Tyler had caught it in his open palm.

He brought it back to the table, sitting it down next to her hand, meeting her flustered gaze. "I handle delicate objects very well," he said, low, as the girls exclaimed over the fortunate catch.

She stared at him. He passed a knuckle over her cheek. "All right?"

"Fine." She drew her head back. Cleared her throat. "Thank you for that important lesson, Mr. Winterman. If you could take your seat now, we'll go on with the tea."

Marguerite waited until he found his chair, trying to still her racing heart, chastising herself for being so ridiculous about his presence here, the amused and knowing looks Tina and Chloe were exchanging, the intuition of the children. She was feeling invaded on all sides and she placed the blame squarely on his shoulders for appearing in her day when he had not been invited. But this was Natalie's party, she reminded herself. That was her focus and her salvation. Just like with Brendan. Immerse herself in the details and the seas moving turbulently within her would calm, even under the unsettling gaze of Tyler Winterman.

"Now, girls, let's talk a little bit about the tea ceremony itself. The chairs we are sitting in were made in 1850 by a master craftsman, Thomas Wilkenson. He put his initials in the design work of each one, in the left arm. You can run your fingers over it, feel it, his promise that each one was hand-crafted. His wife did the brocade work which, while it eventually had to be replaced, was reproduced as she did it. By hand and with the same pattern, by her granddaughter. That's what a tea ceremony emphasizes. The detail and perfection. The care. Imagine it's a hundred years ago and there's so much going on in your daily life. Well, even now. You have very busy days, don't you? Tell me what you do all day."

"School."

"Soccer."

"Dance."

"Homework."

"Piano."

And the list went on. When it ran down, she nodded. "So you see, we are all so very busy. Now, imagine if you set aside thirty minutes of your day for this. A quiet oasis of time, where you could set a mood or tone just by how carefully you planned the ceremony, the enjoyment of those who you might invite to attend, every detail, from flowers, candles, colors...you can do this for your friends, your parents, your sister..."

She held the girls riveted, bringing alive a way of life that had been all but forgotten and perhaps had never existed as perfectly as it was imagined now. But in just the couple of times he'd been here, Tyler could tell how much these details meant to her, as if they were tiny stitches that kept her life perfectly sewn together, so what was inside didn't burst out.

He loved watching her move, speak, but he especially liked her stillness. That was when he felt the energy rolling off her in waves most strongly. Like now. She wore black heels with that cheongsam, a very sexy and yet elegant choice for a woman of her stature and coloring, the formfitting skirt stopping just above her knee. When she'd had her back to him, he'd lingered on the three reminders of even the strongest woman's vulnerability, her fragility. The nape of her neck, the small of her back and the slender anklebones, so similar to and perfectly aligned with the slim heels of her black dress shoes. He wondered how she would react if he touched his lips to that anklebone, caressed it with the heat of his mouth. Then he thought he might better turn his thoughts elsewhere, for if Chloe or Gen asked him to get up to help with anything, he would not be in a suitable condition to be at a children's birthday party.

After the proper amount of time for the seven-year-old attention span, Marguerite concluded her stories about the tea ceremony. The girls had a half-hour to sip their tea, eat their cookies and blow the candles out of their teacakes before Tina agreed that her daughter could begin opening her presents. In a move that was typical for a child without a father but no less capable of tugging at his heartstrings, Natalie commanded Tyler to sit by her while she was doing so. As she compelled him to admire each gift, the other little girls joined her in doing what little girls did naturally, trying out flirting skills that would be honed to dangerous proportions by their early teens but were simply charming now.

It hurt Marguerite to watch it. And it fascinated her. As she quietly worked with Chloe and Gen to clear off the cookie plates and dirty utensils, leaving just the teapots at the tables and a few unfinished cups of tea, he kept them entertained single-handedly. He *would* make a good father, she realized. Some child deserved him. That hurt even more deeply, such that she turned her back on the scene and retreated to the kitchen with her tray.

Ten minutes later, Chloe came in to report that he'd even coaxed a smile out of Debra. Mellowed her such that she was letting Natalie sit in her lap for a few moments, a surrogate older sister.

"And Tina wants you to come out for this next gift. It's a handmade dress from her mother and she wants you to see it."

Marguerite dutifully returned to the floor and found herself directed to sit next to Tyler while Natalie opened the gift. He hooked his arm on the back of her chair, fingers loosely caught in the slats, his thumb idly tracing a pattern on the back of her shoulder, playing with the bra strap under the dress in a discreet, sensual way, the very intimacy of it not lost on her. She thought she really ought to encourage him to use email to communicate with her in the future. Email didn't have hands, a male scent. That mouth she couldn't stop thinking about.

She was relieved when the last gift was opened and she could rise and help Chloe and Gen clean up the wrapping paper. She sent the girls scampering after each scrap of paper, ribbon or bow, though most of the bows were now stuck in their hair, tied onto wrists or made into necklaces with the attached ribbons.

A shriek, a gasp and Marguerite turned in time to see the girls, wound up by the fun and sugar, stumble against Natalie, who in turn stumbled against the birthday girl's table in her oversized ruby shoes. The impact knocked over the rose teapot. The spout broke as it fell over and hit two of the cups. The three items knocked over the bowl of daisies, sloshed out the fishbowl water and all of it spun off the table like pins in a bowling alley. Out of the corner of her eye Marguerite saw Tyler and Chloe emerge from their trash trip into the kitchen in time to witness the glassware, teacups, spilled tea, sugar cookies and flowers crash to the floor all together. The pot, saved by its shape, remained on the edge of the table, a thin stream of tea anointing the wreckage.

Natalie's face was whiter than her mother's and she turned horrified eyes to Marguerite, lips quivering, not the calculated tears of a child knowing how to get out of trouble, but of true dismay.

"Miss M, I'm sorry. I'm so sorry." She bent down and Marguerite realized she intended to get down on those childish hands and knees in her beautiful pink dress to try and fix the damage.

"Oh, no, sweetheart." She caught her up in two steps, lifting her up to her shoulder with some effort. Feeling the thin limbs twine around her waist, she didn't care that the wet tea on the bottoms of those oversized shoes was likely now staining embroidered silk. "Your pretty outfit. You can't mess it up. And broken glass is too dangerous to pick up with bare hands. We'll get a broom and clean it up."

"But…but it's my fault…and you just said how special everything is supposed to be… I wasn't careful."

"No, you weren't," Marguerite agreed, stroking her curls and making those brimming dark eyes look toward her. "And under normal circumstances your mom and I would have you help clean up. But you know what? Sometimes, mistakes happen, when you really, really don't mean for them to. It happens to everyone. And there's this rule that says you can't ever do anything wrong on your birthday."

Natalie blinked. "But I did."

"But it's wiped away, whoosh, like this." She brushed a tear off Natalie's cheek, inspiring a tentative smile. "I want this day to be absolutely perfect for you, Natalie."

"But you won't like me anymore."

Marguerite rested her forehead against the child's. "Do you trust me to always tell you the truth?"

Natalie nodded.

"There is nothing you can do to make me not like you. Why, you are more important than every piece of china in this whole place. And it makes me feel that you are a very, very good friend, to care so much about my things."

"I have an allowance. I get five dollars every week. I can pay you back. I should pay you back." Natalie put her hands on either side of Marguerite's neck, curling her fingers in her hair. She had it pulled back but her braid had unraveled and was flowing down to her waist since she'd removed the clips to pin up Debra's hat.

"All right, then. If you think you should pay some toward the cost, why don't you give me a month's worth of allowance?"

"But the pot is worth like a jillion dollars."

Marguerite smiled. "If that were the case, my friend Chloe over there would have pawned it and sent me a postcard from Bimini."

Chloe chuckled, empting the dustpan of wet glass in the bag Tyler was holding for her. "That's a fact for sure."

The child looked puzzled by the adult byplay but persisted. "I should give you my allowance forever."

"No. When something like this happens, you need to give a friend something they will value. You know what I value, Natalie?"

She shook her head.

"You. Your friendship. So, if you'll give me a month's worth of allowance and promise to be my friend forever, I'll consider that a very, very fair payment for my tea set."

Natalie studied her for a long time. "Mommy," she said at last. "Is that fair? To Miss Marguerite?"

Marguerite resisted the urge to squeeze the precocious child to her heart and never let go. Tina approached, ran her hand up her daughter's back in reassurance. "That's very fair."

"Okay," Natalie said at last.

"All right." Marguerite lowered her back to the floor after Tina ran a quick washcloth over her feet. "And look. All better. They got it all cleaned up. And *what* are you all doing to my hair?" The other little girls, as if released by the license she had given to Natalie, were touching the ends of it, feeling the silk of it around her hips. She spun around in mock outrage and they scampered away, giggling, though this time they were more cautious around the tables.

"Don't you know this is enchanted hair? When I let it all down, I can make the wind blow, the rains fall, or the sun shine. Chloe, why don't you take them out to the back garden and the play area and get some of this energy out? Tyler and I will finish cleaning."

"Mr. Reynolds is here," Gen mentioned. Marguerite turned, looked out through the screen door as a white Lincoln pulled up.

"All right, all the better if the girls go out to play now." She looked toward Tyler. "Do you mind busing tables while I talk to one of my vendors?"

"Not if I'm fairly compensated."

"I just acquired a promise for twenty dollars," she retorted. "It's all yours."

Chapter Fifteen

ɛͻ

Chloe tucked her tongue in her cheek and shepherded the noisy children toward the side entrance to the gardens. Tina hung back another moment, touched Marguerite's arm.

"I am so sorry," she murmured. "Please be sure and add it to my bill."

"It's fine." Marguerite patted her hand, the warm, professional hostess. "You stop worrying and go enjoy them. We'll settle things later." She sent her on her way and turned to meet Tyler's shrewd look.

"And just how much is that tea set worth?"

Marguerite shrugged. "I bought it at auction for six hundred dollars."

"And yet you trusted it with a dozen children."

"Yes, I did. And they're generally very careful, as careful as adults, because I emphasize the special nature of the tea ceremony. One moment of perfection can last a lifetime. That's what the tea parties are about."

"Just as one thousand imperfect moments can make a perfect life," he suggested.

She inclined her head. "So you understand why I used it, as well as why I'm not upset about it."

The door opened and an elderly man stepped in, bearing a basketful of flowers on one arm and a wooden box in the other. He wore a pair of comfortable brown slacks, a striped dress shirt and a baseball cap on his bald pate, which he dipped his head to remove as he crossed the threshold.

"Mr. Reynolds, it's wonderful to see you. I didn't realize it had gotten so late."

"Is this a bad time?"

"Not at all. Come sit down over here and you and I will do our business while Mr. Winterman finishes cleaning up the tables. If he doesn't mind?"

As she sat down with the man and explained the girls' birthday party, the kind of warm chatter indulged when the vendor was a fond acquaintance, Tyler delivered all the silverware and tea sets to the kitchen. While he helped Gen, he listened to the cadence of Marguerite's voice. She reviewed the samples Mr. Reynolds had brought, discussed with him his recent attempts to combine tea types with different flower and fruit flavorings and listened to his description of the conditions in which he'd produced this latest group of flowers for her. When Tyler came back out she was putting a pinch of tea leaves on her tongue. She closed her eyes, inhaled, frowned.

"This is flat, bakey."

"Try this. You'll like it better." Mr. Reynolds, apparently undismayed by her criticism, put another pinch in her hand, watched her bring it to her nose. Rinsing out the taste of the last tea from a water glass, she then put that sample into her mouth.

Tyler took a seat within their line of sight but a table over, taking out his pocket organizer to appear occupied so he would not give the impression that he was hurrying her with her guest.

"Mmmm. Better." Marguerite nodded, her eyes closed. "This one has a lovely aroma. We'll use the clay pots to brew that, bring out that onion and ginger seasoning marvelously." She cracked open an eye. "And did you write down how you put it together?"

He laughed. "You know I just potter with it, Miss Marguerite."

"Mr. Reynolds." She tapped her fingernail on the table. "You must keep a journal, every detailed step of how you do this so you'll know how to reproduce it. What if my customers fall in love with it so much they want more?"

He smiled at her. Tyler saw grandfatherly affection mixed with a bit of a nostalgic crush. "At my age, Miss M, it's not about whether I can do it again. That's the beauty, in a way. Doing it different every time, never sure what to expect." He pinched up the excess leaves, placed them carefully back in their container so none of it was wasted. "Once you do it right once, you don't need to write it down anyway. Your feet will go toward that path again if you don't worry about it or force it." He folded the top, handed it over to her with a beaming look. "Ready for my mystery tea of the month?"

At her nod, he produced a thermos from an insulated carrier and a tiny teacup. Pouring a portion for her, he pushed it across the table and sat back with an expectant look on his face.

She raised the cup to her mouth, inhaled the contents through thin nostrils, her lashes fanning her cheeks, her brow furrowing. Her soft lips parted to press against the cup edge and take in a sip.

It was absurd that he could get hypnotized and hard just watching her drink tea. Tyler had no problem believing what she'd told the girls, that even her hair held magic. The white strands were scattered down her back and over one shoulder, brushing her forearm. He wanted to wrap himself up in them, in her, tangling them together until there was no way to unknot them again.

"It's a Ceylon," Marguerite said at last. "You've added an Assam, just a touch...and rose, I think." She took another sip, then her expression cleared. "You've also added a fruit. Peach, I believe."

He shook his head. "You're uncanny. I've never seen more discerning taste buds. Do you like it?"

"I do."

"Can you guess the color of the rose I brought you today?"

Her eyes warmed upon him. "You know I can't do that. It's beyond even my powers."

"I don't think anything is beyond you, Miss Perruquet." He put the basket on the table and removed the light linen cloth covering them. On top of the carefully arranged group of cut flowers was a yellow rose, the bud not quite open. He extended it to her. "Here you are."

Accepting it with a gracious nod, she rose. "I'll get your check and a bud vase for this."

When she vanished behind the kitchen door, Mr. Reynolds turned his chair, scraping it along the floor, squaring himself with Tyler. For the second time that day Tyler found himself being shrewdly assessed by a protective friend. She was well-fortressed, he reflected. Within and without. Pushing aside the organizer, he gave the man his full attention.

"You know, it doesn't matter what I mix. She guesses it dead-on, every ingredient, every time. None of this, 'I think' or 'I can't quite get that'. Until today."

Tyler met the man's penetrating look. "Was what she told you accurate?"

"Missed the fruit by a mile. It's a mango."

"Shouldn't you tell her?"

"She'll figure it out herself and call me to find out why I didn't tell her right off. I figured she was flustered enough, though. Just like I figure you're the reason."

"I think Marguerite is accustomed to having admirers." Tyler indicated the basket of flowers. Mr. Reynolds shook his head.

"It's not me making her forget her good sense. I assume you have enough to keep her out of trouble until she remembers it."

"Yes, sir." Tyler provided the only acceptable answer under the man's expectant look.

"If I was thirty years younger, I'd squash you like a bug on my way to her, son."

Tyler inclined his head. "You could try." Mr. Reynolds chuckled and Tyler relented with rueful smile. "In truth, I'd say I've already been flattened. She just spent the last half-hour with you, totally ignoring me."

"Ah, son. You're old enough to know women. It's the ones they pretend to ignore that they want the most. That's the way their evil minds work. I don't think that flush in her cheeks is because of me, though for one delusional moment I enjoyed thinking it might be."

Marguerite returned with a check and a suspicious glance between the men.

"Just talking with your fancy-looking busboy here," Mr. Reynolds explained, rising.

"He does more talking than working. I'm afraid his career here is short-lived."

The old man snorted. "That's what my wife said about me. But she kept me around for about fifty years."

Marguerite picked up the tea he'd offered her, took another sip, frowning. "Mr. Reynolds, this... I think I was off—"

"You were," he admitted. "And you were quicker to realize it than I expected." He sent Tyler a significant look. "It's been my experience that women lose their good sense only in temporary spurts. But they can make a man lose his mind forever."

He turned his bright eyes back to a nonplused Marguerite. "You call me when you figure it out, Miss M, if you want. But don't fret about it. Some of my best days came when I couldn't figure out the answer to anything. I'll pick up the basket next trip."

He collected his thermos and cup, made his goodbyes. Marguerite saw him to the front door and waved him to his car. As she watched him drive off, Tyler studied her from his table. The set of her shoulders, the tilt of her head that said she was thinking. The yellow rose sat in its vase on the table, alone, perfect. In a day or two, with the magic that was beyond human comprehension, it would begin to open. Minute by minute it would show a hundred different faces of beauty, inspiring wonder in anyone paying close enough attention to appreciate it.

"Tables all done, boss," he said lightly.

She turned on her heel halfway toward him. The sunlight filtering onto the porch limned the outline of her slender figure. His attention covered all that and more. The length of her forearm, the silver glint of her hair.

"Tyler, what are you doing here?"

"As I said. Missing you."

"I wasn't expecting you."

He stayed where he was though everything about her made him want to go to her. "I owe you an apology. And I have an offer to make, as I said."

The pale blue eyes were wary. "You don't owe me anything, Tyler. You've made it possible for me to continue my membership at The Zone. Thank you for that."

He put the organizer back in his jacket, stood up, watched her eyes gauge his intent. "You know, you have this way of making me feel like a knight riding up to an ensorcelled castle. Guarded by dragons, a deep moat and damn near unscalable walls. But it's those sorceress's eyes that are the most impenetrable fortress of all. It's like you're standing on the top turret, daring me to find a way in."

"Perhaps it's not a dare. A dare implies a desire for the dragon to be fought, the moat to be jumped, the wall breached. Sometimes the message is as simple as it seems. 'Don't go past this point. I don't want you here.'"

Oh yeah. He'd been right. She'd not only recreated her shields, she'd reinforced them to the point the Great Wall of China looked like it had been made out of Tinkertoys in comparison.

She simply looked at him, waiting.

"In all the readings I've done," he said, "there's often this part in the story where a Goddess comes in, full of power and calm. Who has astounding beauty without glamour, the beauty of Nature, all the things that are so powerful in their perfection. And she makes everything better. I look at you and the names come to my lips. Athena, Isis, Freya, Niuka..."

"Tyler—"

"Hush and let me finish."

She subsided, pressing her lips together. He took a step forward, his eyes steady on hers. "I haven't honored you as a Mistress as you deserve. I want to give you the gift you've given me. Please allow me the privilege of serving as your slave for one night."

A charged stillness fell over the room. For several moments, her eyes did not waver. Did not even blink. No part of her moved but he sensed how much was going on in her head. Possibilities, motives weighed. He made sure he was her mirror, waiting for her response with no change in his expression.

Then her gaze moved. Slid down his neck, over his shoulders and chest with the thoroughness with which he suspected her hands could or would. He felt her power roll over him and immediately understood why a sub might feel as if he faced the simultaneously most terrifying and pleasurable experience of his life. This she knew, was familiar with. Excelled at. His cock hardened and he thought of closing the two steps between them to pull her against him, make her feel his need. But he knew how to play poker. He waited.

"At The Zone."

"Wherever you wish, angel."

285

"I wasn't asking."

A smile tugged at his lips. "Name your day and time. I'll be there."

A car door slammed somewhere outside. Something in her eyes shifted. He felt like he was witnessing the turning of a dial that shuttered away one face and produced another, but in that brief moment before the Mistress disappeared those tempting lips formed words.

"Tuesday, eight o'clock."

The same time she always played with her subs, perhaps to underscore that he would be no different. She was carrying around a grudge. With rueful resignation he realized he'd just handed her the means to exercise it.

But when she moved past him, he inhaled her scent and saw the pulse in her throat. He couldn't miss it because it was pounding hard just below that lovely jaw. Without another glance at him, she disappeared behind the swinging kitchen door.

* * * * *

She used a precise method when she washed out the teacups and pots made of glass. Using her fingers instead of a cloth, she worked the soap around the rims and into the cup itself. Then rinsed them under a water spout that came on by sensor. Finally, she turned the cup over on a soft cloth on the counter. She immersed herself in the process, shutting out noise and anything beyond the scope of the square sink full of water. She wouldn't allow her mind to go anywhere beyond the immediate task. She certainly wouldn't allow herself to wonder if he'd joined the children outside. Or if he'd left altogether, his mission accomplished. She gripped a teapot, lifted it.

"Your friend says the more a woman ignores a man, the more it's a sign of her interest."

His breath was on her neck. Marguerite hadn't heard a sound. Not the swinging door, not his footsteps.

"Did he?" The words came out rough and strange. His fingers caressed her shoulders, then came forward, slipped the frogs of the diagonal front-closing neckline of the cheongsam. One...two...three. The fold of fabric dropped forward, half exposing her breast. With a deft hand, he unfastened her front-closing bra. He was methodical and decisive about it, while she was paralyzed.

"We're where people could see us. What are you —"

"Yes, we are. But I haven't given you permission to speak."

She should have been startled, infuriated. Instead, she was starting to shake.

He'd opened her dress like he had every right to do so. Like a Master who wanted to fuck his slave. His hands, capable of sending currents of pleasure up and down her nervous system, were pulling up the skirt on either side of her hips. She heard him mutter a sensual expletive, an explosion of breath as he saw the garters, the thong underwear. What he might have commanded her to wear when she was under his mentoring. A mentoring that was supposed to be over. A lie that apparently was fooling no one, not even herself.

"Why did you dress this way?"

She wanted to deny it. His breath was hot on her skin at the point of her neck again. And oh, God, his teeth were lightly holding her, his tongue now stroking the sensitive bone.

"Speak to me."

"I...liked putting it on, thinking about you seeing it." She'd been her own worst enemy, increasing her sexual frustration by doing things that only reminded her of how much she wanted to be near him. Then he had to appear and discover this.

His thumb slid under the thong, caressing her anus as his other finger gently dipped into slippery heat between her legs.

He rubbed his knuckle through her wetness, apparently enjoying the feel of it. She shuddered, her hips rocking.

"Be still. Be very, very still. You're a statue in my garden, every curve kissed by sun and moonlight." His lips followed the crescent line of her shoulder. Her hands were clenched on either side of the English teapot with yellow daffodil patterns and she could not let go, could not move. All her senses were riveted to his voice, every muscle aware that it existed to serve his Will. Her logical mind and her control were both gone as if they'd never been. In the space of a heartbeat, she'd given everything to him.

All great Masters and Mistresses knew instinctively when the gates fell. When they held in their palm the most fragile part of the sub's soul, beating frantically like a heart. She now understood the look she'd always been unable to fathom in his eye at The Zone, why she'd always avoided him. He'd known he could have this from her.

"Think about those bronze sculptures..." His voice soothed her surge of panic. "How the artists focused on the lines of the body, keeping the lines simple to bring out the life in the art. It's in their very stillness they burst with the power of sensuality. Like you, Marguerite. Absolutely still like this, by my command, you're a Goddess."

He caught the teapot trembling in her wet hand with one of his, eased it down to the counter. Then he brought the skirt up, bunching it at her waist. When he unfastened his trousers, he gave her no time to think before he tore the tiny strap at the leg of her panties, making them drop uselessly to the floor. Cupping his hand over her front, over her mound, he pushed her back into him, into a cock that eased as naturally into her as the knife had sunk into Natalie's moist birthday cake.

"Caress your cunt around my cock, Marguerite. I want to suck your taste off your fingertips."

She reached down, found her wetness between his fingers, the wonder of the velvet hardness of him penetrating her body. When she caressed them both, she heard his groan against her neck, felt the eager shove of him deeper into her body.

She couldn't help the guttural sound of pleasure from her own lips, the admission that her body ached for him. Clamping down on his cock, drawing him in, she welcomed each stroke as he slowly drove into her, withdrew, drove in again. His hand over her mound stroked her clit while the other glided up her body. Palm flattened against her sternum, his thumb traced the crease beneath one breast that felt heavy with need in his hand. Two fingers played in the tender pocket at the base of her throat. His thighs were hard and sure against the back of hers, lean muscle and heat pressed from her ass to her shoulders.

When she reached up, his mouth seized her fingers, sucking the arousal off them. Once he freed her fingers, she caught his shirt at the shoulder, her other hand around the side of his neck. She felt the rasp of his jaw against the baby-soft skin on the inside of her forearm as he bowed his head alongside hers. His breath was hot on her shoulder, her neck, the upper slope of her breast. His fingers and cock worked together in single purpose so she could not deny the man that commanded them. Commanded her.

"Come for me, angel."

As soon as the words came forth, before she could thrust him away, her body exploded, the climax tearing through her, relieving the ache of not having him for the past several days, the thing Chloe had described as summer love. This felt more like fulfillment for all the seasons, including something to warm her in winter.

As her pussy rippled along him, she felt his own release. His fingers dug into her, his strokes sure and strong, driving her down to her elbows on the counter. His body bent over hers, covering her, holding her as his hips pumped against her sensitive buttocks. Her thighs widened, soft whimpers coming from her lips as aftershock after aftershock drove her hips up against him.

At length he slowed but he did not pull away or out. His large hand brushed over her damp back. Stroking her hair off her left shoulder, he laid his lips on that spot. Tasted her, caressed her with his mouth, his hands running down her sides over her bare hips and breasts, their tops unencumbered by the bra. When he drew out, the pressure of his hand brought her up with him. She felt him fasten his trousers before he took the damp cloth from the counter sink, pressing it between her legs before she could protest.

"Ssshhh," he said. "Just be still and lean back against me."

Her arms somehow found themselves back up around his neck as he stroked between her legs, cleaning his seed and her climax off her thighs and the smooth folds of her sex. She pressed her face against his throat, watching him bend his head to the task, the facets of his burnished gold eyes, the sensual set of his mouth.

"I've never had a boyfriend."

"Haven't you?"

She hadn't even realized she'd spoken aloud. "Well, I mean, a lover."

"Mmm." He laid the cloth on the counter again and moved her back a step with him, helping her skirt fall back into place. Bringing the bodice back up, he kept her turned away from him as he re-fastened each frog, adjusted the shoulder seams and smoothed the fabric over the curves of her breasts. When he turned her in his arms, desire still glowed in his eyes. "Well, I think you do now."

Glancing toward the floor, he bent and retrieved her torn panties, put them in his pocket before she could take them.

"I owe you a pair," he said.

"So you owe me a shopping trip."

"That sounds suspiciously like you just invited me on a date, angel." He smiled at her discomfiture, stroked a wisp of her hair over her ear. "Tuesday night, eight o'clock. Anything special I should do to prepare? Which room?"

"I'll leave instruction with The Zone staff as to how I want you prepared and where. I typically don't tell my subs what to expect. It's none of their business what I'm planning, just that they be there on time and submit to it." Why were the words making her shake, as if the ground were about to open up beneath her under that unreadable gaze? "The rest is a surprise."

He nodded. Before he could step back, she caught the front of his ironed shirt and yanked hard. Buttons clattered across the floor. He made an involuntary movement toward her but otherwise held his stance as her gaze coursed down over the muscled chest, the fine mat of hair, the tapered waist.

"Now we're even, on clothing at least." The physical act helped her find her Mistress voice. Deliberately she raised her gaze back to his face, taking time to enjoy the territory in between. "All you owe me is Tuesday."

"A promise that's a privilege to pay." His eyes burning, he took her hand in a firm grip, raised it to his lips and turned it so they brushed her palm. "I'll see you then, Mistress Marguerite. Don't forget me. I'll be waiting for you."

She watched him move out the kitchen side door, which would allow him safe passage to the parking area without the children seeing his state of dishabille. It intrigued her that he'd scoped out her exits in so little time. Then she discovered that the other entries to the kitchen, the one to the garden and the swinging door, had been quietly secured when he came in. Even the blinds on the garden door were closed so no little people could have surprised them in their very adult moment.

He was considerate, giving and courteous in all the important ways. Passionate, demanding and ruthless about getting what he wanted, also in all the important ways.

She bent and picked up every button, lined them up on the counter, stared at them as if they were jewels that had fallen into her lap. She had no idea what she was doing anymore. For some reason, that didn't really matter at the moment.

Placing the tip of each of her fingers on five of the buttons, she moved them across the counter idly as if they were tiny skates, making patterns. Spoke his words aloud, thinking about them.

"A thousand tiny imperfections can make a perfect life."

Chapter Sixteen

ಹಾ

The purple light of The Zone's gold-edged neon marquee threw a wash of surreal light over the parking area. It was a good crowd for a Tuesday night. Marguerite sat in her car, watched the security patrol make its second lap since she'd pulled in ten minutes ago. Apparently the ownership of the club had taken prompt steps to ensure there would be no repeat of her unpleasant experience.

It was yet another of the many ways The Zone made it clear that the protection of their members was a number-one priority. But beyond admirable management style, it was a personal message from Tyler to her. A message she chose to push into a closet in her mind where she wouldn't see it. She needed her focus tonight. She took a deep breath. One. Two. Three.

Tuesday nights were about finding and keeping the balance she needed to run the rest of her life. She harbored no illusion that this night would do that. She felt like a restless sea, waiting for the arrival of a storm to give her the fuel to explode with power and pounding fury. Ravage a coastline, demolish homes, stack up boats like a pile of children's toys.

She'd taken his offer, recognizing it as a high compliment. Her pride wanted to show him what being under her Dominance would be like. And now she felt a way she'd never felt before. Always before, the moment she drove into the parking lot she'd feel a calmness settling on her shoulders, her mind centering on her intentions for the evening, on what she'd demand of the man she would choose.

Tonight she managed the ripples of unease by letting them pass around her like rush-hour traffic on the highway.

She'd let them get by, then find her center as she always did. She'd know exactly what she wanted to extract from Tyler to feed her own soul.

Getting out of the car, she pulled the velvet cape around her body, her pale hair gleaming against the unrelieved black. She didn't take anything else with her. Everything she'd requested would be in the room. Just like Tyler.

She nodded to the doorman. From the barely restrained speculation in his eyes, she understood the reason for the crowd. She'd requested that the ceiling view screen be left open. The staff posted what groups and scenes would be available for viewing via email blasts sent out twenty-four hours before the session. She imagined such an unexpected face-off between the two most powerful Dominants at The Zone would create a standing-room-only crowd.

An audience didn't faze her. In her mind it was always between her and her sub, but the ceiling view could rattle the chosen slave. Especially a private man like Tyler.

Stepping inside, she went through the reception area and straight down the side hall to the private video rooms. As she'd requested, her tape was being queued up, by a Zone staff member named Stacey who'd likely been radioed by the doorman as Marguerite was crossing the parking lot.

"We just finished getting him ready, Mistress. He's ready when you are."

"How long is the tape?"

"About fifteen minutes."

"All right. Please have someone stay in the room with him for the next twenty minutes. I'll be down by then."

The young woman nodded, turned for the door. Marguerite noticed the spots of color high on her cheeks, the averted eyes. "Stacey?"

"Yes, Mistress?"

She knew the girl to be an extremely capable staff member who often earned extra money as a hired submissive for those Masters and Mistresses who preferred a trained, known quantity in The Zone walls. She looked distinctly flustered tonight.

"Did you handle Tyler's undressing?"

"I did, Mistress. A woman to undress him and two men to restrain him, just as you specified."

"Did you enjoy that?"

Her response, though soft, was immediate. "I did, Mistress. Thank you."

"Why did you like it so much? You see things like this every night."

"Not a Master like Tyler. Not being bound, stripped." She drew an unsteady breath, let out a nervous chuckle. "With respect, Mistress, there isn't a woman here tonight who wouldn't want to be in your shoes." She slipped out.

Marguerite shook her head and settled in a chair. Curling her cold hand in the warm folds of the cloak, she let one leg emerge, cross over the other. She pressed the play button.

She'd thought about having one of the male staff do the undressing but realized that as a petty desire to irritate Tyler and discarded it. Then put it in anyway. Then took it out.

In the end, she'd opted for a woman for the very reason she'd almost decided against it. When she focused in on hands on that muscular body on the tape, she wanted to absorb herself enough in it to imagine it was her. Stacey didn't know it but Marguerite would have given a lot to be in *her* shoes. Disrobing a submissive, unbuttoning shirt cuffs, sliding trousers down over a well-defined backside, seeing what type of underwear or socks they chose, those were intimacies she could not risk close-up, hands-on. But she could experience them this way.

He stood in the center of the observatory, her favorite Zone room. The lighting could be dimmed so only a glittering of stars were thrown out for light along the walls of the chamber. The lights rotated as if the bound sub were the center of a moving galaxy. The platform on which he was anchored could also be rotated, all of which helped disorient him while publicly displaying him from every angle. A spotlight would illuminate him but the Mistress could come and go out of the starlit shadows, all of her preparations and tools set up out of sight, increasing the trepidation.

She'd had him brought in blindfolded because she suspected he would look for the camera and gaze into it, guessing she might do this. She saw immediately that he'd dressed for her. Black slacks perfectly pressed, a pristine white shirt, silver cufflinks. Black and white, which set off that raven and silver hair. The lights deepened the ebony shadow of his jawline that no amount of shaving could completely eliminate.

Stacey moved out of that darkness. Marguerite had commanded that no one was to speak to him unless necessary. He was simply to obey their physical nudges to move as they needed him to move. No distractions, nothing but what was in his head to keep him occupied. No attempts at banter to regain some control of the situation. If attempted, he was to be gagged. Since he had received a copy of the instructions, she wondered what his reaction had been to that.

When his nostrils flared as Stacey came near, Marguerite felt the jolt to her toes. He recognized her scent. She'd left some of her tea tree oil infused with lavender for Stacey to mist on her skin. To give him a moment of confusion and to see if he was that sensually aware.

Stacey's fingers slipped the buttons down the front of his shirt, lifted his hands to undo the cuffs. She fumbled a little but then she took a closer hold of the shirt at the waistband of his slacks to free it, her thumbs brushing the well-defined lower abdomen just above the belt line.

Marguerite had seen his upper body during their partial weekend together but she'd been too often distracted by other factors to fully enjoy a perusal of it. She didn't have to be distracted now. The curves of the pectorals, the sectioned stomach muscles were sculpted with the perfect imperfection of one of his bronze statues.

Stacey glanced up at his face. He hadn't said a word but a slight smile played on his mouth. Not a smirk but a reassurance for Stacey. He knew the hands touching him were that of a submissive. The son of a bitch could tell the difference. Marguerite shook her head. Stacey was enjoying herself now, reaching up to push the shirt off his shoulders, her palms following the skin as the shirt peeled away and his arms drew back to let her get the shirt down them, the solid strength of his biceps and rounded points of his shoulders gleaming in the lighting. As she moved away to go hang up the shirt, the two men moved into the light. Three sets of manacles were lowered from the ceiling. They lifted Tyler's well-defined arms to lock the cuffs at the wrists, just above the elbows and the final set right between the swell of the biceps and shoulders. The slack was drawn up to suspend the arms perpendicular from his body, a pose that would limit his upper torso movement far more than just drawing his arms over his head. The pose of DaVinci's perfect Vitruvian man.

Pressing the zoom button, she went in on the chest area as she always did to closely examine every possible angle, to determine if there was an unacceptable level of discomfort to the restraint. There was a second screen and she turned it on now, for it showed a live view of her subject waiting for her. She compared, picked up the headset. "Tony?"

"Yes, Mistress Marguerite? Always a pleasure to hear your lovely voice."

"You and Eli did an excellent job. Would you please raise the biceps restraints an inch? I want a little more strain on the shoulders."

"Right away, Mistress."

"And please start him rotating so the audience may enjoy the view."

Tyler's head had turned at Tony's voice, his head cocking. She wondered if he could hear her voice coming through Tony's earpiece.

She turned her attention back to the replay. No open cuts to concern herself with. She saw the scars she'd remembered from his house, knew there might be more vulnerable joints there and made a mental note to take care in those areas. Then she zoomed out, watched Stacey loosen his belt, free the tongue, dropping the pants lower on his hips, revealing that V line of muscle on either side of his stomach disappearing beneath the waistband.

She wasn't breathing as Stacey unhooked the trousers and took down the zipper. That was why she preferred particularly in this case to view this in privacy. He wore dark gray underwear beneath the slacks, the snug stretch boxer shorts that hugged the ass and crotch, the upper part of the thighs. Stacey had the trousers halfway down his legs before she remembered the shoes. She tapped on one dress shoe with a finger, a silent direction to toe the shoes off. The trousers were loose at the upper part of his thighs, enhancing the artistic display of grace and beauty in his upper body as he complied.

Marguerite was throbbing. Throbbing. She didn't throb, didn't have this uncontrolled pulsing in her cunt keening for fulfillment when she looked at her subs. There was a deep sexuality to their interactions but she was able to keep it locked in a contained space, relieving it in her own way with her own private ritual when she got home at the end of the night. She wanted satisfaction now and all she'd done so far was watch him get undressed, like a peeping Tomasina in a boy's locker room.

Stacey's slender hands were at the band of those gray boxers. Hooking it, she took the underwear down, cupping her hands so she'd be able to feel the curve of his buttocks whisper under her fingertips. Marguerite could hardly blame her. Tyler's head was still. She'd made a calculated error with the blindfold. She wanted to see what was going on in his eyes.

But his stillness suggested tension, wary alertness, waiting for the next move.

She told herself this wasn't about payback, though she could feel a beast in her wanting to tear him down, open him up, make him bleed for disturbing her world, for asking more of her than she'd wanted to give. And she knew he had the audacity to want ten times more than even that from her.

When Stacey got the fabric of his underwear past the curve of the buttocks, she had to bring her hands forward to peel the fabric back and free his cock. It was a mouthwatering size. Marguerite was sure the opportunity to see it for the first time was causing a stir on the main floor among those who'd come to see this show. Somehow the word "show" created a tightness in her body, a moment of sick nausea. She pushed it away, breathed. No. She'd never made her interactions with a sub about a performance, but she'd always made them public because she'd seen no need to do otherwise. Had no desire for the intimacy that privacy could bring.

Tyler said he was honoring the Mistress in her. Giving her the chance to what? To even the playing field, to apologize, or to simply manipulate her?

She rose, not wanting to see Stacey rub the warm oil on her hands and begin to stroke it on Tyler's cock as she'd required. She hadn't wanted the rest of him oiled. Actually she didn't necessarily need that part of him done but she'd wanted him handled by strange hands while restrained to disturb him. Watching his quiet features she realized she was the only one who could accomplish that. He was waiting for her. For her to prove she could take him down as easily as he had taken her.

She put her hand on the stop button but could not bring herself to press it yet as Stacey's hands rubbed that impressive shaft, back, forth, oiling it as it rose under her touch, as she palmed his balls and got them glistening. She would put him in a cock harness, attach it to nipple clamps, make him feel pain, the type of pain that was in her head now, becoming a pounding headache. She wished she had amputated Tim's genitals. If she had, she would not only have a sense of satisfied completion, she'd be in a safe, quiet cell now where these things didn't matter.

She hit the stop button, removed the tape and dropped it in The Zone secure return box so it would be re-filed in the main office. Gathering her cloak about her, she yanked open the door to come face-to-face with Mistress Violet, leaning against the rich wallpaper of the opposite wall.

Violet did not come to The Zone as often as she had before she married Mac, but Marguerite knew they still came a couple days of the month. Usually in the company of friends like Tyler to take advantage of The Zone's topnotch amenities for play. While Violet was barely tall enough for the top of her head to reach Marguerite's chin, Marguerite did not underestimate her.

"Something I can do for you, Mistress Violet?" It was an effort to put courtesy in her voice but she managed it.

As a result of the exposure created by the bust of the S&M killer, Violet no longer bothered with the long black wig and contacts that used to alter her appearance at The Zone. Her shoulder-length curly auburn hair and Caribbean blue eyes were a tempting match for the body she displayed in a black corset. It pushed her small breasts out and nearly over, the garment a complement to the snug purple satin skirt with black filmy overlay that flirted just above mid-thigh. Marguerite suspected that she had made Mac lace the corset, tightening it until she was satisfied with the view. Despite that intimacy, Violet likely wouldn't have given him permission to touch anything yet, wanting to keep him hard and lusting. Teasing him with what was so erotically displayed in the corset his hands had laced and what was barely concealed above the hem of the short skirt.

It was the type of game a good Mistress excelled at, or one intensely experienced with the desires of her slave. Marguerite wondered what it would be to indulge in such loving play with someone. She'd never sought that with a sub, perhaps because she was driven by a very different compulsion. Her dwelling on it now was just another example of how Tyler had managed to fuck with her head. Something that would end tonight.

She began to move past Violet when the woman did not immediately reply but was not at all surprised when Violet raised her hand. "A moment of your time, Mistress Marguerite."

"A moment." She stopped, sighted just over Violet's shoulder and found a photograph of Marilyn Monroe. In a crinoline and bra, smiling her sad, distant smile at the camera. "I have someone waiting."

"I know that." Violet stepped squarely in front of her, blocking her way. Marguerite's eyes narrowed. "I'm asking you to be careful. What you did earlier with Tim, if it wasn't for your relationship with Tyler, you wouldn't be down there tonight."

"I don't have to court Tyler's favor. The Zone can kick me out at any time."

"You'll take care of him tonight."

"The Zone has rules."

"And as you've demonstrated quite recently, every experienced Domme knows how to hurt someone without breaking the rules, especially if they know the ways to keep the sub from crying uncle. The best ones can cripple without even breaking the skin."

"That sounded suspiciously like a compliment."

"My mistake. I meant it as a warning. He's stupid when it comes to you. I'm not."

"I disagree. You're the one standing in my way."

"Mistress Violet." One of The Zone staff members, Mark, had come up the hallway. "With your permission, I need to speak to you a moment."

Violet never broke eye contact. Her lashes did not even flicker. She took a step forward, lowered her voice. "I have a tremendous amount of respect for you, Marguerite. I've learned a good deal from watching your technique. But I love that man very much. Whatever nightmares or demons you're exorcising, you make sure you don't sacrifice him to appease them. You hurt him and I'll tear you limb from limb."

She moved around Marguerite, bumping her shoulder none-too-gently to get to the waiting Mark.

Without hesitating, Marguerite moved onward down the hall, pushing the exchange away, pushing it all away. There was only one thing now and that was the sub. Not Tyler. There were no names, no identities, simply the power and energy she needed for their session. It would be no different tonight. She could not afford to let it be different. Not if she was to protect Tyler the way Violet wanted.

* * * * *

"Ass. Moron. *Man.*"

Mac lifted a brow as Violet sat down in the chair he'd been holding for her. It had a clear view down into the observatory room and of the hundred-and-twenty-inch flat screen on the wall at the deck floor level. Currently it provided a close-up of Tyler, arms restrained out to his sides, legs manacled and spread, ankles secured to the bolts in the floor. The blindfold was still in place. Stacey had reluctantly finished with him, so his genitals were well oiled and well aroused. The audience was currently getting seriously worked up as the platform turned, displaying him from all angles in erotic slow motion. Mac knew all his senses would be on high alert, not just his glands. Waiting for that one noise. The sound of a door opening, the feminine step that said *she* was there with him, the one that was keeping his cock at aching attention even more than the tactile ministrations had done. He knew Tyler was not a submissive but he also recognized the look he'd seen in Tyler's eyes when he'd passed him going down to the observatory. Dom or sub, a man in love was a man willing to undergo anything to win the woman who'd stolen his heart.

The Masters and Mistresses were of course accorded the balcony seats. Their subs, if they had one, were seated at their knees or standing behind the chairs as Mac was now. He leaned down, a long arm on either side of his wife's chair and nuzzled her ear. "What's the matter, sugar?"

She thrust the note up at him, shrugging him off irritably. "Stupid men."

Mac looked down at the note in Tyler's broad script.

Violet, Perry has instructions from me. Nobody is to enter that room until we're done. I'm asking you to trust what I know. Don't interfere. No matter what.

"He's anticipating this getting pretty rough."

"You think?" She scoffed. "The woman tried to chew the balls off a sub not too long ago. The only reason she's allowed to be down there tonight is because she's with one of the owners and because of the crowds she draws. And because Brendan talked Tim out of filing a complaint against her. I know this is a good place." She waved a hand. "But we both know when she performs the bar tabs triple. So I guess we're just supposed to sit here while she neuters him, or just cuts his throat." Her gaze shifted to the screen. "I'm tempted to let her do the neutering. His ability to think might return to his brain where it belongs. Jesus."

Mac stayed in his position over her. He had a fantastic view of her breasts swelling high out of that corset. The glitter dust she'd sprinkled across their tops was making his tongue itch. But she needed something else right now other than his substantial erection pressed against the small of her back. The way she casually rubbed against it with the shifts of her body told him she was aware of it, making him ruefully bless and curse her ability to multitask, to torment him while fuming. She'd closed her eyes, was shaking her head.

"Sugar." When he touched her face, he compelled her to open her eyes and look up at him. "Tyler's an intelligent guy and a tough Dom. He trained you. I think you should do what the note says. Trust him."

"But his judgment is seriously impaired."

"Because he's in love with her?" Mac's silver eyes crinkled. As she always did, Violet got a little lost watching that firm mouth lift in a smile. "Maybe they'll be lucky and find what we found. But we had some pretty edgy moments getting there together. For people like us, for anyone, you have to earn the right to it." He bent a little closer to her. "Just like I'd like to ask my Mistress how I can earn the right to put my mouth on those beautiful breasts of hers. I'd like to suck on her nipples until she comes just from that, as I know she can do. Repeatedly."

She slanted a glance up at him, his attention spreading welcome heat over her skin. "I'll give it some thought. For now you just stand behind my chair and keep that big cock of yours hard for me. Let me feel it against my back, ready to serve me when I call for it."

"That's not going to be a problem, Mistress."

She brushed her cheek against his palm. Taking a light bite on the silver bracelet he wore, her symbol of ownership, she tugged on it. "You may be on different sides of the D/s fence but you and Tyler both try charm for distraction. I think you're in for a long, hard night to remind you I won't be charmed."

"Yes, Mistress," he said.

She kept his hand on her shoulder, rubbing her face against it like a cat, seemingly placid now. But Mac wasn't fooled. Watching her gaze shift back to the man bound in the observatory, he had a feeling what they were about to witness was going to be a problem. He ran a light finger along her neck, a transgression he hoped she wouldn't command him to withdraw, for he knew his touch would help calm her.

Tyler, you better know what the fuck you're doing.

Chapter Seventeen

ℭ

Marguerite stepped into the dark shadows of the observatory, nodded to Tony. He moved past her and the door snicked shut, leaving her and Tyler alone.

Whenever she'd stepped into this room before, she'd had a sense of who the submissive was, a glimmer of something she'd seen in his soul. Something she would use to get all the way in, open him up and use that to balance them both.

She wasn't sure if she'd found that glimmer in Tyler, a key. She wasn't even sure if that's what she intended to do tonight. She was still waiting for her inner compulsion to speak to her as it always did, telling her where she wanted to go tonight.

In the meantime, she let herself look. The video screen didn't do him justice but then she'd known he'd be more potent to her senses like this. The observatory wasn't an overly large room, the shadows covering all the equipment stocked on the walls, the few storage areas. All the focus was on the dais under the spotlight. She didn't look up, wasn't even aware of her audience any longer. The room was silent, as she'd requested, no music. And the audio output was not turned on. Their play was visually public only.

She'd had younger, more handsome men in here. But as her eyes coursed over the rugged lines of bone and muscle, the scars, that fascinating expanse of silky hair layered on his chest and forearms, she knew those bodies had never attracted her the way this one did. Nor the shadows that lay beneath their surfaces. He'd barely even cracked a window for her there, though he'd had no compunction about kicking in the door to her psyche and demanding she offer her soul to him, every black corner.

"I was beginning to think you'd changed your mind."

His voice was as tactile as the touch of his fingers running down her back, raising nerve endings to high alert, but it was also velvet. Like the comfort of a known voice coming out of the dark when walking alone in a graveyard.

"You won't speak unless I command it."

When he was facing her, she flipped the switch that stopped the movement of the platform. Then she moved along the outer crescent to the items she'd had left for her. A downshielded dim light showed her a five-foot-long latigo braided Mexican whip with wooden handle which she used frequently and a tool she used on her more hardheaded subs such as Marius. A thirty-inch-long Scottish tawser that she'd customized. Tawsers were originally used for punishment of schoolchildren, to strike their hands. The tool typically was one or two straps of leather put together and toasted over a fire to make it more rigid. For modern-day BDSM play, they were more flexible and she'd had a trio of cuts made along the length of the strap to increase the sting and maneuverability. It was a highly effective punishment tool, used when the sub's endorphins were rushing high and he needed that ultimate pain experience to push him to orgasm.

Still not speaking, she unfastened her cloak and hung it up, picked up the whip. Swung it, re-accustomed herself to its weight and balance. Stepped into the spotlight with him.

Letting her gaze travel from low to high, she started with his bare feet. The manacles fit snugly around his ankles. She'd requested steel because she wanted the discomfort factor on his bones. Not excruciating for a couple hours but they'd leave red marks when removed. The manacles on his arms were the same, so movement was attended by the clanking reminder of imprisonment. Then she moved on to the calves, knees, long muscular thighs, the cock that had been semi-erect when she entered and was now fully erect. Lower abdomen, broad chest, smooth shoulders. The scars that altered him here or there, the tension in his neck that suggested her biceps adjustment had resulted in the discomfort she'd intended. The firm mouth beneath the blindfold's cover. That fine, dark hair. Aristocratic nose. Clean, trimmed fingernails.

She took her time, standing there for some minutes, just looking at every part of him, enjoying the ability to do so without interruption or interference. She'd had subs that she'd made stand with their eyes downcast while she sat a few feet away, enjoying the visual feast of them, watching them get more and more aroused as her silent regard stimulated them.

The purpose of her sessions was as she had described it to Tim. The attempt to compel stillness in a world that was never still, by achieving a connection with another that went beyond words and noise. But if she took Tyler into that still moment, would she find such contentment that she'd never crave motion again?

She stepped forward, one step, two steps. In a smooth motion she arced the latigo whip, struck his thigh, just below and to the left of the scrotum, exactly where she'd intended it to fall.

He hadn't anticipated that as her first move. She could tell by his start, the flex of his fingers against the manacles. She moved closer, past him, dragging her fingernails across his leg, over the reddened skin, letting the trail of the whip follow and tease his testicles. She stopped, her gaze level with his outstretched arm, her eyes and mouth inches from the smooth, muscular skin. All hers. Offered to her freely.

"When I speak to you, you will answer 'Yes, Mistress'." Her breath moved the fine hair on his arm.

She flicked her glance right, watched his jaw muscle flex, his head tilt toward her. "Yes, Mistress."

She made a precise left turn, walked the length of his arm, circled it. Coming back to stand behind him, she went to work.

First the whip. Across the back several times, different spots. Shoulder blades, lower back, buttocks, striking with the braided thong. Then she stepped back further and used the trail, the single string at the tip, to sting. Then alternating.

He remained silent, his breath coming out of him in short bursts as he managed the pain. She did not speak either, letting the pain she was inflicting be her words to him.

Pain and sensory deprivation together were powerful focus tools. She wanted him mindless, as mindless as she'd been. On a pause, he angled his head, showing he was trying to relieve some of the tension she had created between his neck and shoulders. Moving forward again, she stopped right behind him, the curve of his firm ass against her hip, the tip of her breast pressed to his marked back.

"Christ, touch me," he murmured. Raw. Not begging. Demanding.

Her hand hovered over his flesh as she fought the compulsion to obey. At length, she laid her fingers on him as lightly as a moth landing, at that aching juncture of his neck, feeling the knotted muscle. Not to caress but to determine the status of his discomfort. She reached up, made the adjustment to the restraint, eased it out a half inch, giving him a bit of relief.

"I control your comfort as well as your pain." She noted his cock jumped at the sound of her voice, reacting as if the smooth slick velvet of her cunt had closed over him.

"I don't doubt that at all. Not since I met you."

She slid under his arm, her hair brushing his sensitized skin. Her hand pressed briefly at his side.

As she stood before him, Tyler felt her breath near his chin, telling him she was within kissing distance, but when he stretched out, tentative, she was gone again, a frustrating illusion. No. A fantasy come to life, teasing him.

Just like a covert operation, he knew the goal going in, had prepared himself for it to the maximum extent possible, knowing there would be unforeseen contingencies. She'd been an obsession before their partial weekend together but now that he'd touched her, tasted her, left his scent on her, he hadn't counted on how being this close to her but unable to touch her would goad the alpha in him. It took concentrated effort not to use his full strength against the chains in a futile attempt to burst loose. And as if she knew that, she stayed just out of reach, a distance calculated to madden him.

She moved behind him again and those long nails, the slim fingers, went to his neck, playing in the hair at his nape, but only to release the blindfold. It tumbled from him, the black silk rolling down, spreading out and floating to the floor. Her palm followed the length of his right arm, the top of it, caressing the muscles of his biceps, his forearm. When she reached his hand, she drew away, avoiding the intimacy of fingers touching fingers. Then she stepped around and in front of him, increasing his torture by showing herself to him at last.

The dress she wore was her signature white. No diamonds tonight. It was long-sleeved, high-necked and fit like a second skin, but not like the bodysuit which was seductively tight. This dress molded every portion of her anatomy. The size and shape of her breasts, the bud of the nipple, even the slight uneven transition between the areola and the smooth curve of the breast itself. The stretch fabric outlined her hips, her buttocks. Her legs, bare, smooth, long and fine as a deer's, were tucked into white stilettos with a sharp toe reinforced with silver.

It took him some time to reach her face. She wore no makeup. No adornment whatsoever. Just the dress which quite obviously had nothing under it. With her clear blue eyes and that moonlit hair, what else did she need?

He wanted nothing more than to worship and cherish every part of her body. In that he was sure he was little different from the submissives who had shared this room with her. But he wondered if they noticed other things about her. The fact she so rarely smiled. That there were often shadows under her eyes. How thin her arms were, despite the lean muscle tone. The fragile slenderness of her neck, her wrists, her ankles. Everything he'd observed of her suggested that she lived the life of an ascetic. Very restrained, very controlled. Turning denial into an art form.

When she turned to lay the latigo down on the rack, the dark shadow between her buttocks made his blood boil closer to the surface. The way the fabric creased and moved with her ass, rode up high on her thighs in the back. If she bent over, he knew he'd get a view of her soft, delectable pussy.

He could almost sense the reaction of the crowd above. She was a vision. She always was. Her beauty didn't rest in a feature or group of features. It was in her otherworldly quality. He stood in a room with something not quite of this earth. Perhaps an angel with a broken wing, forever consigned to walk among humans, puzzled by them, never quite in sync.

All the miserable things he'd seen, all the things he'd been unable to prevent, had given him what he needed to be the man who could love her and care for her forever. He knew it. He would fight the demons in her dreams for her, give her back her smile as a gift she'd earned a thousand times over. It wasn't egotism or wishful thinking, he simply knew it as truth. He just had to get her to believe it. When he looked at her he saw his own soul looking back at him, the lost piece of himself.

"I want you."

She stilled for a moment, but then she lifted her arms, her back still to him, to tuck up the tail of her hair in a knot. When she turned around, her arms still raised, he swallowed, noting the way the dress stretched tight over her breasts. She came to him, her eyes on his cock, not acknowledging him or his words. Slowly she moved her body against his, rubbing her mons along the length of his turgid arousal, the fabric of her dress the thinnest of barriers. She bent her knees to rub her nipples against his hard abdomen, then straightened, taking them up his chest, tilting her head back a little so he could not reach her with his mouth.

"I want to fuck you. Now." He growled it.

Marguerite managed, just barely, to prevent her body from giving itself away with a shudder at the words. She was ravenous for him, too. And he was hers to touch, wasn't he? With her free hand she curled her fingers around his oiled cock while his breath drew in. She felt his eyes on her face. After a moment, she ducked under his arm to his back. Running her palms up each side of his tense buttocks, she eased her now oiled knuckle in between the cheeks.

"You don't follow direction very well, Tyler. I told you not to speak. What if I decide to fuck you? How would you like that? What if I want you to come for me? Your seed jetting out into the air. What if…"

She didn't want any of those things. She wanted this. Pressing her body close against his back, she rubbed her pubic bone against the seam of that delicious ass, raised on her toes to seize a handful of his hair in her hand. Yanking his head back, she sank her teeth into the juncture of his shoulder and throat. This was savage need, the desire to draw Tyler's blood and essence into her, keep his taste on her tongue forever, hoping it would still the restless desire raging through her. Her other hand came up, collared his throat to hold him at the uncomfortable angle, pressing, restricting his air as she sank her canines in deeper, tasting his blood, his life.

Focus, Marguerite, focus. The roaring was hard to push back but she did it. Abruptly she released him, listened to him take a harsh breath to pull air back in his lungs, watched his broad chest expand. Stepping back into the shadows, she wiped the back of her hand against her bloody lips as she walked it off, circled in the darkness. Her body trembled, her breath coming as rapidly as if it were her air that had been constricted. She stopped when she was straight across from him again. Her eyes drifted down to find him even more hard and erect.

Obviously, she hadn't frightened him. She raised her lashes and found the same look he'd had when she first removed his blindfold. Possessiveness. Even chained, his eyes made it clear he considered her his. And he was waiting. Waiting for what? Blood ran down his shoulder, over his nipple. She raised a hand to her mouth, feeling it there again, seeing it smear on her hand. Looking down, she saw a stain of it over her left breast.

"You put anything in my ass, angel—" He spoke now, low and dangerous, as if she'd just asked the question. "And you'd better keep me tied until you're in the next state. And even then, I'll find you. You won't walk comfortably for a week."

"I'm not your submissive. You don't spank me. Not ever again."

"I don't need to spank you to make it hard for you to walk."

The amber had become gold fire. Just as a lashing could rouse a slave's submissive devotion to fever pitch, it had fully roused the Master in him, the Dominant male. She knew if he were free right now, there was nothing she could do to escape him, to keep from being shoved to her back, her legs parted and his body thrust into her, fucking her into submission. The thought made her quiver hard and deep down in the dark places of her soul. Something primal was moving in his eyes but a wave of the same was raging through her body, taking her over.

"I didn't give you permission to speak. Do so out of turn again and I'll gag you."

"Do I get to choose what you gag me with?" He cocked his head. "The silk of your hair would make a lovely gag. The full ripeness of your breast, your nipple for my pacifier...your plump cunt. Are you still smooth for me, Marguerite?"

She seized the latigo from the shelf. As it uncoiled with a hiss, she snapped it out of the shadows, making sure the tail struck the base of the scrotum with stinging accuracy.

He flinched but it just increased the challenge in his eyes. When he bared his teeth, she was flooded by the turbulent storm moving within her, driven by hurricane-force winds of emotion. She didn't step back to let it settle. Not this time.

"Is this how you respect a Mistress? Challenging me, daring me to top you like a green submissive? Did you expect me to buy that bullshit line about honoring the Mistress in me?" Her voice did not sound steady, even to herself. She stepped deliberately out of the shadows, every part of her going still, zeroing in on one objective. To give the power within her an outlet.

Focused on the blatantly male display before her, she swung the whip.

His eyes never left her face. Not as she landed strike after strike on his front, knowing exactly what level of pain would be felt. A man could be hit harder than a woman because their skin was less sensitized. Using her well-practiced skills, she striped his body with red marks, never breaking the skin but delivering the maximum amount of pain. While she didn't touch his genitals again, she abraded the skin near them with harrowing frequency.

But throughout the flogging, though his breath began to labor as the pain level increased, he remained still. The more he didn't move, the more the energy vibrated off him until it filled the room with heat, fueling the thing building in her and between them.

His body gleamed in sweat. Her dress had become transparent as she became damp with her own reaction, the stress of the scene, the demand of her own desire.

Stepping back, she picked up the tawser in her free hand. Tyler knew she was considering another round and where to place it. The whip moved with her, coiling around her calves like a sinuous snake permanently enamored of Eve. Or Lilith. His nerve endings were roused, vibrating, affecting his emotions as well as his body. He could admire her ability, her stamina, even as he knew he was losing the ability to hold on to his own control, driven to the edge by pain and his own alpha lust. The desire to become a raging beast, tear the chains from the wall and take her over, was becoming as excruciating as the rawness of his skin.

He could read her emotions through the strikes. Anger. Controlled anger for the moment but definitely teetering on the brink. Frustration. With herself as much as him as she struggled to reach the state of mind she wanted. Pride was part of this, too. He'd mastered her and she needed to balance that, to prove to him she was a Mistress. He'd suspected that would be a component of tonight's session even before they started. He also suspected he'd become the manifestation of the things that frightened her. He'd stirred them up, things perhaps she'd never allowed herself to want. And then he'd let her go, left her to deal with that alone. This was his penance. He wasn't going to leave her like that again, damn it, no matter what.

She lifted her gaze, met his with eyes like a blue wasteland. "Do you know what pain is, Tyler? Really know? You're so fucking determined to be inside of my head. But you give me nothing."

"I'd give you everything, Marguerite, if you'd just let me."

"Don't try that. Don't you dare." His voice, his truth, hit her like a return blow and she lashed back out.

This time she didn't hold back, didn't think of rules, only the fact that she was breaking open, her darkness spilling into every corner of the room. It was going to swallow them both up, so what did it matter?

Two steps forward and she at last brought the tawser into play, the handle wet from the sweat in her palm. A strike on his abdomen earned her a grunt of pain as the strap proved its reputation as a weapon of extreme BDSM play.

But his eyes were calculating. Waiting. Still waiting.

For something she couldn't give him. Why didn't he understand that? Or maybe he did and this was just his special torment for her, to try and pry it from her.

Lashing out wild, control slipping away from her, this time she struck the left nipple dead-on. His jaw clenched, breath whistling out between his teeth. And still that same steady, waiting look. She needed to obliterate it. Her fingers clenched on the handle and she snarled, took him across the jaw with the tawser.

Striking in the face for any reason except with the flat of a hand was a cardinal sin at The Zone. She didn't care. They'd come, they'd stop her, she'd never see The Zone again, she would never see him again.

"Marguerite—"

"Shut up. Just...don't...speak." She spoke through the roar, the white noise in her head so loud that his voice grated across it like a jagged dull knife over a wound already infected. She struck out again, not caring where, just wanting to hurt. She heard a stifled curse and redoubled her efforts. Safe words. There were no safe words. He hadn't asked and she wouldn't give him any. No mercy. Nothing safe. Nothing but pain.

She struck again and again. The face, the torso, his legs. She cried out with each blow, each one feeling as if it were ripping the flesh from her soul.

When she couldn't take any more, she dropped both weapons, threw them from her and spun away, covering her face with her hands, squatting down on her heels in an effort to protect her vital organs, vibrating from the pain she was sure was going to shatter her into a million pieces.

She'd hit him, she'd hurt him. Deliberately, not for pleasure but to inflict pain, to impose the agony that was burning through her. She was dying inside. There was so much darkness, she couldn't see. She was afraid to take away her hands to see what might lie in wait for her in that darkness. And the roaring would not stop, the rush of water behind a dam of memories she thought she'd secured away from herself. They were going to come crashing down, pummel her with an eternity of this mindless, screaming pain.

"Marguerite."

She had no idea how long he'd been saying her name, that gentle repetition. Not angry, not panicked, simply calling to her. A little bit of a hoarse strain to his tone. She had no idea where in the room she was. In the shadows, in the light, it didn't matter. It was all the same.

"Come here, angel. It's okay."

It couldn't possibly be okay. She couldn't see anything. Didn't want to. Didn't want to see the crime she had committed, the pain she'd inflicted on his body merely because she wanted it so much.

"Come here, Marguerite. Now."

She turned toward his voice, that fierce tiger's power, the *mouko*, compelling her at last. She stumbled, stepped out of her shoes, took one barefoot step, another. He'd stopped talking, so she stopped. There was only darkness.

"Right in front of you, angel. Just a few more steps."

He knew. He could tell she was lost, lost in broad daylight. If she could just huddle in that darkness, stay in the shadows, it would pass. She would find herself again as she always did, find the balance she was able to maintain as long as she stayed in solitude. But now she didn't need silence. She needed that voice. Needed it more than she'd ever needed anything, more than she'd allowed herself to need in a very long time.

Reaching out, she found him. It was his rib cage, the skin hot to the touch, wet with sweat. When she blinked, a haze moved through the blackness. Moving closer, she felt his heart beat against hers. Slow. Even. Hers reverberated back. Fast. Erratic. But the pulse of the world was in him, going on steadily even under chaos.

Leaning in, she pressed the side of her face against his neck, smelled blood where she'd bitten him. As she nuzzled the wound and licked it gently, he made a soft sound of reassurance. She had just beaten the hell out of him, broken every rule a Dominant could break but she sensed nothing from him but...sanctuary.

Turning her cheek, she rubbed against his unmarked shoulder area, moving her lips over the rounded end. Bending down, she tasted the slope of his side just beneath his arm. Her hands descended, taking her down inch by inch. She touched each shallow valley between the ribs, reaching the crisp hair that narrowed to a point over his flat abdomen. Down to the hipbone, her palm finding the buttock. Another blink of her eyes and the darkness was slinking sullenly away, clouds defeated by his blazing heat. She felt the golden fire of his eyes like the warm touch of sun on her hair and skin. And like the sun they were something she could not look at directly. Her bare foot pressed on his, her toes digging in to feel it flex under hers. When she sank down, her cheek grazed his cock, still remarkably semi-erect above his scrotum. She tasted him there, a shy kiss. Sliding her arms from his hips, she found a lower circle around his thighs and rested her head just below his genitals. Her mouth, the wetness of her breath against that first mark she'd put on his thigh. Her fingers told her he had welts everywhere. Bleeding in several places, for her dress was stained with it.

She couldn't top him. She didn't want to. She didn't want to be a Mistress to Tyler. The knowledge of it was quietly there, the real battle she'd come in here to fight. What the waiting look in his eyes told her he'd known all along. He'd proven himself her Master even when bound, taking over her senses even without the privilege of touching her.

She was lost in him to the point of immobility, so integral that it went past having to define it as Master and sub.

She had denied what they both knew was true from the beginning, not because she didn't believe it deep in her soul but because she couldn't accept it. But he hadn't let her have any other choice. Her own needs had forced her to face the truth.

Tyler could not find sexual satisfaction with anyone but a woman whose nature could submit to him. She'd known that from the beginning, which made this moment an undeniable truth.

She was a Mistress who needed a Master. Who needed him.

* * * * *

Join Tyler and Marguerite for the rest of their story in:
Mirror of My Soul
Part II of Ice Queen
Now available from Ellora's Cave.

Why an electronic book?

We live in the Information Age — an exciting time in the history of human civilization, in which technology rules supreme and continues to progress in leaps and bounds every minute of every day. For a multitude of reasons, more and more avid literary fans are opting to purchase e-books instead of paper books. The question from those not yet initiated into the world of electronic reading is simply: *Why?*

1. *Price.* An electronic title at Ellora's Cave Publishing and Cerridwen Press runs anywhere from 40% to 75% less than the cover price of the exact same title in paperback format. Why? Basic mathematics and cost. It is less expensive to publish an e-book (no paper and printing, no warehousing and shipping) than it is to publish a paperback, so the savings are passed along to the consumer.

2. *Space.* Running out of room in your house for your books? That is one worry you will never have with electronic books. For a low one-time cost, you can purchase a handheld device specifically designed for e-reading. Many e-readers have large, convenient screens for viewing. Better yet, hundreds of titles can be stored within your new library — on a single microchip. There are a variety of e-readers from different manufacturers. You can also read e-books on your PC or laptop computer. (Please note that Ellora's Cave does not endorse any specific brands.

You can check our websites at www.ellorascave.com or www.cerridwenpress.com for information we make available to new consumers.)

3. *Mobility.* Because your new e-library consists of only a microchip within a small, easily transportable e-reader, your entire cache of books can be taken with you wherever you go.

4. *Personal Viewing Preferences.* Are the words you are currently reading too small? Too large? Too… ANNOYING? Paperback books cannot be modified according to personal preferences, but e-books can.

5. *Instant Gratification.* Is it the middle of the night and all the bookstores near you are closed? Are you tired of waiting days, sometimes weeks, for bookstores to ship the novels you bought? Ellora's Cave Publishing sells instantaneous downloads twenty-four hours a day, seven days a week, every day of the year. Our webstore is never closed. Our e-book delivery system is 100% automated, meaning your order is filled as soon as you pay for it.

Those are a few of the top reasons why electronic books are replacing paperbacks for many avid readers.

As always, Ellora's Cave and Cerridwen Press welcome your questions and comments. We invite you to email us at Comments@ellorascave.com or write to us directly at Ellora's Cave Publishing Inc., 1056 Home Avenue, Akron, OH 44310-3502.

erridwen, the Celtic Goddess of wisdom, was the muse who brought inspiration to story-tellers and those in the creative arts. Cerridwen Press encompasses the best and most innovative stories in all genres of today's fiction. Visit our site and discover the newest titles by talented authors who still get inspired - much like the ancient storytellers did, once upon a time.

LaVergne, TN USA
13 August 2010
193245LV00002B/130/P